Kathleen
A Dublin Saga

Acknowledgments

To Sue Jeremiah, her patient help kept the pot boiling.

To Peter Lavery, who had faith in an idea.

To Jo Phillips, for her help and concern.

To the London College of Printing, for help with research time and library facilities.

KATHLEEN
A DUBLIN SAGA

Brian Behan

St. Martin's Press
New York

To Theo Wood
whose help and encouragement
made it all possible

Library of Congress Cataloging-in-Publication Data

Behan, Brian.
    Kathleen. A Dublin saga.
      1. Behan, Kathleen—Fiction. I. Title.
PR6052.E326K3 1989   823'.914   88-30605
ISBN 0-312-02593-9

First published in Great Britain by Century Hutchinson Ltd.

First U.S. Edition

10 9 8 7 6 5 4 3 2 1

PROLOGUE

Kathleen sat in her chair by the window of the rest-home. From it she could see the broad sweep of Dublin Bay and the sea and, as it was summer, she could hear the far-off distant roar of the waves as they surged up the sand and then down again, breaking into white foam.

She sighed. It was such a long time, such a long long time she had been alive now – Her ninetieth birthday come and gone. How happy she had been to celebrate it with her son Dermot and his many and varied children, all grown up now with children of their own, and even grandchildren. Liam's grandchild now, there was a one! Just like his grandfather with those golden curls and the cheeky grin.

'Great-grandma, I sure think you're great!' he said in his American drawl as he climbed on to her knee. As he sat there she had seen Liam so clearly in him; time had rolled back and she had felt a surge of love towards the child as strong as any she had felt as a young woman.

Dermot was coming again today, she thought, with that tape-recorder of his for her reminiscences. Wanting to take everything down. He was right, of course. All those memories packed inside her head. Her hands automatically fumbled the rosary as she heard the piped strains of the third mass that day, coming through the speaker in the corner of the room. Here, as she looked over the Bay, she doubted whether there was truly any Hell, and sure the priest was nice when he came by.

And so was Ria. She was as good as a real daughter to her mother-in-law. Ever since . . . and now Kathleen's hands shook and she clutched the rosary tightly. Tears started in her eyes. You never forgot, she thought. It might grow less but the pain was still there after all those years . . . and sometimes as fresh as that day . . . Her

*hands were now gripping the arms of the chair. Then
there came a knock at the door.*

It was Dermot.

'Good morning to you, Ma.'

PART I

1

The rain fell softly on to the spongy wastes of the Dublin hills. It moved gently down over the slopes of the green hills of Tallaght and then hammered its way across the narrow Liffey into Dorset Street. It streamed down the windows of a squat, broad-windowed house – and past the small freckled face of Kathleen Corr staring out.

Her mother softly called her back from the window to her place at the table. Then she carefully turned down the gas-mantles until they left just a pleasant dark shadowy glow, sufficient to give the young family enough light to eat their tea. The rain also poured down the half-dismantled sign that bore the legend of *John Corr. Provision Merchant* and washed over the face of the window, almost wiping out the paper sign that proclaimed *Great and Final Sale Before Closure*.

Kathleen was enjoying her tea. It was black and white pudding followed by sausages, and there was a great plate full of homemade bread. She loved this soda-bread best of all: large warm white cakes into which the rich creamery butter melted, turning the white to golden-brown. The warmth around her was that of prosperous people, and a roaring fire in the large grate completed the happy scene. Kathleen watched anxiously as the soda-bread vanished, the great pile dropping lower by the minute. She carefully reached out and swiftly placed a reserve slice near her plate. Just as quickly her older sister Maggie, snatched it back, yelling, 'Greedy pig'. Kathleen leaned after it across the table, almost knocking over the milk. Her mother raised a voice trembling with anger.

'For heaven's sake, don't row – on this night of all nights.' Emboldened by her anger, she stared around at the four little heads.

'I have something to tell you all. Now listen to me

8

carefully. Our house has fallen on a bad day. Your poor Father tried his hardest, but he was a bit foolish at the best of times. We'll now have to leave here and go away for a while.'

Maggie and her two brothers looked up in astonishment. Kathleen paid scarce attention: it must be a game that Mammy was playing. She was far more interested in getting back that last slice of soda-bread. As she slid it towards her plate, she heard her Mammy continue.

'Now, none of you are to worry. It will be just for a little while, until we get everything straight. It will be like a holiday; yes, try and think of it as a holiday. Maggie, you and Kathleen will go to the nuns for a while, and John and Peadar to the Christian Brothers. But, please God, we will soon all be back together again.' She turned quickly away, saying, 'Now let you all get ready for bed: we'll have a good night's sleep. We have a lot to do tomorrow.'

Kathleen slept the sleep of the very young, deep and long, only waking to Maggie's insistent prodding, and then reluctantly dressing herself to escape the chill March air.

Her mother packed their four little cases slowly and sadly. It was a nightmare, a living nightmare: a great fortune of money gone, her husband dead, and her four children away into an orphanage. It was a shame beyond belief. How could she live one day without the little ones, and yet she must live thus not just one day but maybe for years. She tried hard to stem the flow of tears, and failed. Finally she could cry no more, and with a heavy heart put on her coat and prepared to leave her house for the last time. It had been such a lovely house, which she had entered first as a young bride. Now she must go into a single tenement room, all on her own.

First she watched her two sons leave with the small hump-backed Christian Brother. He fiddled constantly with a nose reddened from years of snuff-taking. As he fussed about John and Peadar, he produced from his pocket a handful of holy medals and placed one each around the boys' necks, much to their delight and Kathleen's envy. Like a little black bat he swooped through the door, with his scarf and the boys trailing in his wake. Nora barely had time to wave the lads goodbye before it was the girls' turn. Maggie was stolid and expressionless. Kathleen could barely contain her joy at the thought of going: she was bored with waiting and wished they could be on their way that very minute. She squeezed Maggie's hand impatiently, and almost groaned with pure frustration when she saw her Uncle Ned appear. He was such a talker it meant more delays, when it seemed they were about to be off. Her uncle's tall, broad-shouldered form filled the hallway and she could not blank out his loud, booming voice.

'Now, Nora, it may all be for the best in the long run. When the houses and the business are sold and the books balanced, we will know where we are. But you may as well know now, things seem even worse than I ever imagined. He owed hundreds, maybe thousands; he was owing everyone – or at least they now say so. If you add to that what his own kinsmen robbed him of, yes robbed him, I can't put it plainer than that – robbed you and yours. Now we shouldn't speak ill of the dead, but your husband, John Corr, would have tried the patience of a saint. I can't find rhyme or reason for some of his antics. What on earth was he doing all day at the Law Courts, listening to the trials, when the real criminals were here in his own shop, serving behind your counter with one hand and robbing the eyes out of your head with the other. It's a wonder they didn't come back for your eyelashes. Now it's left to the likes of me to clear up a fine mess. Still and all, the two lads will be all right. In Artane they will get all the benefits of an industrial school. Three meals a day, a bit of education and, above all else, my dear, they will get a trade so that when they come out they'll be able to turn their hands to anything.'

He looked at the girls. 'I suppose these two will learn enough with the nuns to get them a place in service. At least they won't come to any harm out there in Islandbridge.' He sighed. 'Ah, your fella was a right old gom, sure enough. He couldn't have been the full shilling, could he. There must have been a slate loose on the roof. How else could he have squandered so much in such a little time? Ten little houses, one big one and a fine well-stocked shop.'

Kathleen felt angry. She could see her beloved Mammy was getting more and more upset as he went on, his voice thundering. Staring straight at her huge uncle she shouted in her shrill small voice, 'Leave my mammy alone.'

Startled, he looked down at the little freckled face with its eyes fearlessly determined to defend her own. Her two little hands were firmly fixed on her waist, her whole body thrust forward.

Mammy put an arm around her shoulder. 'She doesn't mean any harm, Ned.'

The big man looked down at Kathleen and stroked her hair gently. 'Indeed not,' he began. He was on the point of asking why her late father did not possess half the little one's spirit, but stopped himself. It was no use crying over spilt milk. Nora and John – when God made them he matched them, a right pair. A pair of soft touches open to the winds of the world. But this little one was a different kettle of fish. Well, if she didn't take after her father or her mother, where did she get it from? It must have been from her grandmother. A great strong woman, she could make hay with the best man on the farm till she was past eighty. He bent down and picked Kathleen up.

'Well, fair play to you, my little one. Ye remind me so much of your granny, a great oul wan. She always said, "We never died a winter yet, and the devil out of hell couldn't kill us in the summer".'

He kissed her firmly on the cheek. 'It's you that has the courage and the fire to kick the ball of life along. Come on then, let's make a shape and get you and your mother off to Islandbridge before the nuns think we have forgotten them.'

*

11

The jaunting-car hushed them up as it swayed along, Kathleen and Maggie facing one side, their uncle and mother sitting with their backs to them, facing the other. It was a dull, cold March day but Kathleen was glad to be off at last. The horse trotted quickly down Lower Dorset Street, and Kathleen had to hold tight to the rail to stop herself slipping to the floor. They turned into the broad width of the North Circular Road, past the ten little houses they had once owned.

A tenant slipped out of one to wave at Nora. He shouted after her in a hearty voice, 'I'm truly sorry for yer trouble, missus,' but the sentiment did not fit his tone of voice. Nora simply waved.

As they bowled along at a cracking pace, Uncle Ned gave Kathleen a running commentary on the route. 'Now, gel, here we are on the great North Circular Road. Notice how wide it is: built like that so old Mother England could wheel her troops round our fair city as fast as she liked. Called the circular road because it matches up with the South Circular to go right round the town. Convenient, eh?'

He paused only to hoot at a housewife putting up bunting for a royal visit.

'God bless our Queen,' she retorted.

'Not *our* Queen. Anyway, she's blessed enough already I'm thinking, ruling all our lands from here to Galway. That one doesn't need our blessing. Hell is not hot enough nor eternity long enough to toast her bones.'

The indignant housewife held back until the jaunting cart stopped at a crossing, then ran forward screaming 'God blast you for a bloody oul fenian.'

He spat down on her as the cart moved away, catching her full in the face, helpless with rage.

He roared with laughter. 'Did yer ever see the likes of that, didn't ye? Wasn't that one up her pipe.'

Kathleen jiggled delightedly on her seat. The trip was getting better and better. Soon they reached the cattle market. As far as the eye could see Kathleen saw cows, bulls, sheep, pigs in their pens.

Her uncle waved his arm at them. 'There you are, girls, those are our exports: cattle and men. You put the land to grass to fatten the landlords' cattle, and ye send your surplus ploughmen to England to make another country rich.'

Eventually, they entered the gates of Phoenix Park. 'Now here we are at the Park, one of the largest in the world. Yonder is the Viceregal Lodge, home of Britannia's local despot. On our right the Zoological Gardens. And see over there, the Wellington Monument, though he wouldn't give us thank-you for calling him one of our favoured sons. "Irish," says he. "Why am I Irish simply because I was born there? Well, if I was born in a stable, does that make me a horse?" '

He then laughed so infectiously that Kathleen joined in. Maggie turned on her fiercely. 'What are you laughing at like a pure eegit? We're losing our home and our Mammy, and bad scran to you, all you can do is laugh.'

Kathleen gazed miserably at her, feeling guilty.

'Take no notice,' shouted Uncle. 'She's an old misery-guts. Here, gel, laugh and the world laughs with you, weep and you weep alone.' He turned towards Kathleen. 'D'ye know any songs at all, at all?'

She thought for a moment. 'I know a short one.'

He prodded her in the ribs. 'That's the ticket, let it ring.'

In a thin, piping voice Kathleen sang, 'Canice's School is a very good school, it's built of bricks and mortar, and the only thing that's wrong with it is the baldy-headed master.'

Her uncle was delighted. 'Good on you, gel, your blood's worth bottling.'

Kathleen fell suddenly silent as the cab slowed before the high walls which enclosed the orphanage run by the Little Sisters of the Poor.

'Just a bit further I think, ma'am, to the gates.'

The light was already fading as the carriage drove up to the entrance. Kathleen, revived by eagerness for a new experience, jumped out of the carriage and ran forward

13

– but was stopped short by a tall, gaunt figure in a crisp brown uniform.

'You must be one of the Corr sisters, then. You're late.'

'Sorry for that, I am,' said their mother, almost trembling. She quickly grasped both the girls' hands, and they winced at the force with which she held them.

'Don't leave us here, Mam, please don't,' whimpered Maggie.

'Come along quickly, now. Which is Margaret and which is Kathleen?' The sister took each by the hand and swivelled them round to face the tall, black wrought-iron gates that seemed about to shut on them forever. They walked in silence towards a red-brick lodge to the right of the gateway. A surge of panic gripped Kathleen and she turned round to look for her mother. She felt it rise up her throat like a hand gripping her, leaving her speechless. *Her mother going just like this?* And when would she see her again? She really didn't want to be here. Yes, mother had explained it was all for the best; but now the moment was here, it was like a physical pain, her panic. Who would tuck her up in bed and whisper goodnight? She was so glad that Maggie was there, holding her hand. But she wanted to run to her mother, and hold her tight – throw her arms about her and tell her she didn't want to be left in the Convent. How could she desert them like this?

Mother stood a while unable to move, then she produced two large oranges from beneath her black cloak and held them out. She seemed so far away now, almost in a mist. Then Kathleen seized Maggie's hand and ran sobbing towards her mother.

'Kath, Maggie, be good now. Say your prayers every night, and we'll all be together very soon, I promise you.'

'You must go quickly now, Mrs Corr,' the sister interrupted. 'Come here, girls. Supper's beginning, and you don't want to be going to bed hungry, do you?'

Nora Corr turned swiftly and climbed into the carriage where her brother had remained to avoid the tearful scene. 'Oh, and, Maggie, you look after Kathleen now,

14

be sure to . . .' But her voice faded as the cab moved off. She felt anger as the tears rolled down her cheeks, salty to the taste. Anger that she was unable to care for her own, that she must be separated from them, that her children should be shut away. But there was nothing to be done about it: she had no money to feed them. And her brother Ned was not much use; he had only enough for himself and for the porter, although he had kindly paid for the cab. She hated it all. Deep within her grief and shame were twisting like a coil round her very soul, slowly breaking her spirit.

The girls stood before a spluttering gas-fire, naked and with their heads stinging from the cruel strokes of the metal comb. Maggie's face was streaked with tears, while all the while Kathleen remained strong and defiant.

'Why are we standing here without our clothes?'

'You *don't* speak until you are spoken to, my girl. We have to get rid of the rags from your past and furnish you with decent clothes. Now get these dresses on, and put on your shoes without your socks. We don't have socks here until we have made them; you'll start on those tomorrow. Now, get a move on.'

The walk up the dark lane to the main house was enough to put the fear of God into any mortal, and the two little girls clung to each other as they gazed towards the glimmer of gaslights in the tall windows of what would be their home for years to come.

'Be brave, Kathleen,' whispered her taller sister, whose hair now spread widely over her thin shoulders like a mantle of gold. Kathleen had always looked up to her sister, and now she knew that there could be no life without her. She bitterly missed her mother and John and Peadar, but there was still Maggie.

'I'm Sister Teresa,' said the tall nun, and if you wish to speak to me that is how I am to be addressed. 'Here comes Sister Maria who will take you into supper'.

The large oaken doors were open wide, and from the bottom step Kathleen could see only a large figure blocking the light.

15

'She's as big as old Ma Curren from the sweetshop,' she whispered.

'Silence! I can see you're going to have to be taught a few lessons, Kathleen Corr.' Her voice was neutral, cold but firm. 'You will obey the rules of the Convent while you're here with us. You are not in your own home now. If you do not obey the rules you will be punished, you understand that? Punished for your own good, until you are able to obey.

'Shortly I will take you into the refectory for supper. There you will find that we do everything to the whistle. On the first whistle you will assemble outside in your form according to your age. On the second you will march in an orderly fashion to the refectory. On the third you will stand by your table – that table and that place will be yours and no other till the day you leave us. On the fourth whistle you will sit down. On the fifth you will say grace. On the sixth you will eat your food silently. About ten minutes before your meal time is finished you will hear the seventh whistle then and only then may you speak softly to your neighbour.'

'On the eighth whistle you will stop talking at once. On the ninth you will say grace after meals, giving God thanks for your daily bread. On the tenth you will stand up and wait for the final whistle when you will march out, either to bed or work. That will be your daily routine till it is time for you to go, and with so many girls here, it is essential that you obey our rules without question. Now, come with me.' She beckoned them up the steps.

Inside, the refectory was vast, with hundreds of girls standing silently beside long wooden tables. Kathleen felt dwarfed by the immensity of it. She felt intimidated by the hundreds of heads that turned to watch the two little girls walk half the length of the silent hall.

It was the sea of faces, looking questioning, that Kathleen felt so hard. How different from the comfortable smallness of their own home. The adventure that she had looked forward to with such eagerness was taking on a bitter taste. She felt her feelings of sadness rise. Oh

16

how much she longed to be home and away from this awful place. She felt the tears begin to trickle down her cheeks until a furious Maggie pressed her nails into her hand and whispered fiercely, 'We will cry for no one,' and marched forward with her head held high. In the centre of the refectory floor stood a nun with a whistle poised to her lips as Maggie and Kathleen reached their seats she blew the blast for them all to be seated, and then another for grace. Maggie and Kathleen sat and mingled their voices with the hundreds of others that now filled the empty space.

The girls ate their thin soup in silence. There was no evidence of any further food, and unthinkingly Kathleen called up the table, 'Sister Teresa, is there any soda-bread, please?'

A wolf closing in on its prey could not have moved swifter across the wooden floor. Down swooped the white butterfly wimple on Sister's head as she grabbed Kathleen's thin arm and yanked her up from the bench and towards the refectory door.

'You should be grateful for what the good Lord has given you today, and now I'm going to take you to the dormitory where you can stand ashamed in front of all the other girls until you drop. But first I want Sister Maria to help me bathe you. Come along.'

It was difficult to sort out the jumble of thoughts going through Kathleen's head as, for the first time in her life, she learned the feeling of hatred. She was stripped naked for the second time that night, firmly between the two Sisters as they sat at either end of the large bath and, while the water ran to drown out Kathleen's cries, Sister Teresa put her hand under the tap and with a wet palm proceeded to beat her across her back and thighs. Sister Maria held Kathleen tight.

Then Kathleen was made to stand naked in front of thirty other girls, big and small, as Sister Teresa explained the wretched new girl's ingratitude to the wide-eyed audience. The memory of this humiliation would never leave her, and would even return to wound her when she took off her clothes for her husband on the night she was wed.

When her ordeal was over, and the girls already sent off to their beds, the weeping child was dressed roughly in an unfamiliar nightgown and led firmly down the central aisle of the darkened dormitory to a vacant iron-frame cot. She climbed in and pulled the thin blankets up to her chin.

'Kathleen, are you there?' came a whispered voice later from the dark. 'It's Maggie here, and you're sleeping beside me.'

2

Kathleen walked the yard of the Convent. Despite the heat of a June day, the yard looked cold, dreary, miserable. The weeds that had struggled through the heavy cobble stones looked weary of the fight and nodded listlessly in the heavy heat.

In her mind's eye she found herself drifting back to another day when the sun was out. She was climbing the sweet cool grassy slopes of Howth Head with her Uncle Ned. He strode ahead of her, his long legs easily outdistancing her short steps. She panted in the heat and with the sheer effort of keeping up with him. They passed through the sturdy, low-bellied rhododendron bushes that skirted the top of the hill and finally she sank down exhausted on the short springy turf that covered the sleeping hump of the Head.

Below her, seagulls wheeled with excited cries. She watched enthralled as the crows fought with the gulls for the right to a precarious cliff perch. The gulls finally gave up the fight and, screeching like mad things, wheeled off towards Ireland's Eye. She watched, too, the little puffins, their silly clown faces in strange contrast to their flight: for they flew busily like worried old spinsters, buzzing their wings like bees as they made off to the white Dollymount Strand.

A hawk hung in the clear air above them, suspended as though by a string – and then as suddenly dropped like a stone, and out of sight.

Her uncle raised his arms and took in the air, breathing great gulps.

'Get that down you, girl, that's the real Larry Daly. That will put hair on your chest. The man that can't love Dublin must be tired of life. Feast your eyes on this, girl.'

She followed his arm and, indeed, it was a pretty sight.

In the far distance the Dublin Mountains rose one after the other beyond the southern slopes of the city. There lay Bray Head, overlooking the sea, which began a long chain of hills that held the southern outskirts of the city in a warm embrace. Protective sheltering, the hills rose one after the other, the Sugar Loaf, Kippure Mountain, and then Hell-Fire Mountain.

She pointed out the last to her uncle. 'What is that little square house on top of the hill?'

He laughed. 'Well you may ask! That, my girl, is the Hell-Fire Club where the rich of Dublin wined and dined to their heart's content not so long ago. They worshipped Old Nick and cursed their God. It's said they played cards all the while, until one night they noticed an extra hand and, on looking down beneath the table, they saw a cloven hoof. Well, truth or lies, one of them went mad and another killed himself. That put an end to their club.'

Wondering at this strange information, Kathleen looked behind her to see the gleaming strand of Portmarnock stretch away into the distance. Closer by, near the sea, lay a small graveyard, and her uncle noticed where her gaze was directed. 'All your people are buried there. It's called Kilbarrack Cemetery – one of the healthiest graveyards in the country. People are dying to get into it.'

He laughed deeply at his own joke and promised Kathleen an ice-cream when they reached the bottom of the hill.

As they stared out over the spreading scene, Kathleen felt there could be no place on earth as lovely or as grand as Howth. Her uncle tightly held her hand, and guided her down the series of zigzag paths that led to the bottom of sheer cliffs. Halfway down he suddenly pointed out to sea. 'Sea mist coming in fast. We'd better wait here awhile darling. We won't be able to see a thing.'

He was right – in seconds the whole of the sea was blotted out in a white, cold mist that engulfed everything. She could hardly see her hands in front of her face, and was scared. Despite the lack of vision she could still hear the swish of the gulls' wings as they wheeled above and below them screaming harshly. Unable to see them, she felt terrified, hoping the gulls wouldn't attack them; some of them had wings two feet wide. She shivered. Her uncle pressed her hand warmly. 'Don't worry, sweetheart, this ould mist will soon be gone. We must just pity the poor blind: now we know what they suffer each and every day of their lives.'

Almost as soon as he spoke the mist began to lift and they were looking down again in to a vast expanse of the deepest, bluest sea she had ever seen. Again the sun warmed their bodies as they descended on to the sandy beach that lay at the cliff-foot. Kathleen raced with delight into a large cave. There she crouched and imagined pirates and all sorts of adventures while her uncle sat outside, puffing on his pipe.

It soon grew so warm with the sun bouncing off the cliffs that Kathleen couldn't resist stripping off and gliding gently into a beautiful rock-pool. She pretended to swim, letting the waves rock her gently in the two feet of water. She marvelled at the prolific life in the pool – anemones that opened like flowers; and tiny crabs, one of them as dead as a doornail with his white belly turned to the sun as if for comfort. She gently prodded a pink starfish, and studied the dozens of sea-snails of every colour. Her daydreaming was broken by the rough intrusion of a large wave that rushed a deal of water into her little pool, making it suddenly twice as deep.

Uncle Ned called over to her, 'Tide is on the turn. Best be making our way back up.' As she dried herself, she felt starving.

They climbed easily and soon reached top. The heather was deep, as stringy as a mattress, so they sank down gratefully. Kathleen was tired from her swimming. Her uncle fed her on slices of griddle-cake and cold tea, and it seemed she had never tasted anything like it in her life. Maybe it was true what her mother once said: 'Hunger is the best sauce.' She sank down into the heather drowsily, and in minutes she was fast asleep. Kathleen

21

woke to find her uncle gently prodding her. 'Come on, Rip Van Winkle, we'd best be heading on home. It's the dead of night.'

He was right. Above her, shining down were all the stars of the heavens, spread out in a wonderful tapestry of diamonds.

They made their way back down the hill and into the village.

'Four eyes! Four eyes!'

Her sister blinked dumbly behind her glasses, and Kathleen cried out, 'Don't just stand there, you great mope, listening to that one ballyragging you!'

She launched herself at her sister's tormentor, a girl three years older than herself. Kathleen was all tiger, snarling and scratching with claws out. She screamed as she received a rough pinch: pain shot upwards as teeth sank into her arm. Other girls converged. Shouts of 'Hit her, Mary' and chants of 'Kathleen' echoed round the yard walls. Unseeing rage gave Kathleen the strength of two, and this attack on her dear sister was the spur.

Although she was smaller than Mary O'Brien, she made up for this difference by sheer ferocity, and fought with a fury that came from deep within herself. No mere playground scrap, the fight became more furious, the yelling louder, the onlooking crowd tighter packed; a hysteric edge touched the shouting. Suddenly Kathleen felt her shoulders tightly gripped, her hold on Mary loosening as she was pulled back. Other girls were now holding Mary back, and Kathleen struggled against the nuns, held with all her strength, but to no avail.

'Please, Sister, it was her that started it . . .' her adversary screamed.

'It was never – you were teasing my sister. You're a great big liar, you, Mary O'Brien, and you deserve to rot in hell for your lies,' Kathleen yelled in frustration.

'Kathleen Corr, you stop that immediately, and you'll come with me right now, you will, and we'll see what we'll find for you to do to make you repent your nasty blaspheming ways.'

Sister Teresa held Kathleen in her pincer grip and hustled her into the main building. It was cool in here, even in summer. Kathleen was not at all repentant about the fight; rage tossed her in its billows as she wriggled beside Sister. The nun pulled her along the corridor and into a store-room. All in a jumble inside were the buckets, mops and cleaning cloths, smelling of old floors and old cleaning, vaguely slimy to the touch.

I do not want to touch these, thought Kathleen. I will not clean while others look on; this is not fair. But the nun determinedly filled a bucket with cold water, and handed her the scrubbing-brush.

'Well, get to it, Kathleen Corr, or you'll be here until tomorrow. I want to see this corridor sparkling by teatime, and the stairs and while you're at it maybe you'll repent of fighting with Mary O'Brien.'

Kathleen looked at the bucket and the scrubbing brush, and thought of the long hours of scrubbing and polishing ahead of her. It was too much, it really was; and all she'd been doing was to defend her sister from being teased by that dreadful girl.

Calmly she took hold of the bucket full of water, and poured it down the nun's skirt. The silence nurtured dynamite, then exploded.

'This is it, Kathleen Corr. You've gone too far this time.'

Kathleen could see by Sister Teresa's expression that, yes, she probably had gone too far, but really there was no going back now. She felt herself being dragged roughly along the corridor, and up the stairs to Sister Anne's room. Now she was for it. Oh, but that Sister Anne could punish a girl and make it last!

The senior nun looked up from her desk. It was that Kathleen Corr, again, brought in by a very flustered-looking Sister Teresa. She listened patiently as the story came out, looked sympathetically at the wet skirt, and crossly at the cheeky-faced girl before her. Really, this girl's insolence was too much. She had always been a problem, but this time, well, there was only one thing for it.

'Kathleen, you know you've done a very serious wrong to Sister Teresa.'

'But, Sister Anne, Mary O'Brien was hurting my Maggie and I couldn't let that happen, could I. And I didn't think it fair I should have to clean all those floors . . .'

'QUIET!' The girl needed to be taught a lesson for her own good. She must not be allowed to think she could act this way towards her superiors. Wasn't that what they had always been taught – obey and be passive? The girl was far too spirited.

Wearily, Sister Anne reached into the drawer of her desk and brought out a little knotted rope. She didn't like this, but the present situation required it.

'Hold out your hand, Kathleen.'

Kathleen held out her hand, knowing she would have to take her punishment. As the knotted rope swung up and down she could only hope it would be soon over. Sister Anne struck the girl nine, ten times, swinging the rope in a practised arc. With each blow she saw the child wince and screw up her eyes, but not a tear rolled down her white cheeks. She was a difficult case and no mistake.

'Sister Teresa, she's to go back to the dormitory for the rest of the day and miss her tea.' She watched as Sister Teresa and Kathleen went out of the room, and then she put the knotted rope away. She felt only a little sorry for the girl. After all, she must learn to obey and not to answer back. That was what the little rope was for – she used it on herself sometimes when she felt her own rebellious instincts gaining the upper hand.

Kathleen's hands smarted. Oh, how it hurt, but she was still not sorry for what she had done. She lay on her bed as the tears started and she stuffed her head in her pillow to stifle them.

It was much later that she woke up out of a kind of

half-sleep to see the other girls approaching her bed. Maggie rushed first to her side and looked at her poor aching hands.

'Oh, Kathleen, it's not fair. Why should this happen?'

'No talking now and lights out,' came a stern voice from the doorway.

The lights went out but nothing could stop the girls from finding out about the day's major happening. Now she had an audience, Kathleen told her tale as a conquering heroine, and soon the whole dormitory was giggling silently at the thought of Sister Teresa and the bucket of water.

Kathleen enjoyed their attention. She loved playing to the crowd and her excited whispers rose.

'Well, Siobhan, Sister Anne bore down on me like an avenging angel and seized my hand so tight I felt like a rabbit in a snare . . .'

'Sure that Sister Anne is a right quare old devil if you ask me, Kathleen. She shouldn't hit you like that, that she shouldn't, and I would write to me pa and tell 'im if that happened to me sure I would an' all.' This came from Bernadette, the spoilt one, sent from a family to be at the Convent rather than stay at their farm in the middle of nowhere between the lakes and the hills, where the white of sheep's coats shone bright through the grasses.

'It's all right for you to talk, Bernadette Monahan,' said Eileen, 'screeching to yer father for the least little thing! It's lucky you are to have a father and mother, while the rest of us — 'tis lucky if we have one parent between four of us! Poor Kathleen has only her mother, and her in a worn-out state.'

Maggie spoke in a loud whisper. 'And if we carry on like this, there'll be more than one of us with sore hands!'

As if in response to her words they heard the sound of leather on the flagstones outside. Ghosts could not have moved quicker and quieter than those girls did then, leaving Kathleen alone with her thoughts and dreams.

The summer passed into winter, and with winter came

the damp: the damp that seemed to ooze out of the very walls of the building and penetrate through barely adequate clothing as the girls sat in rows for their lessons.

Even as the cold fingers of this winter began to poke their way through November, Sister Anne lectured them on the meaning and importance of purity. She was most particular on this point. For girls, above all else, the keeping of oneself pure in mind and body was the most important thing. And the sin of impurity could be in thought, word, or deed.

Sister Anne moved easily through the class, bouncing her words left and right, occasionally stopping to finger her rosary beads. These hung in a black sweep almost to her knees. Every so often she would lift the bronze figure of the crucified Christ and kiss it gently. The girls loved listening to her: her voice held them enthralled, particularly as lots of what she said, though it did make sense, had a hint of greater passions only held back from disclosure to them by the very goodness and sweetness of her nature.

She almost spat the word 'Devil' when she told the girl's of Lucifer's downfall. 'He, who was once a Prince of Heaven foremost among the angels, he sat on the right hand of Almighty God and dared to rebel, poisoned by the sin of pride and thinking himself God's equal. He is condemned to Hell for all eternity, and daily works from there to bring young souls like yours to him to hold them forever so that they may never see the sight of God. That is the greatest torment of all for condemned souls, the reality of never knowing God and His eternal grace and goodness.'

The girls shuddered at the very thought of it and listened even more intently.

'Idle hands and minds are the Devil's playground. It is the idle of this earth that he seeks out, knowing that in their idleness he will find ripe fruit for plucking.'

Kathleen watched, enraptured, Sister Anne's gentle sweet face. She looked so proud, proud as Lucifer, defying the Devil and all his works. Sister Anne was surely the most beautiful creature on earth, with that pretty little oval-shaped face and the loveliest pearly-white teeth. Her white soutane framed a strong body that Kathleen could see was fully formed. Her long pointed wimple was like a ship in full sail. She moved easily, quickly and lightly, all the time warming to her task. To have the souls of these dear young children in her charge was a heavy responsibility, and not one she wanted to lose.

She fixed Kathleen with a warm, engaging smile, a smile that sent shivers down Kathleen's spine.

'Your bodies, girls, are temples of the Holy Ghost. To defile the pure body through thought and deed is to commit the sin of impurity, the greatest sin of all against our Divine Saviour.'

She swept twenty pairs of eyes up to a picture, large and bloody, that hung behind her. Almost four feet by three, it depicted the head and shoulders of a tormented Christ, his head framed by a crown of bloody thorns. Kathleen's heart felt a pang of sorrowing love as she gazed upon the face that looked so agonised. Her young mind opened to Sister Anne's call to ease the burden of Christ's suffering through good works and sacrifice. She would not add one iota to His pain.

Sister Anne's voice broke through her reflections. 'I want you to offer your souls to God. God is not mocked. He sees all and hears all. Should the tiniest sparrow fall from the sky He knows of it. But his greatest sorrow is to see one of His own lambs taken in by that Devil, Lucifer, and condemned to rot in Hell. Hell, where the walls are four thousand miles wide; where the fires burn but do not consume; where we long for death but are condemned to ever-lasting life; where each and every day we long for the sight of God but this is forbidden. Hell, where a whole year is but a moment in all eternity. Even on the last Day of Judgement, the impure may stand with their arms outstretched to their loved ones, but we a thousand miles away from them, condemned to hear the voice of God condemning them to Hell for all eternity.

27

Surely anything is better than that, surely it is better to keep ourselves chaste and pure, not to lose our innocence in one mad moment of temptation, and then spend the rest of our lives repenting it.'

Kathleen moved uneasily; the spell was breaking. Surely it was more than a little unfair to have to spend all your life suffering just for one little lapse.

Almost as if reading her mind, Sister Anne went on. 'The last-minute confession on our death bed may not be enough. Should there be the slightest hint of lapse in our contrition, we are doomed. God is not mocked, dear children. His love is great but so also is His vengeance. He threw Lucifer, who had great power, down into the pit in seconds. Each and every day, vow to draw nearer to God. Bathe yourself in the love of Christ and you will find each day of your life will prove better and easier, and you will grow up to be firm Christians and good Catholics — the mothers of Catholic families that will be a credit to you and yours. Even in small matters, remain modest. When you go to the wash room, remember to face the wall, and avert your eyes from the girls on either side of you. Do not be tempted by idle curiosity, for this is really the Devil's work. He tempts you to find in the unclad bodies of others a vessel of sinful desire.'

She ended her lesson with a prayer, then listened to their responses: 'Through my fault, through my fault, through my most grievous fault.' She next led them in the singing of a hymn, with a clear voice that soared heavenwards. Kathleen joined in, with vigour, and their voices mingled in offering their minds to God.

3

The high windows let in a weakly-shining sun. At a low angle in the heavens, it picked out the dust particles in the air. The coal stove sizzling and spitting quietly to itself in the corner. Kathleen pulled her shawl tightly round her. It was a brightly coloured garment, and contrasted strongly with her grey regulation orphanage dress.

She had reached the age of ten in the spring of 1907, and the nuns taught you how to knit when you reached that age. You were allowed to unravel old jumpers which 'the good kind Catholic folk of Dublin' had donated for the use of the orphanage. This was, of course, after you had finished all your other tasks: the washing and the sewing.

Remembering the last, cold winter, Kathleen had decided this would be a clever thing to do: to knit your own shawl to keep you warm. The various knitters would gather round a table when the wool arrived and wait expectantly for the share-out. Kathleen always chose the strongest colours and, bit by bit, stitch by stitch, her shawl became a thing of its own, as bright as a butterfly amidst the brown and grey.

The sisters had tolerated this, recognising that, maybe in this one thing, Kathleen should be allowed her own way and, besides, it kept her busy and out of other mischief.

No longer were the girls transported into evangelical fervour by Sister Anne's lashing tongue, for now Sister Bernadette had been assigned to take their religious classes. She was more than a little deaf, and just carried on talking regardless while the girls whispered behind their hands. Peering shortsightedly over her gold-rimmed glasses, she would drone on about the beauties of Heaven and the horrors of Hell. Without Sister Anne's poetry and intensity, it was as if the light of religion had gone out for Kathleen, and it now seemed a deadly dull dry thing to be sitting listening to the old nun's rasping voice. Doubts began to scuttle, cockroach-like, into the recesses of her young mind.

Sometimes another reality in the shape of men would intrude, though Father John and the ageing Father Ignatius, from the nearby seminary, were the only two who came regularly into the Convent, and virtually the only men whom Kathleen saw until she left, for the girls were not allowed outside the walls.

Kathleen hated going to Confession. Though it seemed right that you should tell God you were sorry for what you had done wrong, it seemed silly to be telling this to a priest when God was supposed to be everywhere, wasn't he? It was claustrophobic in the little box – the grille like a fly's eye. Why God should choose to be there she could not imagine.

Daily routine in the Convent was simple. Breakfast was a welcome sight at eight o'clock of a morning, when light was just beginning to peep through the windows of the refectory. It was a sparse meal of bread and dripping, with a mug of tea. The long tables were scrubbed clean after every meal, so there was no need for a plate. A mug of hot tea was just wonderful on those colder mornings as it coursed down to a rumbling stomach and warmed a body through.

A nun would stand at the end of each table, with a big bowl of dripping and large hunks of bread cut from the brown loaves baked in the convent's own bakery. The scrapings from the bottom of the bowl were thought best, as there gathered that precious jelly which tasted of the meat's very core. There was no guarantee of getting some, but when you did, it was delicious, and the taste would linger the whole morning.

Then it was back to the day's work: sometimes the sewing, at other times ironing laundry or helping out in the kitchen, or doing the washing. The washing was certainly not Kathleen's favourite occupation. The first time had been a revelation to her. Great baskets of laundry were brought to the washroom, where already fires were being stoked up under the boilers. Kathleen had then been told to 'sort' through the baskets.

What came out stunned her. There surely had been a murder going on as bloody rag after bloody rag emerged from the baskets among the sheets, dresses and towels. Kathleen's wonder increased until she could stand it no longer.

'Surely we should tell Sister about this?' she said to the big girl working with her. Eileen turned to look at the smaller girl's face, which was all innocent puzzlement, and she had laughed.

'Go ask your sister Maggie about it, you silly girl.'

Kathleen could scarcely suppress her curiosity. 'Maggie, Maggie', she called out in the yard at playtime, rushing up to her all breathless. 'There's something funny going on, I tell you. We had all these bloody rags in the washing basket and Eileen never turned a hair. She told me to ask you.'

Maggie looked down at her little sister, ten years old against her own fifteen, and she smiled. She herself had already started to use the rags, but at least she had known what was coming.

'Don't you worry, Kathleen. It's all to do with grown-up things you'll soon find out. The sisters call it the curse that's set upon us women, but all I know is that it happens each and every month until we're old.'

'But where does it come from, Maggie, and why does it happen?'

'It just does, that's all. Don't you go worrying your head about it now.'

And that had been that. There was little discussion of these things, except sometimes among the girls in the dormitories at bedtime. But it was not something that loomed large in their lives, as the nuns were careful to warn the girls against too much interest in their own

31

bodies. The body, after all, was but an impure vessel for the soul within.

Christmas was coming and, with it, the annual concert organised by the nuns. Local dignitaries were invited to witness how their money and gifts were used to the good of the poor little orphans of the city.

Kathleen and Maggie were both chosen for this concert, as they had good voices. Maggie was especially good at reciting long poems, while Kathleen had a sweet clear voice. She was to sing a solo, and she learned her part carefully, looking forward every day to rehearsal time. The soloists were allowed off work for a while to practise in the main hall, and Kathleen sang with feeling:

> *What are the wild waves saying*
> *Sister, the whole day long?*
> *That ever amid their praying*
> *I hear but a low loud song.*

Some days she could hardly utter the words for the lump in her throat at the thought of the waves and the great grey-green sea. She had not been out in the wide open spaces since she had entered the Convent, and this singing brought out emotions long kept hidden. The sweetness of the song itself was made more poignant by her own sense of longing to be out on the seashore where the birds whirled and screeched in God's own sky.

Christmas became a favourite time for Kathleen in the orphanage. She loved the little crib with the baby Jesus and the animals standing round. It was so different an image from that harsh one of Christ on the Cross. She could just imagine the agony of Mary when she had nowhere to put her baby safe on a cold winter's night. The shepherds were kind to bring the baby a sheep, and the three kings had come such a long, long way to visit Him.

Christmas, besides, was a time of extra rations, and special cooking and baking filled the Convent with good smells, for an extra effort was made then for the waifs

32

whose lives were confined inside the walls. Kathleen dearly loved mixing currants and raisins in the huge bowls used for the Christmas puddings, and the smell of the fruit brought sunshine into the heart of the huge kitchen, though encompassed all around with hard stone.

Now it was the day of the concert, and Mam was to come. She had been a regular visitor over the years, coming to see her girls on the allotted days. But she had seemed to grow older with each visit, her hair getting greyer and wispier as it straggled out from under her hairpins. Their poor mother was not doing well: she lived in a tenement room and took in sewing to pay the rent. It was certainly not nearly enough to support four growing girls and boys,

This year the boys had come out of the seminary to look for jobs. John had found work on a boat, and was even now sailing somewhere round Europe, God knows where, stoking up the fires of capitalism in the smelly, airless hold of a merchant ship. Peadar had decided to stay in Dublin and was working at the ledgers in a lawyer's office. He was always scribbling something, a snatch of a song here or a poem there, and his mother had high hopes of that son, if only he stayed clear of politics. In a city controlled by the British, to get involved in politics was a dangerous thing.

Kathleen woke up that day in a state of feverish excitement. They were to perform their concert in the afternoon, and then the girls would be allowed to join their relations in the refectory for tea. When lunch was over, they laid the long tables with plates and cups. Some girls would later set out the bread and cakes and make the tea; but the performers themselves would not have time for that.

This was also reporting time, as relatives had the chance to see the Mother Superior and ask how their girls were getting on. Kathleen dreaded this, as she was frequently in trouble for petty misdemeanours like

33

running in the corridor or talking during silent periods, the result of high spirits rather than wilful naughtiness.

The hall was now filling up, and the audience was seated ready. Plumed hats nodded in the crowd as the women talked to one another. The men looked important in their jackets and high collars, sitting holding their hats on their knees. Local dignity abounded.

Kathleen and Maggie peeped through the side-door looking anxiously for their mam. There she was – looking, oh, so tired and weary. Her little black hat looked sad and worn beside the gay plumage of the women benefactors who did good works and could afford more expensive headwear. Her coat was really not thick enough to withstand the damp chill breezes that blew off the sea and into the city.

When there came her turn to sing, Kathleen could feel her stomach churning. Little flutters danced their own tune up and down her ribcage as she walked on to the platform and waited for the pianist to start. But when the first notes sounded, she forgot to feel nervous – and let her whole being rise with the music, just as the waves rose and fell on Dollymount Strand.

> *Not by the seaside only*
> *There it sounds loud and free,*
> *But at night when it's dark and lonely*
> *In dreams it is still with me.*

And all the dark lonely nights she had spent in her small crumpled bed were there in that song as her voice seemed to fly now, up and away over the convent walls, to the beaches where the mighty sea was even now heaving its way up and down Dublin's shore.

Through her emotions, she hardly heard the applause as she finished and went down the steps to join the other performers waiting at the side of the hall. Maggie squeezed her hand and whispered, 'That was truly lovely, our Kathleen.'

Gazing round the hall for her mother, she saw her

34

sitting there with shining eyes, so proud of the daughter who could sing so fine with that lovely voice. It was wonderful to hear a sound like that coming from one of her own.

Later, when the concert was finished, and they sat in the refectory eating bread and cakes and drinking tea, Mam warmly congratulated them, saying what fine wonderful girls she had, and wasn't the Convent looking after them well.

Maggie and Kathleen glanced at each other, with a look of understanding that there mother was not to be troubled in any way.

'You've such a kind Mother Superior, my dears. Just look what she gave me!' She opened her hand and the two sisters saw a shining piece of silver, a half-crown. As Kathleen saw the tears of gratitude in her mother's eyes, a sudden spurt of anger came upon her. Why should she have to be so grateful for charity, like this? They had not always been so poor, after all, and her Mam had walked from her father's farm to her wedding ceremony on a carpet of flowers strewn by kinsmen and neighbours. And now she was so pathetically grateful for half-a-crown. Kathleen vowed in that moment never to have to rely on handouts from anyone.

4

By Maggie's seventeenth birthday, she had grown into a fine young woman with bright green eyes. Since organization was her special talent, the nuns would be reluctant to see her go from the orphanage as she was so obviously an asset to their little community. For if new girls arrived unexpectedly, orphaned by sudden death in their family, it was Maggie who would show them around and help them overcome their first fears at being left alone in the unfamiliar confines of the Convent. It was Maggie who made sure that they soon found someone who would hold their hand and listen in sympathy to their innermost thoughts. Thus she became the sisters' favourite senior. Thus she contrived to attain privileges and recognition unheard of before in the orphanage. For, if Kathleen was busy dreaming and reading, Maggie was eternally seeking to gain respect for herself. Her stay in the Convent she felt was but a prelude to the greater world outside; she was determined to make an impact there and never have to live like her mother did now.

She would have to leave the Convent soon, she knew. She also knew that she would have to find some means of keeping herself, though she could share her mother's accommodation for a while. She could imagine it: a wretched staircase leading up past numerous apartments bulging with human life and debris, a shabby door leading into a dingily decorated room with one small bed in it. There would be only one sink and one tap to serve the whole house, the tap dripping constantly to leave a brown stain on the cracked procelain. And this hell was where her Mam now spent most of her days, peering through the gloom at her endless sewing.

So today was Maggie's seventeenth birthday, and she sat with Kathleen in the refectory. Her mother arrived promptly, her face flushed with excitement. In she rushed and gave both of them a big hug.

'And it's a happy birthday to you, Maggie, and I've brought you the best present of all.'

'What's that, Mam?'

'Good news, good news. They'll be wanting young girls like you at the theatre in Abbey Street. I saw the notice so went down there and asked . . . Maggie, my love, I'm so excited for you. They said you can start this week as an assistant in the wardrobe department, and they weren't too worried about inspecting your sewing because they know all girls from the orphanage can sew. Can you believe it? It's all arranged. I went to see the Mother Superior extra early, and she said you can come right away. You'd better pack your bag now. I'm so looking forward to having you around at home, I can't tell you.'

'What about our Kathleen, Mam?' she finally got out. One glance at her sister was enough to tell her that Kathleen did not care for the prospect of a Maggie-less future. Though silent now, her face was a mirror to her emotions – a raging torrent beneath.

'Oh, Kathleen, my poor girl, come here,' and Kathleen's mother took her hand and held it tightly to her bosom. Looking deep into her daughter's eyes she could see the hurt and pain there, and the dread that now she would be all alone without her sister, who had been the mainstay of her life inside the Convent walls.

'Listen, Kathleen my dear, your sister Maggie has to be the first to leave – she's older than you. She and I won't be earning enough to keep you and feed you yet, my love. But we'll come and fetch you when we can, I promise. And we'll still come and visit you every month, you understand?'

Kathleen felt only deep, dire despair . . .

When Maggie came back, clutching a bag bulging with her few small possessions, she was all bustle and excitement as the joy of starting a new life overcame all feelings of anxiety about her future.

37

Kathleen's face said more than words, but she held her head high, trying hard not to cry as her beloved sister went from her. The nuns came in to say goodbye and wish Maggie well. Sister Teresa with her stern face and work-roughened hands; Sister Bernadette with an unusually kind expression; and finally the Mother Superior, gliding across the flagstones like a queen bee in the hive.

'We're sad to be seeing you going, Maggie Corr, I can't deny it. Who will be so good with the younger girls in the future? Ah, well, good luck to you, and I hope you remain a good Catholic girl now you're out in the big wide world.'

Much flapping of skirts followed as all ten nuns saw Maggie and her mother out of the main door and across the yard to the gate. Kathleen went with them, clinging to her sister as if drowning, but to no avail. Reaching the gateway, she was hugged warmly, with tear-moistened eyes, and then they were gone – and with them seemed to go the warmth from the sun and the light from the day.

It was a gloomy Kathleen who went back to her work and lessons in the weeks that followed. Maggie had provided a secure bedrock for her daily existence here, and now it seemed as if a great gaping hole had opened.

But the seasons passed and Kathleen grew into a sturdy, well-made fifteen-year-old. Her hair had grown long down her back, like a glossy waterfall, though usually tied back to hide its natural beauty. The Convent food was meagre and monotonous, yet the girls seemed to thrive on it, and grew into shining youngsters whose clean, bright faces would have brought a sparkle to the eye of any proud mother. Feelings of restlessness coursed through her now like the spring sap rising in her young body, and Kathleen longed to be away from the tedium of it all. She was tired of the walls which constantly surrounded her: if Hell was here on earth, surely this was it. The smell of cleanliness entrapped her: carbolic and cold water. She knew there must be more to life than praying and being pure and, although some of the nuns had been kind and taken a special interest in her, they had not really come to know the spirit inside her and had never quite forgotten that she was a 'fiery one'.

She had learned a fair amount at the Convent, besides domestic chores such as sewing and cleaning. Kathleen was proud of her neat copperplate writing with its elegant loops and flourishes. She had paid extra attention to this as she knew it might be useful later. There were no books to read except for the Lives of the Saints and moralistic tales, but Kathleen had read these so many times that she knew them off by heart. Indeed, she became quite famous in the dormitory for her rendition of the Lives, since she would add those extra little touches which made the stories seem more real, and the younger girls would always be asking for more. Kathleen would sit in the middle of the dormitory, and her highly embellished accounts would be delivered with so much exaggerated expression that the others would laugh until their stomach muscles ached.

Her Mam and Maggie would visit her at the end of every month, fetching her a little treat of sweets if they could afford it, and otherwise bringing her news from the outside world – news that she longed for as her yearning for the outside grew. But Kathleen also noticed how her mother seemed to grow ever more pale and thin. Saying 'Goodbye', she would put her arms around her, and feel the sharp bones beneath her threadbare clothes. And, after Mam had departed, with Maggie's strong arm like a prop for her matchstick figure, Kathleen would say an extra prayer begging God to make her mother stronger.

It was the end of March 1913 and another winter nearly over, but the winds could still be cruel and Kathleen wore her extra vest to keep out the chill. Easter was but weeks away, and already the girls were weaving their crosses for Palm Sunday. The sky above the yard was dark with clouds speeding across to some unknown destination, heavy with rain. It was a morning such as this that the news finally came.

It was about midday when she saw her sister enter the workroom, accompanied by Sister Teresa. As soon as she saw Maggie looking so grown-up in a black dress and cape, Kathleen knew that something was dreadfully wrong.

Maggie hugged her so tight she thought she would burst, then whispered to her, 'Come on, Kathleen, let's go to the dormitory. I've something to tell you.'

As they sat on the bed side-by-side, she began to explain in a quiet voice. 'Kathleen, our Mam has gone . . . It was very sudden. There was nothing we could do. She must have caught it coming home from her sewing deliveries. She got wet through to her skin, and then it was so cold in the night. I called the doctor, but he took ages to come, and by then Mam was all low and breathing like a rattle. When he came he said, "If I were you, Maggie Corr, I'd get the priest" . . . Oh, Kathleen, it was hard for her, but in the end she was peaceful, with a smile on her face like a young girl. Just myself and Molly Power there was.'

Kathleen's mind raced with painful emotions as she took this in, and then great racking sobs rent her body as she pictured her poor mother in that dismal room, struggling for breath in the dark hours before her death. Maggie cuddled her shaking sister, stroking her hair and murmuring words of comfort until the sobbing gradually subsided and Kathleen raised her red, swollen face to ask, 'But what happens now, Maggie?'

'You're to come with me and Uncle Ned, back to the tenement where she is laid out. And then we must go to the funeral. You'll have to get your clothes together now.'

The Mother Superior came to see her off, her face twisted with concern. For Kathleen the shock was still great, and she listened numbly as the nun spoke. 'Your Mammy has gone to Heaven. She is with our Lord this day, of that we can be certain. For hard-working, good-

40

living women like her have first call on God's good nature.'

As Kathleen sobbed, the Mother Superior went on softly, 'Now, now, no need to cry. It's a happy release for your poor mother from this vale of tears. Our lives here on earth are only a preparation for our real life in the next one. I am sure your mother knew that and found death a welcome visitor.' Lifting up Kathleen's face, she gazed down. 'Prince or peasant, Pope or poor Clare, we all must face death: it is the great humbler. Go home now and bury your mother, and take all our prayers with you.'

5

Maggie led her silently through the Convent gate and walked her towards a hackney-cab. Her uncle's smiling face leaned out of the window, and when he stepped down she flew into his arms. He stroked her long hair; by God, she was a pretty one, and now fifteen. Aloud he said, 'You're a sight for sore eyes . . . Well, here we all are again like Brown's cows, even if it is a sad occasion that brings us together.'

As they bowled along Merchant's Quay and into the city, Kathleen marvelled at the hustle and bustle that surrounded them. How quiet the Convent had been compared to this, with its scrupulously polished floors, the silent swish of the nuns moving swiftly along. Now they were at Burgh Quay and she was fascinated to glimpse the docks in action. Opposite the huge white edifice of the Custom House, men sweated and heaved to unload cargoes from ships tied up right in the very centre of the city. From one vessel men swayed along the gangplanks with twenty-stone bags of grain on their backs. As the cab swayed perilously near the river's edge, she could see on another boat a gang of coal-heavers digging their way down into the bowels of a black heap that only the other day had supported a Welsh mountain. Just further along, a load of slates from Portugal was being stacked neatly on the waggoner's cart.

She could smell the sweet sickly smell of fresh timber being lifted out of a boat on men's padded shoulders, and despite her grief, she watched entranced as the carters started up their horses under the huge loads and the great hairy hooves strained to get the load moving – and then, with a lurch, they were off, sparks flying. How simple it made life that everything Dublin people wanted could be brought by sea.

Uncle Ned looked at her fondly, a young woman now, with a fine young body on her, God bless her. A far cry from the little slip of a girl he had taken to the Convent so long ago – though in some ways, it seemed just yesterday. Their Mammy's passing must be a bitter blow to the pair of them, and yet each human heart must bear its grief. He cleared his throat and said, 'The reason we came down this way is for me to check the sailings to America.'

Kathleen and Maggie turned to him in alarm.

He smiled sadly. 'I am afraid so. It's the emigrant boat for me, like so many before me, and I am sure I won't be the last. I'm off to look for American gold; they say there is bread and work for all. But I would not forget old Ireland were it fifty times as fair.' He stopped for a moment's thought. 'You know how the old song goes: "Go sell the cow and pig, *agradh*, and wander far away, for in Paddy's land but poverty you'll find". I have a job ready for me in New York, and I am told it's the liveliest city on earth. The Irish are doing great there: our own are making fortunes. I have the fare spared from the sale of the last of our land, and as soon as I have made my way and got settled, be sure I will send for the pair of you.'

His heart sank even as he said it. America was over two thousand miles away: a great journey, a new country. Would he really ever see them again? He looked at their sad young faces and his heart nearly failed him. Then he collected himself. Needs must when the Devil drives. He would go. He would make some money, and then he would send for them. His brother's letter told him of the great opportunities that lay in the States if a man was able to take advantage of them. He would get nowhere here, and opportunities only started when you went abroad. He would take his heart in his hand and go for it. He would miss Dublin, for he loved the old town, every stick and stone in it, yet he knew his time had come. Just as this river ran to the sea, so he must follow, to seek his fortune in that distant land.

43

The girls sat before him. Maggie remained expression-less but Kathleen's face was shrunken with fear. 'But what's to happen to us meantime, while you're making your fortune?' she burst out. 'Where shall we go? Who will have us?'

Well, Maggie will be all right where she is, for the Abbey Theatre people will look after her. And, as for you, Kathleen, I'll ask the Sisters to get you a good place in service.'

Still anxious but partly relieved, Kathleen sank back on the seat. Above all else she dreaded having nowhere to go. Without a home or a job, you couldn't leave the Convent. Or, in the heel of the hunt, if you couldn't find anywhere yourself, then the nuns found somewhere for you, and some of the jobs they found were not the best.

As he went off about his inquiries, Kathleen's head was in a whirl. Her mother dead, her uncle going away, perhaps for ever, and herself going to live with a stranger. Was her life never again to be at peace?

Starting up again, they set off down Eden Quay, but soon their way was blocked by a group of men holding some sort of meeting under a flag embroidered with a plough and stars on a field of blue. Many of the men carried hurling sticks, and every time they agreed to some point, they raised their wooden hurleys in the air and shook the steel-banded heads in approval.

As the girls leaned out to listen, a tall young man at the back of the crowd started paying attention to Kathleen and Maggie rather than to the meeting. Turning his back on the speaker, he drifted nearer to the window of the cab. A cigarette dangling from his lips, he smiled pleasantly at Kathleen with brown eyes. 'Are you taking anyone with you in that thing? Is there room for me?'

Her uncle leaned forward into view. 'No, there isn't, and you'd be better off at your work instead of your damned meetings. I know in Dublin you can start a meeting by sticking your finger in the air, but would you mind telling me what is so important here that it stops people like ourselves going about our business.'

The young man answered reasonably, 'It's union business that brings us here, and yonder is the flag of the Citizen Army which has come to protect us from the police. And we, here, are from the Transport and General Workers' Union, the one big union where working men of all countries can unite and we get to the big rock-candy mountain. At the minute our own leader Jem Larkin is calling for a boycott of the *Independent* newspaper after Martin Murphy, the owner, denounced our union in it.'

Uncle Ned laughed and said to the young man, 'Well *you* don't seem to be taking it all too seriously, I'll give you that.'

'No, you couldn't get too involved in any of these things or you'd never see the wood for the trees.'

Uncle Ned looked out at the crowd. 'Do you think we will be here much longer. I have lots to do and I'm off to America next week.'

The young man looked thoughtful. 'If you take my advice, you will get out before then. The employers are demanding we workers sign a document swearing we won't be members of Larkin's union, and that's something no one in this town will ever do. For Dublin is nearly a hundred per cent trade union now – not like it was some time back. Jem Larkin has raised us up off our knees, and we can look any employer in the face now, not at his boots. Yes, my advice to you, sir, is go while the going is good. Come Monday morning there won't be a ship moving in the docks, from the Alexandra Basin to Butt Bridge.'

Even Uncle Ned seemed disturbed. God in heaven, more trouble now. He would have to change his sailings; maybe he could get away still if he left early enough. He thanked the young man for his friendly advice.

'Jack Carey's the name, sir, if ever I can be of service.'

Kathleen listened raptly to their good-natured exchange. It seemed so manly and worldly after the milk-and-water expounded by the nuns who thought of little else except prayers and death. Here were life, strikes, struggles, and great strong men laughing and joking.

They were all startled by a loud voice calling for the street to be cleared. Kathleen peered out the cab window and saw that the voice belonged to an enormous inspector of the Dublin Metropolitan Police. He grasped a long thin cane in both hands, whilst behind him a file of his men were loosening the straps of their short, thick batons. Swiftly, Carey guided their cab through the crowd and into a side-street. 'You'd better be off before they start a baton charge. Take care now.' And he was gone, waving his hurley aloft. Kathleen looked back in time to see the police begin their charge with weapons raised, and bellowing like mad bulls. But rapidly they were swallowed up in the mass of dockers who came streaming down from the boats and into the fray.

Uncle Ned anxiously urged the cabby to drive faster. What a violent people they were, he considered, and no doubt it would get worse before it got better. Still, he was grateful for Carey's tip; the sooner now he was gone from Dublin the better.

The cab soon reached Sackville Street, so wide and spacious, the main thoroughfare of the city. It was full of jostling and pushing, with hundreds of ordinary citizens out walking, talking, shopping, and the traffic streaming endlessly up and down.

Their uncle continued his usual running commentary. 'It's the widest street in Europe, and it has ten fine statues. Yonder is Nelson's Pillar – the tall one in the middle. The monument is over a hundred foot high and Nelson himself stands on top of it. He only had one eye and only one arm, so they put a one-armed one-eyed adulterer to lord it over us.'

As they passed the base of the pillar, Kathleen could see people queuing to climb to the top. She clasped her hands, 'Uncle could we go up there? Please!'

Her fresh eagerness delighted him; it took so little to please the young. 'Yes, indeed, and why not? We will be a long time dead.' He wished he had not said that, thinking suddenly of his poor sister, but hoped they had not noticed. He turned around quickly to bid the cabby wait for them ten minutes.

The two girls hesitated as they came up to the paybox but their uncle stepped forward. 'This one is mine, as the devil said of the dead policeman.' He stuffed their tickets into their hands and the three of them climbed the long spiral stairway to the top. Kathleen shivered. It was cold as only granite can be; and windowless with nothing but blank wall around them until, suddenly, they were up aloft, over a hundred feet above the teeming city.

Here their uncle was again their guide. 'Feast your eyes on that, girls, Dublin's fair city where the girls are so pretty, and yet no Dubliner would thank me for telling him that Dublin never was in a thousand years an Irish city – always some sort of garrison town. First the Vikings; they used Dublin as a base to plunder Europe. Then the Normans invaded, and now, it's the centre of British power in Ireland. For centuries it was surrounded by the Pale that the foreigners sheltered behind, only venturing out now and again to see how things were in the real Ireland. But we bacame the second city of the Empire, and all those fine buildings you see round were built to honour a city second only to London'.

Indeed, Kathleen was too preoccupied in studying the panorama below to pay much attention to her uncle's ramblings. From up here, the street seemed even wider than ground level. Down Henry Street she could see the vendors running up and down offering their wares to passers-by, and even up here she could faintly hear the women's cries: 'Three a penny, the oranges, missus . . . Lovely Howth herrings, all fresh that swam in the bay this very morning. Come on, missus, give him a couple of these and he won't leave you alone for a week.' But one sight caused her great annoyance. From her perch she spotted three gypsy children tearfully imploring money from passers-by. When they struck lucky, they made off down the street a bit and stood in the doorway of a pub until a red-faced man came out, snatched the coins from their hands, and vanished back inside. The children then wandered back to beg and cajole even more money for the drunkard to squander.

Kathleen was sorry to have to come down at all, but the press of people waiting their turn for the view grew with each passing minute. Soon they were all aboard their cab again heading for their mother's tenement room. Immediately they left Sackville Street, it was almost like another world. They galloped quickly up towards Summerhill, past Kennedy's Bakery where she breathed in the warm fresh smell of newly-baked bread. The streets began to look mean and ugly. They passed down Gardiner Street, its steps festooned with chattering women; then into the notorious Diamond. It was a rough area, and there she saw the Diamond public house with not a single window-pane left, every last one of them gone, smashed in Saturday night brawls and by passing hooligans. But still it was packed, even at this early hour of the day. It was hard to think that this district could get any rougher. They passed, too, the Diamond School for boys, with every window wired up like an outstation waiting for an Indian attack.

Finally, they halted in a mean, dirty, airless little street that long ago had seen better days. Kathleen felt her heart sink. No wonder Mammy had faded away like an early spring flower. Here there were no trees, no smell of heather, no rising hills. All was dank and decay – a decay that ate into the very fabric of the shabby houses. These stood in a terrace, with sightless eyes staring out; torn rags adorned the windows where they had any pretence at curtains. This seemed a very long way from Sackville Street, though only a quarter mile. Here were no fine monuments, no clean, prosperous people. Here the residents looked defeated in their struggle against poverty, and king dirt reigned supreme. Dozens of grubby children played out on the street, missing death by inches as waggons thundered by. With a heavy heart, Kathleen made her way towards Number Fourteen. Nearby stood a group of gossiping women, who stopped their discussion briefly to stare and pull their shawls closer as

Maggie, Kathleen and Ned mounted the wide steps. On the door, a small black wreath with a Mass card proclaimed the death of Nora Corr, widow of John Corr, provision merchant, late of Lower Dorset Street, Dublin. It was incredible – from owning eleven houses to renting one grim tenement room. How their poor mother must have suffered. Yet she bore it bravely, never moaning, never doubting that all would be well with her girls in the end: never asking anything for herself.

Kathleen felt bitter. They who ask for nothing will get nothing. That was the lesson of her mother's life. She had been ruined by a feckless man. She had been ruined by a pretence: the pretending that her husband knew what was best when he didn't. Maggie had told her that, like most men, he was a fool. Now Kathleen felt her heart harden as she looked around her, and she swore to herself that no man would ever bring her as low as her father had brought her poor mother. Yet she could not hold hatred in her heart, not even for the man who had done so much damage with his foolishness. So she blessed herself in front of the Mass card and whispered a prayer for her dear departed parents, hoping that at least they might be happy together in heaven. As for herself, no man would ever mistreat her – or, if he did, he would pay for it.

A great fat floop of a woman stood at the hall door, almost completely blocking it. 'What do yous want?' She glared at Kathleen's neat convent clothes, and certainly they did look out of place amidst all the torn skirts and ragged shawls.

Kathleen felt a surge of anger. 'We have come to bury my Mammy, if you don't mind.'

The great fat woman drew back, nervously adjusting her dress which kept falling open in the middle to reveal two emormous breasts. 'Ah, child of grace, why didn't you say? So, Nora was your Mammy – and, look, here's your sister, Maggie. I didn't see you there. Come in, then. You're as welcome as the flowers in May. Molly Power at your service.'

Now she smiled sweetly on them all. 'Ah, you poor forsaken orphans. Well, I'm proud to say that I looked after your poor mother in her last hours. we don't have much in this street, but what we have we share — isn't that right, girls?'

The women by the steps nodded agreement, and one of them shouted up, 'True for you, Molly Power. Never was a truer word spoken. Every man in Dublin must have had a share in you and your girls.'

Mrs Power laughed. 'Oh, those are common as ditch-water, but good-hearted enough. Let's go up and see the poor woman.'

As Molly Power turned in the dark hallway, Kathleen realised that she had only one leg but was able to move with surprising agility, swaying from side to side as she pushed a crutch in front of her. They made their way up a staircase with banisters so broken that all that was left were little stumps of wood like rotten teeth that would hardly stop you toppling over. Kathleen moved in against the wall for safety.

Mrs Power shouted down at them, 'Excuse the state of us, but the house was condemned by the Corporation years ago. That's all they did, condemn it, and then nothing else for the likes of us. Still, they did us a favour. Since we were condemned, we haven't had to pay a penny rent. Isn't that great?'

The room her mother lay in was tidy and neat but very bare. Kathleen could sense that on all but the coldest winter's day the room had been fireless. The grate was far too clean, and had been so for many a long day. Her mam would try to save on fuel, arguing that she had only to put on an extra jumper to keep warm. She would save her penny to buy presents for her daughter in the orphanage on visiting days. But during the last few months, Kathleen was ashamed to recall she had not looked forward to those visits; Mammy looked so ill. She wondered where her two brothers were now — gone but not forgotten. One on the seas, for sure, but the other an idle wastrel, drinking and God knows what else round the town, Maggie had complained, while their mother lay here like this. Like father, like sons; they had inherited all his stupid careless ways. Why did some men never grow up?

She felt moved by the fat woman's concern. 'Thank you, Mrs Power, for all you did for Mammy. Thank you from the bottom of a grateful heart.'

Molly Power turned towards the window and waited a second before replying. 'No thanks needed. We only did what any good neighbour would do down this street. When anyone is in trouble, we all do the best we can to help.' She then walked slowly round the room. 'You know, it's the custom in this street to have a proper wake for our dead. We get in some drink and a fiddler maybe, and then we sing and dance until the early hours of the morning. It's our way of showing our respect, and it won't cost you or your uncle a penny, for the neighbours will have a collection. Then, if we can pick up a few young medical students from the Royal College, we're made. Some of those would make a cat laugh. Oh, you can be sure we will give your mother a right good send-off. It will be so good she won't want to go.'

That night the chilly room was transformed. A great roaring fire swept up the chimney, the coal forming little caverns of red glowing heat. Kathleen sat with Maggie beside the open coffin and watched as each neighbour came and kissed the corpse, murmuring condolences to the girls as they passed: 'Sorry for your trouble, dear.' Kathleen found it very consoling, and began to weigh the empty poverty of these people's lives against the seemingly endless generosity of their natures.

As soon as they had all passed the coffin, the visitors sat down wherever they could and drank dark porter beer from an endless supply. Gradually, as the evening went on, the reverential hushed tones gave way to loud, raucous, merry conversation. When the pubs closed they were joined by a party of young men in fine spirits.

In one corner sprawled Molly Power, attended by a fat little man who kept stroking her leg. She patted him lightly on the back, 'Mr Bloom, aren't you the dirty little devil. Does your wife know you're out?'

Bloom, gave a gentle smile. 'Indeed she does, and if I'm not mistaken, she was away to the races this very day with a very good friend, Mr Blazes Boylan.'

Around Mrs Power sat several of her sisters of the night, most of them looking thin, weedy and underfed. She was their protectress from pimps and police, and provided them with the odd room in which to practise their craft. It was hard to believe that any man could find pleasure in them, yet whores they were, and their lives would be short and sad. One exception was a sturdy girl with a heavy, broad peasant's face. Her clothes were neat: a blue serge dress drawn in by a large black belt. She wore a sailor's hat, and looked as strong as Mrs Power's other women looked weak. She wandered over beside the coffin and introduced herself. 'I am Nora Barnacle. I was told my fella would meet me here, and I hope you don't mind my coming. I didn't know your mother.'

She went on, 'Me fella's a medical student – and a writer. Sometimes I think he's cracked.'

Kathleen looked at her with new interest. She seemed so unlike the others, her rude, healthy strength a welcome blast of country air. Would she wither here in town like all the rest?

Kathleen listened intently as Nora's voice rose over the increasing din. The room was now jam-packed, and a fiddler was scraping a first few notes, getting ready to let the music rip. First he went slowly over the strings, playing an old Irish lament. It was so haunting that Kathleen felt her very soul lift to the sound of it. It seemed impossible that notes of such purity could be summoned up by a human hand. The room had fallen silent and, as the last note died, the crowd burst into loud applause.

Molly Power tapped with her crutch. 'Mullins, I declare before God there is no finer fiddler in all Ireland. You would charm the birds off the bushes. Give that man a drink!'

Those close to the fiddler were begging him for a jig, but he only smiled. 'In a minute. Let me get this jar down me and then I will play "The High Caul Cap", and you can dance to your hearts' content.'

Nora's intrusive voice persisted. 'Did you ever hear the likes of this? Listen to my fella's letter; you'll never hear anything so funny again in all your born days. The man is beyond the beyond. "I told you, my darling, that you drive me wild with desire in a way that no other woman can. But I want you to do more, my cruel mistress. I want you to use me as you would a surly dog. Crush me, bestride me, like a wild mare." God, isn't he a caution?'

'So I'm a caution, then?' the male voice sounded harsh and angry but faintly amused. 'I see you're regaling all the present company with my innermost thoughts.'

Kathleen looked up at the tall thin figure leaning forward on a long cane, and she was surprised to see that it was Nora who was now blushing from embarrassment. Seizing two bottles in one hand and grasping Nora by the waist, he shouted, 'Let us practise what I preach,' and dragged her to a corner of the room where they lay side-by-side downing the drink. Kathleen was bemused by the strange scene she witnessed. No violence, no rebukes, no grudges held. This was certainly an extraordinary young man; he seemed to be utterly self-confident — no trace of self-doubt in his mind.

A large, ungainly youth beside her spoke: 'You're fascinated with my brother, I see. But that's quite usual. Everyone thinks James Joyce is a genius, including himself.'

'And do you think he's a genius?'

The young man answered without hesitation. 'Yes, I do, and I am the servant to that genius. Jim will do great things: it is in him. He puts his art before life itself and that, I think, is just a mark of his greatness. He doesn't want my service, or so he says, but I think he uses me. I know he reads my diaries. And more than once I have heard Jim's friends quote things that could only have come from me. Yet, if I say the very same things myself, I am laughed at. It's a cruel world, isn't it?'

Kathleen was saved from answering by the wild strains of the fiddle that now erupted, setting every foot in the room to twitching. The tapping of feet soon gave way to wild cries as several couples took the floor and faced each other in the dance of life. Their bodies twisted and turned in a four-handed reel that made them spin for dear life in the crowded room.

Kathleen had never witnessed anything like it. The young man might be ungainly, but on the dance floor he was as light as air. The fiddler sped the notes faster and faster until Kathleen thought they were flying; the feet that now beat the floor seemed to shake the house to its very foundations. The dancers screamed exultantly, and it was with disappointment at the end of the reel that they finaly sank back to the floor.

Kathleen gratefully accepted a bottle 'by the neck' from Stanny Joyce. As she choked on the strong black porter, the first she had tasted, she was thinking how full the day had been. Oh, indeed, she was so glad to be free of the stuffy Convent. She was made for this life. Silence and contemplation were not for her – a nun she would never be now. She wanted too much to join in the race for life, to be part of its rich current. She gazed at her poor mother's face in the coffin: *patient unto death*. That wasn't something anyone would ever set on her own gravestone. She turned to look up into Stanny Joyce's face: it was callow, unbrutalised, fresh yet tired and old in another way. He looked so serious that she could not help teasing him. 'You're wearing a face that would stop a horse-tram. What's the matter with you, at all?'

He sighed. 'I know I'm not good company for a young girl, that's what's the matter. Jim gets round women with soft talk, and I am no good for that sort of work. He despises women and yet just look at him now, fondling away to beat the band.'

They danced once again and, as they went round the floor, Stanny was almost crushing the life out of her. His desperation frightened her. When the music ceased he reached out for her again, but she avoided his frantic groping by adroit twists and turns that left him breathless and angry. Savagely, he snarled: 'You're like all the rest, a tease. You lead a fellow on, and then you push him away.'

She said, 'Oh, it's not that. If only you weren't so extreme about it. You give a body no chance to make up her own mind.'

He almost spat out the words, 'You can keep it then and may it keep fine for you.' He was almost in tears. 'Jim has no problem with women — am I to be behind him in everything?'

Kathleen was saddened by the thought of a youthful life so shadowed by a stronger flame. 'Oh, that's a bitter thing to say, bitter in someone as young as you.'

His hands twisted in pain. 'Young! I have never really been young. I have never known the careless hours of youth. I was robbed of those by a drunken father who put my mother into an early grave. But, like some drunkards, he has the health and strength of an ox. Of course, I am bitter. From a house where you had to fight for every scrap of bread. And my brother is like my father; like father, like son. He has inherited all my father's profligate ways. He spends all his own money and other people's, too, as if the world owes him a living. He treats women like dirt and gets away with it. Just look at him now, groping away at Nora, and yet an hour ago she was sneering at him. Look at him.'

Kathleen turned to look. She saw the dishevelled forms of Nora and Jim entwined on the floor, with Nora sitting astride him as you would a horse, her stout peasant body holding him firmly down. Her long hair kept sweeping his face, and her body moved as though to the sound of soft sweet music.

In dismay Kathleen looked away to the coffin then back to this irreverent scene. She was going to make protest when Stanny gently pulled her back. 'They mean no disrespect, Kathleen. In the midst of death we have life eternal. Leave them be.'

She sank back again and, even as she did, the two bodies ceased to move. Mr Bloom got up to gently place a large eiderdown over them.

Stanny spoke softly to her; the terrible desperation was gone. 'You can see now, can't you, why I feel bitter? My brother uses women as objects. He goes from whorehouse to whorehouse and that is something I cannot do. I have never gone with prostitutes in my life, nor will I ever. I want a woman to care for me, to feel for me. And yet, for all my concern for them, women show me none. They despise me. They think of me as a namby-pamby, a mother's boy. Little do they know the great hunger of the soul that devours me, a hunger to love and be loved. Is that a lot to ask?'

Kathleen was deeply moved. He was right. To love and be loved by another was the one thing that we all wanted. Perhaps to deny someone that love was the greatest crime of all.

But, unused as she was to it, the small drop of porter was taking its toll. She felt her head spinning and sat down on a corner of the sofa. As she fell into a half-troubled sleep, she was barely aware of her sister slipping a cover over her, and people slowly moving round and getting ready to leave. She was gone to the world when at last Maggie pulled on the string and the gas-mantle fluttered out.

6

When Kathleen awoke she thought at first she was back in the Convent. The heavy silence was the same, but that was all. Instead of a dormitory full of sleeping girls, she lay in a high-ceilinged room with her dead mother stretched out in the coffin, and Maggie fast asleep on the floor. The guests had gone, and all she could hear was a mouse slowly scratching its way to a bigger mousehole. She began to brood on how her dear mother had spent her days in this room. She would have awoken early each morning on the old brown horsehair sofa, covered with an old patchwork quilt. She would have shuffled her way down to the cold yard and filled her kettle from a dripping tap encrusted with years of rust. There her neighbours would no doubt have welcomed her with, 'It's a grand day again, Mrs Corr. Isn't it fine and well you're looking.' And her mother would have replied, 'It is, thanks be to God.'

Kathleen wandered over to the door. She opened it gently and listened for sounds, but there were none. Instead she caught the pungent smell of bacon and kidneys frying, and licked her lips. She was starving with hunger and dry from thirst. As she made her way downstairs with the kettle, she found herself following the smell, until, looking through a half-open door she saw Mr Bloom at the hearth, gently tickling the underside of a kidney with a fork. He smiled at her and beckoned with the fork.

'Come in, come in,' he said. 'Wasn't I at your wake last night, and weren't your mother and me the best of friends'.

She hesitated, but he called again, 'Come in, child of grace, sure I won't do you any harm. I am old enough to be your father. Come in and have a cup of tea at least.

Sure, you won't refuse me the favour of your company, will you?' Suddenly it seemed as though it was not she who was the beggar, but he wanting and needing company to garnish his dish. She could not resist his kind offer, so she gratefully sat down at the square whitewood table, scrubbed and scrubbed so its face was nearly worn away from time. Many the good meal that table had seen, but it seemed to Kathleen none more than welcome than this one.

Mr Bloom poured her out a cup of tea so strong that you could trot a mouse on it. Gratefully, Kathleen swallowed the scalding liquid, and watched him holding the frying-pan over the last heat of a fire. 'It's not much', he called. 'But of what there is, you're more than welcome to it.'

Not much! Kathleen was staggered at the piled-up plate that he put before her – kidneys, bacon, sausages, black and white pudding in slices, more white than black. The last was a Dublin delicacy, originally introduced to the city by a German family, Messrs Mogerley, famous throughout Dublin for their puddings, sausages and bacon. There was no one to touch them, and their shops so clean you could eat off the floor.

As they ate, she pressed Bloom for more details of her mother's life in the tenement house. He said thoughtfully, 'She was a great old woman, a real Dubliner of the rare ould kind. If she couldn't do you a good turn, she would never do a bad one. She always looked after neighbours who were ill, and many's the time I have seen her go to look after some children for the day while the mother took a sick child to hospital. She was a grand woman. She couldn't do enough for a body, so she couldn't. There was never a bad word between her and me, or anyone else for that matter. God give her rest.'

Kathleen was cheered by this account. In the end good friends were all, it seemed.

Mr Bloom went on, 'I'll tell you, once I was standing out there on the landing when I was attacked by the blackguard, Cuffe. He's always tormenting me, a born persecutor if there ever was one. Well, not saying one thing and meaning another, Cuffe went for calling me a dirty ould Jew and started to ballyrag me, saying we were responsible for Christ's murder, and that if God himself wasn't safe with us, who would be?'

He poured Kathleen another cup of tea.

'Well, your mother came out and stuck up for me like a good neighbour. "Look here," she says to Cuffe, "a Jew is a poor mother's son like any of us, and how do you know there is any God anyway?" Well, Cuffe looked at her as though she had horns on her head, and tried to floor her, by saying "Didn't God make the world? So we all know that there must be a God". "Well," says she, "if God made the world, who made God?" Well, off he went, flattened.'

Kathleen was amazed at this. It was a philosophic side to her mother she had never known.

The room was comfortable, as warm as her mother's had been cold. Heavy curtains hung from floor to ceiling, and glass ornaments lined a heavy sideboard. On the wall Bloom's mother and father, heavy and grave, looked out of a large photograph. Below it stood two candles with a glass in the middle. She wondered if it was a Jewish feast day. Of their religion she knew nothing. Suddenly there came a voice from another room, calling out, 'Poldy, Poldy, are you there? Am I to die this day for the want of a cup of tea? I thought you'd have been here with it hours ago.' She watched Mr Bloom hastily assembling a teacup and a milk jug on a tray. He glanced sheepishly at Kathleen as he hurried to answer his wife's strident call.

After filling the kettle Kathleen walked back up the stairs, full and content. She went over to the coffin and warmly kissed her mother. How she wished she was back among them: there was so much they could have done, so many places they could have gone together. And now it would never be. She walked to the window and looked out into the dingy street as sadness enveloped her.

'And where have you been this fine morning, our

Kathleen? I've been looking for you everywhere and nowhere were you to be found, and this our Mam's burying day, with me left on my own to do everything imaginable.'

Maggie's face was flushed as Kathleen looked round, and she was twisting a lock of her hair in the way she did when she was tense and worried.

'About last night I will say nothing, save that I have spent more than an hour this morning cleaning the place up while you had sneaked out to God knows where — and what have you got to say about that?'

Kathleen let the scolding words wash over her as the memory of the last night's dancing came back and she remembered the feel of Stanny Joyce's arms so big and strong around her. She was silent, and could think of nothing to say, thinking all the while it must have been the porter that made her forget respect for her own dear mother lying in the coffin.

'Well, you keep a look out of the window for Uncle Ned and the funeral men, if we are going to see mother below ground today.' Maggie issued her instructions as one used to obedience, and Kathleen was only too pleased to be doing something helpful.

Outside in the street the children were now celebrating Saturday with a steady chant of 'Janey Mack, me shirt is black, what will I do for Sunday, get into bed and cover your head and don't wake up till Monday.' A group of girls swung madly round a gaslamp on a rope, their heels kicking against the metal pole as they went round. Just below her, Mrs Power leaned on her crutch. When she spotted Kathleen, she waved up a friendly greeting. The children playing catch-as-catch-can jumped out of the way as a short black hearse turned in off the North Circular Road and halted outside. Its two great black horses tossed their long black plumes high in the air. A serious-faced man gathered the reins and deftly tied them round the shaft of the hearse, gazing up at the house. He was joined by another man from the offside of the hearse, and they both donned large black top-hats.

Then, with a heavy, solemn step they mounted the stairs to her mother's room.

There they stood but made no move to screw down the coffin lid. Instead the driver produced a piece of paper, and his friend's eyes screwed up in cunning enjoyment as he watched his partner. Colley was the man for the job; if he couldn't get money even out of them that had none, no one could.

Colley cleared his throat and, jerking his finger at the body, said, 'There will be no taking of coffins until this little matter is settled.' The little matter was a bill for five pounds, and Maggie's face paled.

Alarmed she cried out, 'My uncle should have settled this.'

But Colley was firm. 'It's equal to us, miss. No pay, no play, and them's our orders.'

Maggie was horrified. If only her uncle would come. The shame of it: no money for her own mother's funeral. If only Uncle Ned would come. But Colley could not wait.

One more try; 'Can't you just make an exception in this case, and bury my mother. You know you'll be paid just as soon as we can manage.'

Colley removed his tall black hat and mopped his forehead. 'No can do, miss. No can do. You would be surprised how many people forget their lawful and awful dues once the body is safely down there. No, it's got to be cash on the nail, so it has, or no funeral.'

It was the powerful voice of Mrs Power that drove Colley down the stairs. 'Get out,' she roared, 'you pair of vultures. Get out and take your bad luck with you. We managed before and we'll manage again.' She turned to Maggie and Kathleen. 'Look here, when a child dies round here we don't have a hearse, just a lift on their daddy's back to the graveyard. The last piggyback they will ever have. Now, your mother hardly weighed any more than a little chissler. We could easily carry her to Mrs Brady's yard in Foley Street, and she'll let us have an ass and cart to take her on to the 'Nevin; it's only a hen's race between here and there.' And she hastened to the window to pour further abuse on the startled hearse men below. 'Aren't you the miserable pair of bastards. You'd begrudge a poor old woman a funeral. Arrh, if I had my way and you both became ghosts, you would even begrudge a body a fright.'

Maggie had been stunned by their demand. Five pounds! She had barely five pence to her name at the moment. Anxiously, she watched as Mr Bloom gently screwed down the lid of the coffin. And she raged inwardly at the defection of her uncle. 'Bad cess to him. Never there when he's wanted.'

But the coffin, being longer, was not as easily managed as a child's. Once or twice, going down the stairs, they nearly lost it over the side of the broken banisters. When they finally reached the street, Kathleen was relieved that Glasnevin was not all that far. Mrs Power was right in that, but she could not help carry the coffin, with her one leg. As they started walking slowly if unsteadily, more and more women and children fell in behind, the children cheering and jeering. They turned out from the narrow street into the wide openness of the North Circular Road.

As chance would have it, their route took them past the house where Jack Carey lodged. Peering out the window, at first he merely laughed at the motley throng, but then he recognised Maggie and Kathleen, both supporting one side of the coffin while Mr Bloom struggled with the other, and some children gave occasional support where they could fit in. Jack slid on a jacket and made his way outside. With a smile to the girls, he slid an arm under the coffin to ease the load.

On they went till they came to The Big Tree pub, where Mrs Power called a halt. They set the coffin on a trough donated for the use of animals by the Dublin Horse and Cattle Trough Association and Mrs Power gave the largest of the attendant boys a penny to stand guard while they went inside. Somewhat the worse for wear, the cortège then moved over Binn's Bridge and turned up along the Royal Canal towards Glasnevin and as they reached the gates of the Prospect Cemetery both Carey and Bloom excused themselves and made off at a trot for the Cross Guns Bar.

The gravedigger spat on teak-hard hands and nudged his mate. 'Look busy, here he comes now, old tub of guts. For God's sake, I hope he finds no fault with us this time.' They were referring to the approach of a portly priest whose white soutane covered his black working suit rather badly. He fingered his prayer stole anxiously.

'Aren't they here yet then?'

The gravedigger spat into a corner of the grave before he answered in a surly voice, 'Sure, you can see for yourself, Father, that they are not.'

The priest looked down into the completed grave. 'Well, if the two of you are finished you may as well get up out of that and see if there is anything else you could be doing, instead of idling here.'

As the two men slouched away to tickle a mound of clay, one of them remarked viciously, 'Idling, indeed! He should know. I never saw a skinny priest yet. Did you see the flesh hanging down off that fella's neck?'

Even as the priest stamped his damp feet into the ground with growing impatience, the little procession came into sight. But the priest's relief soon turned to anger.

'You don't have an offering for poor Mother Church? I can be sure you had enough for drink but as usual with you people, the Church and her priests come last. Fill yourselves with porter and then cry poverty at us. Yet you want us to be out in all weathers performing our duties.'

Kathleen answered sheepishly, 'Well, Father, what are we to do, bury my mother without benefit of clergy?' Reluctantly he sighed, raised his hands and began the burial service.

As the words flowed sonorously from his mouth, so did Kathleen's grief begin to pain her. She glanced side-

63

ways at Maggie, but saw her mouth was set in a tight line, and her eyes kept downcast as the service rumbled on. Suddenly the tears began to flow in earnest, and Kathleen struggled to find a handkerchief.

Molly Power came to her rescue with a hand on her shoulder and a miraculously clean lacy kerchief which she pushed into Kathleen's grateful hand. It was soaking wet when the time came for them to throw earth on the coffin as it lay in the grave, and each clod echoed a deathly knell through the chambers of her heart as she said a silent goodbye to her mother and her childhood.

Outside the main gates, Maggie and Kathleen came upon a very sorrowful Uncle Ned. He clasped Maggie's hands in his. 'I can't tell you how sorry I was to leave it all to you, but needs must when the devil drives. I had to look for passage to America, and I failed. There is none. All sailings from the port of Dublin are cancelled, and I can't make the Liverpool connection. Your man Carey was right: nothing is moving. Larkinism is gripping the docks like a disease. They say that man is a mass hypnotist that he is able to bind the working man with his devilish nonsense.' His square frame shook with anger, 'Well, girls, the long and the short of it is I'll have to wait awhile! I'll give it a few short weeks more.'

He linked his arms with the two sad girls and they started back over Binn's Bridge. 'Well, every cripple has to find his own way of walking, and I am no different to anyone else. And walking is what we'll have to do to get back to the Convent. Jem Larkin has stopped all the trams for now.'

Kathleen answered him firmly, 'Well, we carried my mother to her grave, so I don't think it will be any hardship for us to make our way back to the Convent. Sure, we can go along the North Circular, then through the Park, and there we are.'

So they made their way through Phibsborough and out on the the Navan Road, pressing on until they came to the cattle market. There a vast army of beasts lowed and mooed, as if berating their impending fate. A mob of police protected the drovers as they prepared to move the legions out. First came the cows, their swollen udders spraying the hard road with sweet milk made in the fat grasslands of Meath. Then came the sheep, white and woolly, darting this way and that, to be cursed loudly by their keepers. Last of all were the bulls, a man at the head of each gripping firmly the chain attached to a stout ring in the beast's nose. One in particular roared his defiance and tossed his massive head, like a captive barbarian paraded before the Romans. Kathleen thought it was a fine sight; she had never seen so many animals in her life. They were taking the same route as themselves. There were no boats for England, because of the lock-out of the dock workers, so the beasts began the slow parade up Parkgate Street and into the Phoenix Park. Following behind, Kathleen watched as they were driven into great pits, on whose sides stood riflemen. As the animals entered, the guns rang out. She turned away in horror.

Her uncle's face was livid. 'So much for Larkin. Look at the poor things.'

Kathleen couldn't totally agree with his indignation. 'Sure, wouldn't the animals have been slaughtered anyway?' she asked.

'Yes, but the waste of money. We are not a rich country. Agriculture is our main way of making a living. If that dies, so do we all.'

Cowed by what they had seen, they left the park at the Islandbridge Gate and walked slowly across the river to the orphanage.

PART II

7

Sister Monica and Sister Teresa sat together as the May sunshine warmed the air. The office window was slightly open, letting in a temperate breeze which carried with it the scents of morning-fresh flowers.It was on days like these, thought Sister Monica, when God could be felt in the air, and seen in the new green leafiness of the trees. On such a day the Holy Spirit must have come down to earth, down from the cerulean sky as a shining light – a torch to blaze a path for the poor lost souls of humankind.

Eventually the older nun woke out of her reverie and concentrated on the matter in hand, the Corr girl.

'Yes I agree she seems to have calmed down, but do you think it's a good home to send her to. The Nash family are a little *different*, you know. The wife has been dead for many a year, and from what I hear Major Nash has let his daughter Emma run the house herself. And she has travelled all over the Continent with him, and goodness knows where else.'

'You must be aware, Sister Monica, that Kathleen is too intelligent for a life of drudgery. Some of our girls I would say are ideal workhorses, and can labour in the fields like any man. Kathleen has a spark which many of them lack, though sometimes that spark turns into the fire of rebelliousness. This may not be a bad thing in a somewhat unconventional household. And at sixteen she is not a child.'

'But what about Emma Nash herself? Is she suitable to be in charge of the girl? I hear she holds her own salon, and that unaccompanied men come and visit her. Some even say that she mixes with an undesirable crowd, but that may be malice talking.'

Sister Monica was keen to consider every facet of the

household that Kathleen might be joining. It was her duty as the Mother Superior to oversee the placement of each and every one of their charges, and to be sure that none of them entered households which might compromise their Christian faiths and upbringing.

But Sister Teresa held firm. 'Now I have to say I agree maybe the domestic arrangements leave a little to be desired, but it is precisely this difficulty that Kathleen is supposed to overcome. As far as I see it, she is to act as a sort of companion to Miss Nash, as well as lady's maid, so that when the Major has to be away on duty there is another female to accompany her. I also understand that the Major felt an older person would be wrong for his daughter, so Kathleen would seem to be suitable.'

'Well the Major and his daughter are due here at any moment, so I suppose you had better call the girl in.'

Kathleen had been waiting for this moment. She had tidied herself up to look neat and well brushed when Sister Teresa came into the workroom and called her name. As she followed the nun's long flapping skirt across the flagstones, she realised that this interview could radically affect her life. Her mother's death had lain heavy on her mind in the last weeks, while the bitter spring had given way to the warmth and fair skies of early summer. The first flush of grief had passed, and what had once been a sharp pain was now no more than a dull ache. She wanted so much to leave the Convent and start a new life outside its walls. And it was the realisation that these people today held the key to her freedom that made her heart beat faster and her eyes shine.

Noticing her tense face, Sister Teresa whispered a word of comfort. 'Be calm, now, Kathleen. You have nothing to fear. All will be well.'

As they entered the Mother Superior's office, Sister Monica looked up and held out a hand in greeting.

'Well, Kathleen, the time has come for you to leave us

and go out into the world as a young woman. Are you nervous my girl?'

After a little curtsy, Kathleen looked straight into Sister Monica's cornflower blue eyes. 'No, Reverend Mother, I can only hope for God's guidance in this step I am to take.' That should do, she thought, sitting down on the plain wooden chair. But then the doubts began to assail her. What if I don't like the look of them? Kathleen felt her hands become sticky in the warmth, as the minutes of waiting passed.

When the visitors appeared, Sister Monica stood up and shook their hands and introduced Major Nash and his daughter Emma. As the small-talk continued, Kathleen studied her prospective employers carefully. Major Nash seemed a man in the prime of life, around fifty-five. His rank in the army made him part of the British establishment in Dublin, and the effect of constant good living showed in the Major's face and waistline. In the clear May light Kathleen could see the tiny purplish veins threading his cheeks and he smelt distinctly of cigars. His dress was of a style that might have been the height of London fashion five years previously, but was now well worn. The jacket was a cut-down version of a tail-coat, while his waistcoat sported a large gold chain across the front, attached to the timepiece in his pocket.

It was Emma Nash who drew Kathleen's attention, however. Kathleen had thought herself reasonably tall, but Emma towered a good four inches above her, and even made the Sisters seem small and insignificant. She had a strong featured face which many might find beautiful, and in her twenty years had an air of mature confidence about her which impressed Kathleen immediately. Her dark hair was piled high on top of her head and she was hatless, so that those wisps that refused to be tamed straggled down to the collar of her jacket. Her suit fitted her slim figure perfectly, and the tight waist and puffed sleeves emphasised even more her slender frame. Her eyes were hazel-green with flecks of a tawny amber – which reminded Kathleen of a cat's.

Sister Teresa had brought in extra chairs for the guests, and had now gone off to the kitchen to fetch some tea for them. Sister Monica opened the serious conversation.

'Well, Major Nash, I'm pleased to see you here. As you know, we have many orphans here, and it is always good news when we find a satisfactory placement for one of our girls. But, first things first, can you explain to myself and Kathleen what it is you will be asking her to do for you?'

The Major had a gruff voice hoarsened by years of wine and cigars. He coughed slightly before he began. 'I've decided that my daughter Emma should have some sort of companion, as I might have to be going away soon, and I do not want to leave her alone in the house, even though we do have other servants for the basic chores. Anybody who came to work in this capacity should be honest above all, as she'll be caring for my daughter's personal things. Also she should be able to read and write and do simple arithmetic as Emma, bless her heart, is not the greatest hand at dealing with household accounts and paying the other servants. She would have her own room, of course, and a small salary paid quarterly if she turns out to be satisfactory.'

During the Major's speech Kathleen glanced at Emma and caught her eye. To her surprise Emma winked at her, as if to say, I hope this sermon can finish soon, and I am sure we will be friends. Kathleen flashed her a shy smile.

'And Kathleen, what do you think to that, my girl?' Sister Monica inquired.

'It sounds fine to me,' replied Kathleen with sincerity. heartily relieved that she was not expected to act as a drudge like so many of the other girls, and thankful she had practised her neat hand-writing so assiduously.

Sister Monica continued. 'As for Kathleen, I can assure you she has all the skills you desire of her, and is clever enough to learn new things with very little effort. I hope that this will prove a successful placement. I presume you'd be willing to take her immediately.'

'She can come to us today if she likes. What say you, Kathleen?' the Major intervened.

'I'd love to be doing that, thank you, sir.'

'Go and pack your things, Kathleen and we'll meet you inside the main gate in a quarter of an hour. I'll take the Major and his daughter for a brief tour of the convent, so they can see for themselves the work that we do with the orphans.' She knew very well that this ploy was usually enough for the visitor to reach in his pocket for a few gold coins, as a contribution to their funds.

Kathleen flew down the corridor as if driven by terror, but it was joy that lightened her step. In the dormitory she gathered up all her few possessions: her two dresses, her shawl so lovingly worked on, her mother's letters and her *Lives of the Saints*. Her rosary she stuffed right at the bottom of the pile, hoping she would not be needing it too frequently.

Then she went into the workroom and said goodbye to the girls there; and they all wished her well in her new life, and secretly wished that it was their turn to be going out into the world.

Inside the main gate she found her new employers already waiting for her, the Major discreetly sucking his cigar and Emma rapping a rolled umbrella against her leg. Nearby was a carriage with a fine horse waiting. Sister Monica and Sister Teresa both hugged Kathleen in a rare display of affection – and then the gates closed behind them, and she smelt her first real scent of freedom outside the Convent walls.

Indeed it was a perfect day, all greeny yellow and light blue. The trees they passed were coming into leaf, horse-chestnuts breaking out of the confinement of a winter spent inside a sticky bud. A few bright stars of May blossom were showing themselves in the hedgerow, while nestling in the grass below were pale yellow primroses.

Emma was talking in her quiet, relaxed way. The emphasis of her sentences went down instead of up at the end, in an English way. Kathleen could not help feeling this strange, but considered she would become accustomed to it in time.

'Are those really all the things you own, Kathleen? Have you no warm clothes? It can turn cold even on as perfect a day as this.'

'We didn't go out in the winter much, ma'am, so I just had my shawl and wore two extra vests.'

'Please call me Emma. I can't stand being called ma'am all over the place. Well, we'll soon get you sorted out – isn't that so, Father? I can take Kathleen to the shops in Grafton Street so she can have some new skirts and a coat. Don't you think that's a good idea?'

'Whatever you say, Emma,' he replied gruffly. ' I'm sure Kathleen does need some new clothes – but I'd first see if there are any among your old ones which might fit her if they were taken up.'

But Emma was not to be thwarted. 'Well, I really think she needs something new to buck up her spirits. It must have been frightfully dreary in that Convent.'

'Do as you please, my dear. You know you always do.'

From this small interchange Kathleen became aware that the relationship between father and daughter was easy-going to the point where an outsider might think the daughter was actually in charge. Emma's manner was so confident and open, her voice so reassuring, that Kathleen knew that just as the Major had acceded to his daughter's wishes in the matter of the clothes, so he would in many other cases, despite his brusque military manner. He was sitting very upright in the carriage with his head held high, his gaze fixed far along the road. Kathleen hoped he would not prove too demanding an employer; she did not want to be constantly holding her tongue in case of his wrath.

As Kathleen looked at Emma, she sensed she had inherited some of her father's mien: her eyes looked so fearless and determined. This made her face all the more beautiful, with her striking pallor showing off her hazel eyes. Her hair was dark brown with just the occasional hint of red in it, shining now in the bright spring light.

The door to the Nash's house was large and imposing, with a big brass knocker on it and a bell-pull to the side. The major took a key from his pocket and placed it in the lock. No sooner had he done so than a most furious barking sound could be heard from the interior.

'Oh, Kathleen,' said Emma, seeing Kathleen look startled. 'You do like dogs don't you? I forgot to ask. Sligo is really very friendly. He's only barking because we are home. It's his greeting, you see.'

Though Kathleen had seen a few dogs in her life, they tended to be the street curs and mongrels who scrabbled for a living on the periphery of human civilisation. In no way was she prepared for the dog Sligo who now bounded up to Emma and the Major, licking their hands and making a fuss. There was no doubt about it: the dog did look fierce to Kathleen. His very size was intimidating, the largest she had seen. His coat was a basic brown colour, but what was so unusual were the stripes on his back and muzzle, which gave him something of the look of a tiger.

'He's a cross between a lurcher and a greyhound, that means he's very fast, and a hunting dog. He could catch any villain and tear his throat out, couldn't you, Sligo? There's a good boy. Here, this is Kathleen, our new friend.' Emma spoke loud and clear to the big dog, who fixed his eyes on Kathleen as if to say, 'Yes, you can be my friend, but just you try harming my owners . . .'

'You needn't be afraid, Kathleen, honestly. Sligo is a model dog, but he is also a very good guard-dog and I feel safe when Emma has him with her, as I know she will come to no harm.' So said the major on noticing Kathleen's anxious glance.

They went up a grand sweep of a staircase into a drawing-room facing over the park of St Stephen's Green. It was here the Nashes received their company. And here was another surprise for Kathleen, for all along one wall stood a series of cages with all sorts of birds: canaries, finches, cockatoos and the like – twittering and chirping as lively as you please.

'These are my birds, Kathleen. I love their singing and they all know me.' Emma went up to one bird-cage and gave a low whistle. All the birds within responded with their own sounds.

The Major coughed gently to interrupt his daughter. 'I'm sure Kathleen will be interested in all your animals, my dear, but I'll be leaving you now to go about my business. Make sure to introduce her to Mary and the other servants. I'll see you at dinner.' With that he was gone.

What followed seemed a blur to Kathleen, for after so many years in the Convent she was totally unaccustomed to the richness of decoration and furnishing to be found in the house of a well-to-do family. She was shown each room in turn, from the kitchen in the basement dominated by the big boiler which heated the water and the huge range for cooking, to the small plain attic room under the roof which was to be hers. Emma even showed Kathleen her own room, and the wardrobe full of clothes. As she opened its doors she told Kathleen how she would willingly give all these fine clothes away and dress herself simply, like a peasant, but her father the Major Tommy required that she accompany him often on formal occasions where a certain style was required – to Dublin Castle and such.

'You wouldn't believe how boring and stuffy most of those people are. Sometimes it's all I can do to stop myself being rude to them. It will come one day, I can tell you. Ireland will rise and throw off the yoke of the British oppressor, and I'm hoping to be there when it does happen.'

For Kathleen it came as a revelation that an Anglo-Irish woman could be so hard on her own kind.

'But surely as God-fearing people we should respect the law, ma'am?'

'Oh, Kathleen, you have so much to learn. Come we'll

finish the tour of the house, and then sort out some clothes for you. I can see I'm going to be busy teaching you some history in the next few weeks. Isn't it typical of a convent to teach you everything about the saints and nothing about the history of your own native land.'

8

For Kathleen it was a great and agreeable change to be living and working in the Nash household. At last she was away from the nuns who had so much dominated her life for the last seven years; and all that praying and Mass seemed a million miles away from the urbane life led by Emma and her father Major Tommy. Kathleen loved the new experiences which came with every new day. The sights and sounds of Dublin became once more familiar to her as she ran errands for Emma and sometimes for her father. The Major proved to be a considerate man, as long as he had his cigars and port after a meal he was happy. Kathleen would be sent to buy these cigars from the tobacconist's in Dawson Street. She could make a detour and walk past the haberdasher's where trimmings of all kinds were on display in the windows: laces, silk and satin ribbons in such a profusion of colours that Kathleen would marvel at them every time she passed. Past the butcher's she would go, where the dark meat of lambs and cows would hang fly-ridden from bloody meat-hooks, ready for the richer customers to purchase the best cuts and the poorer ones to be content with the offal.

The tobacconist's was run by an old lady who seemed to have been there since the dawn of time, hands delicately fingering the tobacco and snuff as she weighed it out. Her cigars were of the finest, pure Havana rolled, with prices to match. Kathleen was always astonished at the seemingly endless amount of money the Major had to spend on what was to him a necessity but to her seemed a luxury. And when she arrived back home, he would chuck her under the chin and flirt with her gently saying, 'And how's my pretty miss this morning?' At which Kathleen would feel her face going red, and would shuffle her feet while mumbling, 'Fine, Major, thank you.'

She learnt the routine of the house speedily enough, making friends with Mary the maid who was a country girl from County Clare only a few months older than herself, but lacking any education whatever. They shared the attic rooms at the top of the house, the ceilings not even six feet high, and the heat of the summer days remaining well into the night.

About two weeks passed before a note came from her sister Maggie, asking her to beg time off for a most important event. Her uncle Ned was to leave Ireland for America that very week, and could Kathleen come along to see him off?

Emma readily gave her permission for the day the ship was due to sail. It was a wet day, dark clouds hanging over the huge square as Kathleen set off to meet them. She knew she would be sorry to see him go, for, being much younger than her mother, he had come to seem like an elder brother to the girls, despite his bulky size.

They met by the Custom House beside the river, where boats were plying up and down the Liffey through the wet, dank drizzle of a summer morning. As she crossed Butt bridge to reach them, Kathleen could discern her sister standing stiff and upright and her uncle dressed in his top-coat, carrying a large bundle of possessions ready to start on his new life. When Maggie ran up to embrace her, Kathleen returned the embrace warmly. She was full to bursting with news of her new position, and also curious as to how Maggie was now faring at the theatre. Uncle Ned stood patiently and watched as they greeted one another, then broke in. 'And have you nothing to say to a fellow who will be on the high seas before noon, making his way to adventure in the United States of America?'

The quay was all a-bustle as the ship prepared to leave. Throngs of men, women and children were sitting, walking and waiting their turn to climb the gangplank and into the steamer which was to carry them to a whole new life. The chilly rain could not inspire much confidence or hope as it seeped into their clothes and dampened their spirits. Even Ned did not seem his usual self.

'Right girls, I'm ready to be leaving this sinking ship we call Ireland. Just you wait till I write to you about all the wonderful things I'll be seeing in the new country. And when I've scraped enough money together, I'll send for you, just see if I don't, and you'll be laughing all your way to America.'

'But, uncle,' said Maggie,'I'm happy where I am. I've got a good job, and I love doing it. Why should I ever be leaving this old town?'

'Be thankful you have the work, my pretty, and hang on to it if you can. There's many that would be wanting work, myself among them, and when we do get it, what happens? We're laid off as soon as some Protestant comes along wanting a job. It's not like that in America, I'm told. A man can work, whatever his religion; doesn't it say so in their constitution? Besides, I can see trouble coming ahead with all those union marches and all. You listen to me, my girls, and stay out of it. There's nothing to be gained by fighting the British. It's that old, old story of might is right.'

The waiting steamer commenced to blow its horn in warning and they all jumped in surprise.

'Well, Uncle Ned, it looks like this is it,' Maggie said, as a general movement on the quay indicated it was time to board. 'Here, let us help you with your stuff.'

Kathleen and Maggie picked up the smaller bags he had with him and they all approached the gangplank. Shortly they would have to watch him go up into the ship, a forlorn figure among so many others. Kathleen fought back the tears as she said farewell to her uncle, unsure whether she would ever see him again as finally he departed for his great adventure in a distant land.

Standing on the quay, they watched as the last stragglers rushed to board the ship: watched as the water churned when the big engines began to throb; when the last rope was cast off and the ship made its way, behind tugs and pilot boat, to the mouth of the Liffey before setting off for Liverpool and the emigrant boat to America, across the wide Atlantic.

'Well, he's off, Kathleen,' Maggie sniffed. 'And I wish him luck, and may the saints look over him as he goes.'

'Sure it's seems a poor way of doing things that a man like Uncle Ned should have to leave his home and relatives and travel to a land he knows nothing of, is what I'm thinking, Maggie.'

'But that's the way of things. It seems they've been leaving Ireland for as long as any can remember. After all, what's here for a man with no means or land . . . It's difficult to make your way in this country and that it is.'

The ship was already some distance away and Kathleen turned to her dear sister, who was now only a little taller than she. 'And what about you, Maggie? How is the theatre?'

'Oh, Kathleen, I have so much to tell you about it, and if you can spare a couple of hours we could go there, and I could show you where I work and introduce you to . . . Oh, you'll never guess, I've met the most lovely man you can imagine and we are stepping out together, and I think you will like him and I think he likes me . . .'

It was a short walk from the quayside to the theatre where Maggie worked at the corner of Lower Abbey Street and Marlborough Street. The two sisters spent this few minutes discussing their uncle's departure, and wishing him well.

'I'm truly hoping he makes a success of it, but, Maggie, what happens when a man is all alone with none of his kind to be with him?'

'I don't think he'll be all alone for long: there's many an Irishman over in New York. Why, it must be half Irish by the numbers that have gone, and he must be able to meet a few friends who will help him on his way.'

By now they had reached the theatre. Iron railings stood proud and painted along the front, and an elegant wrought-iron and glass porch covered the entrance, extending over the pavement, with ABBEY THEATRE picked out in the same iron-work.

'The main door is shut in the day, Kathleen, but you should see the crowds, all waiting to come in, and the theatre ablaze with light. We'll go in the stage-door at the side. They are rehearsing a new play, I believe, by that man who wrote the one that was hissed off a while back. He and Will Butler are forever arguing about it.'

'Will Butler, is he the manager? A sort of slight fellow with glasses? Why, he comes to Emma's a great deal and I'm thinking he has a strong fancy for her. He looks at her, well you know, just so, like a little soft dog who would just love even to be kicked as long as his mistress did it.'

'Shh, Kathleen, I hear them now. Through the next door and you'll see it all.'

They proceeded along a corridor lined with red flock wallpaper, and Kathleen could hear voices raised. Maggie gently opened the door which led to the rear stalls. She was right: rehearsals were in progress. Kathleen's heart beat faster as she entered and saw for the first time the stage and the auditorium.

Two actresses were on the stage. one with a noticeably low-cut dress. The other an older woman, was shrilly denouncing her and clearly a quarrel was in progress. Then a voice cut in from the gloom of the stalls.

'Now remember both of you, although you are ladies in dress and manners, we are in the scene where all this politeness is stripped away. I want you to let go and really fight. You are both in thrall to the same man and both want him desperately, and you're prepared to go to any lengths to get him.'

A second voice rose up, 'Johnny, Johnny, you know what happens when women are too outspoken on stage. Last time they were booed off.'

'But, Will, this is over five years later. Times are changing, and so are women. They're becoming more independent, and to fight over a man will just show what passionate creatures they really are when they strip off their ladylike manners. We are all animals underneath.'

'Listen, while you two are debating, I'm getting cold here,' broke in the actress in the flimsy dress.

'All right, we'll have a break. It must be nearly lunch time. See you back in an hour.'

As the lights went up they revealed row after row of red velvet seats, and the two men sitting in the stalls. As he stood up, Will Butler caught sight of Kathleen and Maggie hovering by the door. 'Why, it's young Kathleen from Emma Nash's house, and what brings you here?'

Kathleen spoke up loud and clear. 'Maggie here is my sister and she brought me to show me where she works.'

'So Maggie's your sister, is she? Well, she's a credit to you, for everything runs smoothly when she's in charge. Even the costumes arrive on time . . . Kathleen, say hello to Johnny Gilbert. He's one of Ireland's finest playwrights.'

Kathleen bobbed a curtsey. 'I'm pleased to be meeting you, sir.' She was aware of Johnny's eyes appraising her keenly as she approached, and they held her own for a second or two longer than was usually polite. To him she seemed the very embodiment of fresh young woman-hood, perfect and as yet untouched by worldly affairs. Nearing the age of thirty, and still unmarried, he was no stranger to women.

'Maggie Corr, you never told me you had a sister.' He clasped Kathleen's hand. 'Tell me, Kathleen, how do you like working for Emma Nash?'

'She's a very kind mistress, thank you sir, and I could hope for no better position.'

'One thing I'll be telling you about my sister, Mr Gilbert. She has a voice like an angel you wouldn't believe. When she sings the leprechauns dance and the spirits peep around stones to see who can be singing with such a fine voice.' Maggie's tone was humorous but serious.

'Sing for us now then Kathleen. Go up on the stage

82

and sing for us.' Johnny's eyes reassured her with their brown warmth.

Kathleen felt flustered. Maggie brought this on her so suddenly, and the only serious song she could remember on the spur of the moment was 'Dan O'Hara'. As she sang the old tale of eviction and destitution, she could hear her voice rise and fall with the emotion of it. Suddenly she felt a strange confidence sweep over her as she stood looking out at the auditorium of empty seats. When she had finished the three verses she knew, her small audience clapped with fervour.

'My my, Kathleen, what a voice it is you have. I'm sure we can be using such in one of our entertainments. What do you say, Will?'

'We'll see, Johnny. Listen, I've got to be seeing to some financial matters, so I'll have to be leaving you.'

'It looks as though I'm left with you ladies. What about a stroll outside and a small lunch with a glass of beer?' Johnny gazed enquiringly at the two girls, one so mature and capable for her twenty-two years and the other, so appealingly fresh.

Maggie muttered that she would have loved to come but must check some clothes through. She turned to Kathleen. 'I'll be free at ten-fifteen tonight. Jim and I often go dancing in the evening, so meet me at the stage-door and we'll show you some of the lights of Dublin on your first night off.'

Kathleen suddenly found herself left alone with Johnny Gilbert. And how nervous she felt to be alone with a man so famous, about the same age as her uncle and obviously much more worldly-wise than herself.

But Johnny perceived her nervousness, for he was always very sensitive to women's feelings. 'Come, Kathleen, we can still have some lunch. You can tell me about yourself as we walk to the public house.'

Hesitantly Kathleen succumbed to his invitation. Outside the theatre, the weather had changed. The sun was now shining fiercely, having banished the drizzle and mist. The pavements were steaming, and there was a sweet fresh smell in the air. Johnny proved a considerate host, and led the conversation so deftly that Kathleen had no need to feel awkward or shy. Indeed, after the first few minutes, she found herself chatting away as though she had known the man for years. It seemed so natural to be walking out that bright noon-tide with a man at your side, on their way to lunch together.

Johnny knew a discreet bar with separate seating booths where a fellow could enjoy a little private conversation with a lady without the world and his father seeing him. The adjoining public bar was a very different matter, where sawdust on the floor gathered up the spittle of the working men who drank away the dust of their labours. As Jack Carey stood there he had seen the couple reflected briefly in the great engraved mirror which gave a glimpse of those entering the door to the room beyond. Again he admired with interest Kathleen's fresh young face. I'll be seeing more of that girl, he thought to himself as he downed his drink and set off back to his day's labour carrying bricks.

Kathleen looked around her with interest and amazement. The shining mirrors of reflected light, the brass pumps for the porter, and the gleaming, glinting glasses lined up like soldiers for the fray all seemed to make the interior so inviting. If the sisters in the Convent could see her now! They surely would not approve. And so it was with a frisson of naughtiness that Kathleen allowed herself to be ushered to a quiet corner compartment at the back where a wooden partition cut you off from the view of other people. Johnny Gilbert was the perfect gentleman in showing her to her seat.

'I come here quite often,' he said. 'And this seat is one of my favourites. If I sit here I can just hear the men in the public bar. I love to listen to them speak and laugh and sing; it's all good fodder for a play-writer, it is. Now Kathleen, what would you like for your lunch? I can tell you they do a lovely meat-pie, all brown and crusty. How do you feel about that? And a glass of porter with it? How does that sound?'

'That sounds just fine, I'm thinking, sir.'

With a swift but gentle movement, Johnny put his hand over hers and squeezed it softly. 'Don't you be calling me "sir", young Kathleen. Call me Johnny. All my lady friends do.'

Kathleen could feel her neck flushing; she had never thought of herself as a lady friend, and neither had she had much human physical contact with anyone outside her family.

Johnny stood up to go to the bar and order the lunch, returning with two glasses of the foaming dark brown beer.

'Here, Kathleen, you must be thirsty after your long morning out. And after a sup you can tell me more about yourself.'

Kathleen was again surprised how easy it was to talk to Johnny Gilbert. He listened with such a sympathetic ear as she related her life-story to date. It was the first time she had properly spoken to a stranger about her mother's death, and she found she could now speak about it without tears coming to her eyes. It was as if her Mam was safe in Heaven by now, God rest her soul.

'And now I'm working for Emma Nash, as lady's maid and companion. I take Sligo for walks – he's the big dog Emma owns – and I open the door to visitors and take people's coats. Oh, and I help her with the household accounts and sometimes write letters for her. And the Major is ever so kind, and he sends me out on errands, and sometimes he gives me threepence as a tip for just popping round the corner! It seems the man has enough money to paper the walls. The house is lovely, so light with all those big windows, and from my room in the attic I can see the tops of the trees, and when it's windy I feel as though I'm in a tree-house up there swaying away in the breeze.'

'You sound well settled in there, Kathleen, but with a voice as fine as yours I think maybe you could do something better for yourself. How is your memory for learning words?'

'I think I can say I'm, well, as near a parrot as you'd find this side of the Irish Sea.'

Johnny laughed. 'But I'm not looking for a parrot! What I'm thinking is that I've got a new play that I'm writing and one of the characters is a young girl like yourself, basically a country girl who comes to the city for the bright lights. I can't promise anything but it'll probably be finished by the autumn, so I'll tell Will to inform Emma Nash when we're having the auditions, and perhaps you could come along. How does that sound?'

Kathleen, momentarily speechless, was relieved to hear the barman shout, 'Two meat pies!' Johnny went to fetch them, and by then she had recovered her composure enough to say, 'That sounds just wonderful,' and wonder did he really mean it.

They were delicious pies, the meat perfectly cooked, topped with jelly and surrounded by a crisp brown pastry-case not too thick.

Realising she was hungry, Kathleen set to with a gusto which surprised even Johnny, himself not a great eater. As they ate, Kathleen became aware of the sounds all around: the animated conversations in the other booths, the laughter of ladies nearby and the deep-throated voices from the public bar where the workmen were downing their porter. The sounds rose and fell, almost whispering at one moment and booming loud the next. She felt warmed through, and very content.

'Shall I walk you home, Kathleen?'

She was startled at this. Then she thought, why not? And said so.

It was mid-afternoon by the time they were crossing the O'Connell Bridge, Kathleen with her arm through Johnny's and feeling for all the world as though it was just the right thing to be doing. The sun shining on the river made it seem like liquid gold. She sighed as she looked along its length. 'Poor Uncle, I'm hoping he will fare all right across the ocean in a strange land with nobody he knows.'

'It's amazing how people can survive almost anything,

86

and I'm sure your uncle is clever enough to win through. But have you no other relatives, Kathleen?'

'I do have two brothers, though where they are now I cannot say. One works as a sailor; he could be in China for all I know. The other could be in Dublin somewhere, but to tell you the truth I have not seen or heard from either since Maggie and I went into the Convent.'

Johnny could not help feeling sorry for this girl, with no parents to look after her and starting out in life with so very few assets. He thought of his own much easier life cushioned by funds which allowed him to travel abroad, though his income was not large. He compared it with the life Kathleen had been forced to lead, shut up in an institution for most of her young life so far. Yet how resilient she seemed, how full of life and vigour! She was like those peasant women he had seen and admired on the islands in the west of Ireland: yet somehow she had an extra quality, a beautiful voice and an obvious talent. He found himself very attracted to her.

He left her outside the house, St Stephens Green, promising he would write to her if he did not see her again soon. He did not want to go inside. The Emma Nashes of this world were not really to his taste, too sophisticated and overtly cultured to suit his own simpler tastes.

But Emma had spotted him taking leave of Kathleen, from her stance at the drawing-room window. She knew something of Johnny's reputation for favouring young girls who were nowhere near his match in age or experience. However she decided against speaking to Kathleen for the moment. Her disapproval was not altogether based on protecting her employee from harm. Deep down, Emma Nash, for all her vocal support of the poor and the underdog, considered that the classes could never really mix. Kathleen was not suitable for Johnny Gilbert any more than he was a suitable escort for her. Her wild Dublin accent and deprived upbringing meant she lacked that certain polish which came with a life of ease and travel such as Emma herself had always known. Yet she could not readily admit to such feelings in public. She, a champion of the working people of Ireland, could never announce to the world that she really would hate to live with any of the people she spoke up for in public meeting houses. And she had always to diguise a certain feeling of disgust when she visited these people in their squalid homes.

Kathleen came in looking flustered and uncertain, for she had looked up in time to see Emma turning away from the window. Does she approve? – she wondered. But remembering her meeting with Maggie that evening, she mustered her courage and confronted Emma.'Will it be all right for me to go spend this evening with my sister Maggie? We're to go out dancing, and I haven't been out in the evening before.'

'That's all right, Kathleen. Of course you can go out. Did your uncle leave with no mishap?'

'That he did, Emma, and the boat sailed down the Liffey with many a mournful hoot, echoed in his heart, I suppose as he goes to a new life.'

'Good luck to him then, and as it's your day off I won't ask you to do anything here. Get yourself some supper later from the kitchen.'

Kathleen turned up the flights of stairs to her little room, where the sun shone in to mark a square of light on the floor for the shape of the window. Searching through all her clothes, mostly Emma's cast-offs, she found a skirt and blouse which she thought she would look her best in. She took the pins out of her hair and brushed it thoroughly. But feeling sleepy – it must be that glass of beer – she stripped to her shirt and lay down on her bed for an unaccustomed afternoon nap.

9

It was Mary the maid who woke her up. 'Come on, Kathleen, it's seven o'clock.' As she woke, the memory of the day returned, and with it a rising tide of excitement. She had not danced since the wake for her mother and hadn't that been a time indeed. She remembered the fiddler and the wild stomping feet, and now she was looking forward to her night out like any Cinderella going to the ball. She took her time washing and dressing, studying her hair in the cracked mirror to make sure it was all in place. Smoothing down the cream blouse, she thought she might even wear a red ribbon in her hair! Stepping lightly down the stairs in the twilight, she heard the major's voice through the drawing room door.

'And is that Kathleen I hear, tripping out and leaving us? Come in my dear, and let me see how you look.'

Major Nash was a great drinker of heavy-bodied wines. Claret and port were among his favourites, and sometimes at regimental dinners he had been known to down three bottles of the stuff. Tonight he was just feeling slightly tipsy, and the sight of a beautiful young girl was just what he needed to make his evening complete.

'You look stunning, Kathleen. Come and I will kiss you goodbye. Emma's out at one of her goddamn evenings, preaching to the masses, and I'm sore to losing the only other bit of female company in the house.'

He took hold of her hands and drew her to him, leaning across the bulge of his stomach. Kathleen did not like this – smelly whiskers and cigar-laden breath – and drew back as soon as she felt the prickle of salt-and-pepper facial hair against her own smooth cheek.

'Not surprised I am to see you react so, a terrible old fogey like myself. What's a young girl like you want with the likes of me? Off with you now, and not too late, mind.'

After she had gone, he felt a great sadness fall upon him. His youth gone, the woman he loved dead – and now seeing Kathleen's instinctive distaste made him mourn his loss all the more. He took the bottle of port from the cupboard, lit himself a cigar and sat down to read the paper in his favourite chair. His head was soon nodding and his snores echoing through the tall house.

The river was still and the sky clear, with stars just beginning to pinpoint the dusk with their light. The moon, huge and yellow, was rising over the roofs of the houses. Kathleen gazed over the parapet of the bridge to see the water lapping its way along beneath – the continuous motion of the tides drawn by the moon above. The air was heavy, soft and warm, and Kathleen breathed in deeply. How she was looking forward to dancing, music and company.

At the stage-door Maggie was waiting with her boyfriend. Jim Sheehan was a tall man with a tight black moustache. He could have been taken for an English guardsman, such was his posture and stature. He was a man who felt sure he was going to make his mark, and as assistant manager at the theatre he had already made an impression for his efficiency and for keeping calm under pressure. While the artistic managers squabbled endlessly amongst themselves, it was Jim Sheehan who sorted out the wages for the actors and stage-hands. It was he who arranged the cleaning of the theatre and the minor repairs and the decorations which kept the place looking spruce and attractive. In Maggie, Jim believed he had found a girl who would not just be his life's companion but also his business partner. A partner he could trust.

Maggie, for her part was attracted by his quiet demeanour as well as his handsome face, and knew she was ready to pledge herself when he asked. She was now hoping desperately that Jim and Kathleen would become friends.

'Jim, this is Kathleen, my sister.'

'It's pleased I am to be meeting you. And don't you take after Maggie here.' Jim's eyes looked Kathleen up and down appreciatively. She was indeed like her sister: the same trim figure and colouring. But there was something different in her face that he could not quite work out – perhaps because she was younger than Maggie. Younger people tended to be wilder and more rebellious.

As they strolled to the dance-hall they passed a number of public houses with their doors open to the warm night air. The mingled smell of sweat, beer and tobacco could almost be seen, it was so strong; and Kathleen's nostrils dilated with it.

It was down one of the poorer streets that the hall was situated. Long before they reached it they could hear the band playing, the wail of the fiddle, the drum beating its rhythm, the short bright notes of the piano, and the pipe trilling above it all. When they arrived the hall was already packed. Bodies were almost flying round the room, it seemed to Kathleen, as the dancers whirled past her. But the interval followed almost immediately, and she was thankful for that, as the crush of hot humanity in motion was almost overwhelming. She would be glad of some time to take her bearings.

During the interval came some entertainments. First a middle-aged man came to stand beside the band and he sang a beautiful song in Gaelic. To Kathleen the words sounded so poetic and fine that she suddenly felt ashamed that she did not understand her very own country's language. Luckily the singer afterwards explained the song's message.'And that, ladies and gentlemen, was Eamonn an Chnoic.' It's a song written by one Edmond O'Ryan, a brave man who supported King James II. What happened to him? Well King James got defeated, and this poor Edmond was outlawed and his estates confiscated, and here he is poor man waiting and wailing at his loved one's door. If you enjoy these dances and songs, why don't you come to our special meetings? The Gaelic League will tell you all about the things they don't teach in school. We'll teach you the Gaelic so you don't die inside of speaking that foreign tongue, English. And we'll teach you songs and dances long forgotten, too.

And now for your further entertainment we have two young girls who will dance for us.'

The band struck up a sparkling jig as two girls dressed in green came forward. They wore hard-soled shoes which tapped out their own rhythm on the wooden floor. Kathleen managed to slither through to the front, and there could watch their feet moving and weaving. Their legs seemed independent of their bodies, moving as if on strings, while their heads and torsos faced fixedly forwards.

At the far side of the hall Jack Carey caught sight of Kathleen watching the dancers, and his heart leapt within him. There she was, the young girl he had his eye on – and for the second time this day. He began to thread his way slowly towards her. When the music struck up again for the next dance, he got there just in time and turned to her flushed, excited face, 'Would you be liking a dance with me?'

Kathleen saw before her the figure she remembered from a few weeks earlier, but in rather different circumstances. What was his name, Jack! That was it. She consented readily.

He put his arm round her waist and she rested her hand on his arm, and she could feel the hard muscles of a man who worked with his body. The thought occurred to her that here was someone totally unlike her intellectual lunch companion, Johnny Gilbert. As they danced, there was no time to talk, and the music and the dancers took on a life of their own. She could hear the beat of the drum, reflected in her heart beat, and as they skipped and turned she could feel her whole body responding right down to her toes. This was being alive, she thought to herself – and far away from high convent walls.

Their first dance was followed by several more, until

Jim Sheehan came up and requested the chance to partner her. He held her in the same way as Jack Carey, but the sensation was totally different. With Jim she now felt so utterly safe, but with Jack she had experienced a thrill, a flutter, that was new to her.

It was now half-past midnight, and the dancers were thinning out. Maggie was looking suddenly tired, as Jim returned with Kathleen.

'Maggie, my dear, I'll be walking you back home now. Kathleen do you mind if we are leaving you? Or we could walk you to the bridge?'

'I think I'll come with you. My feet are crushed in these shoes and I'm needing an airing. Oh, Maggie, isn't it grand to be out dancing!'

Walking slowly down the street, they heard behind them the clatter shoes on cobbles. It was Jack Carey running after them.

'Kathleen, wait for me . . .' He rushed up panting to her side, then nodded to Maggie and Jim.

'Don't you worry about Kathleen. I'll see her home for you. And where is it you are living now, Kathleen?'

'Over the river and to St Stephen's Green, if you don't mind walking that far.'

'And why should I mind that on such a beautiful night?'

They had said goodbye to Maggie and Jim twenty minutes before and were now walking through the park towards the Nash house. They had found plenty to talk about earlier as, despite earning his livelihood as a labourer, Jack was a well-read man who hoped one day to make his mark as a writer, But now it was dark under the trees and Kathleen could sense Jack's body tall and strong beside her. The thrill she had felt in the dance-hall was giving way to a shiver of fear. She had never been alone with a man at such a late hour. Was this what the nuns had warned her about?

The moon had just gone behind a cloud when Kathleen felt him put his arms round her and draw her face up to his. He kissed her face – her eyes and cheeks and neck – gently at first, and then with increasing passion.

'Kathleen, Kathleen,' he was murmuring.

When he did finally kiss her on the lips she found herself responding, and she could feel her body going weak until she seemed to be falling and he alone was holding her up.

Something was wrong. He had lifted up her skirt and his hand was sliding between her legs. She put her hand against his chest, whispering, 'No, Jack, stop that now. I must be going.'

But the hand didn't stop and he was now clutching her so tight she could hardly breath. He half carried her towards a tree and pushed her roughly against it. She could feel his fingers pulling at her knickers, and the tingling between her legs.

With an almost superhuman effort, she managed to struggle free. Almost in an instant Jack was mouthing words of apology, 'I'm sorry, Kathleen, I don't know what came over me. I'm sorry, I really am.'

'Jack Carey, I never want to see you again, and here I was, a young girl trusting you.'

'Look I'm sorry. Please say you'll see me again.'

But Kathleen hardened her resolve. He had frightened her, and it was romance she wanted, not a roughing-up in the park. She was not ready for such a relationship, and was now prepared to deny this man her friendship on that account.

As he moved away, he turned to whisper, 'You'll come round to me, you'll see. I'll give you two or three more years and then you'll know what a man can do for a woman. I only hope I catch you then. Goodbye to you Kathleen Corr, but only for now.'

Kathleen ran all the rest of the way to the safety of the house with its small rooftop room. She flung off her clothes and lay weeping on the bed. She felt violated.

Yet not a wink's sleep did she get that night, for Jack Carey had awoken her body to passion. Despite her new resolve she knew she had initially responded to him, and

94

in a way which could only have led him to think he could go further. It was partly her fault, and now she felt guilty. She would have to go to Confession the very next morning.

Kathleen was still wide awake when the birds started their pre-dawn twittering; then, as the light stole upon her, she fell into a fitful sleep. Sister Anne figured largely in her dreams and a little knotted rope came down hard on her hands.

10

Summer was reaching its height and the trees were beginning to look dusty and used, like tired flowers in a hot room. Kathleen did not see Jack Carey again in that time. Nor had she gone to confession the morning after she had fled him so hurriedly in the park. She realised priestly comfort was not necessary to assuage her guilt.

Instead she devoted her full energies to supporting her Mistress Emma, accompanying her to political meetings, and watching with admiration as Emma rose up to speak in front of large audiences of city folk, making her points with an urgency and authority which could not fail to convince. Emma knew her history all right, and could surge through the story of the Irish people in little under an hour. The nuns had not taught history like that. The great dog Sligo would sit under the bench, a silent guardian to his mistress, ready to growl and bare his teeth if any should approach.

It was during such public lectures that Emma seemed to rise above herself; and she seemed to take on the voice of the whole Irish nation, in a threnody for lost lands and sacrificed lives.

'And what was it that brought the English here? I'll tell you what . . . Land – that's what. For in those days wealth and power lay with those who owned the land, and therefore the means of food production. And they seized the land of the Irish people and came and settled upon it. I tell you, ladies and gentleman, if such people as yourselves had not been prepared to stand up and speak out, then conditions would not have improved at all. Look what happened in the Land War – when we all stuck together we won back some rights. We can do it again. We must do it again, and soon, and regain control over our own country . . .'

Kathleen would watch proudly as a cheer rose from the audience, their faces filled with hope and wish for change. But secretly she was anxious lest Emma go too far; that she would be arrested any day now for subversion against the ruling British. And after these meetings Emma would seem exhausted, as if she had given too much for a public cause and it had drained everything out of her. Her thin body would be racked with a dry cough, and her eyes would shine with unnatural brilliance, like those of one possessed. Yet she would soon recover after a day or two's rest, with Kathleen in attendance to bring her food and drink on a tray.

Occasionally she witnessed Emma arguing heatedly with Will Butler about her participation in these meetings. Will was no activist, and one afternoon in particular she overheard him holding forth, while she herself was in the garden shaking the crumbs from a cloth.

'I can't understand why you have to go out preaching yourself to death, Emma. You're like a bellows full of old wind. Surely the artist's role is to change the consciousness of the nation through literature and art. What need to go into common meeting-halls, like you do?'

'Why, Will, you're such an intellectual snob . . . you'll never realise! We *must* organise for the future. *You* are whistling while the ship goes down.'

'And *you* will end up being arrested, I'm warning you. There are too many spies about, with ears and eyes willing to go on sale to Dublin Castle in these hard times.'

Kathleen had seen Johnny Gilbert now and again since that first encounter at the theatre. They had even gone for walks together, and she had once posed for him to take photographs in the park. Indeed he was deeply sympathetic, and she found herself growing fond of his attentions, his sad eyes, the way he listened intently to her as if her words were all-important.

There was no doubt about it, Kathleen felt increasingly attracted to this gentle, civilised older man who had travelled widely and enjoyed so many lady friends. She loved hearing him talk about France and Italy – far-off places that seemed to her like dreamland. But most of all she enjoyed his vivid descriptions of life in the islands off the west coast of Ireland, and the people there who lived a simple life so close to the soil.

Johnny was infatuated with these peasants. For hours he could extol the virtues of a life lived under the elements; of fishing on a sea which might swallow you up at any time; of the folk stories told from an oral tradition stretching back over a thousand years. Kathleen would listen entranced to his fine-sounding words, and wonder at them afterwards. There must surely be drawbacks to a life lived in the confines of a small cabin, close to a turf fire throughout the damp of the winter, with the smell of ordure from the cow at the far end of the room. She remembered keenly her mother's life of poverty and hardship, and doubted that all was as wonderful as Johnny seemed to think. Secretly she was glad she had a good position in a fine town-house, working for an employer who seemed to respect her as a person.

Yet even that position was ambivalent. Certainly when they were alone together Emma would reveal her private thoughts and hopes, but in company Kathleen was regarded as little better than a maid, and this was reflected in the attitude of Emma's visitors towards her. Witness Will Butler, for instance, one of the most frequent visitors. When he came bouncing up the steps, he would merely throw his coat at Kathleen, with barely a grunt of acknowledgement in his haste to see her mistress.

Kathleen soon realised that Will's interest in her Emma was in no way lessened by her refusal to even contemplate marriage. She noticed how his dark eyes would follow her mistress hungrily round the room. There he would sit on the chaise-longue covered in green leather, its back to the high windows overlooking the leafy Green, his gaze intense as he declaimed some news and his gold-rimmed spectacles quivering atop the thin aristocratic nose. Then Emma would sit down in her favourite spot by the grand Georgian fireplace, her mouth curling in amusement. And Sligo would lie docilely at her feet, his brindled markings toning in with the predominant brownish colour of the room.

Kathleen had time to observe these finer points in their behaviour, as the conversation was rarely if ever directed at her. Thus was the propriety of the mistress-servant relationship preserved.

Yet, at other times it was ignored completely, and Kathleen felt almost as though she was being treated as an equal. This often happened when they were out alone together in the fresh air; as when they once caught a tram out to Howth to take Sligo for a long walk on the Head. He would love searching for rabbits among the heather and chasing through the rhodedendron bushes, while the breeze from the sea would be welcomely cool.

That day Emma was in fine form, dressed in her freshly ironed blouse, high up the neck despite the heat of the day, and a skirt Kathleen had purposely let out in order to give greater freedom of movement. They could have been taken for sisters, so casual was the nature of Emma's dress. The sun was not yet at its peak as they climbed up towards the top of Howth Head. Emma was in the habit of declaiming history and politics to Kathleen on these walks, and considered this part of the girl's education. Today her theme concerned events during the 1840s.

'And do you know, Kathleen, they died in their thousands, and hardly a hand was lifted to save them . . .' So she continued with terrible tales of the Famine, until Kathleen's head seemed ready to burst with facts and figures. Indeed sometimes Kathleen felt she was being used as an experimental ear for Emma's public speeches. Nevertheless she listened intently. She had heard about the Famine before, of course, but only as a simple tale long ago at her mother's knee. Emma's account was one of such concentrated hardship and degradation, however, that Kathleen protested in shock that this could not all be true.

'Surely, Emma, if there was food in the country, as you say, there must have been some way to make sure the little children did not go hungry?'

'Kathleen, let this be a lesson to you: when Irish children died, it mattered not a jot to the English. And many of the landlords did not care much either.'

At the summit of the Head they sat down, and Sligo ran off in delight. The heather was giving off its own wonderful scent, the sun shone down from a clear blue June sky, and the sea lay below like a glittering jewel in its shifting shards of blue and silver and gold.

'Phew! I'm baked', Emma panted. 'Let's rest here for a while. We can lie in the heather like I used to do as a child. You can see the tumulus from here. Look, it's that little hump. It's where they used to bury their dead on the hill-top. A good place to be buried, don't you think?'

'Yes, I used to come up here with my uncle, and then he would take me for an ice-cream down in Howth. It's a fine place to take the air.'

'You know, Kathleen, it's times like this that help you to forget all the evil that's happened to this country in the past. I feel so invigorated coming up here.'

Emma leaned back and closed her eyes to the sunshine, and Kathleen felt a similar drowsiness coming upon her. As she looked towards the tumulus, she wondered which of Old Ireland's dead had been put to rest under that green hillock. But it was the more recently dead who came to trouble her as she fell into a doze in the heat.

She was on a path leading to a huddle of low buildings. She could see they had no windows, and the doors looked as if they had been bricked up. Along the path towards her came a stream of ragged-looking people, men, women and children. As they passed her, Kathleen saw they were gaunt and thin, with eyes sunk deep in their sockets, and their lips cracked and covered in sores. Several of the women carried pale-looking infants which seemed unnat-

100

urally still. Kathleen caught a glimpse of their wizened breasts, which seemed empty of all nourishment.

When a girl about her own age approached, she asked her, 'Who are all these people, and where are they going?'

'To heaven, I hope, where their lives may be better, as surely no hell could be worse than what we have been through.'

And as the dismal throng of people increased, the girl began to tell her story.

'We grew only potatoes, see. They be the only things we poor people could grow in our own little bit of land. The landlord's wheat, well it was growing tall and strong, and in the summer of that year we little knew what lay before us in the dark days of winter. And as autumn came and the plants were dug up, there were no potatoes; killed off all of them, and nothing to eat. We starved, and my stomach swelled. I even ate grass but it was no good. My little baby brother died in his sleep one day, his stomach as big as a ball, and my mother cried, and we grew weaker and weaker. It was the same in all the other cabins – no food at all. And we watched carts full of grain set off from the landlord's fields that winter to be exported abroad. We felt so helpless. I began to see things, and I told the priest I had seen the Virgin coming to care for us all, and he said it was God's way of comforting us in our trouble. It rained and it was cold. Then illness struck and we were so sick the rushes we slept on smelt of vomit. None of us could move for days.

'Then father rose up and told us the time had come for us to hide our suffering from our neighbours. He would fetch some stones and slowly, slowly laid one on top of the other in the doorway till the little daylight disappeared. His tears were the mortar for that wall of stones which was to cut us off from life. Little by little it rose to blot out a world we would see no more – my mother, my father and we seven children alive inside our tomb. We heard keening from the other cabins as my father, finally murmured, "Tis done".

'The dark fell upon all of us after that, and a blessed

101

relief it was as the Angel of Death came upon us and gathered us up in his soft white feathery wings, and flew up out of that cabin.'

By now there were gaunt and suffering people as far as Kathleen could see, spread over the gently rolling hills and fields. As the girl finished speaking and melted back into the multitude, a moan rose among them all, a cry of pain across the years. 'Do not forget us!' they seemed to be saying, and the women's cries of grief pierced the still bright air.

From among the throng one old woman seemed to be staring her straight in the eyes. Dirty and dishevelled, she seemed to be beckoning Kathleen into the crowd.

Reluctantly Kathleen followed her, and the crowds around her seemed to fall back. The old woman took her by the hand and led her on. She was now stumbling over stoney ground, and there on the top of a hill stood a small shrine with a cross.

'Who are you?' Kathleen screamed.

'I am your namesake — Cathleen they call me. And look, they come to me for help.'

Kathleen stared in disbelief as the crowd pressed in again, and she could feel the mass of people behind her. 'Yes, Cathleen ni Houlihan is my name. Watch me, I will help my children and succour them.' The crone limped up to the shrine, throwing her cloak back over her shoulders. She then climbed up the pile of stones to embrace the wooden cross. Turning, she cried, 'Help me, Kathleen! Let them come to me.' Out of the crowd of spectres, one wafer-thin child was brought forward and lifted up by its mother to suck on the startlingly white breast that fell out of the crone's rags. The child drank greedily and, as Kathleen looked on, she saw the crone's face grow younger, and a beatific smile spread across it — and a light was shining like a halo behind . . .

Kathleen woke and felt a chill to her bones. Looking up, she saw the sun had gone behind a cloud, and the day now seemed altogether gloomier and sadder. The cries of

102

the ghostly multitude seemed still to be ringing in her ears as she sat up, wondering for a moment where she was.

Emma was already standing, looking out over the sea to the boats on the horizon.

'Come on, Kathleen! Up you get. It's two o'clock, and Willie Butler promised he would come by this afternoon with some of his new play. We could have a reading of it, and you could play a part if you like.'

Kathleen stood up and smoothed down her skirt. 'I was dreaming there for a while. I thought I was in some village during the Famine, and the dead were talking to me. May God in heaven bless their poor souls.'

Emma looked at her curiously. 'Kathleen, the dead are always with us. They live on in spirit form, and I'm convinced they do come to haunt us in our dreams. Come, let's go now. Look, the sun is with us again ... Sligo, Sligo, where are you?' Her voice rose to a penetrating yell, and the dog rushed up panting, and threw himself on his mistress with delight. Standing on his hind legs he was almost as tall as Emma herself, and she returned his boisterous greeting with words of endearment. 'There, there, Sligo. There's a good dog.'

And to Kathleen she turned. 'Let's go and have an ice-cream.'

Arriving back home, Emma and Kathleen felt exhausted and were glad to relax. Emma asked the maid to bring them tea as they sat in the shady drawing-room in the heat of the afternoon with the windows wide open. The cries of children came drifting through the windows. Parasols and rugs scattered blotches of colour on the green grass of the park outside, now yellowing slightly in the heat. It was an unusually dry summer, and today was clean, sharp and bright.

When tea was ready, Mary brought it in, with her sleeves rolled up and perspiration gleaming gently on her forehead. The tray was placed on an occasional table covered with a lacy cloth. The china cups were hand-

103

painted with summer flowers, poppies and hollyhocks, delphiniums and daisies, each one a masterpiece of delicate brushwork. The teapot itself was made of silver.

Kathleen poured them each a cup, then sat down attentively in a cushioned chair.

'Willie should be here any moment now,' said Emma. 'I love him dearly, you know, but he's not the sort of man I feel I could settle with. There's one or two things we would disagree on, and I don't like the way he panders to that Lady Gregory — as if being a lady conferred any special talent on one. He's always such a stuck-up prig when he comes back from the country . . . *Ah!* It can't be long now before Major Nash is back from the big parade . . .'

Kathleen was used to these disjointed musings and ramblings of her mistress. It was as if she was thinking aloud and just letting words dribble out with no concern about whether they meant much.

Suddenly there was the noise outside of galloping hooves and a carriage squeaking under strain.

'Quickly, Kathleen, go and look what it is. It sounds like something urgent,' cried Emma.

Kathleen glanced out the window, then ran down the curved staircase to the front door. Two soldiers were in the driving seat, and one leapt off the carriage shouting, 'Call the doctor quickly, miss. The Major has been taken sick.'

The carriage door was flung open and the two soldiers began to gently draw out the supine form of Major Nash. Kathleen started in shock; his face was purple and he seemed to be unconscious.

'Emma!' she shrieked, 'Come at once. The Major is ill!'

Surprised by the noise below, Emma was already halfway down the stairs. As soon as she saw her father and the colour of his face, she ordered the men to carry him up the stairs, and sent Kathleen to fetch Doctor O'Neill, who lived in Clarendon Street just five minutes away. Kathleen sped away as if the hounds of hell were at her heels, weaving through the crowds strolling the pavements of Grafton Street, and turned into the doctor's street. She ran up the steps to the front door, grasping the knocker firmly and banging it down as if she was trying to wake the dead. A maid opened the door and immediately went off into the house to call the doctor, who luckily was in that sunny afternoon.

Doctor O'Neill was used to such emergencies; and to the ways of people calling him in panic and paying him at leisure. He had seen enough deaths and births to know that mostly there was little to be done in extremis save comfort the relatives with the knowledge that they had at least done something positive to help their ailing kin.

Kathleen watched in a frenzy of impatience as he put his instruments into his bag, carefully buttoned up his shirt, then finally walked out the front door. She had never seen anyone look so ill as the Major.

Arriving back at St Stephen's Green, Kathleen could see the whole house was in turmoil; the front door lay wide open and the two soldiers were hanging around the steps, awaiting further orders. The doctor strode past them and made his way up to the patient's bedroom. Kathleen heard a murmured discussion, then Emma came down, her face pale and her eyes shocked.

'What exactly happened?' she asked one of the soldiers.

'Well, miss, the Major was watching the parade, and as you know it's a hot day and he had on his full uniform. Then suddenly he seemed to fall over clasping his throat. Well we were told to take him home immediately, as the regimental doctor was unavailable. Hope he's all right, miss.'

Finally Doctor O'Neill came down the stairs and into the dining-room where Emma and Kathleen sat waiting, with heads bowed, at the table which had seen so many lively parties over the years.

'I'm afraid, Miss Nash, that the news is not good. Major Nash has suffered a stroke, and has lost the use of his right arm and leg. This may improve in time, or it may not, but there is a danger, nay even a likelihood that he could suffer another stroke.' He cleared his throat. 'Keep him quiet in bed. He is sleeping now, so let him rest, and when he wakes up, break it to him gently that he cannot move his arm and leg. He's an active man, and it may come as a shock.'

Kathleen looked over at Emma's face as the doctor's words dropped into the silence of the room, and she felt a deep sympathy for her. The pangs she felt for the loss of her own mother were still fairly fresh. Emma sat stiffly with her arms resting on the table, hands clasped tightly. Her face was drawn and lacked the confidence which normally made her so striking. For the first time she looked vulnerable. Kathleen felt like patting her head comfortingly as a mother would a child, but she retained her distance, sensing that Emma's grief was too private an emotion to intrude upon.

'I'll come back tomorrow and see how he is,' said the doctor.

'Yes, thank you, doctor. Thank you for coming so promptly. Kathleen will see you out.'

Kathleen was instructed to give the soldiers a quickly scrawled letter from Emma's hand. They turned the horses round and trotted off. The house seemed unnaturally quiet when they had gone, and Kathleen returned to find her mistress still sitting at the table, paper and pen in front of her.

'I'm worried, Kathleen, and afraid. If my father goes, I don't know what I will do. He is my dearest friend.'

11

'Is he sleeping, Emma? Should someone watch over him?'

Emma wiped her brow and sighed. She hated the stress of it all. Poor, poor Father, to collapse in front of the regiment and be brought home like a dying dog.

'Kathleen, I'm so frightened. Listen, you go and watch while he sleeps, and as soon as he wakes, shout down for me. I'll take over through the night, so that between us he is not alone. I'll just write a quick note to the theatre, as Willie hasn't arrived yet and I want to put him off. Mary can take it.'

Kathleen went upstairs to the grand main bedroom where Tommy Nash lay in his bed breathing in a ragged, desultory fashion. The curtains were drawn to cut out the evening sun and the room felt very warm and stuffy. Kathleen pulled up the sash window a little to allow in some air. Looking at him carefully, she could see his mouth sagging on one side, as if he had no control over it. It gave him a curiously lopsided look, unkempt even – something the Major had never seemed before. Now he could be taken for one of the city's many drunks who staggered round the streets late at night. It turned Kathleen's heart over with pity to see him thus.

She moved a small wicker chair to the bedside and sat down to begin her vigil. Patiently she waited through the next two hours, and several times she nearly fell asleep herself, tired after their walk on Howth Head. The images of her strange dream hovered at the corners of her mind, stark and seemingly real, as she wavered between sleep and wakefulness.

A clock in the drawing-room below was chiming seven when Emma entered the room. She looked first at Tommy Nash lying so helpless in the bed, and then told Kathleen to go and rest herself, as it was going to be a long night. Kathleen noticed how Emma, normally so much in control of any situation, was now looking haggard and unsure of herself. She touched her hand gently and left the room.

Down in the kitchen the cook had prepared a light meal. Kathleen ate the cold meat and bread without appetite, and then to pass the time went up to the room on the ground floor where the books were kept. Funny that during her time here she had barely had a chance to inspect them till now. It was while she was looking over the titles that she heard an urgent summons from upstairs, 'Kathleen, please come up.'

Upstairs the lights were fully lit in the bedroom, and Major Tommy was rolling his eyes in an effort to speak.

'I've lost her, my one true love, and what am I left with . . . it's no good . . .'

'Kathleen, I think he is raving. You had better tell Mary to go and fetch the doctor again. I really don't know what to do . . . you'll have to help me. Father, dearest, it's going to be all right. It's Emma here, your own daughter. I'm not going to leave you.'

'Emma, Emma, come here so I can see you. The light is very dim . . .'

The Major's voice sounded so strange, the words only half-formed, and Kathleen could hardly understand what he was saying. He lay back on his pillow with his hair all in disarray, his eyes unfocused and staring.

As Emma drew closer, he continued: 'Let me see you, my girl. Ah, it is you . . . I have to tell you something . . . remember this . . . never be afraid of anything . . . not even death . . . Promise me . . .'

His voice was trailing off now, and he sank back into the pillows as his breathing grew coarser and more erratic.

'Damn the doctor, Kathleen, where is he?' Emma sobbed.

'It's a priest he is needing right now, I'm thinking,' Kathleen murmured.

Suddenly the Major's head jerked up, his eyes wide

open. 'I can see you. I am coming,' he shouted, as his neck seemed to stiffen. He brought up his good hand to point into a corner of the room, and Emma and Kathleen frantically tried to hold him still as an awful rattle seemed to come from his throat and blood trickled from his mouth. A moment later he fell back limp, his eyes still staring into the same corner.

In the hush that followed, the door opened, and Doctor O'Neill came in. He went over to the bed and looked down at his patient, then felt his pulse.

'He's gone, I'm afraid. His heart has just given up, poor man.' Gently he closed the Major's eyes and pulled the sheet over his face. He had thought the old soldier had longer to go, but it was sometimes better this way, as men who had seen such active careers rarely settled to an invalid's life with good grace.

'If you like, I'll call on the undertaker,' he suggested. 'He will come in the morning to make the preparations.' Following a death, it was always difficult for the relatives. Amid their own grief they still had to concentrate on arrangements for the burial. Still, Miss Nash should have some help from the army; they would see to it the Major was sent off in style. There was nothing more he could do here, and there was that poor Mrs Kelly about to have her baby.

'I'm sorry, Miss Nash, but I must be on my way, and I'll send you the death certificate in the morning.'

The following days saw the house filled with English voices as the Major's fellow soldiers came to pay their respects before the funeral. The colonel of the regiment assured Emma that everything would be taken care of, and of course Tommy would have a full regimental funeral, with a guard of honour and a volley of guns. The coffin would be draped with the Union Jack and borne on a bier drawn by six black horses. He would be buried in Mount Jerome Cemetery, after a solemn procession through the streets.

Kathleen stayed at home while Emma attended the

funeral, for it would be a very British and formal affair. The curtains were drawn as a mark of respect, and would remain so until the end of the week. There was to be no Irish wake for Tommy; his army friends would mourn for him in public, and Emma would return home on her own. It was near the end of August, just after the dog days.

So Kathleen waited in the darkened rooms. The Major's death had been confusing for her. She surprised herself by feeling so sorry for the man, for she had only known him a few short months. And him a Protestant too, and serving in the British army! He had treated her well, though, with the old-fashioned courtesy he extended to all of the 'fairer sex'. Yes, she would miss his bluff affection and solid presence in the house.

The hours passed and Sligo began to whine. He needed to go out so Kathleen took him into St Stephen's Green and along the north side. Looking up Dawson Street she noticed several trams standing completely still. Normally the road was full of their clanking as they swayed along their metal rails, sparks flying.

'There's no trams today, if that's what you're thinking. They're all marching around the town. They just upped and left the trams where they are. Folk can't move around because of them, and there'll be more trouble before the week is out.'

The speaker was one of the park regulars, an old woman whose face hung in folds and wrinkles like an elephant's skin. Hers was a twilight existence between life and death, just scraping a living off other people's crumbs; and there were many such in Dublin.

Kathleen whistled for Sligo. She smelt trouble.

At three o'clock Emma was delivered home in a carriage. She looked really terrible as she came into the dining-room and staggered on to a chair. Laying her face on the table, she broke down in great sobs.

'They threw things at the coffin, Kathleen. My dear father lying in there on his way to burial. They shouted "English bastards", and the soldiers had to fire off their guns to make way through the crush. The streets were full of people, what with the trams not moving. And yet I've always supported their action . . . and my poor father has to suffer from it.'

When she lifted her face, twisted and contorted with grief, Kathleen could recognise a woman torn between love and loyalty to her family and the same feelings towards a cherished ideal. And now her family was gone, she had only the ideal left to sustain her.

But for this day she would mourn her father, and Kathleen was gentle with her. As darkness came, Emma was still talking through the events of her life with Major Tommy, remembering their travels in Europe in sunnier times. Kathleen provided a ready ear, for she realised, there being no wake, there was no other way of releasing these feelings. It was good to talk about the dead as you saw them on their way. Did the Holy Mother look after Protestants as well? She hoped the Major would not spend too long in limbo, and she vowed she would say a prayer for him that very night.

The solicitor, Mr Rourke, was a man used to imparting important news to the bereaved relatives of the dear departed. Sometimes it would come as a surprise, like today for instance, when he had an appointment with Miss Nash, old Tommy's daughter. A delicate job it was going to be this morning, and no mistake. Still, it would be all over by lunch-time, and there was a good meal and good companions waiting at the Club. He took out his watch and wound it vigorously, slipping it deftly back into its pocket. She would be here soon. Indeed, here she was. The panelled door opened softly and in walked Emma Nash with some young slip of a girl. A fine woman, Tommy's daughter; a wonder she didn't get married. Mr Rourke walked forward to shake Emma's hand, and motioned to the two to sit down. The wood panelling on the walls gleamed with frequent polishing. The papers on Rourke's desk were ruffled by the slight breeze through the sash window, open at the bottom.

111

'I'm afraid the news is not good, Miss Nash. I've been going through your father's papers, and it seems that apart from his army salary he had very little money of his own.' The solicitor folded his plump arms on the desk and leant over. 'All in all, there is very little left for you. But the one good bit of news is that I have a letter from your uncle in Kerry, who is also a client of mine. Apparently he saw the army obit. in the paper and took it upon himself to write. Here is his letter.

Dear Mr Rourke
I saw the news of my brother-in-law's death in the *Irish Times*, which saddened me although we had not communicated for many years. I am writing to you to offer my niece a home here, as I know Tommy was not rich on his own account. Please show this letter to her and tell her to come to Kerry as soon as she likes.
Yours,
Edward Burke

'So you see, Miss Nash, I have at least that comfort for you, for as it stands there is no way you can continue your present lifestyle in the city. There is no funding for it. I would advise you, therefore, to rent out the house in St Stephen's Green and to take up Mr Burke's offer of a home.'

Emma laughed bitterly: it was all too ridiculous. Left with only an unknown uncle's charity. Then she saw Kathleen's face, white with strain and worry.

'Don't worry, you'll be looked after Kathleen. I'll go to the country and take you with me.' She slipped her hand into the younger woman's and squeezed it to reassure her.

The unprofitable meeting with Mr Rourke seemed to have galvanised Emma out of her depression. In a way, action was her ideal comfort. After sending advance warning of their arrival to Uncle Edward, she became a whirlwind of motion through the rooms of the house. With deep regret she told Mary and the cook the sad news that she could no longer offer them employment.

Then Kathleen set to sorting and packing, as they were to go by train to Galway the following Monday. First day of a new month and a new life.

Saturday came and they were still in disorder when the message arrived, its carrier a skinny young lad of scarcely twelve. Cocky and sure of himself he was, and Kathleen listened carefully to what he had to say.

'Tell Miss Nash there's to be a meeting in Sackville Street tomorrow at one. Jem Larkin is in hiding, but he should be there with the Countess.'

'And is that all you know?' said Kathleen.

'That's all I've been told to say, and I'm not saying any more. I've done my job and I'm off, for it's dangerous times these are.'

Emma received the message with excitement. 'So he's in hiding is he, that Jem Larkin? With the Countess, indeed. We'll have to attend the meeting, Kathleen, but I'm worried . . . there are notices up banning it, and the police will be there. But we *must* support Larkin . . . though how he will get in to speak to the people, I do not know. He will certainly be arrested if anyone recognises him.

Sunday was steamy. The day seemed to have wrung out a towel and left the droplets of moisture in the air. But Emma and Kathleen were ready waiting outside the Imperial Hotel in Sackville Street at the time the great union leader was due to appear. Kathleen felt the press of ordinary people all around her: working men locked out from their workplaces because they had dared speak out against the bosses. Kathleen could feel their mood of frustration and anger. Sleeves rolled up, their caps pushed back, they were waiting quietly to see if their hero and spokesman would really turn up.

The police had silently moved in behind them and now menacingly surrounded the crowd. Bells began to ring and Kathleen could see the noon Mass crowd coming from the Roman Catholic Pro-Cathedral in Marlborough

113

Street. A hush of expectancy fell upon the crush, though nothing at all seemed to be happening. Then suddenly a woman came out on to the balcony of the hotel. A cheer rose up from the assembled crowd and they threw their caps in the air to see the 'woman' take off her hat and veil and start addressing them in a loud male voice. It was Jem Larkin himself.

'I know this meeting has been banned, but I'm here to talk about the cause of Irish freedom . . .'

Suddenly police appeared behind him from inside the hotel and began to haul him back. The crowd surged forward, becoming like a thing alive, writhing this way and that. Kathleen had lost control over her movements, and could feel herself being carried towards Prince's Street by the side of the General Post Office.

As she stood up on tiptoe to see what was happening, she caught a glimpse of batons descending. There was screaming, and another surge backwards, and she realised she was trapped in the throng. There was no sight of Emma, and Kathleen felt more than a little frightened – yet exhilarated as the violence of the moment pumped adrenalin into her veins.

People were pushing past her now, with blood bright red on their faces.

'Goddamn the police! The bastards are laying out everywhere.'

She realised that something had gone very wrong, as many of the victims now trapped in the fray had not come to attend the political meeting at all, but were innocently emerging from Holy Mass.

To and fro the action went and none knew which way to turn to escape the police, so ready to charge with their batons raised. All was total chaos, which the police should be preventing, yet it was their own lack of organisation which was the main cause of the fracas. If only they would let the people get free. Amidst the panic of the trapped crowds, Kathleen could smell their fear. Brave words counted for nought in this crush; she herself was screaming along with the rest.

It seemed like eternity before order was reestablished, and the throng was able to disperse. Some could hardly walk because of the injuries they had received, and, although she did not know it then, two had been killed. Later her heart ached at the waste of it all.

One distraught woman begged Kathleen to help her support her wounded husband home, a few streets away. 'And wasn't I telling him not to go to any banned meeting, and just to come to Church with myself. And look what happened to the both of us, just walking home after a service to our Lord and we gets beaten for our pains. May they rot in hell, those policemen.'

Kathleen shivered at the sight of the blood on her dress as she made her way back across the river.

12

There was no sign of any carriage to collect them when they reached Galway station. After waiting impatiently for half an hour, they luckily found a carter to take them and their luggage to Uncle Edward's house, called Springmount. Kathleen was tired now, for the long train journey had exhausted both of them. Emma had gone very quiet, and seemed incapable of dealing with the minor exigencies of travelling, so Kathleen had taken over. Even Sligo had been unhappy on the train journey, but now was ready and eager to run.

The country town of Galway came as a shock to Kathleen after the relative sophistication she had known, if only briefly, in Dublin. Here there was mud in the streets, and the almost clownish ruddiness of the people's faces showed sign of their outdoor life. Though probably no less deprived than their Dublin cousins, they certainly looked less pallid and wan.

She sympathised with poor Emma. The events of the last week had been a great shock to her, what with the death of Major Tommy and then the bloody riot. But, then, she had begun to realise that Emma was the type of person who did go through cyclical changes of behaviour: at one time extremely active and outgoing, at the other hiding morosely within herself. She was now entering a period of gloomy inaction which left Kathleen to deal with all the practical matters that confronted them.

Ah, but it was good to be out in the country again. And as the cart left the town behind and travelled along a country lane, Kathleen breathed in the clean air with an intoxication she had only ever felt from the few glasses of porter she had drunk in her life up to then. The very wind seemed to be caressing her face and softening her skin. One moment she saw a rabbit start from the hedge, its small tail bobbing as it dived into the nearby field. Sligo saw it, too, and went bounding in pursuit. Too late. The rabbit dived into another hole, and deprived Sligo of a tasty dinner. Then they passed a rookery where the birds were beginning to settle down for the night, wheeling slowly as they argued and scolded each other. The sun was a golden globe in the west as they reached the last incline; the sky was mackerel painted with a rosy blush.

"Tis a fine evening we're having,' said Kathleen to their driver's back.

He looked round, his cap pushed askew on his head, 'Set fair for tomorrow, I would say; and we're needing all the sun we can get, as when the rain comes you'll be thinking you'll never see the sun again. His voice had a faint twang to it, something Kathleen could not recognise, but was in fact a slight American accent. The man had been over the water and come back again with enough money to set himself up with a house and a wife.

'Are you staying long at the big house? That Mr Edward is a quare ole person and no mistake. Looks like a fox, he does. Doesn't move like one though.' Here the man laughed. 'I'd like to see him do a day's work like some round here. He wouldn't survive it I'm sure.'

'I don't think I need your comments on my relations thank you.' Emma's sharp retort startled Kathleen. She had been silently sitting on the other side of the cart on top of her baggage, and her sudden interruption cut through the amiable atmosphere growing up between Kathleen and the driver. It was as if her very presence demanded that they all observe the roles put upon them by birth and rank: mistress, servant and hired man. Indeed Emma looked her part. Though her hat was pinned on securely, its plumes were waving as the cart jolted along. Though this looked almost comical, her face retained its tightness, and her eyes had a shrewd and hooded but empty look about them.

After that Kathleen remained silent until they turned

through the gates to Springmount. There was no one to greet them at the gate lodge and obviously no one lived there. The tall grass growing round the gates looked as if it had been uncut for many a year, implying that the gates themselves lay permanently open and unattended.

The same air of neglect hung over the drive up to the main house. Tall beech trees hid the light, their smooth grey trunks like pillars of stone.

Finally they reached a Georgian country villa of modest proportions. In the eighteenth and early nineteenth centuries many such houses had been built throughout Ireland as visible symbols of the rising wealth of the English landlords who had decided to make their home there. Emma's mother had been born in this house, one of a large family which had since dispersed across the world, leaving Edward the second oldest brother to preside alone over the house's decline.

At first glance it retained its pristine look of grandeur, but closer inspection would reveal that not much had been done to it in a hundred years. Paint was peeling off the windows and sills, and bare wood was starkly visible in many places. There were cracks in the rendering everywhere, especially in the upper storey, which gave the house a wrinkled look as if old age had withered it, rather than the weather.

The carter finally reined in his horse, and jumped down to give the ladies a steady hand as they descended from the back of the cart. His eyes scanned Kathleen briefly and smiled. With Emma he was more circumspect, and he doffed his cap like a paid servant should. After lifting down their bags he accepted his money from Emma with a 'Thank you, ma'am.'

Kathleen gazed at the house with a growing sense of unease. There was no sign of welcome, though Emma had written to warn of their coming as soon as she had returned from the solicitor Mr Rourke. No lights glowed in the elegant bowed windows; no doors were thrown open with a cheery welcome; and there was no sign of anyone to help with their luggage. The cart turned to go and the horse, sensing its homeward run, set off at a brisk trot. In the silence Kathleen and Emma could still hear its hooves as it turned out of the drive back on to the lane.

'Well,' said Emma at last, 'I suppose the only thing to do is knock on the door. Uncle Edward is obviously not looking out for us.'

It was now getting dark, and the pretty pink of the sky had given way to the shadows of the evening. Kathleen could see columns of midges on the grass beside the drive. An owl hooted and a damp chill rose from the earth. Emma approached the double doors on which there was a fancy brass knocker shaped like a claw, green with neglect. Above the doors was a fanlight, elegantly and intricately shaped. Emma's knock seemed to resound very loudly through the still air.

Several minutes passed, and Kathleen was beginning to doubt that there was anybody in the house at all, but then she saw the guttering of a candle shining faintly through the fanlight.

The door opened and a face appeared. 'What is it you're wanting at this time of night?'

'I've come to visit my Uncle Edward, and would you kindly let us in. I'm Emma Nash.'

The candle lifted to reveal the face of a shabbily-dressed man they subsequently discovered was the butler, Smith. It was, in fact, hardly fair to call him a butler as he had become more like a personal friend to Edward Burke, having worked with him ever since he had married that awful woman who had died young. Smith was himself no longer young; his bushy eyebrows were now white where once they had been deepest black. His originally slight figure had filled out over the years, and now he was of considerable girth. The fact was that he had been dreading this encounter ever since the master had warned him of it. He already felt jealous of Emma; and, as for the chit of a girl she had brought with her, well he would soon have her cut down to size – there was plenty of family silver to be cleaned.

'It's Smith here at your service, ma'am. I'm sorry for the delay.' This was spoken with such obsequiousness, such unction, that Emma grimaced with distaste.

'Thank you, Smith. Thank you very much. Could you show us our way and carry the luggage.'

Sligo growled as Smith approached the bags, but Emma summoned him to follow her, and obediently, with tail down, he did.

The hall was full of shadows and they could barely see the curve of the staircase which carried the eye up to a ceiling dome where light came in.

Emma was obviously growing impatient; used as she was to prompt action, she seemed to have emerged from her contemplative mood and was ready to take charge again.

'Uncle Edward, we're here!' she called, once, twice, and then again. There was no reply.

'Your uncle's in the dining-room.' Smith gestured briefly. 'The room on the left there. Dinner was at eight so you're late, though there may be something left for you.'

Emma walked to the door and opened it. The two women entered, Sligo following behind.

At the end of a long mahogany table sat a man considerably older than Major Tommy. His grey hair had grown long, and was tucked behind his ears. The only light in the room was a three-branched candlestick placed immediately before him so that his face took on the shadows of a death-mask. To the right of the table was a sideboard on which sat a few serving dishes covered with matching tops.

'Tommy's daughter, is it?' the voice said querulously. 'Come over here and let me have a look at you.' Emma drew closer into the pool of candlelight.

'A pretty enough woman, I suppose. Shame you never got married, what? And who's this with you?'

'It's Kathleen, Uncle. My companion. I couldn't leave her behind, and Mr Rourke said you didn't have a large household so I thought she could come in useful here.'

120

'Off you go, Kathleen, into the kitchen. Smith will look after you.'

'I'm sorry, Uncle, but Kathleen has always been treated like one of the family. She is not quite the common servant you take her for. She will stay with me, as will Sligo.'

Sligo was forgetting his manners, and just at that very moment had managed to dislodge one of the lids from the serving dishes. A piece of meat swiftly disappeared. The clatter of the dishes alerted Uncle Edward to the dog's actions.

'Let's get one thing straight before we begin, Emma. I will not tolerate a dog behaving like that. For one thing it is unmannerly, and secondly my dinner service won't last too long.'

'Sligo, come here. And sit.' Emma's voice was shrill and shaking.

The dog guiltily avoided its mistress's eyes as it sat down beside her.

'I suppose you'd better get yourselves plates and sit down, then.' Edward waved a tweed-clad arm towards the sideboard. 'You'll find it all there.'

Kathleen said nothing during that first meal at Springmount. She swallowed the cold meat and cold vegetables, but avoided the congealed gravy in the silver gravy-boat, and she thought gloomily about their prospects for the future. She would miss seeing Johnny Gilbert for one thing, and she didn't suppose that there would be any like him so far away from the Dublin circles she had got to know. Emma, she was sure, would miss the social action and her meetings after a week or two. Images of the Sunday's riot played behind her tired eyes: blood spouting from cut heads and bruised polls; the shouting and confusion as she was pushed hither and thither in the crush.

She sat up suddenly at the sound of raised voices.

'My dear Emma, it's all due to Popery. You can't have any civilised nation which bows down to a mere man. The sooner the agents of revolution are rooted out the better, I say; and may they be hanged for their pains, as it's treason to plot against our King, God save him.'

There was no arguing with such vehement prejudice, and Emma soon realised it. It was going to be a difficult time for her if Uncle Edward was going to press his views so obdurately. And him showing no respect for the Holy Father! Normally Kathleen would have been quick to defend her religion, despite some nagging doubts, but instinct convinced her that now was not the time to do so.

That first night was a sign of what was to come. Edward Burke proved to be a wearisome companion at meal times, either moaning about the estate and its workers, or railing against the Irish in general. Emma eventually arranged it so that she and Kathleen could eat certain meals much earlier, and left Edward to himself as much as possible. He did not seem to mind. It was as if he considered he had done his duty to his dead sister by offering his niece a roof over her head, and after that she could fend for herself.

Emma had changed. As the weeks went by, Kathleen began to worry about her condition, as she hardly went out and stayed in bed much of the day. She had also taken to talking obsessively about her past life, her visits to France, her social life in Dublin, as though those days would not return.

For her own part Kathleen spent much of her time out of doors. The grounds of the house were not large, and the gardens which had once been treated with loving care and attention were so grown over that few flowers bloomed except the weeds and the straggling last remnants of roses. Autumn came early that year, and while the first few weeks at Springmount had been characterised by bright sunshine, as soon as the equinox came in September the winds blew and the rain fell continuously. The slates on the roof rattled and the windows let in draughts; damp patches appeared on the walls, returning after a brief summer's absence; moulds flourished in dark corners.

The servants of the house, Smith and Mrs Crook, didn't seem to bother about such things. The kitchen was just about the only warm room in the house, and they alone benefited from this. Edward was as mean with his money as he was in spirit, and refused permission for any other fire than that in the dining-room, and that just a small one. Emma began to cough again.

Yet there were occasional breaks in the clouds, days when the sky blued over and the holly-tree gleamed bright green, and on such days Kathleen would try and persuade Emma to go out with her.

'Emma, you're going to fade away, sure you are, if you don't take an interest and come out a little. Look at you, pale and white and looking unhealthy, and how are you going to help the cause of Irish freedom if you are ill.'

'Kathleen, I can do what I like, but I am dependent on an uncle who I cannot agree with, living out here in the middle of nowhere and with no friends to comfort me.'

'Let's go into the town, Emma, and see what can be seen. Three weeks to Christmas and we have nothing of cheer. Your Uncle, I believe, could not care less. And anyway I have a letter to post.' Kathleen could not conceal her impatience; she was now longing for the town visit. Three and a half months had gone by, and she had received but one letter and that from Johnny Gilbert.

Dear Kathleen

Just a little note to tell you I'm going to France for a few weeks and will not be back until after Christmas. I'm missing you, but don't see how I can be with you until the spring, when I will be coming to visit my old friend out on the island. Things in Dublin are not good. The people are hungry and there are many helping to give out food. I also think that we are in for a big war in Europe very soon. My new play will be finished when I see you, so I hope we can read it through together and that you enjoy it.

Much love to you,
Johnny

Her heart had lifted when she recognised the writing on the envelope – and how she wished she was back in the city! But somehow she felt tied to Emma, at least in this time of her mistress's 'sickness', which was how she had come to think of it.

'If we go to town,' she persevered, 'we can see if there's letters at the post office, and I can post mine, too. Surely Will has written by now.'

'What care I for news of a place I cannot live in, and where once I felt I was doing something useful. Now I am but a useless parasite.' Emma reacted with her now normal bitterness at first, but suddenly she pulled herself up straight and said firmly,'All right, then, we will go together. We'll take the small trap and the quiet horse.'

This they did, and set off on a fine December's morning to Galway. The hedges hung with jewelled raindrops, and a faint mist still lingered in pockets of land. Emma's face took on a wild expression as she gripped the horse's reins to drive the trap. Something seemed to be forcing her into action after the previous lethargic months of grieving, her will forcing her to renewed frenzy, her restless eyes darting here and there.

The town was busy as the shops did a brisk trade in their wares. Most of them were serving drinks, and already drunken shouts and songs could be heard. Several boats were in from the offshore islands, and news was circulating fast of the funeral taking place that day. Emma made inquiry as to what had happened.

'It's bad luck come upon some of them, I hear. One poor man has lost two children in no less than a week, may God have mercy on their souls. It seems one boy fell over the cliff. Found him in the sea, they did, but would you believe there was not a mark on his body. And then the little daughter goes and dies of whooping-

124

cough two days later, poor soul. And imagine how his woman must feel, bringing the two of them into the world and all come to naught.'

This sort of talk acted like the elixir of life on Emma; now hearing of others' woes she was ready to forget her own.

They went to buy their supplies with new energy. Uncle Edward had reluctantly given them some money to buy what he called 'necessities': flour, tea, sugar, oats, and such. These they found in the general store down by the quay. They even had a little money left over.

Most of the shops stretched along the side of the harbour, and there the main traffic of the town congested. Boats were tied up against the harbour wall, some with nets on board as a sign of the fishing which was a local occupation all around the coast. The quayside was full of the women who brought the fish to sell on. A brisk trade was being conducted that day, with goods fast changing hands while a great deal of alcohol was consumed by men unused to much cash in their pockets. More than a few wives would be disappointed that night when their men returned home with less money than they expected.

It was hard for them to avoid a drink, as at each little shop there would be a few glasses for the customers, and the wheels of trade were oiled with whisky and porter so that the shopkeeper could sell his wares more easily. Old debts were similarly repaid or favours done in previous weeks: a hand with digging the turf here, a night's help with fishing there. So the male community met together and exchanged news from farther-flung places. But the women rarely came with their menfolk on trading days, having enough to do caring for their broods of children and the animals. Today, however, there was a sprinkling of women from the islands, because of the funeral. Not for them the fine clothing of the Dublin ladies, or even the cheaper copies that poorer girls might wear on a night out. These had flaming red petticoats under long black skirts, a shawl over the shoulders for warmth, and a look of the sea in their eyes.

Emma and Kathleen stood and watched respectfully as the little procession carrying two small coffins moved out of the town towards the cemetery. The priest walked alongside, his black vestments blowing in the breeze. Kathleen crossed herself as she watched them pass, and muttered a blessing.

'It must be a terrible thing to lose two children like that, one on top of the other.' She glanced up at Emma, and was surprised to see tears streaming down her face. She gripped Kathleen's arm,

'Kathleen', she sobbed, 'the boxes are so small. All come to nothing – so much love gone to waste.'

They were just leaving the outskirts of the town when the storm hit them. Rain like steel pins drenched their clothes, and they were soon wet through. The horse was willing enough, but had trouble working against an oncoming wind so it took them nearly an hour extra to reach Springmount, and by the time they arrived darkness had fallen. Sligo came running round the side of the house, barking his welcome. Having been locked out, he too was soaked through, and looked like some alien black dog whose ribs stuck out unnaturally. Kathleen led the horse round the back of the house, where the old stable-hand took him off for a rub-down and a good hot bran-mash.

No such welcome was waiting for Emma and Kathleen. Uncle Edward came shuffling out of the dining-room at the sound of their entrance to inspect the goods they were supposed to have bought.

'Hours late and the food wet! Emma Nash, you may be called my niece but such stupidity argues you're no relation of mine.'

'Uncle Edward, I am sure you can replace the order. Kathleen and I will go again.'

'It's lucky I'm not like that lot in town. Shiftless the lot of them, they don't do any work or get off their backsides to help themselves. The men go drinking and

126

sup away what little they have, and then they have the cheek to go to their Confession the next day so their religion lets them do it all with a clear conscience. I've no sympathy, I can tell you. They should work harder and have fewer children. Take your 'companion' upstairs with you. I don't wish to see you again today.'

'And where's *your* Christian charity, I'd like to know,' Emma snapped. 'It's a convenient sort of religion that can sit at home surrounded by comforts and only worry about a few bags of spoiled flour.'

'Away with you!' Her uncle's face was growing redder by the second, and Kathleen feared he would have struck Emma then if she had not turned and tripped up the stairs. Without delay she hurried after her mistress. Their clothes were drenched and clinging to them, so their first thought was to change into something dry. It was after Kathleen had brought some tea up from the kitchen that she noticed Emma was wheezing slightly and shivering.

With a hollow laugh Emma said, 'I don't know what's come over me, Kathleen. I'm all hot and cold.'

'Get to bed with you Emma. I'm thinking you don't look well, and must keep as warm as possible.' Kathleen looked at the empty grate and decided to beg for some wood for a fire.

But Uncle Edward adamantly refused to allow a fire to be lit. 'She's wasted enough money of mine today, and now she wants a fire, too. No, I say.'

That night saw a frightening deterioration in Emma's condition, until she was coughing fit to burst. The grey light of dawn was seeping through the curtains when Kathleen stirred from her vigil at Emma's bedside. Her patient looked very pale, barely asleep with lids half-closed, and breathing in irregular gasps. Thoroughly alarmed now, she went downstairs to catch Uncle Edward before he went out.

'I think she's needing a doctor, sir. Emma may look strong, because of her size, but she isn't.'

He was silent for a moment, looking out of the window

at the grey mist surrounding the house. All the dampness of yesterday's storm was evident in the vapour cloaking the house so that even the drive was invisible. 'She doesn't deserve it, Goddamm, but I suppose you're right. I can't let my own relative die in this house for want of a doctor. Get Peter to go for him, then.'

When the doctor came, he examined Emma carefully before he went downstairs to report to Edward. He had left some medicine and given Kathleen instructions to nurse her carefully, and not let her get excited. Even from the bedroom Kathleen could hear him yelling at Uncle Edward. 'Are you stupid or something that you could leave her on the verge of consumption without a fire in the dark days of winter. Shame on you! She must have a fire at all times, or I won't be responsible for the consequences.'

So the fire was lit by a reluctant Smith, and so began a long illness which lasted through until the following March. Sligo kept constant vigil beside Emma's bed and Kathleen was in regular attendance until the worst was over. Christmas had come and gone with little cheer at Springmount, and it was only gradually that Emma was strong enough to rise from her sick bed and take an interest in the outside world again.

Meanwhile two letters were delivered which contained news of some interest. Kathleen's sister Maggie was now engaged to be married, and the wedding would take place the next summer. And Johnny Gilbert had sent Christmas greetings from Italy, though these arrived very late.

My very dearest Kathleen,
As autumn came I decided to make my way south to the sunshine. I went to Rome and Naples – both of which were so crowded I decided to travel even further south. And here I am in Catania, Sicily, a world away from you and my beloved Ireland. I have rented a little house which faces on to a courtyard, along with several other houses. The courtyard is always full of chatter and children until late at night. There are some

beautiful buildings here but the countryside around is like a scene from the Middle Ages. The peasants grow their own food and take olives and oranges to market. I have seen oranges on trees, and picked and eaten them straight from the branch. You cannot imagine how fresh they taste!

These people are very devout and pay great attention to religious festivals. On All Souls' Day they march in procession through the streets with statues of the Madonna, and eat sweetmeats which are very sticky.

Last week I hired a horse and went up towards the volcano called Etna. The roads here are all surfaced with black volcanic paving stones. You can go right up the mountain, which is covered in snow at present. I saw smoke coming from the summit, and at night I have seen red lava glowing.

The people do not seem to worry about it. That's the will of God they say, and St Agatha will protect us. She is the patron saint of the town, who stopped the lava enveloping it a few hundred years ago. There is a shrine at the place where the lava halted, and I must say it is quite spectacular, with a wall of black volcanic rock. It's as though the hand of God reached down at that point and forced it to stop sharp its destructive advance towards the town.

I have been to the opera, too. Such magnificence for what is really only a small town! It made me quite homesick for Dublin and the Abbey Theatre. And most of all for you, my dear Kathleen. And I'm also envious that you should be living now so close to what is one of my favourite places in Ireland, indeed in the whole world.

In the meantime Happy Christmas to you. I'm coming home in March, so I'll come and see you then.

Much love and kisses,
Johnny

Kathleen had read and reread his letter, marvelled at the strange foreign stamp, and put the missive into her

129

drawer for safe keeping. She was uncertain as to what Johnny wanted of her; he seemed so affectionate and loving it warmed her to him. But then she would remember that disturbing incident with Jack Carey, and how her body had almost betrayed her. She tried hard to put Jack out of her mind but she had too much time to think and brood through the days when Emma lay abed recovering from her illness. In spite of her desire to forget the episode she would find her mind turning towards it and going through every detail.

13

Then the spring finally came.

It was a perfect April day when Johnny Gilbert arrived in a small trap from the town. It was very unusual to have visitors at Springmount so, her curiosity roused, Kathleen had made her way to the front of the house at the first clatter of hooves and wheels.

There she saw Johnny, smiling down at her, his face tanned by southern sunshine. She instantly felt embarrassed and shy, for they had been apart long enough to have become almost strangers. Yet he leapt from the cart and took her in his arms and kissed her in greeting.

'Oh, my Kathleen, how I have longed to see you again. And now I'm here, and I want you to come out with me today. I have some food and we can go for a picnic and enjoy the spring air. Come on, Kathleen, I have so much to tell you.' With scarcely a word, Kathleen dashed into the house and up the stairs, arriving breathlessly at Emma's side.

'Johnny Gilbert's here, and he wants me to go on a picnic with him. I hope that's all right? You will be able to manage, won't you?'

Kathleen was surprised at the cool tone of Emma's reply. 'Yes, you can go if you must, but make sure you're back before dark.'

She was not to know that Emma's coolness disguised a certain jealousy. Emma herself was yearning for some news of Dublin, of the theatre and the political scene. She would have to devise a way of returning there soon.

At seventeen Kathleen was ripe for romance; ready to open like a flower after the long winter. Johnny Gilbert's coming on that bright April day was thrilling in itself, but to spend a day out with him was an unexpected joy.

131

Riding in the trap they made their way down towards the sea, and as far as they could go before the track ended. There they tied the pony to a bush and unloaded their picnic. They did not have to wander far before they found an ideal spot and set down the baskets. Johnny had brought a rug for them to sit on, but he darted about like a child in wonderland and kept pointing out different aspects of the wildlife: the gulls screeching and squabbling over nesting places lower down the shoreline; cormorants diving for fish, their smooth black bodies cleaving the water like knives. And the sea itself, today heaving gently towards the land, where the water of the mighty Atlantic spilled over the rocks on the shore.

The cliff was not very high, so they could pick their way down to the flat, where the spray was fresh in their faces and the smell of salt was strong. All around them rock plants were flowering in crevices; their precarious existence triumphant in their flowering season.

They sighted a seal further out, its head held above the water, its great doe eyes scanning them searchingly, with whiskers that would bring pride to any city gent.

'They live in underwater caves, those seals, Kathleen, and men from the islands come and hunt them. They have to dive way under and catch them in their lairs, then drag them up to the surface and the boats.'

'The poor seals! Why they did no harm to anyone! Why do they deserve to be killed so?'

'It's brave men that do the work, Kathleen, and that from necessity, for seal meat can be dried and salted and provide many a good meal for a family, and their oil can light their homes. Yet they do retain a respect for their prey. Some nights the seals come out on the rocks and sing to each other: an unearthly wailing chorus that would put the fear into any man that heard it and didn't know what it was. I've heard it myself when I've been out in the boats with them. It's uncanny that such beasts could sing like that, as if they were sirens luring men to their deaths on the rocks. Of course, by the morning they have all disappeared into the sea again.'

132

Kathleen watched the seal swim away, lifting its head up to look at them now and again. Perhaps it had its young to protect, smooth calves born to life underwater; sleek and swift when swimming, ugly and lumbering on land.

They walked back up to where they had left the rug and their picnic. Johnny had bought fresh loaves and some cheese made locally, and something Kathleen had not tasted for a long while – wine. Drinking it made her feel quite guilty. She had not been to Mass all winter, and here she was drinking wine on the cliffs for pleasure!

Johnny had chosen well, and the red liquid eased its way into her blood stream and made her feel talkative and jolly. She told him all about Emma's illness and the long dull days she had spent at her bedside.

'Emma Nash does not realise what loyalty she elicits. She's a strong personality, Kathleen, and you mustn't let her dominate you. Watch her carefully, for she has a sting in her tail and is not always as grateful as she should be for what people do for her. Yet she is a woman of contradictions, because I can never say she has ever been unstinting in devoting unselfishly her time or her efforts on behalf of the Irish nation.

Kathleen heeded his warning thoughtfully. 'But I have no choice at the moment, as where would I find a better position?'

'When you return to Dublin you must work in the theatre, like your sister. I'll find work for you, my dearest. Don't worry.'

So they talked on as the sun reached its zenith and the wine took effect, and Kathleen offered little resistance when Johnny reached over and put his hand under her chin to draw her close, and kissed her on the lips. In shock she felt his wet lips on her mouth and the roughness of his tongue against hers. It was like waking after a long sleep, as Kathleen felt desire surge through her body. Johnny continued kissing, and they were soon locked in a tight embrace. There was no denying it, she was enjoying this warmth and affection and the feel of another body next to hers. But Kathleen was also aware of the stories she had heard in the Convent – how a man will just want to use you, then throw you away. Wait until you're married before letting him have his way with you, a small voice warned.

Her present situation with Johnny seemed so natural though, and him so loving that it was hard to resist. The sun was warm on her face, and Johnny's whiskers tickled her neck. She found herself stroking his head and murmuring as he gently slid his hand into her blouse. As he held her breast she felt her nipple grow until it became the source of the most exquisite feeling she could have imagined. Suddenly he withdrew his hand, spat on it, and quickly it was back where it was before, only this time rubbing, rubbing in time with his little cries of 'Kathleen, Kathleen.' He was now lying so close beside her that she could feel the hardness of him. And then he slid his hand up her skirt and she felt him touch her between her legs. A finger was just reaching its goal when the two lovers heard little shrieks from close by. Some local children out walking had crept closer for a better look.

Johnny stood up, red-faced. 'And what is it you want, you little rascals, creeping up on our private business! Be off with you!'

The children yelled something in Gaelic and ran off laughing, but the moment was spoilt. And Kathleen learnt that afternoon that romantic moments in life are few and far between, and difficult to sustain. When Johnny sat down again he seemed to have lost his urge, and started to pack up their picnic things. But, even so, they sat for a while longer and watched the clouds passing overhead, dissolving gradually in the intense blue of a sky washed clean by the winter's rain. She felt a sudden surge of affection for Johnny, and tried hard to imprint these images on her memory so that she would be able to recall this day whenever she pleased.

Despite the warmth earlier in the day, it was now getting

134

decidedly cooler as a sea breeze had sprung up, rippling the surface of the water to look like a lamb's fleece. Johnny and Kathleen stood up and shook from the rug the crumbs left over from lunch.

Then he looked her straight in her eyes and, grasping her hand, softly spoke words that Kathleen would, in a way, have preferred not to hear – but which sent a thrill through her all the same.

'I suppose you've guessed by now, Kathleen, that I'm very, very fond of you. I would like you to marry me, and for us to share our lives together. But I realise I'm quite a bit older than you, and I don't want to force you to answer straight away. So I'll ask you again when you are older.'

On their way home they sang old songs and kept warm by huddling up to one another, Johnny's body forming a windbreak for Kathleen's slighter figure.

He dropped her at the end of the Springmount drive as the golden western sky was turning purple, and she ran all the way to the house, still feeling intoxicated by the wine and the sea air. To see the horizon so far off on the ocean had given her a much needed sense of space, and Springmount now seemed totally claustrophobic in its sheltered dell amidst the rolling hills.

'You're very late!' Emma was standing on the stairs when Kathleen entered the front door.

'I'm sorry, Emma – but Johnny had something important to say to me.'

'I can't imagine what that would be, and I really don't think it's a suitable relationship at all.'

'He's asked me to marry him, that's what.' Kathleen could scarcely suppress her indignation. For what did Emma Nash know about love anyway, she who devoted her life to hollow political causes.

'So you think he will marry you, do you? Let me tell you, little Kathleen, Johnny Gilbert has had at least three engagements that I know of, and not one has he married.

135

Oh, he loves the idea, indeed, but he'll never tie the knot. Just you wait till you meet his mother . . .'

Kathleen was about to retort, when Uncle Edward came in, hot and flushed from his ride to town.

'Here's a letter for you, niece, from Dublin,' he muttered as he strode past.

Emma's eyes lit up as she took the letter and opened it. After studying it for a minute, a delighted whoop came from her lips. 'Oh, Kathleen, it's such good news. Major Tommy wasn't so poor after all – they have found new deeds and some invested money. Not a lot, but with the interest I'm to be an independent lady at last!'

After the first surprise, Kathleen too could feel the excitement. She would be able to go to Maggie's wedding in June – and perhaps even audition for the theatre. Yes, things could turn out a lot better than at present.

It was only later that night, when she was alone in bed, that she could go through the events of the day, mulling particularly over Johnny's proposal which was not a proposal. She remembered how he had held her close, and how safe and cherished she had felt, with not the least trace of fear. Yet, if there was no fear, neither was there the thrill she had once experienced in Jack Carey's embrace. It all seemed very confusing as she fell asleep with the sound of the ocean echoing through her dreams.

PART III

14

Returning to Dublin was a joy for Kathleen: to be back in the busy streets amid so many bustling people again. To some extent she had come to terms with the country, but it was not really to her taste. She loved the infinite possibilities that the city threw up, and always the possibility of meeting new people. Then there was her own sister – and Johnny Gilbert returning shortly from the western islands.

The house in St Stephen's Green had been opened up before their arrival: the dustsheets cleared off, the furniture and floors rigorously swept.

Emma was back on form, and enjoying her new-found status. She had hardly entered the old house again before she was sending out messages to all her old friends, particularly to her special friend Will Butler at the theatre.

Kathleen carried this last message, with strict instructions not to dally. She needed no extra bidding for she was thrilled to be out of the confines of Emma's companionship. The intervening months in the country had sorely tried her patience with the woman.

She skipped over the O'Connell Bridge with the welcome sound of the trams clattering beside her, and she sucked in the city smells with intoxication, as if they were the most expensive perfume in the world. Here were so many ladies and gentlemen, ordinary men, women and children all out in the May sunshine. One thing her enforced absence had taught her was the meaning of the word *provincial*. Dublin, by contrast, had life, lights and action.

People were everywhere about their business this fine day. Maids on their way to do errands, their sleeves rolled up in the May sunshine, hands reddened and raw from scrubbing laundry. Gentlemen strolling into the city to complete some business transaction – gentlemen whose suits were pressed by the selfsame maids who had scrubbed their shirts.

In Sackville Street she could see the shop awnings down to provide welcome shade for the strolling shoppers. It all gave a fine appearance of wealth and stability. But Kathleen herself knew all about the dismal tenements which lay so close by, the crowded rooms where the light of the day scarcely reached, and the children who spent their days with bare feet and dirty, ragged clothes; their nights huddled together in a single bed with all their sisters and brothers.

Some of those same children were out today, begging the odd bit of money from any rich-looking passer-by. And they were not the only beggars. There were also men for whom there was no hope – shambling and shuffling through their days, living from one drink to another, companions in dereliction as they spent their last coppers on yet more whiskey. The city's underbelly was not a beautiful sight; poverty hung like a cloud over it, and the people who lived there.

It was just after midday when the two sisters left the theatre behind and walked to Maggie's lodgings in Capel Street.

'So tell me all the news, Maggie. I've been hidden away in the country for so long, it's like coming out of the Convent all over again. And all these men in uniform . . . what is happening?'

'You've been away a good while, indeed. It's been a winter and a spring, and no mistake. Now, let me think – when was it you left us?'

'In September. Just after that riot.'

'That terrible Sunday was just the start of it. We've had plenty of marches and rallies. There's been arrests and imprisonments, too, as well as injuries and deaths. The poor have been hungry because of the lock-out. Martin Murphy and the other employers have locked out every man in Transport Union unless they sign a docu-

139

ment swearing they will have nothing to do with unions. The situation is so bad that Jem Larkin wants to send the starving children to Liverpool, but the Archbishop is against that because he says the poor children will be tempted away from their religion if they go. The whole city is in turmoil. Those men you've seen marching about with the funny hats on and the white bands around their jackets – they're the Citizen Army which has been formed to protect the workers from police harrassment. Murphy is trying to take on scabs to break the strikers' picket-line, but now the workers have their own men to protect them from the police. The National Volunteers are another lot . . . Sometimes I think our men are all luna-tics; they're spoiling for a fight which will have many a bloody nose and weeping mother at the end of it . . . But let's not talk about that now – and me getting married next month.'

Kathleen gazed with interest at her sister, whose eyes were so sparkling and merry. Her chestnut hair had been cut shorter, and now sat prettily on her shoulders.

'And aren't I glad I'm back here in the city to see it. You must be so happy.'

'Kathleen, I'm speaking seriously now, I think I've found the most wonderful man in Jim and I want to look my best for him. When we get home I'll show you my collection, as I call it . . . By the way, that man you met at the dance . . . Jack Carey was it? He was over at the theatre a few times asking after you. He tried to get one of his plays produced there, but Will Butler refused him. Apparently he's gone off to England to work for a while . . .'

Kathleen's heart lurched in her chest. Jack Carey asking after her? Would she like to see him again? Her face burned with shame at the memory of their last encounter.

Soon they came to the house where Maggie lodged. The landlady lived on the ground floor and was forever popping her toothless head round her door to check who was coming and going. She kept what she considered 'a decent house', and she wanted no riffraff entering her decorous abode.

'Who's that with you, Maggie?' she called round the door.

'Only my sister Kathleen, back from the country this very day, Mrs Riley. And it's a good day to you.'

'Silly woman she is,' Maggie whispered to Kathleen as they climbed the stairs. 'One day her nose is going to grow so long it will reach over to England!'

Maggie's room was on the first floor and overlooked the street. It was of good size, and stretched the full width of the building. It contained a bed with a quilt thrown over it. Two chairs stood on either side of the fireplace like guardians. The table was strewn with Maggie's papers, covered with figures and doodles.

'Sit yourself down, Kathleen, and I'll be bringing you some tea. We're allowed to share the kitchen if we're good and clean.'

When Maggie fetched the tea, the sisters set to catching up on each others news. Maggie was surprised that Kathleen had been seeing and hearing so much from Johnny Gilbert. She wondered whether to warn Kathleen about his reputation as a man who courted young women but never married them. She decided against it, however, for the present. Instead she showed Kathleen her trousseau, the sheets and blankets and table-cloths all bought with money saved out of her wages from the theatre.

'And what might these be?' said Kathleen, holding up a bunch of little nightdresses.

'For the first baby, of course, you silly. If I'm to be married to Jim, I'm going to have babies, aren't I? You do know all about that, don't you?'

It was a much wiser Kathleen who left her sister that afternoon to return to St Stephen's Green. Maggie had told her all she knew about making babies. She had also confessed her own fears about the wedding night . . . did it hurt when you made love for the first time? These considerations had never occurred to Kathleen, and certainly not in such detail. It certainly gave her cause to brood on her own marriage plans.

The thought of her sister's wedding, however, filled her with excitement; it was to be a big event. As Maggie had no family of her own to provide, Jim's family had decided to give the pair a wedding to remember. The Sheehans were a responsible lot, solid respectable Dublin burghers whose status was assured. At first they had been doubtful about their son's choice of partner, but had soon been charmed by Maggie's appearance and manner, and had no doubt she would prove a good wife to him.

Mrs Sheehan had nursed artistic ambitions as a young girl, and it was she who had encouraged her son Jim and given him his proud and upright mien. She knew that the theatre was not always the most steady of careers, but she has persuaded her husband that Jim would be successful in whatever he did, and even more so if his heart was fully in the enterprise. Maggie could not have wished for more sympathetic in-laws.

If that was so for her, it was not to be so for her sister Johnny Gilbert returned to Dublin shortly, and Kathleen was again the subject of his amorous intentions. And it was not long until Johnny fixed the dreaded day for Kathleen to meet his mother.

Doris Gilbert was a staunch Protestant and, like many of her religion in the Catholic city of Dublin, she was amongst its richer denizens. Her husband had died the year Queen Victoria had visited the city in 1900, so she was a long time a widow. She had not come out of mourning and still wore black – of the most expensive quality of course. She had only one son, Johnny, and she loved him with a love that smothered and imprisoned. She would always want to be completely involved in his life. Considering that no other woman could possibly understand her son the way she did, she was not now prepared to have him throw himself away on a mere chit of a girl, and a Catholic at that.

The Gilbert residence stood in the more salubrious part of the city, amid houses thrown up as the Victorian age advanced in prosperity and confidence. Johnny met Kathleen, at the tram stop in Rathmines Road, and soon they were walking up the hill to Palmerston Villas.

Kathleen wore her very best outfit, and was feeling exceedingly nervous. Her clothes were clearly not those of a well-to-do girl from a respectable family; rather they had a cast-off look about them which Kathleen had attempted to conceal by skilful reworking and a good pressing. The skirt had been one of Emma's, but the material had faded through much washing; so, although it had once been of good quality, it now was past its best. Luckily the weather was warm enough not to require a coat, for Kathleen would have felt ashamed of her own.

'Oh, Johnny, I feel so anxious. What will she think of me?'

'Don't you worry. Mother will be all right. She knows I love you; haven't I told her so many times? She will see that I'm happy to be with you, and that should be enough for any mother.'

'But you said she is a stickler for the proprieties, Johnny. Are you sure she won't disapprove of me?'

'Don't you worry, my sweet. Mother is a lamb really. Look we're here already.'

The house in Palmerston Villas was a residence designed for family living. Now the house was inhabited only by Mrs Gilbert and her cook-housekeeper, helped out by a daily maid who cleaned and kept the place spotless. This was not difficult, as nothing much ever happened in the house. Mrs Gilbert rarely had guests except for her son and, apart from her assiduous church-going, had very little social life. A few ladies would come to tea occasionally, but usually she kept to herself.

She had produced Johnny when she was already forty, so that she was now what she considered to be a grand old lady. Her husband had made some shrewd investments a quarter of a century ago, and on his death had left her with enough income to sail through the rest of her days with little worry.

As Kathleen went up the path, she felt her heart

pounding. The maid ushered them into the drawing-room, where a fire was burning in a sumptuous grate even at this time of year. Kathleen heard the rustle of skirts and there stood Mrs Gilbert, dressed all in black and holding out her hand.

'Good afternoon, Kathleen. I've heard so much about you.'

They all sat down and a short silence ensued – one of those uncomfortable little pauses in conversation which often happen when people have nothing in common.

'Well, Johnny, you're looking well after your visit to the islands.' It was Mrs Gilbert who broke the silence.

'Yes, mother. The spring was just perfect, and the islanders as fine and brave as ever.'

As mother and son continued talking in a desultory fashion, Kathleen found time to glance round the room. Heavy curtains at the windows shut out most of the sunlight, so the room had an almost subterranean air. Knick-knacks stood regimented in their preordained positions along the mantelpiece and on occasional tables. They were treasures of the British Empire, such as the ivory elephants from India, a reproduction pair of Chinese vases, a bust of Gladstone. A giant palm grew from a heavily decorated pot-holder in the corner next to the window, and a number of other plants crowded themselves on to a hexagonal table. The sofa and matching chairs were covered in a heavy brocade, while over the backs lay lacy antimacassars to prevent soiling.

'And what about your family, Kathleen?'

Kathleen started at Mrs Gilbert's sudden question. 'Oh, my father and mother are gone now, God bless their souls, and my uncle is across the water in America. But I have a sister in Dublin.'

'Kathleen must be thirsty, Johnny. Why don't you go out and see to some tea for her?' Mrs Gilbert gave him a pointed look, and he dutifully left the room.

Mrs Gilbert continued in her clear, precise tones. 'I'm so glad, Kathleen, that you have come to see me. I have been looking forward to this meeting, as I would like to clear up any misunderstandings. How old are you, Kathleen?'

'Seventeen, Mrs Gilbert.'

'You do realise, of course, that my son will be thirty this year, and so is what I might call a mature man already. I'm sure you understand what I am trying to say, that you are still very young, so I hope you are not thinking *too* seriously about my Johnny.'

'Oh but, Mrs Gilbert, I don't think age is such a problem, do you. I'm very grown up, I think, and Johnny can be quite the young fellow sometimes, you know.'

Mrs Gilbert sighed. This might prove a difficult case. Perhaps the girl really did have her heart set on Johnny. But now for the trump card . . .

'Well, I do think it would be wise to wait until you are twenty-one before you begin to think seriously about him. And another thing, I believe you are a Catholic? You must be aware that I would never consider it right and proper for my grandchildren to be brought up in the Catholic faith.'

At this point Kathleen became aware that the older woman was totally antagonistic to her, and that nothing would change this attitude. But she could prove herself equal to the challenge. For if Johnny and she did indeed get married, she would make very sure that any children of theirs were brought up as Catholics.

She spoke crisply. 'Mrs Gilbert, I think it is for Johnny and me to decide, and I can be telling you I don't need your advice as to what is right at my age. Johnny says he loves me, and that is enough. I don't see why you should put obstacles in our way.'

Mrs Gilbert reddened with anger, and was just about to make some retort when Johnny came in, carrying a tray. He instantly sensed strong feelings in the air, and could see that both women were visibly agitated.

'Tea, mother?'

'I'm sorry, Johnny, but I don't wish to take tea with this impertinence. And I'll ask you not to bring Miss

145

Corr round here again, as we have nothing to say to each other.'

Johnny looked in dismay at the two women, one so young and lovely, and the other crimped into her pattern of old age and narrow-mindedness. He was appalled at what may have happened while he was out of the room. Why couldn't Mother try just a little harder to like the girls he favoured? And Kathleen, staring down at her skirt and twisting her hands round a handkerchief, why, she was positively distressed.

Suddenly she stood up, her eyes burning with anger and shame.

'Oh, Johnny, please! I think we had better go. Mrs Gilbert doesn't seem to want me here . . .'

The journey back on the tram was spent in recriminations. Kathleen was deeply hurt that Johnny had not warned her fully of his mother's prejudices. He, on the other hand, was upset because the two women had failed to communicate.

'Just wait, Kathleen. Another four years and you will be twenty-one. We can wait that long, and by waiting Mother will see I'm serious about you. Then she won't be able to say a thing against you.'

But Kathleen knew that almost anything could happen in four years, and it was from that day on that she began to recognise Johnny's weakness of character and his tendency to cave in before his mother.

On 28 June 1914, far off in Sarajevo an Austrian archduke was assassinated, setting off a fatal chain of events which would sweep like a hurricane through Europe.

On the same day Maggie Corr was married. It was very much a theatre wedding, with all the company present at the party afterwards. Mr and Mrs Sheehan were proud of their son so tall and handsome, and they thought that Maggie looked a picture in her wedding-dress and veil. Kathleen cried in the church when she thought about her unfortunate encounter with Mrs Gilbert a few weeks before. Still, perhaps it was for the best, she brooded;

perhaps she and Johnny were not really suited in temperament. She admired him; that was true. After all he was a successful playwright. She was attracted to him; that was true also. But she could not help suspecting that any man who remained so tied to his mother could never make a totally devoted husband. She was also beginning to doubt if she had any true passion for him; although she loved his hugs and kisses, she never felt she yearned for him totally.

The wedding party was such great fun. They danced and sang and ate for hours, until it was time for Maggie and Jim to go off to their unknown destination. Kathleen hugged her sister with tears in her eyes.

'Good luck, Maggie. I'll see you in a week.' And then they were gone, with the company cheering the carriage as it set off for Kingsbridge station.

Mr Bloom was among the guests, and reflected to himself how it was just two years ago that he had accompanied the two sisters to that sorry funeral. Time flies like an arrow, he thought and chuckled. Now it was good to see a wedding. Good luck to them, he thought, I hope they are happy.

15

Maggie's wedding was the start of many changes in Kathleen's life. Emma had been very active since their return from the country, regularly giving her lectures and talks on the subject of Irish freedom. Indeed she had felt that victory was almost in sight when the news came through that the British Parliament had finally passed the Home Rule Bill.

'Just think, Kathleen, an Ireland about to govern its own – and after all these years and all these struggles. As if we hadn't been capable of it!'

But Emma was also aware, that history was not on her side. Every day she read the foreign news with increasing alarm, and in her darker moments expressed those gloomy fears to Kathleen.

'What if war breaks out? What does that mean for our menfolk? I'm hoping they won't go and fight for the British. What have the British done for them except oppress them and starve them for hundreds of years. But I have no confidence in Irish menfolk; they have a very strange sense of patriotism. Just you wait and see.'

For Kathleen the issue seemed quite simple. It was obvious that should England go to war, then it was no business of the Irish.

When the declaration of war finally came at the beginning of August, breaking the lull of expectancy, it was almost a relief. Suddenly the streets took on a busier air, and there were soldiers in khaki everywhere. Just as Emma had predicted, young Irishmen were soon joining up and getting off to France.

September came, and Kathleen was to visit her sister's house. She always enjoyed such visits, as Maggie's and Jim's rented rooms seemed an oasis of order away from the teeming streets outside. They had not been able to afford much to start with, just a couple of rooms in a tenement block. The staircase was typical, dark and smelling of old cooking and damp. In one room stood the marital bed and the trunks the two kept their clothes in. The floor was well scrubbed and there was an air of decency and neatness.

Maggie welcomed her sister with pleasure. Marriage obviously suited her; her face had filled out a little and she looked radiant.

Kathleen sat down in one of the chairs and studied her sister more closely. Despite the obvious bloom, there were faint signs of stress. She kept pushing back wisps of hair that fell in her eyes, and fiddling with a sleeve button.

'And how have you been keeping, Kathleen? Have you been seeing anything of that Johnny Gilbert?'

'Not much, after that visit to his mother! I used to see him once or twice a week but since then, well, I haven't bothered too much. I've begun to wonder if we're not suited to each other after all.'

Maggie smiled inwardly; so her little sister was coming to realise what Johnny was made of at last. It must be a sad discovery, but still she was only young and would recover from it all. Kathleen moved on to talk about the war.

'Well, I'm having cause to think about it myself, Kathleen. Jim has joined up to fight. At this very moment he is down at the army centre. It's evil this war, I know, but we must defend the country.'

Kathleen saw the worry on her sister's face show more openly now, and she could not quite believe her ears. 'How can he do that, Maggie? How can he fight for a cause which is not ours but that of our oppressors?'

'Don't be naive, Kathleen, and grow up. The Germans are wicked, and it's much better that we join up with the English to fight them. Besides, the British are bound to give us our freedom, when it is all over, if we fight with them now.'

Maggie, I can't believe this. You're not thinking straight. Your Jim could die for the English – what use

149

is that to you or to Ireland? Emma says "England's difficulty is Ireland's opportunity", and I think she is right there. While they are tied up in Europe, it should be easy to overthrow them in Ireland.'

'Kathleen Corr, you've become just a little mouthpiece for that Emma Nash! I think you've been living with her far too long. In *your* narrow circle you may think that what you believe is true too for the rest of Ireland, but not so. Look around you. See how many of our men are joining the British contest. Think how much worse the German yoke could be, "England's defeat is Ireland's also". You'll find most people think like I do. And I can tell you that if the Irish did revolt, they would have very little chance of success.'

Kathleen was surprised at the vehemence of her sister's views. She had thought that they believed in much the same things, but suddenly she saw her sister as part of the majority prepared to forgo the cause of Irish freedom for the moment. The two sisters were red in the face with their arguing by the time Jim Sheehan came home. Kathleen hung her head at the sight of him; she did not want to argue with her brother-in-law. What was done was done. He looked so smart in his uniform, she had to admit. Faced with him, she could vent her anger no longer, and her feelings turned to concern lest he might not return, and leave her sister a widow.

'When is it that you're going, Jim?'

'The day after tomorrow we sail to Liverpool. Then training for two weeks in Salisbury, and we should be in France by November at the earliest.'

Kathleen felt saddened at the news; her sister scarcely married and to lose her husband so soon. Yet when she looked at Maggie, she seemed to be so proud of her Jim, gazing at him with glimmering eyes.

This would be their last meeting all together before he departed, so how could she spoil her sister's last days with her husband through argument and bitterness.

But the weeks and months leading into that cold winter

gave Maggie some cause to regret her strong words to Kathleen. Letters from Jim were few, but what there were convinced her Kathleen's viewpoint held some justification. Jim was an intelligent man, and perceived the full force of English disdain for the Irish. His letters recounted vividly his life in the army, and showed signs of being heavily censored. Maggie could only read between the lines and guess at what her husband was going through.

My dearest darling Maggie,
It seems so long since I have seen your face and held you in my arms, and I miss you so. How are things in Dublin? Is the theatre managing without me?

We are camped in the town of XXXXX I have been placed in a regiment full of English. They call me XXXXX and XXXX, and have no respect for our religion. There are no Irish officers here.

We are digging a trench so that we can hide away from the Germans and lob gunfire at them over the top. Inside the trench it is getting damp and muddy, so please send more socks as I never seem to be able to find dry ones.

How can I describe my feelings for you at such a distance? Every night I lie awake in my bunk, hearing the sound of guns and wishing I was back with you in our little room up the stairs, after the last folk have gone home from the theatre. . . . and then I feel the cold so keenly and wish I was lying warm in our bed and stroking your silky hair and holding you close to me.

Let's hope this nonsense will soon be over and we Irish boys can return to our own country and have done with this bloody struggle.

Some wounded came in yesterday, and there was one poor boy from Donegal crying out for a priest and there was none. His leg was XXXXX and there was XXXX everywhere. It seems there is little . . . for such as him as the XXXXXXX finishes most of them off.

And now, my darling, I must go because it is my

151

turn to take the watch. I will write again as soon as I can.

All my love,
Jim

Maggie read and reread the letter and it was, oh, so easy to imagine what it must be like for him. A pit dug into the land with men living and dying in it. Poor Irish boys dying without a priest, their legs torn from them, the red blood spurting and then congealing. Gangrene bringing a creeping death. She shuddered at the thought.

She showed these letters to Kathleen, who looked at her sister in alarm; for despite their occasional arguments they were now as close as ever. Kathleen was glad, at least, that Maggie was kept so busy – she had taken over many of Jim's duties, and was proving to be an even more capable administrator than anyone had expected.

But the war did not end so swiftly, and the following summer found it continuing apace. Emma's activities had taken on a thoroughly frantic air, and to Kathleen it seemed she herself was forever running messages to and fro at Emma's bidding. Closed, sealed envelopes had to be hidden on her person as she went about the Dublin streets delivering them to houses shuttered and blank. Uniforms were everywhere; there were in fact three armies. The British Army, the official force of law and order, was everywhere in evidence; aware that there must be no opportunity for rebellion in Ireland. But there were also the private armies, the nationalist Volunteers and the socialist Citizen Army all seeking to defend their own interests. It seemed as if all the menfolk were dressed up for wargames, and there was an atmosphere of tension which was almost palpable.

It was another hot summer, as the dry dusty streets and trees cried out for rain, when one day in August the body of an old man was to be buried.

'And who is this man whose funeral we're attending?' Kathleen asked Emma.

'He's Jeremiah O'Donovan Rossa, an old Fenian leader come back from America to find rest in Irish soil. He was one of the first of us dedicated to the cause.' Emma drew herself up tall, and her eyes glittered as she spoke of the Fenians who had pledged themselves to overthrow the English way back in the middle of the previous century. Emma Nash was convinced the time was coming when the English would leave her beloved Ireland forever. If force was required, so be it. After all, had not the English under Cromwell taken the land by force in the first place? Had not the poor peasants been *forced* off their land until political agitation had given them back their rights?

Kathleen drank in the air of rebellion; it now seemed as natural as breathing to her. There could be no doubt about it, Emma was surely right.

The next morning the two of them set off with the procession, following behind the bier to Glasnevin Cemetery.

'Who's that at the front of the crowd, Emma?'

The man leading the procession was dressed in the uniform of an Irish Volunteer, the collar standing up, the leather belt crossways over his chest, the peaked cap held under his arm as a sign of respect.

'Why it's Patrick Pearse,' Emma whispered. 'You have taken letters to him, you know, though he hasn't ever been to my house. That would be far too dangerous, what with those two fellows constantly on the watch outside.'

So that was Patrick Pearse, leader of the twenty thousand Volunteers.

In the cemetery the grass grew high around other graves, with white stone Celtic crosses everywhere. It was a sad place on this August morning. There was a curious hush amongst the crowd, as if expecting something special to happen: not exactly the raising of the dead, but certainly the rekindling of the great man's spirit amongst them somehow. Kathleen watched in awe as a silence came upon them, and the man Patrick Pearse prepared himself to speak. At first she could not hear

153

what he said, then she suddenly understood why this was so: he was speaking in Gaelic. Yet everybody listened intently to Pearse and, as she looked round, Kathleen could see their rapt attention to his words. Though unfamiliar, they were words which seemed to unite the crowd in a common humanity, a love of their country and its language, and a resolve to see it free of its chains.

And then suddenly, across the hushed throng, her eye caught sight of someone she recognised. Could it be? She stood on tiptoe to see better. Yes, it was . . . Jack Carey! And what was he doing? Scribbling in a notebook for all he was worth, it seemed. His head and shoulders stood above the others, and Kathleen caught her breath as he pushed his hands through his hair when the wind blew it over his face. Now she knew she had not forgotten him . . . oh no. Even as she saw him the memory of that disturbing night came flooding back to her, and her knees began to tremble.

'May we think about the death of this famous man . . .' The priest intoned the funeral service flatly, yet the crowd seemed to hold its breath in awe as earth fell on to the coffin. They remained thus silent for several minutes before they turned to leave, stepping between the quiet gravestones and returning to the busy city.

'I must have a word with someone, Kathleen, so, if you please could you return to the house and take Sligo for a walk?' These were words from heaven for Kathleen, as she joined the crowd leaving the cemetery, and pushed her way through until she reached his side.

'Well, if it isn't Jack Carey appeared from nowhere!' Her heart was pounding as she boldly said the words and looked up into his face.

He stood looking back at her in amazed silence. The young girl he had escorted home all that time ago seemed now a self-confident young woman. Almost automatically his fingers traced the outline of her chin, and Kathleen was surprised at the surge of feeling this provoked in her. She laughed it off nervously.

'And aren't you still the same as always, Jack Carey, taking liberties with a girl?'

He smiled at her, and his eyes smiled too. 'And where are you living now, Kathleen?'

'Still the same place.'

'With Emma Nash? Well, I'd be careful there, Kathleen. I hear of conspiracies afoot, and there could be danger in it. I'd have nothing to do with them. But hush now; there could be unkind ears around.'

Changing the subject, they chatted inconsequentially until they came to the canal. Jack had to file his report with the newspaper he now worked for, so they arranged to meet again later that week.

They went dancing, and Kathleen thrilled to be held in his arms again as the music played. But this was no repetition of the previous occasion. As Saturday night followed Saturday night, Kathleen found herself growing more and more in love with Jack, for now he was the soul of discretion and never again attempted anything physical which might frighten the girl. He was content to play the waiting game, convinced she would soon be his.

In November, Kathleen was given her first chance to appear on the stage. Johnny Gilbert had influence in the theatrical world, and had fixed for her to audition for a pantomime part in one of Dublin's other theatres, the Queen's in Lower Abbey Street. Though he realised there had been a cooling-off between himself and Kathleen, he seemed to bear no grudge. Indeed he still found her attractive and fascinating, but was relieved she had not pressed him further about marriage. It was always easier to give into his mother. Yet his sense of honour made him guiltily aware that he owed Kathleen some favours. So Kathleen went to the audition, and was given a part. Even Emma was encouraging. She had furtive business of her own to occupy herself, and as long as Kathleen was at home until four in the afternoon, she could then go to the theatre for a few rehearsals. To Emma it seemed no serious diversion for Kathleen to play the part of a chick. She was to wear a fluffy yellow costume and sing her song while little Jack Horner sat in his corner. Anyway, the pantomime would have a run of a mere six weeks after Christmas.

Kathleen, however, felt instantly at home in the theatre – and as the run progressed she grew more and more confident, and the applause grew louder and louder. Her sister Maggie attended several times, and was deeply struck with the beauty of Kathleen's voice, which seemed to have developed out of all recognition under the expert tutelage of the chorus-master.

It was one night in January when Jack Carey came to watch Kathleen perform. Afterwards he met her at the theatre door, and offered to buy her supper. They went to the neighbouring public-house, which was full of performers, some of them singing round a piano at the far end of the room. Other members of the company smiled warmly at Kathleen as she entered, and she found herself enjoying the comradeship only a theatre could bring. Yet soon she hardly noticed those around her as Jack vied for her attention and plied her with whiskey. At first it made her gag, but then began to slip down as freely as Liffey water on its way to the sea.

As her intoxication increased, she found herself gabbling away to him as though he was just a waste-bin for her words – and he listened so patiently, just like a priest. Like a priest! The thought checked her; surely this was not right . . . a respectable girl like herself! But one look at Jack put even this thought aside, and she reached out across the table and took his hand and raised it to her mouth to kiss.

He answered her touch with gentle pressure, and it was as if there were only the two of them in the world – as the rest of the bawling, rollicking people faded from their ears, and she stared into his eyes. 'I think I love you, Jack,' she said suddenly – and instantly regretted the words.

A curious smile played across his lips, and he patted her hand gently. 'I know. Come, let's go.'

Out in the street she could see the stars. A wind was blowing off the sea, bitter chill so that it nipped through her clothes and took whatever warmth was left from her skin. The perfect crescent of a moon hung in the cold firmament, half a ring of rock suspended in the deepest blue. Jack held her close, and she could smell the whiskey on his breath and feel his hard body next to hers. The drink made her soft and pliable.

'Why don't you come back with me tonight?'

The enormity of his proposal suddenly struck Kathleen. How she loved him . . . yet how could she now resist any advance he might make.

'I think not, Jack. I must go home. I'm so tired.'

'Sure, that's just an excuse. You're afraid of me, that's what. In one moment you say you love me, and the next you want to run away from me'

For Kathleen it was suddenly as if two people were at war within her. One voice was urging her to stay with him and love the cold night away; while the other, the clear cold voice of conscience, was urging her to leave him now before it was too late.

'It's a fine thing for a girl to say she loves a man and then to deny him the comfort of her arms. Come, Kathleen, no one can see us. No one will know.'

As his warm eyes looked into hers she felt her resolution dimming. Oh, yes, it would be all too easy to give way to him, and how she wanted to – how she longed to walk through the streets arm-in-arm and up the stairs to his shabby room. And how she wanted just to let him hold her in his arms and touch her all over, like it had begun that first night they were together. Her mind reeled with the criss-cross of emotions she felt.

Jack Carey could see how she was hesitating, and he pressed on. 'It seems you're like all the other theatre floozies. You lead a man on and then dump him. It's sick of you I am, Kathleen Corr. Three months a-courting and a good-night kiss is all I see for it.'

'And what do you offer me, Jack Carey? A night in a

157

dirty bed I should think. No mention of love. Courting indeed!'

'So it's marriage you want, is it? What do you think I'm offering you but a love that's free as the wind?'

'But love can't be free!' she cried.

'Well, if you're going to be stubborn . . .'

'Stubborn! You're calling me stubborn. I tell you now, Jack, I wish I'd never met you. You're bringing me misery like the cold wind that's biting through my clothes right now . . .' Jack saw Kathleen toss her head in rage. She was so beautiful right now he could crush her in his arms and love her forever . . . Her eyes were wild and her face flushed from drink. But he was bitter . . . surely she was deliberately goading him?

'Well, I can tell you I've had enough of you. I dare say your attitude has something to do with those nuns of yours — may they go to hell! They do more to interfere with men's and women's deserved happiness than is right . . . dried-up celibates with withered brains, the lot of them. What do they know of normal life?'

'Jack Carey, you be quiet now. I won't have you speaking like that.'

'Oh, won't you . . . Well, it's goodbye to you, Kathleen Corr,'

She had no time to reply as Jack turned away from her, walking away down the street where the pools of lamp-light left dark shadows to hide in.

She was alone in the windy gloom. A few scraps of paper rustled round her legs. The crescent moon hung still as a few dark clouds passed over its slim shape. Icy drops of rain blew into her face.

Was this all that was left?

She could hear the tinkling piano in an eating-house where the steam on the windows hid the occupants, who were singing noisily. She leant back against the wall, feeling the bricks rough to her cheek. As some people came out, the noise increased: shouting and the chink of glasses. Light spilled on to the pavement, along with cheerfulness and warmth from the open door.

A man and a woman passed by her, and she saw the man's arm dart round the woman's waist. She was laughing heartily.

'You're a one and no mistake, Tom. Just you wait till I get you back to my place . . . we'll see who's mistress then.'

'And I'll give you as good a time as any sailor, Sal.' He reached over to dive his hand down the front of her dress. Kathleen watched fascinated from the shadows as the woman smacked his hand away.

'You be getting your cold hand out of there, young Tom. You can drink at the fountain soon enough.'

'And smother me head no doubt in between them.' Their laughter lingered behind long after they had vanished down the street – echoes of a happiness denied to Kathleen. She shuddered, pulled herself away from the wall, and set off across the river.

Approaching the house in St Stephen's Green she could see that the shutters were closed, with only chinks of light revealing that someone might be inside. Emma had given her the key earlier, so as not to disturb her. There were no live-in servants now, as Emma increasingly felt the need for utter privacy. She often pointed out 'the grey men', as she called them, who stood in the shadows by the park railings. 'Come from the Castle to spy on me, a patriot! We'll get round them though, Kathleen. My secret visitors will have to crawl over walls and through gardens to get in here.'

Entering the hall she could hear the muted sound of conversation in the drawing-room upstairs. Emma's quick and high-pitched voice a counterpoint to a deeper, more sonorous tone.

As she crept past the room, Emma cried out, 'Kathleen is that you?'

'Yes, Emma, it is.'

'I wasn't expecting you until later – but, heavens, it's near midnight already. Come in, then.'

Kathleen entered the room and found just two of them:

159

Emma in her favourite jade-coloured blouse standing tall and proud next to a tall man with black hair and a handsome face.

Ralph Bailey was an Englishman, bred like a racehorse for distinction. It transpired his family had been part of the fabric of the British army since the great battles of Trafalgar and Waterloo. His father had been a typical British bulldog: xenophobic, moustached, and bibulous. Ralph, the dutiful son, had spent his days at Marlborough and then Sandhurst without questioning his future as a professional soldier. But then his father had been killed during a tiger hunt in India, and Ralph's mother had assumed more importance in his life. She was Irish by birth, and found the sudden freedom from her husband, combined with a steady income, a heady brew. Liberated from being an army wife, she had returned to her home county of Wexford and bought a small country estate. Ralph was fond of visiting her during his leaves, and with the soft Irish air in his lungs he had began to take the Irish cause to his heart.

Now he was about to plan the great mission of his life. He had even crawled over garden walls to reach Emma's house, and was glad to find her waiting. Such a proud and beautiful woman to be alone in the world!

Kathleen took one look at this man and guessed he was part of Emma's master-plan. But she felt as though she was interrupting something as intimate as a love scene, so quickly made her excuses. Yet she was curious and, careful to shut her bedroom door in an obvious way, she lay in her narrow bed and strained her ears to listen. Though she could hear very little of the conversation, what she did hear gave her a clue to its content . . .

Germany was one word which repeated itself; money and guns were two more . . . Was Emma going to use this man to secure guns and ammunition from Germany for her rebellion? My God, it was a dangerous undertaking!

It *was* dangerous and no one understood this more

than Bailey himself. It meant a complete break with his English past. He would be dubbed a traitor by men he had once known and fought with. If the mission was unsuccessful he would face the ignominy of death by hanging. As he left Emma's house his soul trembled at the thought of the perils to which he was exposing himself.

He had taken the King's shilling and was now going to break the oath of allegiance he had once made. But why? Hatred he supposed; revenge on all those smug bastards who had mocked the homosexual in him, who had humiliated him and forced him eventually to resign his commission. He felt no loyalty to them any longer. Power, maybe that was what he craved – power without responsibility. The reckless heady power of the conspirator, of the assassin who plots the destruction of the state that has rejected him. Or greatness – maybe that was it. A promise of greatness if the rebellion succeeded. Against all the odds, if they won he would hold power in the new republic. With Britain heavily engaged with the German armies now was the hour, Englands' difficulty, Ireland's opportunity. Now was not a time for faint hearts. He summoned up all his courage and strode off into the darkening night.

16

In the Pro-Cathedral the daffodils trumpeted the return of Christ; their yellow and green gleaming in the spring sunlight. It was Palm Sunday and Kathleen was at Mass. The music struck chords within her which had played since an early age; the nuns had done their work well.

The priest was inviting prayers for all those engaged in the war, and Kathleen responded with an invocation for her brother-in-law. It was three weeks since Maggie had last heard news from him.

'Let us remember and honour those whose names are even now being carved on memorial-stones up and down our land; those who have died for a just cause. Let us thank God that they have gone out to fight the evil that is Germany.'

The sun glinting through the great windows told of the start of another growing season and the return of warmth. Perhaps Emma was right when she said the Church was just a reflection of ancient paganism.

That morning Emma had set off to some Union meeting, scarcely able to conceal her excitement at the events which were unfolding. Whatever happened, it would mean changes, and big ones at that.

Blinking in the sun outside, Kathleen set off down Sackville Street. Huddles of people talking together gave the thoroughfare an air of anticipation. She looked up and saw a tricolour flag fluttering – over the General Post Office – green, white and orange. So this was it: a gesture against the authorities, an unfurling of the flag, a symbol of Ireland.

'Kathleen!'

She turned round – and there was Johnny Gilbert of all people! But changed ... so changed. It had been a full three months since she had last seen him, and now he seemed a shadow of his former self. His eyes had the look of a sick man; sunk into their sockets, they looked as if a light had been turned off and all happiness gone. What on earth could have happened to him?

'Kathleen, it's a long time since we saw each other, and I know I have even not written. But I can see you notice it: the change in me, I mean.' Johnny hung his head. 'I've been to all the doctors, you know. Look!' He lifted his hat and Kathleen looked with horror. What had once been a fine head of hair was now reduced to a few wisps and tufts.

She struggled to think of something to say.

'Johnny, I'm so sorry. I should have written, only . . .'

'I know, I know. My mother says I must go to England to see a specialist in London. Damn it, Kathleen, I can't concentrate on my work. I wake in cold sweats most nights. But for the last week I've felt a little better so I've come to the city — to visit some friends from the theatre.'

As he paused for breath, Kathleen quickly changed the subject. 'Have you seen the flag, Johnny? Sure it's a stirring sight to see it fluttering.' Johnny turned round to look. 'There's trouble coming, Kathleen, let me warn you. I would leave Dublin over Easter, if I were you. The British are not going to take this lying down, what with the war in Germany and all . . .'

'And where would I go to, Johnny Gilbert, may I ask? Isn't Dublin my home and I have no other? Am I to desert Emma and leave just when things might get exciting?'

'I can see you have your heart set on staying. You always were a headstrong girl. Well, I can only wish you luck if there's going to be a fight. Me? I'm too weak to be of use to anyone. Anyhow, I'll be on my way. Goodbye, Kathleen.'

Johnny took her hands in his own and squeezed them with a look of pain in his eyes which reminded Kathleen of Sligo — questioning and sad.

'Johnny, I wish you well and I mean it.'

She watched Johnny walk away into the crowd, and it was almost as if a shadow passed over the sunshine of the day. How terribly changed he was! Somehow she sensed she would never see him again.

17

Ralph Bailey was sick and tired of being confined in the submarine. He had been inside this tin-can for a whole week. Occasionally they had come to the surface while fresh air had been pumped into the cabin. How intoxicating it had seemed – more exhilarating than the finest of vintage champagnes. In their dark underwater world the harsh accents of the German crew had begun to grate on his nerves and the two Irishmen assigned to operate with him obviously preferred their own company to his. He was after all a stranger and, worse, an Englishman. So, he was helping the Irish – but could you really trust him?

He thought again about the smooth body of the German sailor, no more than a youth, with whom he had shared a narrow bed three nights before. How he had embraced him in the night. That's how he liked them, young and inexperienced, and the feel of their satin skin next to his own as he marvelled at the grace and beauty of youth.

Ralph pushed back his black hair traced with silver and peered through the periscope. There was land ahead – the Irish coast! Soon they would be landing the guns. With luck the long-planned rebellion would be under way in a couple of days. Tomorrow was Good Friday . . . so the arms should reach Dublin by Saturday night. He already smelled success. It had been a very delicate task to persuade the Germans. It was only when he had convinced them that the whole of Ireland was like a powder-keg just waiting to have a fuse set to it that they had relented and made provision for the guns and ammunition to be shipped. He shivered involuntarily. The work he was up to was that of a traitor – conspiring with the King's enemies. In Germany he had formed an

Irish brigade from captured prisoners of war, and they would be ready to follow him once he had landed. The risks were great, but the cause of freedom was greater.

He would be glad to get out of this hole. How did they stand it, the crew, to be under water nine-tenths of the time, crowded together in this submarine. The smell, when you first entered the thing, was indescribable.

'*Achtung, achtung* . . . Prepare to land!'

His ears popped as the vessel slowly surfaced and broke water. At last a heavy clanking signalled the opening of the hatch, and fresh air poured in. The engines had stopped their throbbing, and the submarine was gently moving on the slight swell.

Ralph stripped off his jacket, shirt and trousers, revealing a fine, well-muscled body. They would have to swim the rest of the way, as the submarine could not enter the shallows. His two companions also stripped.

Up the metal ladder and then into the water. It was freezing cold and the shock of it took Ralph's breath away. But he struck out immediately; he was a good strong swimmer and would easily cover the half mile or so to the shore. Eventually he heard the swoosh as the submarine dived behind him. Looking back, he saw no sign of it left but bubbles and ripples. Reaching the beach, he lay flat on the sand warmed by the sun.

It was then he felt the cold tip of a revolver held to his temple . . .

'Gotcha!'

Thinking this was some kind of joke, he swung over to brush the man aside. Instead he saw the familiar uniform of the British Army, and his heart sank as a vicious kick caught him in the privates. 'Here's the bloody traitor – we've got him.'

Two shots rang out. His two Irish companions slumped to the ground.

'We're going to draw out the agony for you, my son.' Rough hands hauled him to his feet. 'We'll make you squeal until you wish you'd never been born.'

The sun had hardly cleared the tops of the trees in the park when men and women appeared with spades and shovels to dig out a command post. There, too, was the Countess Markievicz about whom Kathleen had heard so much, wearing a wide hat to shade her from the sun. It was she who was giving the orders: 'Come, hurry now. We must be finished by noon.'

'Will you look at that one there digging as if she was a gardener, and in the middle of a public park! Sure she must be a crazy old madam to be doing that!' Workmen perched on the scaffolding nearby had taken to jeering; but the Countess was undeterred.

'Instead of your mocking, why don't you come down and help us. We're doing this for you – and for Ireland!' No sooner had she spoken than she fired a pistol in the air to show she was serious about her intentions. These were the first shots Kathleen was to hear that day – and the workmen decided it was wiser to flee.

Emma was nearly ready to join the diggers, dressed in some old clothes of Major Tommy's she had kept for such an occasion. The trousers were much too loose, and were tied round her waist with a piece of cord. She had bound her hair up and tucked it under a cap, so, wearing a jerkin on top, she now looked the picture of a fresh-faced country youth. She had urged Kathleen to dress similarly. 'You can run faster in trousers, and that's what I'll want you to do – run like the wind to the middle of town and report back on the developments there.'

Kathleen decided against such an outfit – she would tuck her skirt up so that it was shorter. There could even be some advantage in that; at least a soldier might hold his fire for a woman.

Maggie should be here now, Kathleen was thinking – my sister should be here to fight alongside me for the sake of Ireland. She's hiding, I know she is, worrying about that husband of hers, and here we are about to face the troops . . . A churning in her stomach reminded her how nervous and frightened she was of what might happen. Was their victory as certain as Emma seemed to think?

They had been waiting an hour in St Stephen's Green before Kathleen was bidden to hurry to Sackville Street with a sealed message. She was totally breathless as she crossed the river. It was about noon and the sun so high in the sky beat down with unseasonable warmth. She was already damp with the perspiration of running.

Suddenly she heard the sound of marching feet, and there she saw a column of Volunteers marching down the street. She pushed her way frenziedly through the crowd which watched in incredulous silence. It was when the marchers reached the General Post Office that the fray began – glass was broken and shots fired, and somehow the men seemed to get into the building with little resistance.

The crowd around her broke up as if suddenly coming to life, and swiftly spread out along the street. They were throwing bricks and stones at the shop windows! Glass was soon everywhere, and the crowd was no longer an amorphous group of people out for an Easter Sunday stroll but a frightening mob bent on destruction and looting. Cries and yells filled the air and people surged to and fro, pushing their fellows aside with scant regard for each other's safety.

In the midst of all this Kathleen managed to struggle through to the door of the Post Office, where a group of Volunteers questioned her, 'What is it you want with the high command?'

'Please, I've got messages from the Countess down at St Stephen's Green.'

The door opened and she was hurried along to the main hall. A little fat man with a huge moustache was sitting next to the one she recognised as Patrick Pearse. He took the message, opened it, nodded, and spoke in a hoarse voice with a Scottish accent. 'Just wait a minute and there'll be a reply.' From his appearance she assumed this must be James Connolly.

Kathleen took the envelope and was shown out of the

building by a side door, and began to find her own way back to the Green. She crossed by Grattan Bridge instead of the direct route, for she could hear guns firing and much yelling from the main street.

It was nearly two o'clock when she arrived back to find the St Stephen's Green sector of the rebellion well entrenched and boldly waiting for the British to arrive. Spirits were high as she told them of the taking of the General Post Office and the gunfire and looting across the river.

'We'll beat them yet, Kathleen,' Emma crowed. 'It'll all be over soon. We'll give them such a hiding as they've never seen when they come down here – Sligo get down!'

The big dog was thoroughly excited by all the activity and started to bark frenziedly as a small group of soldiers approached them across the park.

'Quickly, Kathleen, take this and hurry. It's another message, and you'd better be away before the trouble starts. Sneak off and make yourself invisible . . .'

For the second time that day, Kathleen started the hazardous journey to the city centre. She could see smoke before she even got there. Again crossing by the Grattan Bridge, she approached the area cautiously; she was glad now that her woman's skirt gave her some anonymity.

Glancing downriver she could see a large fighting boat making its way upstream against the pull of the tide. It had a Union Jack flying, and her heart sank. This meant the British were about to use the big guns.

All was desolation on streets that before had been so smart with their many fine shops. Their broken windows now left huge sightless eyes to gape upon the scene. On every side she semed to hear the clump of marching feet and the ping of bullets. Kathleen kept her head low and prayed, 'Holy Mother, protect me in this my hour of need . . .'

It took her much longer to reach the GPO this time, as she ducked and dodged between shop doorways. She saw occasional bodies, too, and folk helping with the wounded. She was thoroughly dishevelled and tearful by the time she handed her message to the rebel leaders.

'They'll be lucky to get any help from us. The extra arms from Germany have been seized, we hear, and there is no more ammunition in the stocks. It's all a disaster!'

A note was hurriedly scribbled and thrust into Kathleen's hand. And then she was in the street again.

It was well after four o'clock as she crossed the Green towards the dug-out. Hearing sounds of confusion and shouting, she hid behind the trunk of a horse-chestnut and peeped round to see what was happening. Kathleen could just see the Countess being hustled towards an army wagon, her head held high. As she tried to struggle, one soldier struck her a swinging blow.

Kathleen watched as the wagon was filled with the brave souls who had chosen to fight, then it slowly lurched off to the main road. A terrible silence fell on the Green.

When she looked over at Emma's house, she saw windows smashed in and the door battered down. Cautiously she headed towards it. Little knots of people were gathering to survey the damage.

And then Kathleen saw the form of Sligo slumped on the steps. His jaws were slack, his eyes dull and glazed. He was a very dead dog with a bullet through his head. Sligo who once had quivered with life had obviously been killed trying to defend the house. And what was she to do now? Where could she go now that Emma had doubtless been arrested?

Kathleen walked into the park and sat with her back against the rough bark of a tree. Though she felt like crying, no tears came. She could hear booming in the distance now – that boat with the big guns on it. The sky above the city was glowing with an unnatural light – though it was not a visitation from the Lord but a manmade phenomenon that produced it. There were fires raging in buildings wrecked by both sides in the struggle.

She would have to go to Maggie.

As she sadly made her way there, she saw many a

wounded man coming from the fight, aided by his womenfolk and friends. There must be many others who now lay with faces turned to the sky and eyes filled with emptiness. But there was no way she could reach her sister's as there were barricades across the streets. A great and powerful tiredness was upon her, as if her spirit could scarcely keep her legs moving. Yet she continued walking in a daze until she reached Chancery Street and cut through to Dorset Street. Like a somnambulist walking sightless along the way, unaware of her appearance or her direction.

As she pushed northwards she finally reached the intersection of Lower Dorset Street with the North Circular Road. On the latter a troop of soldiers was marching along, and she remembered what her Uncle Ned had said all those years before, when as a little girl she had been on her way to the Convent. He was right – the British could move their troops at will along its wide avenue.

Not looking where she was going, Kathleen suddenly collided with another woman. She was a stout body and no mistake; wild grey hair flying out of a bun, black marks on her face, and a light in her eyes as is found amongst those who hold causes deep in their hearts. Kathleen was silent as she brushed herself down.

'Here, are you all right? You look as though a thunderbolt hit you from the sky! What are you doing out in the middle of all this?'

'And what business is it of yours, I may ask?' said Kathleen recovering her spirit.

'I am only on me way to be of use. Mrs Furlong's the name, and I'm out to look for poor wounded Republicans to give 'em a helping hand.' She peered at Kathleen in the gloom. 'Well, you might as well come with me, my girl. I can see you're looking lost and forlorn – don't bother telling me your story now. Too much work to do, and me very own Patrick in the thick of it, God Bless his soul, and all the others down at the factory!'

It was as simple as that. Kathleen, lost and wandering, had found someone who would take charge. So she joined forces with the redoubtable Mrs Furlong, and they spent the better part of the night of that Easter Monday helping injured rebels back to the Furlong house in Railway Street. All three floors of the house were soon full of wounded; mostly surface injuries which needed bathing and bandaging, rather than major lesions which they left for the hospitals. Mrs Furlong had the energy of a steam engine, and she kept Kathleen from even thinking of the horrors she had see by driving her to heat up water and make endless tea. 'Nothing better for a shock like this than a strong cup of hot tea,' she kept saying. Finally at about three in the morning, with the guns still booming only a few streets away, Kathleen sank exhausted on a couple of cushions and fell into a fitful sleep.

She had fought well that day. Yes, maybe the battle had been lost in terms of martial victory, but that was not the only type of victory. What had risen up that day was herself, dressed in new green clothes, proud of her people and their doings. Cathleen ni Houlihan shook the bright ringlets from her face. The days to come would be black and sorrowful, as many a poor Irish mother and family would lament the loss of their loved ones.

She herself had never felt finer, as though from the death of those sons who had fought for her she was like a phoenix reborn, arising out of the fires of the crumbling city. She would spread out her beautiful wings like a dragonfly and dry them in the heat of those very same fires, so that soon she would be able to soar up to the heavens and forget the chains that had shackled her through the centuries.

The overlord had thought he could destroy her, but even in that moment of destruction she had been able to evade him and be reborn as a thing of beauty. So beautiful that people would once more marvel at her and heed her call.

*

'Wake up, Kathleen Corr. It's six in the morning, and there's errands I want you to do for me and the cause.'

Kathleen focused her eyes on the stout woman she had met only the evening before – Mrs Furlong.

She rubbed her eyes.

'Get up and you can take some food to them at the garrison in Jacob's biscuit factory. You'll have to be a quick thinker, but I'm sure a girl like yourself will cope, an' all. Here, take this to the factory, and good luck to you. Ask for Patrick – he's my son, and he'll vouch for you.' She held out a parcel of bread, but where she had got it from Kathleen did not know.

Kathleen set off as she was bidden, hiding in doorways and scuttling along the streets until she got to the back door of the biscuit factory. The guard let her through when she asked for Patrick Furlong.

He was a young man blessed with good looks. His dark hair was pushed back from his face, and he had such gentle eyes that Kathleen's breath was quite taken away. Maybe it was the circumstances under which they met, the heightened awareness brought on by danger, which made her heart leap when she saw him; or maybe it was on the rebound from her previous experiences with both Johnny Gilbert and Jack Carey, both men older and more sophisticated than herself. Unlike them, Patrick Furlong looked as if he needed looking after and caring for, his soft eyes vulnerable and his slight body swamped by the oversize uniform.

He politely took the parcel from her, and the instant she heard him speak Kathleen made up her mind she would get to know him better when all this was over.

'You'll be going back to my mother, will you? Tell her we're doing all right, and we'll be with her soon enough.'

She saw Patrick several more times during Easter week, as she was sent hither and thither by Mrs Furlong – who would have made a capable general if she had been a man and in the army. She was a formidable organiser and made sure that all round her knew exactly what they were supposed to be doing and where they were going.

173

She had a list of houses sorted out where the wounded cold receive succour from sympathisers, and though not directly involved in the fighting she was amongst the first line of support for those who were.

Kathleen would find herself gazing into Patrick's eyes when they met, as if hoping for an extra gleam of recognition. She tried hard to recall his face every time she left him, and would bring it to her mind's eye each night in the moments before she slipped into sleep. She was so painfully aware that every day might be the last, that she might never see him again, and each night she prayed in her heart to the Virgin that Patrick Furlong might be spared.

As that week progressed, it became obvious that the rebellion was failing. The big guns were doing their work, and though there was courage enough to win the battle, ammunition and supplies were short. By Saturday afternoon the fighters seemed to totally weary, their spirits crushed by nearly a week of bombardment.

18

The wounded and their helpers at Mrs Furlong's house were quiet and subdued; no patriotic songs were now sung as news came in intermittently of rebels captured and buildings destroyed. There was a feeling of despair hanging in the air like a veil.

Mrs Furlong had been a great one for keeping their spirits up — especially in the mornings after a night of pain. 'Up with you, lads, those who can. And those who can't, smile for us all, because it won't be long before we are declaring that Ireland is free!' But even Mrs Furlong's cheerfulness seemed to flag as the days went by, and finally on the Saturday she had to tell Kathleen that she could find no more supplies of food. 'For the damned British have cut 'em all off, and here we are going to starve, and the poor wounded men you see about you have nothing to nourish them. It's a sad day, is this, Kathleen, and we're not likely to forget for a long time . . .'

The week's fighting had brought much destruction to the city. Even the rebel headquarters had been moved from the GPO, which was now a gutted shell, with smoke-blackened spars sticking up into the sky like beseeching hands. Elsewhere the vultures of war were picking through the debris for what they could find. And other folk were on more merciful missions, taking up the dead while the guns were not firing.

That same Saturday morning Kathleen was sent to the new rebel headquarters to take yet another message to the leaders Patrick Pearse and James Connolly. They looked as if they had been awake for a week, and indeed they almost had. Connolly especially had the red-rimmed eyes and darting look of an insomniac, a man driven by a ravaging spirit to deeds almost beyond his strength and endurance. She waited on one side as the men conferred over a written document, murmuring between themselves. 'How does this sound? "In order to prevent the further slaughter of Dublin citizens, and in the hope of saving the lives of our followers now surrounded and hopelessly outnumbered" . . . all right don't you think? Oh to hell with it. We'll have to sign it . . . Where's that girl that was here a minute ago? . .'

Connolly shouted across the room, 'Here girl – what's your name anyway?'

'Kathleen Corr, sir.'

'Well, Kathleen, we want you to carry one last message. And it's with a heavy heart it is that we do, for it's nothing but the surrender document that you will have to take over to the British. Do you think you can do that? We'll give you a stick with a white cloth on it.'

'I'll do it, sir,' said Kathleen bravely, her heart sinking at this admission that the struggle was over – the end of their hopes and dreams, and probably their own lives.

Kathleen ran nervously through the street, ducking her head whenever she heard the whine of bullets. She was terrified by the danger of this errand, but sheer panic kept her going – for now nowhere seemed safe. Over to the left she could see where the GPO was on fire, from a bombardment that grew heavier by the minute. She guessed that the gunboat anchored on the Liffey must now be tearing the heart out of the city with its deadly fire. In a way she was driven on by the thought that the note she carried would end the suffering of many brave men and women.

When she reached the British barricade, she was met with jeers from the soldiers, 'Is there nothing better than a chit of a girl to send? I suppose there's none brave enough to show his face round here; as a traitor he'd probably fear ending up with a bullet in his heart.'

Refusing to rise to their scorn, Kathleen held her head high until she had handed the document to one of their officers. Now Dublin Castle was victorious, and the job of clearing up could begin.

Just one week and it was all over. Kathleen found it hard to stomach. The GPO gutted by fire. Sackville Street barely recognisable under heaps of rubble. Men in chains sent down to the quay to be taken off to English prisons; their heads bowed, feet shuffling, hands chafing at the handcuffs.

Worried about Emma's fate she had gone to Mr Rourke's office to inquire. To her surprise, he had received a telegram from Switzerland: it said little, but at least Emma was safe. Kathleen wondered how she had managed to escape. Maybe she had used some old connection of Major Tommy's to get her out of Dublin and on the road to Rosslare – or maybe bribery.

The whole city was electric with tension. It was as if the people were waiting only for each day's news – hungry for sensation and titillation.

The first executions began on the Wednesday, and more soon followed. The rebel leaders were taken out of their cells and shot one by one. But as each day went by, sympathy grew among the ordinary folk.

'I must say I feel sorry for them,' said Maggie on the following Sunday. 'If you'd asked me a week ago, I would have said they'd been engaged in the most stupid and foolhardy venture of all time. But when you hear of what the British have done to them; why they're even going to hang that brave lady, the Countess . . .'

'And do you know I've something else to tell you,' Kathleen finally interrupted.

'And what's that then?'

'I've met . . . well I've met a man I like.' Kathleen looked at her sister pleadingly – wanting her to listen and sympathise. 'His name's Patrick and I met him during the Rebellion!'

Maggie smiled to herself as Kathleen chirruped on. Oh yes, she'd heard it all before: Jack, Johnny and now Patrick. Would she never settle? Was this one for Kathleen? 'Tell me about him.'

From Mr Rourke Kathleen eventually discovered that

Emma Nash did not intend to return to Dublin, and it certainly did not seem to be in her own best interests. Consequently Mr Rourke was to see to the house, have the damage repaired, and let it. This defection of Emma's meant that not only was Kathleen homeless, she was also jobless. Maggie, of course, had offered her sister shelter for as long as she liked – well at least until Jim came back from the war. Kathleen did not want to overstay her welcome, but she had very little money of her own so was very grateful.

Luckily the Abbey Theatre had not been damaged, and when it reopened it was almost busier than before, as people tried to forget the horrors of Easter week.

Maybe she could audition for another stage part, and she inquired about the play Johnny Gilbert had been writing – was there any chance of a part?

Maggie looked at her sister sadly. She had read the play two or three times; and she did not know whether it was the illness that was tightening its grip on him, but he really seemed to be losing his touch.

'Kathleen, I'll be frank with you. Johnny has written the most fantastic plays in his time. Sure I'm not about to be claiming that I'm the one to judge him – that's Will Butler's job with his artistic committee – but I've seen enough plays produced to know that Johnny's latest is not the sort of play our theatre-goers will like.'

'Do they have to like it, though, Maggie? If there were only plays people liked, then we would never see anything that was the least bit new.'

'Whisht, now, just because you've sung in the panto-mime, don't start thinking you can be a star in the real theatre. I'll see what jobs are going first, and when you're earning your bread and butter, then you can think about the bright lights.'

Crestfallen, Kathleen fell silent and drank her tea. How this Sunday was dragging on. She looked out of the window at the steady rain falling like a grey shroud. It beat against the windowpanes and ran down in droplets.

'And here you are worrying me about a part in a play

while my very own Jim is away on foreign soil. The names creep up the memorial every week, and we don't know a thing about what's happening over there.'

Oh yes, Maggie knew how to put the needle in and turn it to make a body hurt. For Kathleen instantly felt contrite as anything as there was, her sister sitting in her chair with the tears starting from her eyes like the raindrops falling down the window. She went over and put her arms around her.

'I'm sorry, Maggie, it's just . . . well, I'm so confused. Listen, if the rain clears let's take a walk out in the fresh air. That'll cheer us up.'

As the weeks passed into summer, gradually things returned to their everyday normal. Good news arrived with a letter from Jim, and Maggie seemed like an angel blessed with good fortune when she received it – her eyes dancing with happiness and her face taking on a glow which had been sorely lacking for many weeks.

'And he tells me that everything's all right and he's pleased that summer's here, and he should be home on leave in July. Kathleen, I can't believe it – Jim coming home for a whole two weeks!'

Kathleen looked up at her sister and caught her staring . . .

'Oh, Kathleen, I've just thought. If Jim's coming home, you couldn't, I mean – is there nowhere you could go for a spell . . . Well, you know, it would be extra wonderful if Jim and I could be alone. Not that we wouldn't want to see you, of course . . .'

'I'll go and talk to Mrs Furlong. She runs a lodging house and she might need some help.'

And what a very good idea that was on the spur of the moment, thought Kathleen; seeing Patrick every day might make him notice her more. She had been round to see Mrs Furlong a number of times, and though Patrick had spoken to her amicably enough, he had shown no special attention. He was a shy one! And yet she yearned to stroke his white neck and smooth back his hair. These were new feelings, Kathleen realised, since she had never before felt so protective towards a man. Patrick was so different to Jack Carey. Where Jack had been forceful and domineering, Patrick was almost timid, and in no hurry to assert himself.

'I don't know about July, Kathleen, but I could do with some help right now, cleaning and cooking and all. You could have the room off the second landing. It needs a good clean out, but it should suit you for a while.' Mrs Furlong was quick to understand what Kathleen needed. She liked the girl, and was not unaware of the glances that went young Patrick's way. Perhaps a little proximity would do the trick, though heaven knows Patrick was slow on the uptake.

Mrs Furlong's house contained a surprising collection of people who lodged in various rooms on three storeys. It was one of the better tenements, which wasn't saying much; but by the standard of the day it was a good, clean, decent house, the sort a working man would go a long way to find. The stairs rose through the middle of the house, with two rooms back and front on each side; there were also rooms off each half-landing, and there was a kitchen on the ground floor at the back where all the occupants could cook for themselves.

Mrs Furlong herself lived in the basement, having her own enormous bedroom with a double bed in it, left over from her days with her 'dear departed Harry'. She had two sons, in fact. Harry the elder had been named after his father, and to her loss and chagrin he had actually volunteered to fight with the British army. He took after his father, big, and redfaced, with hands that seemed to flatten out at the end and finger-nails which were wider than they were long. Harry was the type of Irishman who had built the railways in England, America, and Australia, and anywhere else that needed them.

Patrick on the other hand had a wiry frame and long nimble fingers which he used to advantage in the printer's trade, picking up and placing pieces of type with astonishing speed and accuracy.

The other men who lived in the house pursued a wide range of occupations. Michael Flynn, labourer, worked all hours using his muscles to earn his pennies; his shock of red hair ever falling into his eyes. Desmond O'Malley, a lawyer's clerk, was studying to better himself, and was for ever trying to wash his shirts clean in the kitchen sink while pleading with Mrs Furlong to hang them up to dry in the tiny back yard. And then there was Peter O'Grady who worked on the quays, and had moved thousands of tons of cargo in and out of boats, but now spent more time shouting hoarsely to the other dockers since he had risen to be foreman. These were just three who had made their homes with Mrs Furlong, preferring the decency of her house to the dirt and fecklessness of others, despite the strict house rules she imposed.

Mrs Furlong liked a spot to drink herself – and kept a bottle of whiskey especially for when she was feeling a little low – but she could not abide a man who could not hold his drink. The traditional Irishman who staggered, lurched and bellowed out songs was not to her liking. Nevertheless she enjoyed a good time, and every Monday night there was a big gathering of twenty or more people in her large basement. These were Republican supporters mainly, people who thought and felt like herself, and wanted only one thing – the end to British rule on Irish soil. There was much singing and dancing at these meetings, and Kathleen enjoyed them immensely. Here she learnt the songs of the Republic, and sang them, in her sweet voice so that her audience was entranced.

Even Patrick began to notice there was something special about this girl who had come to help his mother. Following her up the stairs, he could not help notice that she had a pretty turn of ankle, and at twenty-three he judged himself entitled to take an interest in the opposite sex – if only he did not become so tongue-tied in the process!

Kathleen was determined to carry through the plan

that had grown in her heart since the day she had first met him. Here at last was someone who did not seem to want to dominate her and yet to whom she felt irresistably attracted. Furthermore he was not much older.

Patrick featured increasingly largely in her dreams when she lay down to sleep. His face kept appearing in her thoughts, and she fell to imagining his arms gently holding her – oh yes, she knew he would be gentle and firm and kind, all at the same time. She could not really explain why she felt so drawn to this quiet, unassuming man, and she wanted to look after him, take care of him, and love him. When he was about, the day would seem a little brighter, her step a little lighter. Yet she would blush furiously when he did talk to her, and came over so shy that she would curse herself afterwards for being so stupid. She would sometimes catch his eye on her when she was singing at the Monday gatherings, and feel herself almost melt that he should be paying such attention to her. Occasionally they would be seated side by side, and she would become acutely aware of his wiry frame next to her, longing to rest her head on his shoulder and stroke his dark hair. Maybe then he would turn and kiss her? But as such imaginings went through her mind, Patrick himself remained silent. He was seemingly unavailable, and this made him seem more interesting.

They were like two people groping in the dark to find each other, and not quite getting there. Sometimes Kathleen felt she would burst with her pent-in feelings, that she would shout out, 'Patrick – here I am! Look at me!' But instead when they met on the stairs he would merely say, 'Good morning, Kathleen,' looking at her in that blackbird way of his with his head to one side, and Kathleen would briefly reply, 'Good morning, Patrick' and hurry by.

Jim Sheehan's leave came and went. Maggie was all a-flutter then, radiant for the two short weeks he was with her, and distraught when the time came for him to go. And when he departed, Kathleen did not move back in with her sister, but continued to live at Mrs Furlong's.

*

182

Then on one of those glorious September mornings when the sky seems to be singing and the trees just showing a hint of their autumn colours, Kathleen finally took the plunge. She had just returned from Mass with the Furlongs, and suddenly heard herself suggesting to Patrick that they catch a tram to the seaside and take a walk. 'Autumn is on its way,' she flustered, 'and we'll be stuck inside for many a week in the winter with the rain pouring down. Let's go and take the air while we can!'

Such a bold young hussy, she felt in embarrassment, but Mrs Furlong gave her instant encouragement. 'Yes, go on, Patrick. A bit of the ould fresh air will clear your lungs out.' From then Kathleen understood that Mrs Furlong was on her side.

They went to Bray Head and walked up the hill among the bushes and the heather, and suddenly it seemed easier to talk. 'Look, Patrick, at the sea, sparkling like a diamond! And if we're lucky we'll see the ferry from England.'

'Aye, it's a grand day to be out . . .' and here he hesitated as if he was not quite sure what he wanted to say '. . . especially with a goodlooking girl such as yourself.'

Kathleen turned to face him, and looked in his eyes which were lively and loving, and she took his hand in hers and held it tight. He didn't resist this gesture — instead he gave her hand a little squeeze.

Kathleen's heart soared with the skylarks as she and Patrick continued up the hill. She remembered another afternoon by the sea with her Uncle Ned as a little girl. And where was *he* now? As good as dead, as they hadn't heard a word. More likely he had vanished on to skidrow and was ashamed to admit it. And then there was that time with Emma, when she had experienced that extraordinary vivid dream about Ireland's suffering.

'You look sad, Kathleen. What is it?'

'Memories, Patrick, memories . . . of times when I've been here before.' When she told him of the peculiar dream about the Famine victims, he warmed her with such a sympathetic eye that it was as if she was unloading

183

the memory upon him – as if the burden of it had gone from her.

'It's hard to get rid of such thoughts, Kathleen, I know. It's as if they're burned into your mind. I used to have bad dreams as a boy – I used to think the devil was after me. They've a lot to answer for, those teachers. Sometimes I would wake up with the feel of hellfire on my neck, and a little prick of the devil's fork in my back. And I'd cry and cry so that mum would come and cuddle me.'

'What a poor little fellow you must have been, there in your bed in the middle of the night, screaming to the moon!' Pretending indignation he chased her up the slope then in the golden light, until they were breathless and laughing too much to carry on.

'You're a fine girl, Kathleen,' said Patrick, panting. 'I'm glad you came to stay with us!' As he stood with his back to the sun, Kathleen could see the light shining through his curls, and she ached for him to take her in his arms, and she wanted him even more because he seemed too shy to do it. It maddened her that she could not will him to embrace her, to kiss her lips, stroke her hair and speak words of love in her ears. His very shyness emboldened her as she took his hand again and pulled him up the hill behind her, listening to the skylarks singing high in the blue, her heart up there with the little brown birds.

She kissed him then, and he seemed to respond . . . and then it was as if he had come to life and was kissing her neck, her ear, and finally his tongue was making little darting movements in her mouth, so that Kathleen felt as if she was about to fly off the hill like the larks above her. As they lay down his hands were soon stroking her hair, her neck, her arms, so that shudders were running through her body . . . and finally she felt his hand on her bodice. She looked at his soft brown eyes, and he looked at her as if beseeching. The moment was still and unmoving between them and Kathleen felt her nipple

184

harden under the blouse. Patrick was trembling as his excitement seemed to spill over.

'Not now, Patrick, not now,' Kathleen murmured as his hands rubbed her breasts.

'Kathleen, my love, Kathleen,' he panted.

With a soft moan, Kathleen leaned towards him, and felt him hard against her thigh. His knee moved between her legs and his hand moved down to stroke her leg. Now she was gasping and kissing him with passion.

'Patrick! Patrick!' she was crying softly . . .

It was a rustling in the heather further down the hill which stopped them. Startled, they looked at each other and saw that there was Kathleen with buttons undone and skirt above her knee, and Patrick's hair sticking up wildly. They gazed for a long moment in each other's eyes, and Kathleen saw Patrick smiling at her as she hastily put her clothes straight and sat up next to him as a young couple came up towards them.

'Good afternoon to you,' said Patrick; and Kathleen lowered her eyes before the man's insolent stare and the girl's laughing gaze. They had passed in a second.

'Kathleen . . .' Patrick murmured. 'Kathleen – you will be my girl, won't you? We'll go out together and we'll be friends?'

As they stood up, he put his hand under her chin so that her face was tilted towards his. She leaned forward and put her head on his chest, feeling the taut strength beneath his shirt. Then she drew back and gazed afresh at his face, just showing the faintest sign of an afternoon shadow. She would always remember him as he was that day, eager and loving, earnest and soft at the same time. She loved him for his look of vulnerability; the white skin of his neck disappearing into the whiter skin of his shoulders. Her insides churned.

'Put you arm around me, Patrick Furlong.' And Kathleen drew his slim body to her in an energetic hug, so great was her happiness. And she kissed him so that it was he who now blushed and looked flustered.

*

185

On their return home Mrs Furlong could sense that something had developed during their outing, and she was pleased; though she determined to keep a good eye on the young couple as she didn't want any hanky-panky in her house, but she did not have long to wait, as hardly four weeks went by before her son Patrick came to tell her he was intending to marry young Kathleen.

'And I hope you'll be very happy,' said she, thinking of all the preparations she would have to make for the wedding day, as the poor girl had no parents of her own.

19

'Maggie! Maggie!' Kathleen was shouting up at her sister from the street. It was about ten in the morning, late in October, when the streets were crisp and clean. The faint mist of the early morning had cleared to leave traces of damp on the roofs and pavements, so they shone with a neat dullness in the flat grey light.

'Come on up, Kathleen,' a voice cracked with sleep came from above.

A woman, standing on the steps with two small children, looked Kathleen up and down, 'Didn't yer used ta live 'ere?'

'I did that! And a grander place you'd go a long way for!'

The woman stared hard at Kathleen, her small dark eyes scanning her as if counting her worth by her appearance. Mrs O'Shaughnessy was never one to let an opportunity go by for a little begging. That Maggie Sheehan might be all right up on the first floor but herself – well there wasn't light in her room and the walls were damp, and Roger – sure he was a good man but he spent most of what he earned on the horses. And there was always the odd copper to be got out of a friendly face . . . 'You wouldn't care to give a poor woman a penny or two?' Kathleen remembered this one of old, and being in a carefree mood undid her purse and pressed three pence into her hand, then she ran up the stairs to where Maggie stood peeping out of her door.

'Good morning, Kathleen, and it's well you're looking!'

'And the same to you, my sister,' – and then hardly able to stop the words from spilling out, she twirled round the room and her skirts whirled up. 'Good news! I'm going to marry Patrick Furlong!'

Maggie's eyes opened wide, 'And isn't that what I've

187

been expecting all along. Why, you haven't been to see your poor old sister for three weeks, and the last time I saw you, you went all doe-eyed when you spoke of him! So when's the wedding then?'

'November. Just before the really short days come, and we shall be together for Christmas, you just see. Mrs Furlong says we can have one of her rooms, and Patrick's set the date at the church . . . Oh, what shall I wear?'

Maggie gazed at her sister with her eyes shining and her cheeks flushed, and she thought back to her own wedding-day and how happy she had been. And now? A lump came into her throat and a tear to her eye as she thought of Jim – but she must not spoil Kathleen's happiness.

'I'll make you a dress, of course, you silly! And you'll look so beautiful as you walk down the aisle that Patrick will count himself the luckiest man in all Ireland that he should be having such a girl for a wife!'

So they were married at the end of November, on one of those bleak twilight days when night takes a long time to turn to day and changes back to night in the blink of an eye. Maggie had made Kathleen a gorgeous dress out of material left over from the theatre costumes. She was pleased with her sister and thought Patrick a good match for her, so making the dress had been a joy and helped her to forget about the war a little. If only Jim was home! Each little bead she had sewn on with loving care, and she had ransacked the theatre's vast trunks and baskets for some antique lace.

The church had been built at the beginning of the nineteenth century, retaining its classical glories, albeit in a faded state. The panelled ceiling showed the skill of the plasterers who had worked on it all those years ago; while the fine proportions of the building brought an air of calm stateliness to the occasion.

Kathleen had moved in to stay with Maggie for the week before, though of course would return to Mrs Furlong's to live with Patrick after the wedding. They were to have one of the back rooms, away from the noise of the street.

Outside, the wind was blustering. It wuthered round the roof-tops and blew in between the cracks of the window. It howled its sorrow down the chimney so that the fire guttered and the flames were reluctant to leap. Mrs Furlong's basement offered a haven away from the early evening chill. She had provided the food – roast beef with bread and pickles. To go with this she had sent out for a few jars from the local public house, and had called in a friend of hers who could play a fair fiddle to liven up the party. Maggie had come along, and Mrs Furlong had invited her own cronies from the street . . . oul' Mrs Henessey with her gouty leg, sworn off the drink but maybe just this once . . . some of the Republicans who had been given shelter during Easter Week together with their wives or girlfriends . . . as well as friends of Patrick's from work, and a few of Kathleen's from the theatre.

Jigs and reels were played with gusto while the guests drank to the young people's happiness, and a flush began to appear on Kathleen's cheeks as she drank her share.

'Here's good luck to a fairer pair I haven't seen this side of Liffey for many a day!' cried one of the guests, and the whole of the party kept cheering until Patrick had to get up and speak. 'I'm very grateful . . . I mean, thank you all for coming and . . . and wishing us happiness . . . and I'm sure we will be!'

And suddenly it was ten o'clock and time the bridal pair went off to their room. As Kathleen and Patrick climbed the stairs they could hear the noise of the party behind them, the shouting and laughter and singing coming up the stairwell. Patrick opened the door and lifted her into the room.

Kathleen lit the candle at the side of their bed and the flame flickered through the darkness, casting a glow around the room, with fantastic shadows leaping as it glimmered.

She sat on the side of the bed and began to undress.

'And what are you staring at Patrick Furlong?' she turned round as she felt his gaze on her.

'At my wife, of course!'

'Shouldn't you be getting undressed, too, instead of staring at me?'

'I will, I will, but I must say my rosary first.'

So it was that Kathleen's wedding night began with prayers as Patrick fingered his beads, muttering the time-worn phrases and she shivered between the sheets. She was almost dozing off when he slid in beside her and reached out his cold hands to touch her. 'It's freezing hands you've got, Patrick,' she said. 'Can't you rub them together a bit.'

'I'm sorry. Oh, I'm really sorry . . .'

And then it was she who reached out and touched him and felt his ribs, counting them down his body. She stroked the back of his neck and snuggled up to him, blowing in his ear so that a shudder went through his body. Then he was all wild passion kissing her and wriggling around like a mad thing until he rolled over on top of her.

There was a great deal of fumbling around then Kathleen felt a sharp pain as he entered her. When their passion was spent they lay with their arms around each other, and the candle went out on the night as the two bodies slept.

In the weeks that followed they grew to know each other fully, as the winter winds were blowing the chill of December. Kathleen found how Patrick's body could mould itself so perfectly to hers, how his hard leanness was the perfect foil for her slight softness. It was as if she had entered a new world, and each time he looked at her or touched her hand under the table at mealtimes, she would feel the strength of renewed passion. Most nights they went to bed early and continued to explore each other's bodies so that soon Kathleen felt she could sculpt his shape blindfold, could remember how his long fingers caressed and touched her till all she wanted was for him to possess her totally.

*
190

Kathleen felt sick. Every morning recently she would wake up and lie just waiting for the sickness to pass. Patrick was very considerate, bringing her some sweet tea before he went off to work; looking all concern at her with his dark eyes troubled.

'Are you sure you're going to be all right? I mean, you don't need a doctor do you, Kathleen?'

'Aren't you the silly one, Patrick Furlong. What do you expect when you leap upon me more nights than not? It's a baby we're having, you know. Maggie told me this will pass, so don't worry about me — I'll be all right. Indeed I was thinking of getting a job, you know, just to help us along.'

'But, Kathleen, you work for my mother, there's no need to go out and about to work.' Patrick looked genuinely concerned. He did not want Kathleen to slave in some office; but he knew that once she had set her heart on something she would let very little stand in her way.

'I've already spoken to her, Patrick; and sure she doesn't mind at all. She says it will get me out of the house, and a change of scene is what I'm needing right now. "Time enough to be in the house when the baby comes," she says to me, and "We don't want you carrying no heavy washing around right now." So I'm off to an interview today. You can wish me luck.'

'What can I say to you? You've made up your mind and you must go . . . but I'm not happy, that I'm not.' As Patrick rose to go he looked so concerned that Kathleen called him back and kissed him. She smiled and whispered, 'I'll be fine. Don't you worry at all.'

Bleak February it was when she finally took the tram to Kilmainham. It stopped outside the prison and she alighted as the bitter wind blowing up the river cut through her. Just by chance she happened to look up at the windows of the gaunt stone building and a flash of movement caught her eye — some birds hovering around one particular window.

As Kathleen strained her eyes to see, a white hand

191

appeared at the window, throwing out crumbs, and then a face – it was the Countess! Unlike the birds she was trapped in a prison cell. In her present happiness, Kathleen shuddered to think the same could have happened to herself had she been still at the Green with the rest when the British soldiers came. But at least the Countess had escaped the death sentence.

It was about eleven when she reached the office and went up the stairs to the first floor. There were two desks in the outer office. At one sat a mousy-looking girl checking figures in a ledger. She looked up when Kathleen arrived, and nodded a greeting. Her face was that of a person who spent her life being walked over; white and pasty, as if she had never seen sunshine or wind but had spent her life cooped up like the Countess.

'Good morning. Mrs Kathleen Furlong? Mr Gibbon is expecting you.'

As soon as she entered his office, Kathleen felt apprehensive. The man was older than Patrick, about thirty perhaps, and wore a tight moustache which seemed to curl in a sneer at the corner. His hair was greased down tightly and parted at one side, and the suit he was wearing was what Kathleen would term 'the sharp sort' - too fashionable in style yet made out of a material obviously of the cheaper kind.

'And what sort of job is it exactly, Mr Gibbon?' she asked, after the preliminaries.

'You know, the usual sort – looking after the boss!' As the interview progressed, Mr Gibbon seemed to ask the most peculiar questions.

'And do you think you could please me as an employer, Kathleen?'

'I'm not sure what you mean by that, Mr Gibbon, but I have a neat hand and can add up figures accurately.'

'Let's hope your hand is as neat as everything else about you. Tell me, have you worked for many employers?'

'Only one, Mr Gibbon, and I'm afraid she is abroad now.'

192

'Ah, that would mean you have few references, am I right? Well, I have to tell you that I would have preferred someone with a little more experience, but if you are willing to work hard and please me I will take you on.'

Despite her doubts Kathleen was pleased, 'Why thank you, Mr Gibbon. Thank you very much.'

Suddenly he leant over towards her and grasped her shoulders and drew her to him. His lips crushed down on hers, and his moustache bristled against her upper nostrils. Though Kathleen wriggled, he held her tight, and what was worse she could feel his free hand fumbling with her blouse. Kathleen struggled hard and managed to get free.

'Mr Gibbon! Do you mind! I am a married woman and will have nothing to do with such things.'

'You must be a pure one then. All my other girls will do more than that to keep their jobs . . .'

'I don't care what all the others do. You can find someone else to work for you . . .'

As Kathleen hurried out, she felt ashamed and humiliated. To have come all this way and then be treated so! It was too, too degrading.

All the way home on the tram she kept brooding: should she tell Patrick? She decided against — he might be angry enough to deal with Mr Gibbon himself, and she wanted no violence. So she kept her secret and pretended she had failed to get the job because of her inexperience. Instead she went to her sister Maggie and pleaded with her to find her something to do in the theatre.

'You know there's no point in you dreaming of the stage, Kathleen — and certainly not in your condition. But since you're my sister I'll see what I can do. Perhaps you can help my assistant in the wardrobe department.'

So Kathleen ironed and mended the costumes. It was drudgery but she was glad to be back in the theatre again. She frequently saw Will Butler dashing in and out, and learned that he had found himself a new wife; so he had finally given up hope of ever claiming Emma as his own!

Gossip had it that Johnny Gilbert was still in England, attending a special clinic. In fact the theatre backstage was a hive of gossip and tittle-tattle which she picked up from the company as she helped to dress them for their nightly performances. She began to regret she had not pushed herself a little harder to make it a career, but now here she was a married woman carrying Patrick's child.

She had first felt the child move one rainy day in April, and that night put Patrick's hand upon her swelling stomach so that she could see his eyes light up as he too felt the quickening of life there.

But while new life was growing within her, many others were being lost over in the muddy fields of France. Letters came irregularly from both Patrick's brother, Harry and from Jim. One day Maggie came in to work looking pale and exhausted, as if she had passed the night without sleep at all. Kathleen was quick to notice the change in her sister. As they sat at the long table where the costumes were inspected, she held out a letter to Kathleen, who wordlessly read it,

My darling, darling Maggie,
It looks as though I have copped it this time, as they have shot away my left leg. I am in the military hospital in XXXXX, and at the moment I can't move for the pain of it. They cut it off at the knee. If I pull through this they will send me home, so keep praying for me, darling, and please above all keep cheerful. I'm not finished yet!

Yours evermore,
Your loving husband, Jim

Yes, Maggie had plenty to worry about for sure. Losing a leg was a dangerous thing; she had read in the newspapers that gangrene was a danger for those whose wounds took a long time to heal. And death could not come too quickly for those who were affected by the rot; smelling their own bodies putrefying as they lay helpless amid the flies. And what could the two women do about it – nothing. Nothing except pray to God in heaven to

194

have mercy on him and bring him back to Maggie alive. Kathleen saw her sister's eyes fill with tears and she comforted her as best she could. Better he came home without one leg than not at all!

The baby was due in September and Mrs Furlong had helped Kathleen make some baby clothes. By high summer, at the beginning of August, Kathleen was so big that workmen in the street would whistle and shout, 'I bet *you're* hot, me darlin!' And she would waddle along as best she could, indeed feeling hotter than she had ever done in her whole life. The child seemed to really heave itself about, elbows and knees sticking out, like moving round her stomach in some stately dance. Patrick was gentle with her now, and let her sleep in the big bed alone while he returned to his old bed in the basement. Kathleen found nothing strange about this, and when he kissed her goodnight she was grateful for the space in the bed and thankful that on these hot nights he was not tossing and turning beside her.

As she woke up in the mornings, responding to the movements within her, she felt as if her whole time was being co-ordinated to the child's needs. She was not sure which she would prefer, a boy or a girl, and just hoped instead it would be born safely.

Mrs Furlong was full of motherly if sometimes alarming advice. 'Sure, you'll know when it's happening; it's a pain like no other and you'll recognise it when it comes.'

'And how long will it take?'

'Oh, that depends, Kathleen. There's some women who can lie screaming for a day, while others just take to their beds and the babby slips out so smooth like a young seal.'

'I just can't believe that a baby could come out of me. I just don't seem wide enough . . .'

'That's what it's all about, my dear; a body has to stretch. That's why it hurts so, and the first is usually the worst. Each one is different, so they say. Why, didn't

195

young Harry tear me half apart, while Patrick came out all slippery like an eel?'

It was about five in the morning and the sun was just peeping over the rooftops. Kathleen woke feeling rather strange, and then she felt it, the pain. It was like an iron band was being wrapped around her back and was slowly beginning to crush her. She found herself panting and crying out with the pain of it. Patrick must have heard her, or had some sixth sense, for there he was at the door.

'Quick . . . get your mother,' she gasped. 'I think this is it . . .'

'But it can't be – there's a month to go yet.'

'Get her quickly, Patrick . . .' she groaned as again she felt the pain squeezing her till she felt she would burst asunder.

Mrs Furlong appeared immediately and, as ever in a crisis, took control. She ordered her son to run out for a cab, as his wife must surely go straight to the hospital. She herself packed a bag for Kathleen, and helped her to dress.

The cab journey was one that Kathleen would never forget. As the horses trotted smartly over the cobbles, every bump and lurch seemed to resound through her body and multiply a thousand times. At the hospital there were nuns in white habits who received her and led her up to a small room. They told her to get undressed, and left her there. Patrick and Mrs Furlong were to wait downstairs, as no visitors were allowed.

Then the midwife came and talked to her. She told Kathleen to put her legs in some weird stirrup-type arrangement, and Kathleen felt so helpless lying there, flat on her back with her legs up in the air as the pain coursed through her. Hours seemed to pass until she noticed the pains came more frequently now.

Eventually the midwife returned and inspected her again. 'Not long for you now, I would say.'

And then Kathleen was crying out, willing for it all to

196

be over, as she felt the baby passing out of her. She saw the midwife pick up a purple-looking object with a white rope wrapped round its neck like a pearly necklace. Her baby? She heard the slaps from behind her, but no cries came. No sound or joyous scream of life or movement of tiny limbs. Strangled they said she was. Strangled with the umbilical cord. Nothing they could have done - in fact it happened quite frequently. God sometimes acted in mysterious ways. She mustn't worry; there would be others. There was absolutely no reason why there should not be others.

For Kathleen it was like her whole world had been torn apart. Instead of going home with a new baby, she had nothing for her pains but bitterness.

Patrick came to visit her that day, his dark eyes like a wounded deer's. 'Here, I've brought you some flowers,' he had said as he handed her three red roses that he had picked from a rambling bush growing bravely on a derelict site. They had put the roses in a jar for her and she had watched the petals fall as if the very flowers were dripping blood in sympathy. She would never look on a red rose again without remembering that day in the hospital.

Other women lying around her in the hospital all had their babies, and Kathleen could hardly bear to be there, to watch them chattering gaily to each other as they talked about his little feet or her tiny fingers, and doesn't he look like his father/mother/brother/sister. It was a club she could not join, and she lay hunched under the bedclothes with her eyes closed, willing the time to pass so she could be out of the place with its long line of beds full of happy women with their babies.

God acts in mysterious ways! She laughed bitterly at the thought of it. What sort of God was he, then? One night a dream came to her of a God looking like a demon, who held a baby in his arms and was beckoning to her. She felt herself, in her dream, go towards him, and then the baby would fall from his arms and she would see that the back of its head was missing.

197

She had woken up screaming and the nuns rushed to her bed, begging her to keep quiet or she'd wake the little ones.

'I hate God,' she said coldly as they tried to shush her. 'I hate Him. I don't believe we go to Heaven or Hell — there isn't any except here on this Earth. And I'm in Hell now because your God has chosen to take my baby away!'

'That's enough now,' said one of the older nuns, and sat down on the bed. 'That's enough! Here drink this — and you can go home in the morning.'

Kathleen drank the potion and fell into a dull aching sleep.

So they had watched the tiny coffin being lowered into the ground. And the poor little soul would not even go to Heaven but would have to wait until the Judgement Day, restlessly wandering in the twilight world of limbo. This hurt Kathleen more than anything, that her little girl should have no rest or peace.

Patrick mutely shared her grief, and watched as his wife plunged into sorrowing and pain made all the worse by the outward signs of motherhood that had to be suppressed. For bandages wound tight round her chest to stop the milk coming cut into her skin and made her sore.

20

Mrs Furlong tried to keep her busy, and so distract her from her grief.

'Come on, Kathleen, bestir yourself. No good sitting in the chair now. We've work to do. Here, wash these sheets for me. Take them out in the yard and give 'em a scrub, will you. The washboard's hanging behind the door.'

So, scarcely a week after coming back from the hospital, Kathleen was out in the yard behind the tenements, pouring buckets of hot water into the tub and rubbing the sheets on the corrugated board. Though her hands kept busy, that did not ease the sorrow in her heart, and mixed with the hot soapy water were salty tears when she thought of her poor baby, gone and wandering now in limbo with all sorts of other lost souls.

Patrick had done his best, she felt. He had been kind and gentle with her; treating her like china almost, as if she would break into a thousand fragments at the slightest upset. She could feel his steadiness through her grief, but she knew he was paying the price with private pain. They would hold each other tenderly as they lay in the big double bed, and then would lie back to back, Kathleen with her eyes staring into the dark. On one occasion, when he thought she was already asleep, she felt his body shake with sobs.

'Patrick, my love.' She rolled over to put her arms round him. 'I can't bear it that you should be crying too!'

'It was the sight of the baby's coffin, Kathleen; the size of it, and into the ground with it!'

She pulled him towards her then, and gently licked the salt tears from his cheek, and held him close till his sobs subsided.

Their lovemaking was different from when they were

first married, when all had been innocence. It was as if they had eaten of the apple of life and seen its rotten core.

The weeks passed and another winter was upon them; barely a year had gone by since she had married Patrick, and so much unhappiness. November now, and it was two months since the birth. Kathleen was still prone to a quiet weep when she thought no one was looking, and the black cloak of despair had not lifted from her shoulders. Walking down the street had become an all too painful reminder of what she was missing, as the children played and shouted around gossiping mothers.

'Sure enough, yous should see him of a night when he comes home from the public house; rollin' he is . . . and I sez to him, what do yous think yous are doing a comin' home at this time, and no money for yez work? "Well," he sez, "come off it, woman, there's bread a-plenty around and if yez can't feed three or four chisslers with that, it's a poor do" . . .'

'My Dennis is the same. Sometimes I wish I'd never had 'em, the children, I mean. All four of them draggin' me down, and now look at me . . .'

Kathleen couldn't bear to look, as she knew the second woman had a stomach like a football. How dare she complain? Nevertheless, she realised that with Patrick she had a good enough home. Those very children she heard talk of were probably sleeping in the same bed as their mother; an iron bed in a dark room where little light came, and the chorus of their coughs in the night presaged an attack of bronchials or tuberculosis.

It was Christmas 1917, and Jim Sheehan came home two weeks before. Maggie and Kathleen went to the quay to meet him. It was a bright morning and the sea was shining with reflected sunlight as the boat came in from Liverpool.

Kathleen had mixed feelings about Jim's return. Of course Maggie was happy to have her husband back –

for her the best day of her life since her wedding, with Jim home safe from the war! But Mrs Furlong had spent too many evenings bemoaning her son Harry's enlistment. 'Against his own mother's wishes and all . . . sure he will bring disgrace to the Furlong name fighting for those English!' Yes, she was glad for her sister, but she could not quite regard Jim as a hero, even with leg gone while trying to rescue a British officer.

Waiting at the quayside as the boat came in were a number of other families in huddled groups, wrapped up against the winter air, the women with shawls over their heads, and the older men with cloth caps pulled down over their ears.

With a slight bump the boat was up to the quay, and the ropes were slung out to tie it up. The gangway was let down, and off came the passengers. There were Irishmen returning from work in England, with strong muscles used in war work, and paid enough to feed themselves and have a bit left over for their families back home if they didn't drink it all away in the English public houses. Among them came soldiers on leave, springing down the gangways to their families' welcome.

And finally those returning from the war who would never be fit to wear uniform or fight again. Kathleen watched them sadly: some with limbs missing – an arm here, a leg there; others with bandages covering sightless eyes and unhealed wounds.

'There he is!' Maggie shrieked and pointed.

Jim was now at the top of the gangway. When he saw Maggie he waved, and then started the laborious descent on crutches, swinging along his one good leg while the other stump hung uselessly. He had clearly changed from the upright young man who had gone off to the war, and Kathleen was aghast. She could feel Maggie stiffening beside her. Jim had the look of a hunted man; his eyes were sunk in their sockets and looked flat and dull. Above his lip the moustache was no longer shiny black as before, but peppered liberally with grey. He was also missing a front tooth, which gave his smile a comical, lopsided look as he approached.

Maggie smoothed back her chestnut hair and ran to throw her arms around him so enthusiastically that he nearly lost his balance.

'Steady, Maggie! I've only got one leg now, you know.' He had to grip hard to his crutches as Maggie clutched him to her, sobbing.

'Oh, Jim, I never thought I'd see you again. Thank God in his Heaven and all the saints for bringing you back to me safely again.'

Jim's eyes took on a look of one possessed. 'You can thank them as much as you like, Maggie, but I'm afeared that God and his saints have left this earth and gone away, after all I've been seeing these last years. Come, let's be getting home again. We'll take a cab – I can't walk far with this blessed thing. And hello to you, Kathleen. It's older you're looking, too.'

He closed his eyes in weariness as the cab sped along the quay and back through the city.

It was a long haul up the stairs for Jim. 'We'll have to be moving to the ground floor, Maggie. I can't cope with this every time I go in and out. Mind you, when I get my new leg I should be a walking dynamo!'

Jim's experience of the war had been no different to that of thousands like him. A blatant disregard for human life on the part of the generals had produced the opposite effect on soldiers closer to the action, so that some had gone mad with the images of death that swam before them every time they went to sleep. Jim was one of the lucky ones – he was not dead, and that he was thankful for. Nor had he been gassed, like some of those he had met in the hospital, their skin falling off them to reveal the raw flesh underneath. He was lucky indeed to have had a strong constitution which saw him through that nightmare day when his leg was reduced to pulp. And also the day following, when the surgeons had shaken their heads and got the saw out, its cruel teeth glinting in the makeshift light before he passed out with the shock of it.

Yes, he considered himself lucky to be missing only half his leg, and to come home with his mind still intact. Yet, on some nights he would wake up in a cold sweat when the faces of dead comrades returned to haunt him like ghosts.

As Maggie bustled around to make some tea, Kathleen engaged Jim in nervous conversation. 'And were there crowds waiting when you returned from France to England?'

'More than here, Kathleen, and a might lot more of the flag-waving, I can tell you . . . but it turns me queer now to see it all. You start off thinking you're fighting a just war, and you finish up thinking what a terrible waste. You can keep your glory-mongering as far as I'm concerned. It seems fighting does little good – look what happened to the Rebellion.'

'But, Jim, men may have died, but it did Ireland's heart good to struggle . . .'

'Whisht, Kathleen, don't you be talking your politics to Jim, and him hardly off the boat. Let's think of something brighter to talk about'

'Come here, Maggie my love, and sit beside me and let me tell you my plans. Sure, didn't I have plenty of time to think about them while I was lying in that hospital with the wounded and dying all around me?'

Maggie sat quietly by his chair while Jim, with his stump sticking out, began to talk animatedly. The dull look vanished from his eyes as he excitedly told the sisters of his plans to entertain, astonish and amuse the great Irish public.

'I tell you, we'll be the talk of the town. We'll draw together the best talents of the country and we'll pick the best plays and musicals, for people will now be wanting a little colour in their lives. It's all wretchedly drab, this war business. What do you think, eh?'

Maggie and Kathleen were soon caught up in his enthusiasm.

'Why,' Maggie said, 'you're right. People will be wanting to come out and see good shows, and who better qualified than ourselves to stage them. We know how to hire the theatres and deal with all the arrangements, and I should think there will be a few pennies in it afterwards for us.' And Kathleen suddenly became aware of the iron will which drove her sister on, a will to work any hours if the reward was success.

'Well, that's settled then. I'll get meself a new leg and we'll be off to the races . . . so to speak.'

Jim was not one to talk big without following up. It took slightly longer than he expected, but with Maggie's help and the assistance of an artificial limb maker he was relatively mobile within the month, and the new year saw him much returned to his old self as the new Druid's Theatre was formed.

His return affected Kathleen in a positive way for his enthusiasm for his new projects was catching, and she even became prone to boring Patrick with details of their plans.

'Kathleen, you're talking about the theatre again, and that's the tenth time this week. Can't a man come home from work without a body plaguing him with all that?'

'Let her talk, Patrick. Better that than weeping.' Mrs Furlong stood there with a wooden spoon in her hand, her grey hair straggling down her back and her pinafore tied tight round her plump waist. She was pleased Kathleen was becoming more like the girl she used to be.

Despite his chiding, Kathleen and Patrick were happy. In their room at night they shared the big bed and tumbled around like a pair of puppies. Kathleen grew to enjoy their lovemaking again, and her passion would quickly rise when he approached her in his own tender way. She became aware of the power a woman has over a man, to encourage his passion or turn the cold shoulder, and Patrick readily took her lead. Part of their attraction for each other was the fact that they were both learning something about each other every day.

There was a shadow hanging over them, however, as

the muttered threat of conscription grew. Kathleen could only pray that her Patrick would not be taken away from her. Why Jim had left part of his leg over there, and Harry Furlong was still at the battle-front. Was there any more sacrifice one family should make for an alien cause?

The war did seem to be in its final phase, but an invisible enemy was now sneaking across Europe to bring devastation in its wake. Unseen this enemy wreaked its havoc in its victims' lungs, and their defences were few against its ravages. No guns or ammunition could stop it; no sandbags or camouflage could deflect it, nor bomb destroy. Its name was Spanish Influenza.

It was a wet April and the damp penetrated even the warm basement. If Dublin could sparkle in the sunshine so could it lower in the gloom and hunch its shoulders against the wet wind or dark clouds weighed down on the city and the spirits of its inhabitants. The weather had been thus for almost a fortnight when Patrick came home one night looking hot and flushed.

''Tis nothing, Kathleen. It will pass. I'm just feeling hot and cold, that's all.'

Kathleen put him to bed and ministered to him. But when he cried out in the night, feverish and flushed, and his pulse raced dangerously, Mrs Furlong sent for the doctor.

He had seen a few like this already, and suspected there would be a lot more. Influenza took many forms, but this one looked a killer. Nevertheless he tried to sound cheerful. 'Keep him warm and make sure you wash him down often with a cool cloth. That should help with his temperature. There's no medicine I know of that can help much, I regret.'

It was like a nightmare as Patrick came and went from her during that awful night. Frequently she put her hand on his forehead and felt him burning. Mrs Furlong, too, kept up the vigil that night, fetching cool cloths to lay on him as he moved restlessly to and fro in the damp bed. Her face was white with exhaustion as the dull light of dawn was breaking through the window.

'He's going to be all right, isn't he, Ma?' Kathleen pleaded as she watched Patrick tossing as if to avoid the cooling flannel.

'I don't know, Kathleen. I'm worried stiff. The fever is on him now, and who knows when the good Lord will see fit to take it away.'

All the next day Patrick remained in this half-conscious, tormented state. Occasionally the women forced water down his throat, Mrs Furlong holding him up firmly while Kathleen held the cup to his lips.

When the doctor came again, he did not seem quite so optimistic. 'Your husband is very sick indeed. I'm afraid there's nothing can be done for him except to pray.'

The crisis came the following night, in the cold hours between midnight and dawn. Both women were there again as the man they loved as husband and son began to rant and groan, with an ominous rattle in his throat. His fevered eyes recognised neither of them.

Then about four o'clock in the morning he sat up suddenly and cried out, 'Yes, I'm coming. I'm coming,' and fell back on to the pillows with a smile on his face.

'Patrick!' Kathleen shrieked and threw herself on him, shaking him again and again as if to make his spirit come back – until her mother-in-law had to prise her away, and they both sobbed into each others shoulders as another day began.

'Shh . . . my pet, he's gone to God now.'

'It's not true, Ma . . . it's not true . . . God doesn't need Patrick now . . .'

Maggie and Jim held her upright at the funeral as the tears spurted like ever-lasting streams. Inwardly she raged as the prayers were intoned, angry that yet again the God she had believed in had deserted her. Another funeral – her happiness dashed once more.

PART IV

21

'Get that bloody wagon over here. We'll need it!'

'O'Flaherty, have you laid the nails? What do you
mean you couldn't find any. Go to Tom the roofer —
he'll have 'em. Take a bag of 'em and go down that
bloody road and make sure they're spread even like. We
don't want any reinforcements rushing up now, do we?'

'Packin' the tins are you? Put plenty of scraps in 'em.
Tie the bolts tight at either end.'

'We're gonna have to fire the roof. Let me think, now.
The creamery wagon. That's it! We'll pump the incen-
diary through! Fire the roof so the bastards surrender
and we have 'em surrounded.'

'Watch that gelly, mate!'

The beige sticks were softening gently in the tin can.
You couldn't be too careful at this point; a false move and
it would be curtains for them all. Yet when he thought of
yesterday's little debacle, his mouth tightened grimly. The
whole family shunted out of their home . . . not just one
of them but the whole row of houses which huddled up
to the hill. The soldiers in khaki and the Royal Irish
Constabulary in black, fucking vultures they were. Set
fire to the houses, leaving the women and children crying
by the roadside, kept away at gunpoint. Then they shot
the little boy — no more than twelve he could have been
— and he was only trying to put out the fire.

Must be organised. No good attacking just like that.
Brigade must report to HQ. Waste of bloody ammo and
volunteers otherwise.

The RIC had it coming to them. Came out in the
bloody dark, didn't they? Sticking together in a little
huddle and snatching any suspect, guilty or no. To be
shot, there and then.

Think they'll break us down, they do . . . drinking in

the pubs they've damaged the day before ... then throwing hand-grenades about in the villages as though they were confetti. What a bum way to fight ... not like men at all. Attacking the women 'an chisslers ... Goddam them to hell.

And now the British say that for every loyalist house that's burnt they'll burn three of our lot. We'll fight back. We'll win. Ireland will be ours. We'll fight to the end and rid ourselves of the foreigners.

'Get back in the haggard, and keep yous mouths shut, for God's sake. Saints in heaven they'll never learn, these hill men.'

The gelly was ready. He started packing it carefully with a fuse.

Twice nightly, 6.30 and 8.45. Dress Circle 2/-, Upper Circle 1/3, Gallery 4d. KATHLEEN MAVOUREEN or, A DREAM OF ST PATRICK'S EVE. A Domestic Irish Drama with Music.

This was Kathleen's life now. Two performances a night, with Jim running the company like clockwork so that it produced what the people wanted. 'By popular acclaim' were the right words to describe it. Meanwhile a new war was being waged in Ireland, with the Black-and-Tans – the black of the Royal Irish Constabulary mixing with the British Army tan – fighting against the Volunteers, the troops from the 1916 Rebellion who had fought under Patrick Pearse and were now called the Republican Army or IRA. But as the show continued night after night, Kathleen had hardly time to think about savage hill ambushes outside the city. Nor did she know about gelignite sticks warmed gently so that they gave off no gas. As she sang on her fairy crag to the delight of the Dublin audience, her thoughts were concentrated instead on sustaining the high note and warbling the tremolo.

Singing was what had attracted her to Frank Kearney all that time ago in Mrs Furlong's Monday gathering. The first night he attended she had met a dapper man, small and neat with a well-trimmed moustache. And when he stood up and sang she had been totally entranced by his voice.

'Dance with me, won't you?' His eyes laughed as he gazed at her, and she couldn't help but be charmed by his winning smile. 'You're Patrick Furlong's widow, aren't you? A very brave man for the cause, he was. Met him in the factory during the Rising.' Kathleen's heart contracted, yet she could not blame Frank for the painful memory he'd brought her.

They were dancing together now, Frank guiding her gently. There were several other dancing couples among the many gathered there. The basement door was open; fresh air spilling in from the yard. The violin-player kept the waltz going lively as Kathleen and Frank twirled round the big room.

'You're not a bad dancer, are you? But could we pause a while till I cool off?'

Kathleen did not resist as he took her arm and they walked out into the warm evening air.

'Shall we take a stroll, then?'

And why not, thought Kathleen. Frank seemed as kindly as she could wish for. She had observed him across the same room for weeks now, and thought she would like to know him better. He was always a centre of attention, laughing and joking and throwing back his head to reveal a fine set of teeth. There was something comforting and real about him, and she liked that. She was lonely and needed some comfort, so she allowed him to take her away from the hot, smoky room, and they walked down towards the river.

There was still daylight, but the sun was slipping down behind the houses, with a trace of pink cloud in the sky.

'Will you look at that! It's shaped like a castle!'

'So you have an eye for beauty, do you?' Frank smiled, and took hold of her hand and kissed it. 'Like myself, you might say. I too know beauty when I see it!'

Kathleen was not sure how to take this.'You're a tease, Frank, you are.'

'And what if I am? You'll grow to like it.'

This was preposterous; this very air of confidence was enough to make any girl want to laugh . . . and yet she had not felt so merry for ages. She readily matched his bantering tone, 'And then again perhaps I won't, mister.'

They talked of many things, and time slipped past into the dusk, as Frank slipped his arm round Kathleen's waist to walk her back to Mrs Furlong's.

What was it about Frank Kearney that had attracted her so? He was charming and gallant, in a rather old-fashioned way; the opposite to Patrick in that he had none of the gaucheness of her former husband. He liked company and could sing and laugh, telling jokes to keep a roomful of people amused all night. He was a very sociable man, enjoying the life and the camaraderie of the pubs of Dublin. He was merry and lighthearted, and made her feel happy and young again.

If she felt increasingly drawn to him now, it was perhaps as an escape from the gloom of the past year or so; a return to normal living where you didn't weep every night as you went to bed. And clearly Frank was equally attracted to her.

They enjoyed a wonderful time that summer, as she walked out with him in any free evening she had away from the theatre. He took her round and about the city, so that she met dozens of people in his favourite bars. He knew how to treat a lady, too! A few romantic words and then a little joke, so that nothing ever became too serious. He would nibble her ear and kiss her till she did not want it to ever stop.

The moment came one evening as they walked together on Dollymount Strand. They had even taken their shoes off so that the salt water puddled up between their toes while they watched the golden globe of a sun hover like a great round kite before plummeting into the sea.

'Kathleen, you're a wonderful girl, you know. If I was a marrying man, and I'm not saying I am, I might be asking you to marry me.'

211

Kathleen's heart beat faster. The sun glittered on the swell, and the gulls cawed and croaked.

'Is it a proposal you're making, Frank?'

'You'd have to come and live with me at Ma's, mind.'

Kathleen turned to look at his smiling face. 'And will we be happy, Frank?'

'Well, and sure why not? We can sing our cares away when times are hard, can't we?'

'That we can, Frank. And I'd work to make you a good wife.'

'Come here, then, and kiss your husband to be.'

He kissed her then and held her tight, and they swayed together until they almost fell over into the shallow sea.

In the dressing-room now she sat at the long bench with the other girls. They were all excitement and chatter – a sharp contrast to her own feelings. How happy she had been just before the wedding!

She took off her make-up and changed from her flimsy costume and into her own clothes, a skirt and a simple blouse. She was glad women's clothes were becoming easier to manage; these shorter skirts were safe from the mud and puddles in the street, and there was none of that endless lifting up which was necessary with longer skirts before the war. You could even run upstairs now while carrying something in both hands.

'Night, everyone.'

'Goodnight, Kathleen!' a chorus of voices answered.

It was ten past eleven as she closed the stage-door of the theatre behind her. Glancing up, she saw the outline of her sister in the office window. Maggie would work on until late; it was her way to make sure that nothing could possibly go wrong with the production. She and Jim were untiring in pursuit of their successful enterprise.

She had arranged to meet Frank in The Horse's Head, a pub not far from Russell Street where they now lived, renting a room off his mother. Frank's mother, Mrs Kearney! Up the same stairs they had gone to meet her the day after he had proposed.

It was a gloomy room where Mrs Kearney held court. And there she was, a woman of about sixty lying in bed with a much younger man at noon in the day!

'Here's Kathleen, Mam, the one I was telling you about. I've brought her to meet you.'

'And a more miserable-looking thing I have yet to see, Frank. Tell her to come closer. You know I can't see as well as I used to without me glasses.'

'You'd better go a little closer, like she says.'

The woman sat straight up in bed, punched the man lying next to her with a curled fist, and grabbed at Kathleen's hand as she stood by the bed.

'Turn round then, woman!'

Kathleen was speechless, but turned round.

'Not too bad, I suppose. She can help me with the house — clean the stairs and such.'

Kathleen eyed this strange woman and her streaming black hair streaked with grey. Her nightgown was grey to match; the grey of unwashed cotton. But her eyes were bright and darting, as if eager to memorise every detail of the woman about to marry her elder son.

'Have yez got nothing to say for yerself?'

'I'm pleased to meet you, Mrs Kearney, and I'm hoping we can be friends.'

'Hark at her, will yez all . . . Mrs Kearney, eh? You can call me "Granny". Everyone else does, except my two sons here. One as fine a specimen as yez'll find this side of the Irish Sea, that Frank there; and the other' — here she grasped the ruffled hair of the man beside her in the bed — 'Well there's not much to be said for him, my other son Neal. Except that he's a decent enough hot-water bottle. Aren't you that?'

'Yes, Mam. I'd be saying that. I'm a splendid hot-water bottle.'

'Here, Kathleen — whatever your name is, take this and get it filled up.' The Granny handed Kathleen a teapot. The spout was cracked.

'Where will I find the kettle, then?'

'Kettle? What kettle? Frank, take her down and tell

213

her what to do, will you? I'll be needing the pot any minute now.' Then the Granny started to heave herself out of the bed.

Kathleen fled. She had no desire to witness what came next. 'Where's the stove, then, Frank?' she asked at the top of the stairs.

'It's not a stove you be wantin' but a silver piece. She likes a dram or two of whiskey after noon.'

Later, when Kathleen pressed Frank for information about his extraordinary brother, he laughed. 'Isn't it comical for him to be in bed with the ould one? He must be forty if he's a day. Do you know he will never rise till the streets are well aired – but there's no harm in it. She just keeps him in that bed to save the rent of a room. While he's there she can take in an extra tenant. There's no flies on that one!'

The Horse's Head looked busy as Kathleen pushed her way into the public bar. Men and women were talking and joking at the table, and the heat seemed to exaggerate the smell of sweat combined with tobacco smoke and yeasty porter. Scraps of conversation caught her ear.

'They say there's not a single Catholic left in the ship-yards in Belfast now. All five thousand of 'em gone!'

'Came in second, didn't it. Limped home like a donkey. I tell yous all, I'll never take a tip from him again . . . '

'They say these Orangemen up north are driving Cath-olics from their homes and looting their shops . . .'

'Nice little filly. In the chorus I hear. You could do a lot worse than her for an evening out . . .'

Finally she reached the bar. 'Have you seen Frank Kearney this evening? I'm supposed to be meeting him here.'

'Well, now you're asking. Come to think of it, he was here earlier. Dressed up very smart, with his hair brushed like he was meeting someone important . . . What was the name of the place, now? The Diamond perhaps?'

'Thank you,' she said to the barman with the rolled-up sleeves. 'If you see him, tell him I called by.'

The barman smiled. That Frank Kearney, he had all the women asking after him. He watched as Kathleen made her way to the door. But that was his wife, wasn't it? The one that worked in the theatre? Somebody should tell her what was going on. None of his business though. It was not a barman's place to comment on his customers' behaviour.

There was loud music emerging from the Diamond. Kathleen could hear the piano from the far end of the street, and when she got to the door itself, there was such a crush she could not even see the singer. But she recognised the voice all right. It was Frank! She listened thoughtfully as his familiar voice sang an old Irish air with the lilting passion which reminded her of their nights together. Fuzzy, flowery talk about love – that was Frank. Full of talk and no action. Slumping on top of her after having his way, then snoring through the night.

When the song was finished, there was a general movement towards the bar. Suddenly Kathleen did not want Frank to see her. She hid behind a pillar and watched as the crowd thinned out. There he was now, at the bar, fetching two drinks. Her eyes followed her husband as he wove his way across the room to a corner. Who was that with him?

Through the crowd Kathleen could now see familiar blonde hair and red lips. He was smiling at her and she was throwing her head back to laugh. It was Bessie Burgess. She was well enough known in these parts, as a woman who did not work yet somehow had money enough for fine clothes and fancy outings to the races and the theatre. What would her Frank be doing with the likes of her?

Kathleen felt a deep tiredness overwhelm her. The night's performance had already drained her, and she could not confront Frank right now. She would leave that till later.

But what had happened that night soon laid down the pattern of their life. When she did confront him later, he merely brushed her aside.

'Can't you see a man's got to have a little company in an evening? There ain't no harm in it as far as I can see. Why, you go off to the theatre and do your act, and what's left to me but to sit at home and listen to me Mam banging on the floor from two floors up that she wants the chamber emptying? Whisht, woman, it's no life for a man. Not that I'd want you to stop work though, for we need the money.'

And that was true. Kathleen knew Frank worked hard at his painting and decorating, but where did all the money go? He never gave her more than a few shillings, so she had to pay for all the food he ate. Well, he must spend a fair amount each night in the pub, but even so surely he could give her a little more. She could not bare to think he was giving money to that woman, that Bessie Burgess, whose voluminous bosom was the talk of many a crude mouth. And why should he be giving her money? Kathleen refused to follow that thought through, as if she were a blinkered mare who laboured in harness and plodded round unseeing.

Yet when she was between shows, and there were no rehearsals to attend, he would make a decent fuss of her and take her out, and they would sing duets in the pubs like in the old days. Except, of course, when he was off to some secret meeting with his Republican brothers. This was the serious side of Frank, and he did not talk about it much. 'I'm off,' he would say, and she understood he could be back at any time during the night, creeping around quietly so as not to alert any of the other tenants. Their neighbours were a mixed bunch, who came and went, but you can't be too careful was Frank's motto.

Then came that night in December 1921 when the news came through of the Treaty. Ireland to have its own government at last! They were to have freedom of sorts . . . but also partition. Freedom for twenty-six counties in the south, and the other six in Ulster to be decided about later. The Treaty was hoped to end the terrible guerilla war that had been tearing the country apart. The Republican leaders were forced to sign under

216

a threat from the British Prime Minister that refusal to agree would mean the stepping up of the British offensive into a terrible and bloody and total suppression of the whole country. The news filled Kathleen with great joy. Wasn't this what they had all hoped and struggled for – an Ireland free from the hand of English government?

Frank remained sceptical. 'Wait until you hear the full story woman, before you start rejoicing. It seems the British are to keep six counties to themselves. It's all to placate the Protestants and Orangemen – those who've burnt down Catholic houses and killed our folk. Why, thousands of our Catholic brothers are right now sheltering in stables and cowsheds, turned out of their rightful homes. What hope have they of receiving fair treatment from the piping Orange bands?'

Frank continued bitterly: 'We went out for a republic for all the thirty-two counties, and what do we get but a country split in two. Those fellows who signed the Treaty had no mandate from us. They are traitors, every last one of them, and they have signed their own death warrants.'

Cathleen ni Houlihan sighed. She felt as though a limb had been amputated, and her blood even now was pouring into the Irish Sea.

The overlord had left her now; for that she could only say she was thankful. But he had taken some of her children with him, and now the rest were all set to quarrel with each other. How long could she endure them slowly killing each other like this – hiding in bushes to leap out, and set upon their brothers. Mothers would weep as their sons slashed each other's flesh, and hurled explosives to kill and maim.

And the rich would win, as always. It was the poor who fought and suffered. The rich citizens and land-owners would enlist the overlord's help to quell the struggle for a complete republic. And the hand of Rome would lie heavy on the land, so that any effort to change the order of things would be discouraged, for Rome liked things to remain just so.

Cathleen ni Houlihan wept for her country.

22

The baby looked distinctly yellow – a golden shade as if he had been out in the sun too long.

'Just a spot of jaundice, dear. It will soon clear up. You just look after him well and he'll be all right, you'll see.'

There he lay next to her. He had little wisps of golden hair curling round his head, and his little fists clenched and unclenched in his sleep. She marvelled at him: so complete and perfect. Each little toenail a small miracle. And then when she held him to her breast, his greedy little mouth would fix on to her and suck and suck like a little leech.

The nuns were brisk with her. 'Make sure you keep clean now when you go home!'

Kathleen was only sorry that Frank could not be there. The police had come and taken him off in the night a fortnight previously. Suddenly, with no warning. Fast asleep in their bed they had been when the pounding at the door made Kathleen sit up in alarm.

'And what could that be in the middle of the night? Why it's enough to waken the dead in Hell. Lord preserve us, Frank, wake up. It can't be one of our own, for they would make less row.'

A few moments later Kathleen heard voices at the door . . . 'Come out here, Frank Kearney, where we can get a good look, at you . . . And who else have you in there?'

Frank was now wide awake, and yelling angrily. 'It's just my wife and I lying in our bed, and what right have you to be coming here of a night to disturb a God-fearing couple?' Even while he was speaking he was pulling on his trousers and shirt. And then he was gone.

Kathleen rose and hurried down the stairs. A rough

hand grasped her elbow and kept firm hold of her as she stumbled into the street. There was her Frank with his back to her and his hands up against the wall. She dared not cry out, though a scream rose to her throat. The policeman in charge began bawling orders to his five subordinates.

'You two, go in to that miserable hovel and check if there's any more traitors hiding there.' Turning to Frank he growled, 'As for you, you bloody Republican, we'll soon see what you've got to say for yourself. Hands behind your back and we'll put the cuffs on.'

Kathleen heard a click as the cuffs were fastened. As Frank turned to look at her, she felt her heart go out to him. But his gaze was sardonic as if to say: I'll soon be finished with this little lot, just you wait and see. Instead he called out, 'You look after yourself now, Kathleen. You've got a young Kearney right there with you.'

Badly shocked, Kathleen went back into their room and sat at the small table. She had always feared this moment.

The tap was dripping: plip . . . plip . . . plop . . . plop . . . But she did not notice, neither did she care. Instead she leaned her head on her hands and sobbed.

Morning broke and a pale sun forced its way through the window before Kathleen rose from the table, rinsed her face, and began another day. And now Frank was in prison with some of his IRA comrades, betrayed by an informer. She would take the baby to see him as soon as she could.

She was to go home today, so she was dressed and ready. The long ward of the lying-in hospital was full of women in labour or mothers with their babies. It had been a noisy place with the infants all waking up at different times in the night.

Here was Maggie now, to walk home with her, wearing a new dress.

'Why, Kathleen, isn't he a dear. What are you going to call him? A little beauty like that needs a splendid name.'

220

'I'm thinking of something short and neat, like Liam. Nothing too fancy.'

Back in Russell Street the women gossiping in the sunshine gathered round to see the new addition to the host of children who lived in the dismal rooms around.

'God bless 'im!' one cried.

'Now yer troubles are only just starting!'

Kathleen was surprised to find the Granny up out of bed, and it only ten in the morning. Furthermore she had cleaned out the room, and there was even tea laid out. She looked a curious figure, her greasy hair hanging loose halfway down the back of her old green blouse. Kathleen had seen scarecrows looking smarter, but she had made an effort, for sure. The oilcloth on the table had been wiped, and the window opened to let in air. The street sounds of summer came floating up, cries of the tenement children playing tag round the lamp-post. In the evenings these would be lit by the lamplighter, and then they would shriek after him, 'Billy with the lamp, Billy with the light, Billy with his sweetheart out all night.'

The pub on the corner, Fannin's was opening, and those men who had finished work were ready for the first drink of the day. Their deeper voices came floating on the breeze, to blend with other sounds.

The Granny had even scrubbed out a drawer for the little one to sleep in. As she bustled around the baby, Maggie hurried off; she had no particular liking for Kathleen's mother-in-law. She and Jim had just put down the money for a house in Rathmines, and secretly she was appalled at the condition of the house and surroundings her nephew was to live in. The doors of the tenements lay open to the street, so that drunks on their way home of an evening would stop to relieve themselves in the hallways. On summer days like this the stench could be terrrible. And her sister with just one bed, a table, a few chairs, a dresser with a few plates and cups, and a chest to store clothes. She blamed Frank for this.

You would never find Jim Sheehan out drinking until all hours.

The Granny surprised Kathleen that day, sure she never expected her to take much interest in the baby. But the older woman was only too eager to pick him up, cooing at him as if he was her very own long-lost child.

'He's to be called Liam,' said Kathleen.

'Is he now? Little Liam. He'll be my little lamb, my little lambie, won't you.' And, as if responding to the Granny's attentions, the baby gave a toothless grin and hiccuped.

'See, he knows his ould Gran already! The little lambie knows who loves him and will teach him all about life.'

Kathleen had felt a little doubtful about that. She could smell drink on the Granny's breath even that early in the morning. Intoxicated by the fumes on his grandmother's breath, and him only two days old! She would have to watch the old woman carefully.

Those first weeks with the child were so busy she hardly had time to think. Liam needed feeding six or seven times a day, and then there was all the washing of diapers. Yet she did not mind waking to the baby's cries at four and five in the morning, because she could hold him close in the bed and feel his soft baby skin and little body next to hers. There was peace and pleasure about this that was worth being woken for.

The Granny would poke her nose in very regularly to look at her 'little lamb', before and after forays out to meet her cronies at the various hostelries in the area. She would even bring them in to see her grandson, and Kathleen would stand by nervously while various women of uncertain age would gaze rapturously down on Liam and drink him a toast out of her chipped cups.

'It's a good thing for them to wet the babby's head, is it not?' the Granny would say as she tipped her bottle of porter over the cups and shared it with her unsavoury friends. Of these Kathleen most disliked Meg O'Higgins, who seemed particularly attached to the Granny, following her every word and nodding vigorously. She

222

had no teeth so her mouth had a soft, shapeless look about it, and she would grind her gums together in a way that irritated Kathleen to distraction.

The Granny loved all the attention Meg gave her, but abused her cruelly in front of the others. 'Look at her, now, did yous ever see the like? A dribblin' eejit she is, an' no more 'an that. Come, Meg, give us a song now.' And Meg would open her mouth and out came a thoroughly tuneless sound, mixed with much slurping and slapping of her loose lips. It was infuriating, and the Granny did it on purpose. But Liam seemed to thrive on all this, despite his mother's misgivings.

It was her husband Kathleen worried about most. Since that night they had taken Frank away she received letters from him. He was in Kilmainham Jail with some other IRA detainees, and it horrified her to think that as soon as they had seen the back of the British, their own people could resort to this. She heard terrible tales of cruelties done: Free-Staters strapping live IRA prisoners to the front of their trucks so that if they hit a land-mine they would go up first; dismembered bodies found in the Phoenix Park with their hair, teeth and tongues pulled out. May the Lord be thanked that Frank was safe from that! She would wait eagerly for his letters.

Dearest Kathleen
As you know, I can't say much because of the prying eyes of our own brothers. I'm really glad to hear that little Liam continues to do well. Here every day is much the same: get up, clean out, eat gruel. Weather getting hotter, and the smell of the unwashed more noticeable. Write soon, and if you could find your way to send me a plug of tobacco and some papers I'd be grateful. I know you haven't got much, but maybe Mam would let you have some money. Looks like I'm in for a long spell. They don't let us have visitors as such, but wives come to the wall at about three in the afternoon to wave to their husbands. They don't seem

223

to mind as long as the women are with children. Hope to see you there soon.

Your loving husband,
Frank.

His next letter brought news of a different kind.

Darling Kathleen,
Many thanks for your letter. I'm really glad to know you and the baby are well, and he is growing fatter by the day! I had an interesting time yesterday, and I have some news for you which might give you a surprise! You know how I'm interested in anything to do with the fiddle, and wish I had learnt it myself. Well yesterday they brought in a new man. I thought he looked familiar but couldn't place him. Anyway, I heard him singing and went up to say, 'That's a wonderful song you've got there. Is there any chance I could learn it meself, as I'm a bit of a singer.'

You're not going to believe this, but he looks at me and says, 'Thank God someone else in this camp likes music. Pleased to meet you. Peadar Corr's the name.'

Well, as you can imagine, I ask him some more and it turns out that he is the very brother you haven't heard from for an age and a half. Seems he went to America soon after you went into the Convent, and stayed there until after the war. Been living in Cork, he has. Isn't that a thing now?

Not only that, he's a grand singer and writes his own songs. He's teaching me a few airs and we practise near every day. It helps pass the long hours.

That's the good news.

It also seems that John, the brother who went off to sea, ended up in the drink off a place called Borneo. On his way to Australia he was, when he caught something called Yellow Fever and had to be buried at sea. May the Lord have mercy on his soul!

Until later.

Much love and kisses
Frank

224

Liam was about six weeks old when Kathleen decided to take him to see his father. It was a tram ride away.

'Yous just take care now, with my little lamb. I don't want any harm coming to him. Anything can happen with the civil war going on out there. Sure, they don't know who to kill next.' The Granny was reluctant to help her with this trip in any way, but finally gave in and pushed the tram-fare into Kathleen's hand.

The terminus was very busy, with men in uniform controlling the crowd. The Free-Staters were out in force – the men who supported the settlement and Partition. Men dressed in old British army uniforms with the insignias ripped off moved among the crowd looking in baskets here and checking suitcases there. They had the ragged air of those not quite comfortable in their clothes, knowing they were cast-offs from another bitter conflict.

Kathleen boarded the tram and settled into her seat. Liam started crying so she unbuttoned her blouse. She loved the baby at her breast; it was a time which was theirs alone, which no one else could share. Liam lay next to her content; occasionally breaking off for a gulp of air before settling down again to his steady rhythm. Kathleen half closed her eyes as she enjoyed the sensual pleasure which engulfed her.

Frank never made her feel quite like this. When they had first married it had seemed heaven on earth. Frank was no fumbler like Patrick had first been, and from the start he had treated her body as his own, caressing her boldly and expertly, touching her so that she cried out in passion as she clung to him and pushed him deeper within her. Then gradually he had seemed to want her less often, and as her workload in the theatre increased, they began to see less of each other. He would stumble in at night and fall straight into bed beside her and begin snoring loudly. Nevertheless, some nights he would take her roughly, and without consideration, and then seemingly take pity and cry out in his climax 'I love you', so she would respond with the same and feel as if he

225

belonged to her again. Liam was conceived on just such a night. She sighed.

'Haven't I met you somewhere before?' She looked over and saw a woman peering at her from the opposite seat. She was about Kathleen's age but looked rather downtrodden, with lines of weariness etched on her forehead. A small hat perched on her piled-up hair gave her a faintly ridiculous air; and her too-tight jacket looked as if it would pop its buttons at any minute.

Kathleen was puzzled for a moment, then she remembered. All that time ago at her mother's wake — the woman with one of the Joyce brothers.

'It's Nora, isn't it? It's long years since we met. You were with Jimmy Joyce.' The tram moved off, creaking, clanking and grinding its way along its metal rails.

'I'm still with him, to my everlasting misfortune. And what's your name? I've forgotten, I'm afraid.'

'Kathleen Kearney, but Corr was my name then. You've maybe seen my name on the posters for the theatre. I used to sing there before the little 'un came along.'

'I wouldn't know. I've been out the country too long. That man of mine says he can't stand it any longer, and he refused to come back. Too busy scribbling all day, as if that will help to bring in the money! Why he can't get a proper job, like a teacher, I don't know . . . How far are you going, anyway? I'm just off to see an old aunt who needs a visit. And it's good to be back . . . at least people understand you here when you speak the language of your childhood.'

Kathleen briefly explained her own mission before Nora's voice took over again rising shrilly over the clatter of the tram.

'This civil war business, though, isn't it a thing? It ain't safe for a Christian woman to go abroad. Why, I was on this train last week and there was a sudden jerk and, would you believe it, I fell right off my seat on to the floor! Then I peep over the window — but see nothing but bushes and trees. Then I heard men shouting up the

226

track, and the screams of other passengers. Then the sound of trucks approaching, and suddenly bullets were flying this way and that. I got right under the seat like a rabbit in its burrow.

'Saints preserve us, it must be an ambush, I'm thinking. Jimmy said I shouldn't come. "You just watch, Nora," he said. "The Irish love nothing better than a fight, and it will all be for nought in the end, as the Church will triumph and they will all go back to their womenfolk with their tails between their legs." Anyway then there's more shouting I could hear through the window: "We're going to murder you traitors. Crawling to the British for supplies to kill your own brothers, you deserve something worse than death" . . .'

Kathleen's stop was fast approaching, so she interrupted the tirade. 'I'm getting off here, Nora, so I'll say goodbye.'

'Good to meet a friendly face, it's been. Good luck to you and yours, Kathleen.'

'And to you.' Kathleen gathered up the now sleeping baby and climbed down from the tram.

The prison walls looked just as grim as they had those years ago when she had spotted the Countess's face at a window. She had since been freed, and was still a staunch Republican – elected as a Sinn Fein MP.

Kathleen looked up at the rows of windows. Frank had said he would be looking out at three every afternoon in case she came by. It must be nearly that time now.

Liam was stirring. She looked down at him. Will he look like his Da or like me, she wondered. It was hard to tell at this young age.

The windows of Block B were all wide open and she could hear someone singing.

Oh, all around my hat I wear a tricolour ribbon–oh,
All around my hat until death comes to me.
And if anyone should ask me why I'm wearing that
    green ribbon–oh,
It's all for my true love I ne'vre more shall see.

She then heard a dreadful banging, as if the whole block was using slop buckets as a chorus. She sang the words quietly to herself, for she knew the song well.

> He whispered, Goodbye, love, Old Ireland is calling,
> With his bandolier around him, his bright bayonet shining,
> His short service rifle a beauty to see.
> There was joy in his heart though he left me behind him,
> And started away to make Old Ireland free.

Kathleen had been there to see the British finally leave Dublin Castle, marching down to the boats, and yet here now was her own Frank imprisoned by his fellow countrymen. Suddenly she saw him leaning out of one window. As if knowing his father was there, little Liam suddenly woke up, Kathleen held his tiny arm up in a fist salute.

23

'And do you know, the little one's knuckles go white when he pulls himself up on the chairs. He's a determined boy, he is, that Liam. Sturdy little legs he's got on him, like a pony. I just wish Frank would pay more attention to him, but he won't. Or look after him sometimes, maybe. But he leaves it all to the Granny. "Mam," he says, "it isn't a man's work to be harking after chisslers, and I'm off to look for work every day, so while Kathleen is helping out that sister of hers, you wouldn't mind, would yeh? And could yeh lend me a few pennies, just for the fares." The Granny has a soft spot for her Frank, but she's even more eager to help out now, so she can get her hands on Liam.'

Maggie smiled at her younger sister. She got into some messes, and no mistake.

'Liam will be all right, you'll see. Why, many a little'n is looked after by relations while the man goes out for a bob or two. And whisht with your talking now, Kathleen. We've got to finish these by tomorrow. It's dress rehearsal and Jim will be breathing down my neck again. Do you know, it's now the fifteenth show he's put on since the war. The man's a powerhouse.'

The sewing-machine whirred. The iron steamed. But Kathleen still fretted about Liam. Stuck up in that frowsty room with only old lags for company, it couldn't be healthy for a boy so young. And then when she got home some evenings the Granny would turn up in a cab, her words slurred, with Liam dirty from head to foot as though he had spent his day crawling in the mud.

'A little bit of dirt does a child a power of good,' the Granny would say, and Kathleen had to admit the boy never seemed to fall sick at all, and loved being with her. His first word, uttered only last week, had been 'Gangan'.

Still, it was good to have Frank out of prison, even if he didn't help much with the child. For twenty months they had held him, and then he had only been released with the general amnesty.

At lunchtime that day she was meeting Frank in a pub after he had finished some union business. As soon as she entered, she recognised it as the one Johnny Gilbert had taken her into at their very first meeting. Poor Johnny. Right to the last he had been trying to launch that play of his, but his illness had dragged him down. She heard that he had faded away to nothing before finally dying in great pain. A great sadness fell over her at the thought.

'Kathleen! Are yeh in a dream or what?'

There was Frank, looking his usual neat self, leaning out from one of the cubicles. She moved over to join him and he went to the bar to fetch her half a pint of porter. For a while they chatted inconsequentially. It seemed there was very little work for him at present – just a few days here and there.

In the mirror reflecting the pale January light, Frank suddenly spotted a blond woman walk in. It was Bessie Burgess . . . and he thought back to those pleasurable days they had gone to the races, while Kathleen was in rehearsal. Hand up on creamy thigh to stocking-top. A little tickle and a slap on the wrist. Frank mumbled, 'There's someone I want to see,' and left her abruptly.

Facing the other way, Kathleen had not noticed. But, left on her own, she started to look around her. Minutes later, when she glanced across to the public bar, her heart started to race. Jack Carey! He hadn't seen her, thanks be to the saints! It gave her time to compose herself.

He was ordering something from the barmaid, leaning over in conspiratorial fashion and gazing down at her ample charms displayed as she bent over the pump. Then he looked up, as if from an invisible signal, and spotted Kathleen. Collecting his drink, he stepped swiftly through the interconnecting door.

'And if it isn't Kathleen Corr, looking quite the grown-up woman now, and married I see,' he said, inspecting her ring.

'Yes, I am that, and Frank my husband is here this very day. I'll introduce you to him if you like.' She looked around for Frank. There he was, over there with that blonde! Laughing with her as if she was his only one. Kathleen felt a spasm of jealousy pass through her despite the heightened excitement of seeing Jack Carey again. She decided to be arch.

'And where have you been these long years since I left you in the cold dark street, Jack Carey?'

He took up her bantering tone. 'If I remember rightly, Kathleen, I left you snivelling against the wall – but no matter. It's good to see you again! And myself, I've been a travelling man from here to there, keeping clear of the wars and the shooting in the streets. I told you there'd be trouble, now didn't I? I've worked in the shipyards of Glasgow and the steel-mills of Doncaster, using these hands to earn me an honest crust. I've come back now, though, and I'm on my way to the Abbey Theatre to see that Lady Gregory, in case she can do anything for me. I believe it's a good play this time. And you, my little pantomime chick, how is your own career on the boards?'

The unexpected endearment brought a flush to Kathleen's cheeks. 'Oh, this and that – singing mainly – though I've done some acting as well . . . I'm just helping my sister Maggie sew costumes at the moment.'

'And here's a promise from me! If this play goes ahead, you can try for the big part. You're just the right age. I can't promise, though, and you'll have to audition with all the others, but I'll give you my vote if you're any good, and I'll try and persuade the others. Let's drink to that.'

So they clinked their glasses together, and under the table Kathleen felt his hand on her knee. She hesitated – then reached down with her own hand and pressed his. If Frank could have his fun . . . her stomach somersaulted.

231

'Well, and who be this then, talking to my wife while I'm off on some business?'

'Jack Carey, Frank — an old, old friend I met before the Rising.'

The two men eyed each other, then shook hands. It was the last time they would ever do so.

'Right now. Come in stage left . . . saunter across the stage . . . Come on, Kathleen, you're a woman of the night now. Hitch the dress down a little at the front, and off the shoulder . . . That'll do nicely . . . And as you turn towards him, make sure there is a glimpse of flesh . . .'

The part was demanding, there was no doubt about it. It was strange for Kathleen to have to act so wanton and lewd, and to speak such vulgar lines. 'Come 'ere, my lovely, and I'll show you what life is really about. Only two pounds and yez can do what yez like with me . . . I keep meself fresh, not like some of the oul' hooers round and about.'

Yet, for all that, she threw herself into the acting with gusto. Frank, too, was happy for her, sensing a life of easy money ahead. But she felt herself increasingly attracted by Jack Carey as he hung around the rehearsal with an eager watchful eye. His dominating presence was felt by the whole company, as if some restless spirit was presiding over the auditorium. It was a powerful play set amid Dublin lowlife: a parable of Ireland as the lady who would sell herself and her charms to a foreigner. Kathleen was not too sure that the Dublin audiences would like it much. They were a conservative lot basically, though there was some loosening up among the middle classes who patronised the theatre. Their social life had opened up again. The talk was all of *cocktail parties*, and *what to wear* at functions. The wars over, the English gone, and Dubliners were reclaiming the parts of Dublin which had been the preserve of the British. The old Vice-regal Lodge became the focus of many an aspiring bourgeois wrapped up in top-hat and tails and feeling ill at ease with the unfamiliar protocol of these occasions.

232

Opening night finally came, and Kathleen was all a-fever in the dressing-room. In the midst of her panic she suddenly received a little note from her brother Peadar.

Dear Kathleen,
Good luck with the play. I'll be watching from the gallery.

Peadar

Kathleen smiled. Since he had been released from prison, along with Frank, Peadar had teamed up with Jim Sheehan to help with a new show.

But this was no time to be thinking about family matters. Her costume was there, ready to wear, and a more sorry bundle of rags there never was! She could hear the audience clapping as the curtain rose, and as she pulled the dress over her head she breathed in deeply to slow her heart beat in preparation for her entrance.

The play was all about Dublin's fighting poor, their loves, their joys, their struggle to survive . . . about Dublin women and their great courage, and their never-ending attempts to keep family and home together. It drew a vivid, shocking picture without fear or favour, showing both the whore and the wife. She was sure it would be a great success.

But at the end of the play there was a strangely muted response from the audience, as if they did not know what to think of it. Kathleen felt let down, deflated, and not a little humiliated. She had given her all to this play, and knew Jack Carey longed for its success. Though she had reservations about parts of it, indeed, she felt it was a play that deserved attention.

The leading man poked his head round the door. 'Funny audience tonight, weren't they? I reckon we'll have to wait until the critics have sorted it out. Dublin audiences seem to need guidance from on high.'

Kathleen was depressed and did not feel like celebrating that night, so she quickly dressed to go home. She hoped the Granny had put Liam to bed early enough, at least before she set into her bottle for the night. In less than ten minutes she was out of the theatre, and up Marlborough Street past the Cathedral.

Taking the short cut through Mountjoy Square she heard sudden laughter and slowed down when she saw a couple walking arm in arm just ahead of her. She recognised the female laugh and the low male laugh, even at a distance. It was Frank. With that Bessie Burgess, swaying along together and singing snatches of old songs. Turning aside she headed round the south side of the Square and up Charles Street. She was now almost running and her heart pounded with the exertion, and with the anger of seeing her husband cuddling with another woman.

Kathleen burned with the shame of it, that her husband should be out philandering for all the world to see but two streets away from their home. Well, Frank Kearney, a time will come when you will regret this. I'll see you do.

Backstage on the second night the atmosphere was totally different. The house was full – but what a crowd. They were soon shouting and booing. The critics had not been kind.

'Jack Carey's new play takes a look at the seamy side of life. It suggests that an Irish woman would be capable of selling her body for money, and in doing so brings to the stage dialogue and situations which are wholly unsuitable for the public to witness. The management of the theatre are to be execrated for their willingness to stage a play which had no perceivable artistic or literary merit.' So said one of the more wordy theatre buffs. 'SLUR ON IRISH WOMANHOOD' screamed another, more popular rag. 'The Archbishop of Dublin spoke out strongly today against the staging of Jack Carey's play *Down in the Streets* by the Abbey Theatre. "Never should such sacrilege be allowed to have a public airing. It shows the irresponsibility of the theatre's management that such snivelling rubbish should be staged in public. I heartily condemn it and whoever acts in it." '

234

The noisy reaction from the audience was incredible. During the interval, Jack came into the dressing-room, and he stood behind her chair. As they gazed at each other's reflections, he laid his hand on her shoulder and impulsively she took it and placed it next to her cheek.

'They sound as if they're baying for blood out there.'

She smiled sadly and he reached down and kissed her behind the ear. Looking up at her reflection in the mirror, he murmured softly, 'Maybe we could meet and talk afterwards?'

Kathleen swallowed – scarcely able to speak.

The performance continued to be a disaster that night. There were so many interruptions from the audience that it hardly seemed they would ever finish. Kathleen found it increasingly difficult to speak her lines as the catcalling rose to a crescendo. Suddenly she felt an egg smash on her.

Finally the police were called in and order was restored when the persistent hecklers had been seen out. But it was a dull and sullen audience who watched the remainder of the play, though Kathleen gave what she considered the best performance of her life.

Outside the theatre afterwards she had to cling to Jack's arm as they pushed through the menacing crowd, and she kept her face lowered to avoid recognition. Once they were clear, he leant down and whispered, ''Tis only a short way to my rooms. Come with me now if you like.'

Swirling through Kathleen's mind was the thought of Liam sleeping peacefully, as he always did, and Frank . . . Who knew where he was? Probably out with that woman again.

'I'll make you some tea, and we can recover from this little lot,' Jack continued.

'All right, then,' she said. 'I'll come for an hour, but I must be back by midnight.'

As they sat in Jack's rooms, gently sipping from his two china teacups, they did not say much – as if both knew what was to come, and the atmosphere grew tense

235

with anticipation. Finally Jack moved over to her chair and knelt down in front of her. Lifting her skirt, he softly kissed her knee before burying his head in her lap. Kathleen responded by stroking his hair and his neck, still so dear to her after all this time, while his hand reached up with busy fingers.

He seemed in no hurry as he began to unbutton her blouse and the bodice underneath. His lips circled her nipple and like a baby he sucked, slowly at first but then with more urgency as he tasted the full sweetness of her.

Jack's face held a dreamy expression as he pulled her up by the hand and led her to his bed. Unbuttoning himself he leaned over Kathleen and she clasped him in her hands so that his sex grew large. At first he held himself still inside her, so that she cried out for him, and then they moved together so that they forgot the disastrous evening at the theatre, and lost themselves in a passion neither would ever forget.

That night set a pattern for the months to come, though Kathleen was careful to avoid the evenings, when she should be back with her Liam. In daytime she would make some excuse about going for a costume fitting, or to do some shopping, so that she could take an hour in the afternoon. And off she would hurry to Jack's room, and there they would renew their love for each other, while the street sounds came through the open window with the blind down. She scarcely stopped even to consider what was happening to her. It was as if a new hunger had entered her life, a hunger for physical pleasure and a delight that was mutual. Frank her husband seemed oblivious, returning later and later each night with another woman's smell upon him. She knew this situation could not last – but her happiness now was such that she blinded herself to any consequences.

24

Autumn came with gusts of rainy wind. The trees in the Dublin parks were dressed in all their golden finery, showering autumn colours on to the ground where they collected in great heaps and rustled and bustled as the wind picked them up and tossed them down again in its irregular patterns. Evenings grew long now as dusk fell earlier, and the cold cruelty of winter was stepping lightly back into the homes of the poor.

Frank had spent what he considered a tip-top summer, thinking mostly about Bessie Burgess. What luck to have found such a woman! And the funny thing was that Kathleen never seemed to mind if he said he was off out again on a Saturday evening. She would merely smile and say, 'You might as well go and enjoy yourself, Frank. You've had a hard week.'

It happened on one such Saturday evening when he was all dressed up ready to go out. Liam was sitting on Kathleen's knee and while reaching across the table for some bread, he knocked the salt all over Frank's plate.

Frank was suddenly furious. 'Can't yez be learning that child some manners? Put him off yer knee, woman and give him a seat of his own!'

Accustomed to having exactly his own way, Liam set up a wail that could be heard down the street.

'And it's all the fault of your Mam, I'll have you know, Frank Kearney, she who spoils him while you're out enjoying yourself and me away at the theatre. Don't come complaining to me now, Frank. Go off to your fancy woman . . . what's her name? Bessie Burgess. Every man's favourite lady!'

Kathleen surprised herself; she had not meant to say such a thing, and she was even now fighting back the tears which came whenever she lost her temper.

Still enraged, Frank stood up and spoke very coldly: 'All right, I'll go then – and don't expect me back. There's another who will want me, that's for sure!'

The door banged behind him and left Kathleen sitting stunned with the crying boy.

Though it had been such a minor row, for Frank it seemed the ideal excuse to move over to Bessie's place in Clarendon Street. It was a better part of town and her rooms were plush compared to the drear drabness of Russell Street. Hers was a cushioned existence of floral carpets and comfortable chairs, where a man might feel at home and enjoy a little jolly conversation before taking off to the large double bed where the delights of the flesh could be savoured at ease. No tiresome child or interfering mother to interrupt their dalliance. And Bessie had always encouraged him to think she waited only for him. So it seemed as nothing whenever she asked him to help her over a little difficulty with the rent, or the bill for a new piece of furniture. And he paid up gladly when they went to the races, jaunting off in one of those new motor-cars.

Yes, he would go and live with her, and she would welcome him he was sure. Besides an attractive woman like that needed a man for protection and companionship.

He rang the door bell and stood back, till Bessie's head, complete with curling papers, appeared at the upper window.

'Well, if it isn't Frank Kearney. What do you want, Frank? We made no arrangement for today, did we?'

'Just a word with you, Bessie . . . but important. Come on, girl, let me in.'

'Just you wait there until I'm ready. I don't receive unless I'm dressed, Frank.'

Frank sat on the step, his mind full of visions of his new life. The evening chill made him pull his jacket tighter round him, and he looked up again to see the lamps being lit. He longed to be allowed to enter the warm cosiness above and relax his limbs in a comfortable armchair. He had had a hard week on a private job, up and down five flights of stairs with much stretching of arms and ladder-climbing.

When the door finally opened, Bessie's maid, a buxom young country girl, let him enter. In the softly-lit room Bessie sat on her couch smoking a cigarette. The lights were placed to show her features to their best advantage, and a loose-fitting dressing-gown revealed the famous cleavage that many a working Dublin girl would envy. Peeking out, her toes were neatly pink and clean, and as she moved on the couch Frank could see her shapely legs and a glimpse of thigh. A fire was burning in the grate and a rosy glow seemed to suffuse the whole room.

'Tea, Frank?' she asked.

'A tot of whiskey if you don't mind, Bessie.'

She frowned, and lines appeared on her forehead which he had not seen there before.

'And what do you want to see me about, Frank? I haven't got much time, as I've an appointment later this evening.'

'Let me sit next to you, Bessie, and I can say it much easier.'

'You stay where you are, Frank, I don't want myself messed up right now.'

'Well, it's like this, Bessie. I've been thinking . . . you and me's been seeing a lot of each other over the summer, and I've got to thinking that maybe we could sort of make a go of it together. That is, we could live together . . . and I could move in here to be with you all the time, instead of just when I can get away from Kathleen.'

O lawks, thought the woman. He's gone soft on me. My little bit of rough has gone and taken a real fancy to me. Well he's not having me. For a start he has no money to speak of. And I don't want to be a decorator's moll with him unemployed half the time. And that wife of his . . . what a shrew she could be, I bet . . .

Bessie blew a ring of smoke into the air and gently tapped the ash from her cigarette into a waiting ashtray.

239

'It's a very serious thing is leaving your wife and son, now isn't it, Frank. I would hate to break up the home of a married man, that I would.'

But Frank was determined to press his case. 'Just think of it, Bessie, you an' me together all the time. No hiding any more, and I could redecorate for yez every year!'

'Frank, my dear, I think you have misunderstood the nature of our relationship.'

'It's love, I'm telling yez, Bessie. This is *it* for me . . .' Frank was pleading.

If there was one thing that Bessie Burgess hated above all else it was a cringing man. Nothing could more inspire her to sarcasm than the spectacle of a man on his knees grovelling before her. She liked her admirers to understand exactly their place in the scheme of things – that they came only on their prearranged days, and that they paid up when asked. Nothing so crude as to ask direct payment for her favours, of course, but a little help with the bills or some new clothes was always welcome. Frank was not playing the game now, most definitely not, and she could feel herself begin to lose her temper. 'Frank, you must know what you're suggesting is right out of the question.'

Feeling himself losing ground, Frank pressed on, 'And why is it, I may ask? Couldn't I look after yez now?'

'Frank, you're being an imbecile, you really are. So I'm having to tell you that, although I'm very fond of you and all that, I could never say I love you. You're just a bit of fun for me . . . and I could never contemplate life with a man so obviously . . . well, working-class?'

And then it came upon Frank like a bolt of light in the darkness. She had been fooling with him, and he was her *plaything*, and he had been paying her for the pleasure.

'You're nothing but a goddamn whore.'

'Now, now, Frank,' she said in her teasing tone. 'Don't let ourselves down . . .'

His sort were all right for a good time in the pub and a little smack and tickle after, but they just didn't seem to know when enough was enough. Now the more respectable type, the gentlemen, they were something different. They would never dream of leaving their families and children, but came to her for favours when the wife was confined with yet another baby. And she was only too glad to oblige as long as they were clean . . .

Frank was standing now, his self-esteem bruised beyond words. His words sounded choked, so great was his emotion that he should be rejected by a whore. 'I'll be going then, Bessie. I can see you don't want me here. Goodbye.' At least there was dignity in his exit.

Out in the street the wind was blowing up. The evening was well advanced, so the bars would be full of warmth and light. He would go and drink until he was deliciously, uproariously drunk, and then go home to his wife and apologise for walking out on her. In fact he would wait for her outside the theatre and walk her home . . . that might please her.

The porter slipped down well that night as Frank sat in the snug which smelled of thousands of spilt glasses which had cascaded down on to the floor and over the table-top. He encountered a few mates from sites he had worked on, now spending their money on a good Saturday night out. They talked politics, women, horses, religion, theatre and songs in no particular order, but all with an earnestness which would have impressed many, and with an irreverence which would have shocked many more.

It was already eleven o'clock when Frank realised he should have been away to the theatre by half-past ten. The cold air seared his lungs as he left the warmth of the pub. He was staggering a little, but pulled himself upright, and he reached the theatre door by ten past eleven. Some of the chorus were coming out, flighty little pieces who were new to the place. Brought in specially for the new musical, he assumed.

'Yeh haven't seen Kathleen Kearney, now, have yez?' he asked one as he leant against the lamp-post.

'Ooh, isn't she the lucky one . . . two boyfriends an' all. Well you're out of luck. She's already gone off with

241

her other one . . . you know that Jack fella whose play got booed.'

If Frank had been feeling drunk before, he now saw things with a terrible clarity. Both his women had been deceiving him! Now he understood why Kathleen did not seem to mind him coming home so late . . . she had been carrying on with Jack Carey. He would strangle the pair of them . . .

Inquiring the address from the stage-doorman, he hurried along the streets to Carey's lodgings, Frank's emotions were in turmoil . . . he would floor the bigger man, he was determined. As in his own house, the street door was never locked, so he ran up the stairs to number seven and shouldered his way in, breaking the door-catch.

There on the floor lay Kathleen's dress and under-clothes. By the light of a single candle wavering in the draught, Frank could see his wife's horrified face peering out over the bedclothes.

'Frank!' she gasped.

Kathleen was too shocked to act; and it was Jack Carey who had his wits about him sufficiently to prevent the scene from becoming murderous. He leant over the side of the bed for his trousers and started to pull them on rapidly. His voice was calm, almost soothing. 'I suppose it's your wife you've come for is it, Frank Kearney? Well, here she is.'

Frank seemed stunned by Jack's cool behaviour, and stood in silence while Jack walked across the room, to pick up Kathleen's clothes and throw them on the bed. Then he was out of the room in a flash, leaving husband and wife alone together.

Kathleen was filled with dread as she saw Frank swaying slightly. He's drunk, she thought, pulling on her dress as fast as she could, not caring if buttons ripped or lace was torn.

'You bloody bitch!'

Suddenly she felt a stinging blow on the side of her head as Frank's fist caught her. It set up a pounding in

242

her ears and she found herself whimpering, which only seemed to enrage him more, as if Jack's rapid departure had left him without a punchbag on which to vent the rage welling up inside him. Again he struck her, and again. The walk home was a nightmare, as Frank dragged her along, gripping her arm so roughly that the bruises would not fade for a fortnight.

'Frank, please let go. You're hurting me . . .'

'And so I bloody should, you whore. I knew that theatre would do you no good . . . Well, you're coming home with me now, and that's where you'll stay. I'll make sure you do, and all.'

The city streets were full of Saturday-night crowds on their way home, singing, shouting, arguing. They would have no time for Kathleen's problems, and anyway their sympathies would lie with Frank. For Kathleen had betrayed her role as wife and mother; the sacred role of the female, and not to be laid aside lightly.

All the way home he kept up his muttering. 'And just you wait till I get yez home, Kathleen Kearney. I'm going to teach you what a man is . . . So I'm not good enough for yez — is that why you have to go off with Carey and lie in his bed . . . I'll show yez something that will make yez pant and scream . . .'

They were coming up Russell Street now, and Kathleen was relieved that Frank was not shouting his threats for all to hear, and adding further to her shame. They were up the stairs and into the living-room, with door slammed shut.

'Before you start, Frank,' she pleaded, 'let me go and check if Liam's all right with his Gran . . .'

'Yez can go and fetch him when I've finished with yez. Get yer clothes off, woman, and into the bedroom.'

'Frank . . . not now . . . please . . .'

He grabbed her arm and twisted it cruelly behind her back so that she could not resist, then pushed her towards the bedroom. There Frank seized the back of her blouse and ripped it off, leaving her naked. Pushing her backwards on to the bed he unbuttoned himself and roughly took her. Kathleen was not ready for him savagely thrusting inside her, and he was hurting her dreadfully. Finally he shuddered in climax, and slumped his dead weight on to her. But it was as if discovering her in bed with Jack Carey had given a challenge to his virility, for scarcely had he finished with her once than he turned her over onto her stomach and began again, so roughly that she screamed into the pillow with pain until he had finished.

It was then the angry blows rained down again, till she could feel her eyes beginning to swell and taste her own blood as it dribbled down the side of her mouth.

But Frank's cheeks were also wet with tears as he fell asleep that night: tears of rage that his wife had gone to another man's bed, and tears of shame for his own humiliation.

At the top of the house Liam stirred in his sleep in the makeshift cot in the Granny's room, and he woke up wailing from a nightmare, 'Mammy . . . Mammy . . .' He felt wet and miserable, and it was so dark.

She came to him with a candle, and when the little boy saw his Mammy's face he laughed – she looked just like a clown.

The Granny turned over in her bed, but said not a word, for if she was awake she pretended not to be. Neal, her younger son, just continued to play at being a hot-water bottle. It was none of his business.

25

'I think I'm pregnant again.'

'And isn't that a piece of good news, Kathleen. Sure it's wonderful to have a proper family.' Maggie was smiling, happy for her sister. She had been shocked the day Kathleen came into the theatre with two black eyes and her mouth all swollen up. She had heard the rumours, of course, that Kathleen was seeing a little too much of the playwright Carey. Frank must have found out, she supposed.

'It's not as simple as that, Maggie . . . I mean . . . well, I don't know who the father is.'

'Oh, my God!' Maggie was truly horrified. Such behaviour was not thinkable within her own ordered life, and she bristled with disapproval. 'Well, what can I say? You must go to Confession and tell God you repent of your sins . . . that may help to lighten the load . . .'

'A fat lot of good that's going to do. The priests cannot possibly understand a woman's feelings . . . and it won't stop the baby coming.'

'Kathleen, you're not suggesting . . . I mean you're not going to try and . . .'

'No, I don't think so.' Kathleen's emotions were in turmoil. She would have to tell Frank soon, a prospect she did not savour. Jack Carey she had not seen since that dreadful night, as if he was keeping clear of her, and she had not wanted to go to him with a face bloated with bruising and turning yellow and purple like a violently sick sunset.

'There's nothing much I can do for you, Kathleen, and you know there won't be much work as you get bigger. You've made your bed and now you must lie on it.'

'And is that all you have to say to me, Maggie . . .

when here I am in trouble and might be needing some extra money, with another babby on the way.'

'I can't be saying otherwise. We run a business, not a charitable institution, and Jim would not have it. But I'll bring round some clothes for you when the baby's born.'

Hot, stinging tears pricked Kathleen's eyes as the hard reality of her situation hit home.

As if to avoid a scene, Maggie bent her head over the ledger which contained her accounts all in correct order with their neat rows and straight columns, so that a person knew exactly what was going on in the business. Kathleen's life seemed so *messy* compared to the double-entry system where everything was pigeon-holed and filed neatly the way she liked it.

Sadly Kathleen made her way out of the theatre and into the grey street. January, with not a hint of the spring to come or of the autumn left behind. The dead time between the seasons, when the streets seemed to give off a dampness which pervaded the halls of tenement houses and the lungs of their tenants. Why, only yesterday they had taken away that girl from next-door; sobbing she had been, as if knowing that she would never come back again. And when she coughed, Kathleen could see the red flecks spraying the pavement. Another tubercular case en route for the cemetery.

She would go to see Jack Carey and tell him her plight. Then everything would be all right. He would welcome her in and they could leave the city together. But in her heart she knew this was no answer, for how could she leave her other little one – her Liam.

She could hear the typewriter tapping in Jack's room, and a faint light showed under the door. Suddenly he was there before her, clasping her in his arms. 'My darling, I'm so happy to see you . . .'

Inside, the room seemed a warm haven away from the bleak January outside, with the rain just beginning to play its tune on the window-panes. The lamp on the table created a pool of light around the pages he had typed. The fire was lit, and the room was much warmer than her own in Russell Street ever was on these cold winter days.

'Sit down, Kathleen. I'm sorry I had to leave you that night . . . I wasn't going to fight him for you, like two dogs brawling over a bone.'

Kathleen sat down on the high-backed chair. 'I have come to tell you something, Jack.'

'Look, Kathleen, I know what you're going to say. You're probably right: we shouldn't go on seeing each other. It's not fair on you, as after all you have a little one to look after.'

Kathleen felt a great and powerful weariness come over her. So Jack was crying off. He did not want her, and was politely making excuses.

'Jack, I'm pregnant and I don't know who the faher is.'

In the silence that followed she could hear the clock on the mantelpiece ticking gently, and the muffled sounds of the street outside rising up through the closed windows. He was staring at his hands, clenching them together so that the knuckles showed white. At last he spoke with an air of weary cynicism.

'I can have nothing to do with this, Kathleen. I'm sorry. I'm off to England soon, for my career. We can have no more to do with each other.'

'I thought you loved me, Jack.' The pain cut through her.

'Kathleen, we enjoyed each other's bodies for a time — and now it is over.'

'But it's *not* over, Jack. Your baby might be with me in August.'

'We don't *know* that it is mine, and I'm not going to be here anyway.'

Kathleen felt suddenly full of despair. Bile filled her mouth and she gagged.

Jack was quickly at her side, stroking her hair and whispering softly, 'I'm sorry. I'm sorry. It just won't work, that's all. I have my writing to do, and I can't afford a family, and anyway it could be Frank's, couldn't it . . . I mean you're not sure yourself, are you?'

'But I love *you*, Jack.'

And then he became stern. 'Kathleen, love is not practical. What you feel is an impossible romantic attraction. It cannot be sustained, so we must say goodbye.'

And then it was as if something snapped in her, and Kathleen stood up to face him, wiping away her tears. Taking a deep breath to calm herself, she looked at Jack Carey for what was to be the last time. She saw a man so dedicated to his own way of life that he would allow nothing to come between himself and his ambition. There had seemed space for a short time for someone like herself to love him, but now it was all over and she would have to cope without him. So be it. She would shoulder her own burden and bear it.

'It's goodbye, then.'

'Yes. Goodbye, Kathleen.'

She went out and slammed the door before she could break down again. Love was unimportant now. Survival was the main thing — for her, for Liam, and for the new baby on the way.

And there was still Frank to tell . . . Ever since that brutal night she had noticed a softening in him. It was as if he was trying to apologise to her, though not in actual words. He would come dutifully home from work, eat his food in silence and hardly speak to her. Yet once or twice he reached his arms around her in bed, as if in a conciliatory gesture. On such occasions she had shrugged him off, curling herself up away from him. But in the last week or so she had found him looking at her with eyes similar to those of the young man she had married. Kathleen's was not a nature to be unforgiving and as the bruises had faded, so had her outrage.

Liam, of course, had helped divert her attention from her troubles. He was learning new words daily it seemed, and was very much the darling of the tenement house. They all seemed to love his cheeky face and golden curls.

The Granny continued to take a great interest in the

child's progress. She would almost beg to be allowed to take him out with her, knowing how all her friends would admire her growing grandson, and perhaps see their way to buying her a drop or two. 'Been walking into a lamp-post, 'ave we?' had been her only comment on Kathleen's bruised appearance.

Now Kathleen would have to go back to Russell Street and tell Frank her situation and she prepared herself as she laid out his dinner. Meat and potatoes – there weren't many vegetables available at this time of year. Today was the last day on his present job, and who knew when there would be more work, the time of year being a lean one for the decorating trade. Come March and they would be all out painting the window-frames and doors of the weather-battered Dublin houses and shops. But now, in January, there was only inside work, and not much of that.

'Well, woman, is my dinner ready? A man needs some-thing hot inside of him to carry on with life.' He lifted Liam up and threw him in the air with a jolly, 'Hello, my little 'un!' The child was none to keen on this, and signalled his displeasure with a piercing yell. Frank set him down. 'Well, don't bother then, son. Run and see your Mam . . . too many women in your life, there is . . . You'll grow up quare if you're not careful!'

As they ate, Kathleen asked Frank the usual polite wifely questions, though she really wanted to shout at him about the new life growing inside her.

There was a knock on the door, and it was her brother Peadar. 'Listen, I'll tell you what I'll be doing. Yous be giving me that jug of yours, then, and I'll be off to Fannin's for a jar. Be gettin' the strings tuned will yezs, and I'll be back with the oil for the voices.'

It was no use telling Frank now; better wait until after Peadar had gone and they were alone. This was the kind of evening Kathleen enjoyed most when they were at home, and maybe a few friends would come round. Peadar knew all the songs and more, while Frank would play his fiddle sometimes, and sing sometimes. This was their first session for a long time, and reminded Kathleen of the way things used to be before she and Frank had fallen out. They even sang their favourite duet, a song that took Kathleen back to her days in the Convent:

Brother, I hear no singing;
'Tis but the rolling waves.
Ever the great wind blowing
Over the ocean wave.

Frank had looked at her then and clasped her hand, and despite all that had been said and done in the past she had squeezed his hand back. And suddenly everyone was gone and Liam was asleep in the armchair. She gathered him up and went into the bedroom, laying him softly in the bed and drawing the blankets over him so that only his golden curls could be seen peeking over the coverlet.

Back in the other room Frank was humming as he laid his shoes by the dying embers of the fire.

I wish I could say I was sorry. I wish I'd never done what I did to her. It wasn't right . . . and now Bessie won't even see me, and Kathleen's like a block of ice. Perhaps tonight I'll tell her I'm sorry.

He heard Kathleen's voice behind him. 'Frank, I've something to tell you and it's very important. There's another child on the way.'

So this was how she had done it, thought Kathleen: told him to his back so he couldn't see her face.

Frank laughed and turned round. 'And I suppose you're a-wondering who might be the father of the new offspring?'

'I am, indeed.' Kathleen surprised herself with her own confession. It was better this way, to have it all out in the open rather than keep Frank worried with dark imaginings right through until the child was born.

He laughed again. 'And a fine mess this is, that I a working man might have to support Jack Carey's brat . . . Or are you going to tell me that you're off and away with him?'

'I'm not.'

250

'Wouldn't have you, heh?'

'There's Liam to think of.'

'Liam, Liam, what a spoilt little brat he'll be with all these adoring women surrounding him. Whatever happens, the next one will not be so mollyfied. I'll see to that!'

That summer saw her grow large with her second child. As it moved around within her, she would think back to those events which seemed so long ago now: the passionate afternoons with Jack — and the ending of it all. There was not a word from him, not a note or a letter. She was hardly surprised, indeed would have been almost taken aback if there had been any communication.

As midsummer came and went, Kathleen felt suffocated in their rooms in Russell Street. She hated the other women outside who seemed to have nothing better to do than sit all day on the steps of the tenements. As they watched the comings and goings of the street, they knew everybody's business, and they were an early-warning system for trouble or illness — two of their main topics of conversation, as there was a good deal of both.

Finally one day in the dog-days of August she felt the pains, and called out to the Granny. 'Can you look after Liam and send for Frank. I'll have to be goin' to the hospital.'

This time the child came quickly. It was Saturday and one of the neighbours had found Frank in Fannin's, and he had followed her after a while to the hospital. It was another boy, a brother to Liam.

As Frank came into the hospital room, he looked down with distaste at his new son, swaying gently as he had downed a few extra whiskies before coming. 'I'll be needing a little bit extra for this one especially,' he had told his Saturday lunch-time drinking crowd, so that by the time he reached the hospital he was more than a little unsteady on his feet. Kathleen lay holding the new baby in her arms. She had scrutinised him carefully, and although new-born he seemed to bear the unmistakable family likeness of the Granny.

Doesn't he look just like your mother,' she exclaimed to Frank.

'He's goin' to be lucky if he does,'cause if he looks anything like that Jack Carey, his life will be all the more miserable for it . . . '

Kathleen spoke gently, 'How can you say that, Frank. He's only a little baby and it's not his fault. You should be loving him anyway.'

Frank peered over at the scrunched-up, bunched-up, red-faced infant. The sun shone through the windows of the hospital ward, to light up the rows of metal beds containing their precious loads of newly delivered and expectant mothers – women ready to suffer the greatest pain to bring forth new life.

'Doesn't look like anything to me', he muttered, 'but they all look the same, don't they?' He swayed gently, then sat down with a jolt on the side of the bed. The baby's eyes opened wide and a healthy squeak issued from his lungs.

'And, there, haven't you woken him up now, Frank?' Kathleen held the child close to comfort him, reassuring the tiny new-born that everything was fine in this strange new place where the spaciousness of it all could shock a body used to the close confines of the womb.

'Well, I'm off now. I'll see you when you bring him home.' And with that Frank stood up, steadied himself, and walked purposefully down the ward past all the other beds, and past the sister, who watched him go with a knowing look, as hadn't she seen many a man in that state when confronted with his own offspring?

26

This second baby was different from the first. Kathleen had known it when she was carrying him, and when he was born she had stared at him long while trying to recognise whose features were present in his face. He looked like the Granny; there was no mistaking it except for the colour of his hair, which was set to be a striking auburn.

Even when little Dermot was brought home, Liam remained the star performer. And as Dermot grew up his perpetual shadow, Liam found a ready audience in his younger brother. Kathleen looked in vain for some likeness to Jack Carey — for some reminder of their brief life together — but there was none. The dice of genes had fallen in favour of the Kearneys, in appearance at least. But, just as he was conceived in anger, so Dermot seemed to be full of it.

Downstairs in their room one day, Kathleen heard signs of uproar from above — such a laughing and a joking. She tiptoed up the stairs, mindful of the Granny's uncertain temper, and listened carefully.

'Will you look at the mite Liam, now, and him only five years old! He could act the hind leg off a donkey, sure he could!'

'I'll act some more for you, if you like!' shrieked Liam. 'Watch me now, I'm the lady down the street!' Kathleen could hear the stamping of small legs on the rug. The lady in question walked with a limp.

'It's cruel you are,' a small voice cried out, 'to make fun of Mrs O'Grady like that. Stop it now.'

'You're a spoil-sport, you are, Dermot, and I hate you, I do.'

'Shush now, Dermot, and let Liam get on with it — he's a funny lad. If you don't shush, I'll clip you over the earhole, that I will!' A shriek followed from behind the door, and the handle rattled. Kathleen fled down the stairs, and Dermot soon followed. There he was, red with the rage of it, and crying now.

Kathleen took this second son on her knee to calm him. This was the way it was going to be, she could tell – all through their lives. Liam the entertainer and Dermot with his anger. Liam her golden boy whom everybody admired and loved; and Dermot his follower, the younger brother whose name they forgot. He would carry that burden all his life.

Yet these were happy days for Kathleen, for she loved both the boys without reserve and revelled in their closeness to her and their changing behaviour as they grew older. She loved to take them down to the beach where they would run wild and free in the open air, and she would sing to herself the songs she loved. They would run to her, legs all wet and salty, and leap up into her waiting arms and she would clutch them to her as if she could not bear the moment to pass and wanted it to last forever, their little bodies pressed to her in unreserved affection. And then she would watch them return to digging in the sand or running into the sea, and could wish for no greater happiness.

Even Frank enjoyed himself when they were all together. They would take the boys out on Sundays almost as a ritual, and Frank then played the loving father for an hour or two.

He and Kathleen began to make love again when Frank came home from the pub, more than a little merry. he would sing to her, slurring his words, and then flopped into the bed and caressed her determinedly until she responded. He knew all the tricks that would make her moan with pleasure and want him despite herself. When he lay with his head across her body, she would still marvel at the smoothness of his white skin, for Frank burned so easily he never took his shirt off in the summer sun. Others in his gang might turn golden, but Frank remained stubbornly white. She would shudder beneath him as he came inside her, clasping her tightly with his strong arms. But then would still turn over and snore away loudly.

Despite their semblance of new-found happiness, still they lived in the direst poverty. It dragged at her and gnawed away so that some days she could not fight back the tears when she looked around the threadbare room. Oh, how right Jack Carey had been: love was a romantic illusion and could not survive these hard times. Yet she felt renewed affection towards Frank and, rare as it was, she would respond eagerly to his caresses in the marital bed. For he was all she had. If he still saw other women, she did not know, and often thought she really did not care. Pondering on the past was a luxury she could not even afford herself.

Occasionally she even fell to thinking about her life with Emma Nash – before Frank, before Patrick – when she had been a young girl with everything before her. Life had been so easy then, living in that big house facing St Stephen's Green. In those days she had never needed to stand with her arms up to her elbows in cold, dirty water. And the simple little errands she ran for the Major! The birds twittering in their cages, poor things! How it all came back to her.

Emma, as she knew from her friends in the theatre, had returned to Ireland, and was living again in the big house she had so hastily abandoned. Her crime of rebellion was long forgiven and forgotten in this new Free State. What if she approached Emma for her old job? Kathleen decided to act. She ran through the tenement searching out some paper, then began to write in her neat hand:

Dear Emma,
I've fallen on hard times. It hurts me to do this, but if you could see your way to helping me I would be very grateful . . .

Two days later there came a brisk knock on the door,

while Kathleen was elbow-deep in sudsy water, trying to scrub clean the clothes they had worn to past patching. It was Emma Nash herself.

'Kathleen, my dear, I received your letter. I've brought you a basket of fruit.'

And there she was, Emma Nash, approaching forty now but with still the same instinctive grace and hauteur which had characterised her back in the days when Kathleen had known her so well. Her hair was cut shorter, just brushing the collar so white and elegantly scalloped that lay flat across Emma's proud shoulders. She was wearing a chain of multicoloured beads which laced their way exotically down to her waist. To Kathleen, used to the deprivation of Russell Street, Emma seemed a vision of riches come from another world. That was a world where a body did not shiver with cold in the dark days of winter, where there were no cries of hunger from children, or illnesses which went untreated, and where want did not raise its ugly, unwelcome face – and so appreciation of art and literature could blossom in enviably pleasant surroundings.

If the sight of Emma was a vision to Kathleen, so was Kathleen to her former employer. Emma's eyes flitted quickly round the room as she took it all in. The stained oil-cloth, wiped clean a million times, which covered some of the bare boards on the floor; the single gas-mantel; the sparse furniture – just two broken-down fire-side armchairs and the upright chairs round the table; the picture of the Virgin relieving the dullness of walls undecorated for as long as any could remember. And Kathleen herself – whom she remembered best as a young girl almost untouched by life – now well into woman-hood, with her hair tumbling from its pins on to an apron which had seen better days.

Kathleen glanced at the basket. She did not like having to receive charity, but she said nothing. The fruit, gleaming green and red apples, the first of a new crop, plums, magnificent in their purple glory, and all those gooseberries – they looked so inviting and wholesome, and surely would do the boys good.

'Well, thank you, Emma. It's very kind of you to think of us.'

'Kathleen . . . please don't take this the wrong way. I'm not here to play Lady Bountiful, but have come for an entirely different reason. I was wondering if you could see your way to doing a little work for me . . . you know, receiving people into the house and welcoming them as you used to. Just a few afternoons a week?'

'Yes, I'll do that,' Kathleen's voice trembled in gratitude, 'but sit down please and I'll make us some tea, and the boys'll be awake any moment and you can see how they are growing into great strong lads.'

Kathleen moved the bowl of washing off the table and motioned her guest to sit down while she seized a cloth to wipe off the excess water. Emma sat holding her handbag on her knees as though she was about to flee, but waited patiently as Kathleen bustled about.

'So you're not working in the theatre, then, Kathleen?'

'More's the pity I say,' said Kathleen as she set the kettle on the grate over the fire. 'You must know yourself . . . after Jack Carey's play . . . and of course then I had Dermot . . . and somehow it seems more difficult with two of them to look after . . .'

Emma knew only too well, as she had been there on that fateful evening. The woman had taken a chance playing such an unpopular role, and now the theatre management was none too keen to have her back – particularly now she had filled out a little and lost that waiflike innocence which had been so appealing.

'Do you still sing, Kathleen?'

'And how could I stop, Emma? I sing when I'm busy here, and Frank and I often sing duets together when we have our friends round . . .'

After the tea was made, Emma began finally to reminisce. 'It's ten years since the Rising, Kathleen, and doesn't it seem like yesterday? Do you remember that chap I introduced you to? Ralph Bailey? It was a shame he had to die. And they called him a traitor, when he was only trying to serve his own country and was a true patriot. I really thought he wouldn't be hanged, you know.'

'It's always a terrible shame when a good man dies, God bless his soul, especially when it's for his country! I cried meself when the news came of Michael Collins's assassination in 1922. He could have been one of our great leaders, and look who we've got . . . the long fellow, that De Valera . . .'

'Still, Kathleen, Ireland is much better off without the British.'

'In some ways that's right, Emma, but I'm thinking are the people themselves any better off? The poor and hungry, I mean.'

Suddenly there were sounds of feet on the stairs and into the room came Frank and her brother Peadar with a man Kathleen had never seen before.

'And what's she doin' in my house, I'd like to know!' Frank muttered at the sight of Emma in her fine clothes. 'Come to lord it over us all, I suppose.' Frank was in fine bellowing form and becoming truculent.

Emma pulled herself up to her full height and turned to go.

'I'll be letting you know whether I can come as arranged,' said Kathleen. 'Don't take any notice of Frank . . .'

Emma swiftly departed, leaving a trace of her perfume behind as well as the fruit on the table.

Kathleen felt her anger rising, but did not want a row in front of the stranger who had come in with Frank and Peadar. He looked a bit flash to her, with a fully tailored suit and a hat, a silver-topped cane and shiny new shoes. He was smoking a cigar which filled the room with its pungent odour and he flicked the ash on to the floor.

'Aren't you going to introduce me?' Kathleen asked.

'This is Walter O'Neill, come with news from America of Uncle Ned!' Peadar was excited and flushed, as if the newcomer had made a big impression on him; but

258

Kathleen guessed from the look of Frank that he had been impressing them with glasses of porter.

'I'm here looking for men such as your husband, Mrs Kearney.' He spoke with an American drawl. 'We're needing them in our organisation back in the States. Men who know how to handle weapons and can be trusted as good sons of Ireland. Well, I met your husband and brother in town – and what a coincidence! It seems your relative works for us. Your Uncle Ned.'

'He went to America years ago, and we haven't heard a word from him since he sailed off in the boat.' Kathleen was flustered and puzzled.

'I have good news for you, then. Your uncle is alive and well, and he works for us in one of our little concerns. Well, I'm here on a recruiting drive, you might say, to find some more trustworthy folk like him.'

'Tell me what he wants, Mam. He's not one of them bailiffs, is he?'

'Whisht, Liam, be quiet now. Listen, you and Dermot go and play now . . . or go up to your Gran with some of these plums.'

The two boys scampered out of the room, clutching the fruit as though it was treasure, and she could hear them arguing their way up the stairs to the top floor.

Kathleen turned back to listen to the men's conversation. Frank seemed to have recovered from his peevish outburst, and was now asking all sorts of questions about the nature of the job and what he would be required to do. Peadar was also clearly interested, but as he was currently employed at the theatre, and about to move his wife and children up from Cork, he was not in such immediate need of a livelihood.

Kathleen now heard all about an organisation involved in supplying liquor despite prohibition. Prohibition in the States meant a growth industry in the production and sale of forbidden alcohol. It seemed Uncle Ned now worked as a barman in one of the new clubs which sold this stuff – and what the American gang leaders needed was fresh recruits to help protect this illicit trade. The stranger was very open about it all.

'What we're really looking for, Frank, is men used to handling guns, and not afraid to use them if need be. Now, I understand you're part of the brotherhood, and could manage a job of that sort. We also need people who can keep their mouths shut, and that again is something you're accustomed to . . . Now, are you interested?'

'I can't say right now, as it would mean a big upheaval for me and the family.'

Kathleen heard these words with relief, but clearly Frank was tempted by the thought of steady employment and a sure livelihood in a new land.

'Not to worry. I'm sure that you, and more of you from this city, will be more than willing to come back and work for me. You know where I'm staying and you can contact me there. So I'll be saying good-day to you all.' And with that, twirling his glistening cane, he stalked lightly from the room.

No sooner had he gone than the three of them fell to discussing the proposition. Peadar was adamant now that he was not interested, but Kathleen could sense that Frank was still tempted. After all, he had not seen work for two months – and him President of the Painters' Union, too! She herself was pleased to learn that Uncle Ned was alive and well, but that was all. This other business, she knew it was illegal, and the thought of Frank carrying a gun badly frightened her.

Fortunately, as it turned out, Frank found some more decorating jobs in the days following, and Kathleen began working three afternoons a week for Emma Nash, so there was no longer any pressing need to consider the American's offer.

Kathleen was not back at work for long. No sooner was she back into the routine of the Nash household than it seemed she was pregnant again. This time there would be no gaps between, as Sean, Patrick and Shelagh were born one after another at yearly intervals. With interest

Kathleen now listened to the women gossiping in the streets when they discussed how to avoid the inevitable. How one, for instance, would jump up and down on the cold floor after her man had had his way with her. Some even whispered darkly of certain *ways and means* which helped a woman make her bleeding recommence when overdue . . . Yet there was no real information, and most were resigned to their fate as they grew big each year and there was another mouth to feed.

Kathleen loved her babies when they came, and took each one into her bed until the next came along. The rooms in Russell Street were always full of drying washing, and although she tried to keep the place clean, that was difficult with the constant demands of her small children and the crumbling state of the building. No repairs were ever done to it, as the Granny felt that was throwing good money after bad. Frank came and went, and had very little to do with any of his children, so Liam grew up with the notion of his father as a distant creature who came in only late at night, bawled around the place for a bit, then snored in bed next to his mother.

Kathleen sighed. Those were the happy days, she felt, when they had been all together and as a family. They would never come again. That day when they had all gone walking by the sea, and had lost Liam. Why, he couldn't have been more than eight. She saw them now, Liam sturdy as an oak tree and Dermot like a young willow. Sean, a five-year-old, with little Patrick. The younger boys, usually overshadowed by their elder brother Liam, had taken this opportunity to run off into the heathery hill to hide among the bushes.

Frank was holding Shelagh's hand. What a gorgeous mite she was! How she had cried as a baby, and suffered from having all those big brothers. Frank was over-protective towards her: 'Daddy's little darling'. Yet who could fail to love her as she danced along beside her father and pointed eagerly at the seagulls? Liam and Dermot were nowhere to be seen. In her memory she could see other people dressed in the clothes of those times. And what had she been wearing that day – oh, that stupid long skirt and shawl. Frank was looking smart though.

They had their picnic on the sands below the slopes, and finally it was time to go home. 'Liam, Dermot, Sean, Patrick,' she had called them in turn, and three voices had replied. Three small bodies had appeared. But where was Liam?

'Frank, where's that Liam?'

'He'll be all right. Don't you worry.'

'But, Frank, he's not come when I called.'

'He's hiding, more like!' Dermot panted from the running.

So they all had looked for him – and no sign.

Kathleen grew desperate. 'Liam!' she had shrieked.

And then they heard him. 'Will yeh come and rescue me, bejasus!' And there he'd been not a quarter of a mile away, up to his neck in an old dug-out hole swearing and cursing like a soldier. 'Get me out of here!'

They all had to heave and pull to get him out. And then how they had laughed! The smaller children giggling at Liam's discomfort, while Frank threw back his head with a guffaw. Only Kathleen could barely manage a smile – the incident had shown her the narrow edge between family mirth and the abject misery of losing her first-born.

Those were the times she now liked to think of best, sitting in her chair by the window overlooking the sea.

PART V

29

De Valera, the long fella, was fighting an election. It was 1932. With his great beaky nose and heavy-rimmed glasses he looked like the great teacher he was. A legendary figure reprieved by the British from the firing-squad, he alone remained of all the leaders of the 1916 Easter Rebellion. The rest filled graves packed with lime in the martyrs' yard in Kilmainham Prison. He carried his aura of wisdom and sagacity well. His voice spoke out in Gaelic and English: 'We will create such prosperity that we will have to call back the emigrants from America and Britain to fill all the jobs. As a result, in every village, in every town, in every street they were singing. 'We will crown De Valera King of Ireland . . .'

In Russell Street Kathleen watched the bonfires lit as her two eldest, Liam and Dermot, shouted and sang with excitement. Sean, Patrick, and Shelagh, stayed close to her skirts, and looked on with the great round shining eyes of childhood.

Meanwhile, in other parts of the city, men and boys were dressing up; they wore blue shirts and felt very smart, echoing their German Fascist cousins whose shirts were brown.

These were happy days for Liam and Dermot. They went everywhere together and explored the surrounding streets so they knew every doorway and every alley. Racing along the Drumcondra Road they would fling stones into the horse-trough, and watch the sun dance through the strong clean water, as the horse delicately nudged a bit of straw aside before sucking it up through square brown teeth. They swam in the canal. In 1933 they went to see the Pope in Phoenix Park, and their father fell asleep on the tram home.

And then Liam joined the Young IRA, encouraged perhaps by all the revolutionary songs he had heard his mother Kathleen singing. Marching along with his little green hat, he tried to look as big as possible when they were asked to form a guard of honour for the Republican Women, the female branch of the IRA.

It was Kathleen who led the Women to protest at the rise of the Blueshirts. Liam could not really understand why, but these Blueshirts were somehow the enemy, and they followed a man called Hitler, and raised their arms to the sky as they paraded stiffly through the streets.

Life was seeming just about perfect until, in the hottest June Ireland had ever seen, the Granny died. Arriving home from school one day, Liam sensed that something was wrong. He was puzzled by the wreath on the door. After opening it, he was mortified to see Dermot, bold as brass, walk over to kiss his Granny on her dead lips as she lay stretched out on the large bed. When Kathleen tried to drag him in, he would not go; he would not pass through the door.

Later, Liam flew at Dermot as they went down the stairs, punching and kicking him and shouting all the time, 'She's my Granny, not yours!' until his parents had to separate the pair – and decide whether he should go to the funeral at all.

Finally he was dressed in his Confirmation suit, when the time arrived for the hearse to appear. They were grand ones, when they did, great fat-rumped horses sweeping round in the street with the plumes dancing on their heads. His Granny had insisted: 'For God's sake, Missus, if I have to go, and I can't see any escape, let me go with four fat-bummed horses, none of them skinny. None of them skinny ould knackers! There's nothing looks poorer for a body than to be pulled by skinny auld things nearly as dead as yourself!'

Liam was put in the second carriage, along with his uncle Neal, who had even got dressed for the funeral and looked pale after spending so many idle years in the bed beside his mother. Then they stopped at nearly every pub on the way which his Granny had partronised, and drank her health. At the Big Tree, Liam sipped a glass of porter and remembered the many days he had done so with his Gran. Sitting there just a bit apart from his immediate family, he could overhear two old fellows talking about Uncle Neal's new inheritance.

'Nothing between him and heaven, but still a warm man.'

'Warm, you're joking. I hear he's boiling, red hot, coming into the ould wan's money and not a penny for the brother Frank. She was worth thousands, saved all that money from the lodgers she did.'

Presently he could hear his mother and father arguing about the same topic. Frank had adopted a couldn't-careless attitude which was driving Kathleen to goading him further, until finally he flung down his glass and bawled out, 'Look, hell is not hot enough nor eternity long enough to roast that ould bitch! Now leave me alone!'

And he abandoned them there with the hearse and he went off on his own, leaving Kathleen with the three younger children flanked by Dermot and a grim-looking Liam. He would never forgive his father those words spoken in wrath beside the coffin, while Kathleen started sobbing at the thought she would never escape from the slum of Russell Street, while the Granny's money was poured down Neal's throat in the public houses.

Kathleen had been going regularly down to the Housing Department for ten years now to ask for new accommodation, Doctors' letters, visits from the sanitation inspector, and the fact that the Russell Street tenement had been condemned for five long years, nothing had seemed to make any difference.

But then one day on a visit to the Department she was handed the key to a new house, and told she must look it over and make up her mind within twenty-four hours. Out of the city they went to Crumlin, way off to the south-west of the city, where there was mile after mile of unmade roads and half-finished houses and no streetlamps. Kathleen was determined. She opened the door and drank in the smell of new paint, new wood and cleanliness, then went down to collect the new rent book that very afternoon.

Frank complained bitterly about the move; for him it meant further to travel, extra fares, and paying rent for the first time ever. But Kathleen would not let him deter her. 'Frank Kearney, you're never in the house. You're either at work or at the pub, and it's me has to spend my days in this dark ould cellar, going slowly mad and blind. I'm not putting up with rats' dirt and filthy lavatories for one single day longer.'

Liam was amazed at her resolve. For him the slums represented familiar warmth, lads to play with, and dark convenient corners where little girls would lift their dresses and let you play with them; he really could not see what ailed his mother.

They moved at night, leaving the bills behind them, and set off to the bleak new housing estate, where the wind whistled and blew up the rubbish in clouds. And this was to be their home now! Crumlin, the very name was enough to put doubts into a soul. It was a graveyard of all ambition and hope, with its great grey streets stretching endlessly over the hills and slopes.

'Well,' thought Kathleen as she moved her few bits and pieces into the new house, 'better make the most of it!' But her soul shrivelled up at the thought of the journey into town and the lack of any but poor dislocated neighbours around them.

'So they shove us out of the way where we won't be inconvenient,' she said to Frank.

''Twas you that wanted to come here in the first place, I'd've stayed in town, given my way.'

'Stop harping, Frank! There was nowhere to go! They were pulling down the tenements and they offered us nothing else. On *your* wage, a fella and his wife has no choice!'

Liam grew to manhood on the Crumlin estate, becoming

267

more and more politically idealistic while the news of fighting in Spain began to appear in the newspapers. He started playing at being the little IRA man, and at fourteen considered himself grown-up. Once he terrified Dermot by dragging him out of bed in the middle of the night and forcing him to his knees. 'I want you to swear that you will die for Ireland. Swear, now, that we will both die for our country.' He had tears in his eyes.

Dermot thought he was crackers and pushed him aside; he had very little time for Liam's idealistic vapourings.

It was not an easy life in Crumlin – and even worse in the lean years. Eamonn De Valera's promises were as nought, and there was not much work and a lot of mouths to feed. Kathleen could see now how well off they had actually been in Russell Street. Dirty surroundings, yes, but safe always with the Granny to borrow off, with neighbours in the house who would look after the children, and no rent to pay. In many ways their new house was a burden. And she sorely missed her sister, now living away off in Rathmines with her own three children. Maggie never came to visit her any more, considering her sister had called all her misfortunes down on her own head by marrying Frank Kearney in the first place. Kathleen felt completely isolated from the theatre world and, cut off from her whole previous life, as if it had never existed. her trips to the pawnshop became more frequent, and now another great war seemed to be looming, with the business in Spain as a mere prelude.

Liam told his mother he was going away to England just a month after the second great war began. As she looked at her son, her golden boy, tears came into her eyes.

'Liam,' she said, 'What use will it be? England will never let you get away with it. And you could kill people. Don't forget that every person you kill is some poor mother's son or daughter.'

'Whisht, Mam. Nobody would ever right injustice who spoke like that. Haven't you always been a great Republican yourself? We must fight for the cause.'

And end up rotting at the end of a rope, thought Kathleen as with a heavy heart she realised the inevitability that he would be gone from her soon enough.

The newspaper reports said it all: IRA bombing campaign, many arrested. When Kathleen saw her son's name, she cried out with sorrow. And there, too, was her first mother-in-law's name – Mrs Furlong. She had been telling the truth then, when Kathleen had seen her packing to go off to England . . . and she was to go to jail now, all of eighty years old because of running a safe house for Republican dynamiters. But lucky, lucky Liam, he was classed as a young offender and would be put in an open prison eventually. Kathleen thought back to the long months she had waited for Frank to come out of jail, and she settled down patiently to wait for her first-born to return.

30

Liam's life in the cell was surprisingly acceptable, despite the number of hours he spent there. Shut up from twelve noon on a Saturday to nine the next Monday morning, the three inmates had plenty of time to get to know each others' personal habits, idiosyncracies and life histories.

Macken had been a childhood hero to Liam. He remembered well the slogans written on the walls all around Dublin: RELEASE THE REPUBLICAN PRISONERS. FREE EDDIE MACKEN! Over the years they had gradually faded, till the letters had almost disappeared. Macken was now an old lag as far as prison went; he knew all the dodges and wheezes, which he readily passed on to Liam. He seemed to have the run of the jail, managing to secure a job in the library, so that he was here and there all over the place.

Liam was envious of his freedom. Sometimes he would see Eddie walking past while he himself was sewing mailbags, with a warder looking on. It was hardly heroic work, yet to refuse it would bring punishment on himself and, worse, would mean no money to buy the little necessities which made prison life more acceptable, such as the small packet of tobacco eked out from weekend to weekend.

Another inmate of Liam's cell was a Cockney. Reggie Wallis was a petty thief who had been at it since an early age. His was the pale, pale skin of the city slum child who never saw sunshine, and if he did he would turn a bright lobster-red after just an hour in it. He was proud of his body and wanted to keep it in good shape, considering it the essential tool of his trade. Whenever he was 'out' he would run for miles through the streets of the richer areas, sussing out likely houses to rob, and then back to the East End where he lived. While Eddie

Macken and Liam were engaged in what he called 'Irish talk', Reggie would be practising press-ups on the floor of the cell, stretching and re-stretching his limbs and muscles to remain in good shape. Reggie would often regale Liam with stories of his successful times: times when he had money in his pocket and a girl on each arm. It made Liam's criminal charge seem quite paltry in comparison. He thought back to the little exploit which had landed him in jail. How pathetic it seemed now. It was a damned stupid thing to try and blow up Blackfriars Bridge. Clinging there shivering while they tried to set a mine to the bridge support . . . and then dropping most of the explosive and watching it float down the river. His two IRA companions had fled then, leaving him with the job of trying to fix the remaining explosive. His hands shook, his head pounded, he had been terribly afraid. He had known then what fear and cowardice meant, in those few moments before he fled and left the whole job in a complete mess. What a farce! All those weeks spent training in the Wicklow Mountains had led to nothing. The patriot game looked more glorious in the warm snug of a Dublin bar than it did on the windswept English streets. Only his speech in the dock had made it seem a little better – and thank God that reporting restrictions had not been lifted, so his IRA friends did not know the true extent of his bungling. His Da would have scorned him for the fool that he was

Macken was taken away early one morning. And then Liam was left alone with Reggie again. But not for long. One afternoon the warder took him along to the Governor's office – he was to be allocated to an open prison. Reggie Wallis would be going too.

'It's not so bad in those places, I can tell you. Cheer up, lad. It'll be better than this dump, you'll see.'

It was different, for certain. Liam had known that from the moment the battered bus had drawn up to the gate. Beyond the wire fence he could see the huts: low, single-storey affairs with windows all along. And young men hard at work painting them. Well, at least he would be able to practise his trade while he was here!

Liam found he made friends easily there. Nobody seemed to care what he was in for, and there was a camaraderie which had been lacking in the separate cells of the normal prison. Reggie was in his element, and soon revealing more of his various talents. He could shuffle a deck of cards with the speed of light, and had a fantastic memory so could remember every card that had been played. He became undisputed king of the poker school — as well as main dealer for any extra supplies that came into the prison.

One man especially attracted Liam's attention. Jay Langtry was small, fine-boned man with hair so fine that Liam thought it might blow away in a strong wind. Jay was a 'conchie': a conscientious objector who refused to fight to order. And, now the war had begun in earnest, he was viewed with suspicion by his fellows. Jay was different in other ways too; notably in his reading taste in the books from the library. Not just crime or thriller fiction like the others, but serious books that Liam could term literature.

As the months passed, Liam had opportunities to converse with the man, even quizzing him once on his motives for refusing to fight in the war. Jay's face lit up and he responded in a voice that entranced Liam with its gentle passion. 'Mine seems to be a crime worse than murder at the moment, with so many young men volunteering to go. But all people hear is the martial music; they don't hear the cries of pain, see — the agony of the wounded. Once again we are guilty of slaughtering a whole generation in the name of race, party and religion.'

'That's all very fine, Jay, but what if a fella came and hurt your own family?'

'I would protect them, of course, but I feel the same about the families of the enemy. I don't want to harm them either . . .'

It was after this unusual conversation that he and Jay

Langtry began to spend more time together. As time passed Liam discovered that Jay had a very great knowledge of literature which he was prepared to share with him, and they would discuss the subject of books for most of their free time together.

'You don't write yourself, do you Liam?'

This question took Liam by surprise. Why should he? But why not, indeed? Hadn't he always produced the best essays at school? Hadn't the Young Republican even published a few of his adolescent musings?

Why not, he thought again. He could give it a try. Maybe a story about the prison — he would call it 'The Young Prisoner'.

Liam found himself growing closer and closer to Jay, until he even found himself physically attracted. He would try to suppress these feelings, assuming they were because he had been shut away from women too long. But, even so, he would catch himself watching the long artistic fingers as they turned the pages, wishing he could hold those hands in his own and stroke that fair skin. When this happened he would force himself to tell stories, stories from his childhood in Dublin when his Granny took him out on their jaunts together. Strange, wonderful stories from another age it seemed.

As Jay listened he watched, entranced, the young man's face light up with the pure joy of story-telling. The youthful uncertainty had vanished. Liam was on his own territory here, and his confidence showed. Jay felt an overpowering urge to hug him close.

Instead he spoke softly. 'You've got a wonderful ear and eye, you know, Liam. You must write all this down so that others can share it.'

They were sitting out of sight in the wood, taking a break from cutting and pruning trees. Liam looked round at his friend and felt so overcome by his praise that he scarcely minded that Jay's hand was now stroking his thigh. When he felt himself respond, he blushed. Jay looked at him questioningly, then placed his hand just there, so that Liam felt fit to burst. He felt the hand slip

273

inside his trousers and then it all happened so suddenly, and it was the most delicious feeling he had ever experienced.

As the weeks passed Liam felt the bonds growing even stronger between them, though it was not something he really wanted. Inwardly he was terrified he might be queer. In Dublin society such fellas were objects of scorn, and subject to beatings and kickings. As he lay in his bed he thought about how he had felt towards Ria . . . and that night before he had left for England, when he had pleaded with her to let him have his way, and her so prim and nice!

'You just leave me alone, young Liam, until you've decided to buy me a ring and we're married in the church like all good Catholics.'

Ria Fitzgerald came from a more prosperous class, and he had first met her at a meeting of the Gaelic League. She had seemed attracted to him, so he had made his initial play. He could remember now her bright, curly ginger hair falling round her face, her green eyes looking at him in surprise that he should dare to touch her! And her a girl from a respectable family!

But when later he finally lost his virginity, the night before his bombing attempt, it had all seemed so natural. The landlady's daughter was a great big girl from County Cavan. From the start she had made a dead set for him, in front of all the lodgers. And then that final evening she had come to his room and sat on the bed as he ran his hands over her large thighs. Lustily she had moved with his thrusts till he had cried out in delight for a brief moment, and then she had left him feeling just a little dissatisfied.

Could a man love both sexes he wondered? He couldn't see any reason why not. It was just in that town he came from, if they ever found out a man had even looked at another fella, they would tear the living flesh off your bones with all their ballyragging.

His mind churned on, when suddenly he felt a tug at

274

the blanket. Jay was there, finger on lips. Tired of resisting this irresistible urge, Liam quietly followed Jay to his narrow bunk and, taking off his pyjamas, lay down beside him. Jay's kisses were wet and inquiring as he stroked Liam till he felt himself responding with fervour. He was in capable hands and Jay guided him so that he learnt quickly, and shortly reached a climax like no other.

31

Ria Fitzgerald brushed her hair at the dressing-table. Staring in the mirror, she admired the way it curled so, in the fashionable way of the moment. She was still wearing her slip, uncertain what to wear for this first visit to Crumlin. She smiled to herself; they wouldn't like it, her parents – they wouldn't like it at all that she should be mixing with known trouble-makers. She had never told them anything about Liam and their correspondence. Inded, what was the point when he was now so far away? But now he had written again and insisted she go and visit his Ma.

They would never understand, they wouldn't. Here she was, all of nineteen, yet they wouldn't let her go to work or even apply for further education. And what had she seen of life? Nothing. But she was determined this situation would change. It was no fun at all to be stuck in a great big house like this with no one to talk to except her parent's friends and their sons and daughters, who came to occasional parties and dinners. They were all so . . . bourgeois, that was it. Insisting on the right clothes, the right spoons, the right forks and the right accents before they would even consider a body worthy of serious attention.

The war was tiresome as well. Too many young men had gone off to fight, which meant there were lots of girls her age who were missing out on their first romances. She opened the wardrobe with the mirrored front and studied her clothes inside. Carefully she chose a plain suit and blouse. That would make her seem respectable, for she understood that, though poor, Liam's mother was the very model of propriety. She then selected her best silk stockings, the ones Daddy had brought back from a business trip, and, checking the seams were straight, she trotted downstairs and out the front door.

It was a cold day, and a biting wind blew down from the Hell-Fire Club and swept through the cold cheerless streets of Crumlin. The new double decker-bus stopped at Dolphin's Barn, and the conductor called out, 'Anyone for the ranch. This is where they play tip-and-tag with hatchets; and they don't bury their dead, they eat them.' Ria headed slowly up Sundrive Road. Stopping to draw breath, she gazed out over the bleak windy waste of the slob-lands. Clouds of seagulls contended with the children for the scraps that fell from the tipper trucks. These children risked life and limb climbing through the descending loads of Fyffe's bananas and Fry's chocolate. Bananas in great bunches, most of them over-ripe and black rotten after too long in the store, but some of them green and good enough to fill bellies that never saw fruit of any kind. And the great sacks of chocolate condemned by some zealous inspector as unfit for human consumption, but still eatable by those that never saw sweets or sugar. With all sweets rationed, the good bits of chocolate could be sold.

The gulls pecked savagely at little hands that just as determinedly reached out for the treasure. With a war on, chocolate was rationed and nearly everything else was scarce. Even in Ria's comfortable, middle-class home things were tight, and for the poor on this sprawling estate the rubbish tip was a source of life. Coal you could not get for love or money, and she watched older children dig deep into the slag-heaps for cinders. Down they went like little moles into the bowels of the earth. She walked over, fascinated to see that some of the holes were ten feet deep. Generations of dead coal were being exhumed and dragged out by little hands and loaded into sacks. A group of girls even offered Ria some. 'A tanner a bag, miss. Ah, go on now.'

Ria just smiled, afraid to speak. Afraid that her middle-class accent might expose her to low taunts.

Some other girls were dragging along a box-cart. In it, twisted like an old sack, was the shrivelled figure of a young boy. His eyes were the liveliest part of him as he watched the girls start to dance round his cart singing, 'Janey Mack, me shirt is black, what will I do for Sunday, get into bed and cover my head and don't wake up till Monday.'

The two older girls then approached the cart and started to snigger. They leaned over and waggled their breasts tauntingly towards the lad. One of the smaller girls protested shrilly, 'Get out of that, ye dirty bitches. Don't do that to a poor cripple.'

The older girls ignored her, and one of them screamed with laughter. 'Oh my God, Lilly, look, he's just like all the others. You could whip an elephant out of a sand-pit with it.'

Their coarse talk attracted and repelled Ria at the same time. Vulgar though it was, it was so full of life, so honest about the things that mattered, that she was fascinated. If her mother ever needed to know why she was attracted to the Kearneys, it was because they were part of this elemental struggle for survival, in a way that passed her by in that sedate madhouse she called home.

As Ria passed a public house called Flood's, though the locals called it 'The Bloodpan', she peeped into its dark interior and marvelled that anyone could get drunk in its cold dispensary-like atmosphere. Yet, even as the barman stood idly polishing glasses, two drunks staggered past her, slapping each other on the back in comradeship.

The estate was vast and treeless, since every tree planted by the Dublin Corporation had long since been cut down for firewood. The houses were mean and small, and in all their thousands offered only two different types: either plain brick or pebble-dash. The glum hand of a soulless bureaucracy had arranged street after street in endless uniformity.

As she strode along Kildare Road she pitied anyone condemned to such dreariness, until she saw another group issuing from another pub, their arms laden with large brown packets of bottles – no doubt determined to live a little as they were sure they would be a longtime dead. Suddenly Ria realised that it was she who had to be pitied. It was people like her who had lost the spark of life. It was she who had to come to Crumlin to rekindle her tinder from a family locked into real existence. These were Dublin's fighting poor; for them, to eat was victory, to survive was everything.

Kathleen awaited Ria's visit with some trepidation, but Frank had reassured her. 'She will have to take us as we are and as she finds us. Either that or just leave us alone.' He was right, of course, so Kathleen smoothed back a greying hair from her temples and threw another shovel of cinders on to the fire. They made a nice warm glow and fed the back boiler so that there was no shortage of hot water in the house. As she eased the damper in to control the draught, she glanced up at the pictures over the hearth. There was a tormented Jesus Christ in the centre, and on either side likenesses of Jem Larkin and James Connolly. Seeing her gaze at them, Frank had once chuckled. 'It's Christ between two thieves.' Kathleen did not like that, and said so: they were good men, one of whom had given his life for Ireland. But Frank had retorted: 'Missus, you take everything awful serious. Sure the two of them weren't Irish at all. One was Scottish and the other was from Liverpool. And, if you want to know, Patrick Pearse was an Englishman and Michael Collins, our golden boy, the Commander-in-Chief of the Irish Republican Army, was born and reared in London. The English needn't blame the Irish for the rebellion since it was themselves that led it.'

Kathleen ignored him, she knew he had a few pints taken, and when the drink was in, the man was out. Better to ignore him, but she hoped he would not make a holy show if he turned up while Ria visited. He was a good man but terrible foolish in drink.

Her thoughts were interrupted by a knock on the door,

and she ushered Ria in, and sat her down at the old wooden table. Brought by Kathleen's mother from her farmhouse in County Kildare, it had seen many a good dinner eaten off it.

Well, that's the way with sons, Kathleen supposed: one minute you're dangling them on your knee, and the next there's posh girls chasing after them!

'So Liam told you to come and visit me. Did you see a lot of him? You know, before he went away.'

'I used to meet him often at the Gaelic League, Mrs Kearney, and we became good friends. I was hoping maybe to talk about him, as I've been missing him so.'

'He's a good lad, Liam. He'll be all right once he gets out of that prison and back into Dublin where his family can mind out for him.'

The conversation ebbed and flowed, and despite their differences in background and age the two women soon took a liking to each other. The older one thought how pretty young Ria was and what a sensible girl she seemed; and Ria herself warmed to Kathleen's charm and wisdom.

They did not have long to talk, though, as all in a tumble the younger children returned: Sean, Patrick and Shelagh, all bearing the family likeness. The place was soon like a hive, so full of life all buzzing round the queen of it all – Kathleen.

Darling Ria,
My third Christmas inside. I won't know what it feels like to hold you any more. I hope you will still see me and that we are still friends when I come out, which should be some time this year.

The camp is *freezing* and the wind howls through the windows like there was no glass there. Even the stove that stands at the end can hardly keep us poor fellas warm! I'm glad you went to see Ma and got on with her well. She is the most splendid person in the world, my Ma is. Did she sing you a song? She ought to have, for she can sing like a bird!   *Love to you,*
Liam

For Liam the affair with Jay Langtry racked his mind and spirit, even though their private meetings were few and far between. It was quite some time before Liam resolved that he should end their liaison – and that the strong feeling of love he felt for the other man he should now root out of his deepest being. Knowing his release date was near, he tried to avoid Jay, and instead devoted himself to helping with the camp concert. He was to play the strolling Irish vagabond, and he enjoyed the preparations. How many afternoons he had skipped school to go to his uncle Jim's theatre and watch the old music-hall blinds come down on show after show! He had no fear of walking on to a platform in front of four hundred other prisoners, and his comic singing, strong and clear, brought the house down.

As Jay watched Liam singing out so heartily, he thought that he had never heard anything so free and expressive, and was deeply moved. After the show he sought out Liam backstage to congratulate him.

'Oh well, yeh, me Ma was always singing, you know, singing in the morning and the evening. She didn't have a drink to sing, like most people. Not Ma. She could raise the dead with her voice.'

Behind the stage they stood in almost total darkness, and Jay moved closer to him. 'Will I see you before you go?' He reached out to touch Liam's hand tenderly.

Liam pretended not to understand. 'You'll be seeing me every day, I think.'

'You know what I mean, Liam. Like we were before . . . You've been avoiding me. Don't bother shaking your head; it's unworthy of you. Don't turn against a natural part of your being.'

Liam merely laughed with embarrassment. Jay was talking like a woman.

Jay drew back. 'Well, so be it! Your mind is obviously too narrow to understand something so beautiful.'

Liam was stung by this suggestion that he was some kind of narrow-minded bog man, and he struck back sharply, his voice squeaking with tension.

'It's not natural. How can one man making love with another be natural? It's against God and nature.'

There, he had said it, and he felt, at least for a moment, the better for having said it. It was like he felt after confession; clean, pure and wholesome. Then the doubts started creeping in. Christ, why was everything so complicated? Guilt again hung about him like a shroud, for he could feel his desire for Langtry even as he walked away. Liam clenched his fists tightly. Was he to be haunted all his life with internal strife? Torn between genuine fondness for another man and yet afraid to taste again that forbidden fruit? He thought of Oscar Wilde, his fellow countryman. *He* had suffered for the love that feared to speak its name. Poor Wilde, it was he that had it both ways: a sweet proud prince just like Lucifer, and just like Lucifer cast down into Hell – the hell of Reading Jail.

He lay awake in bed that night, feeling lonely and forlorn, and in the end he tiptoed softly to Jay's bedside. Either the man was asleep or pretending. As Liam prodded the body softly, he just moved further away. Liam coughed as loudly as he dared, but there was no response. He could see the prisoner in the next bunk stirring, so he raced back to his sad little bed and cried himself to sleep.

Next morning, he was called first thing to the Governor's office. A placid, fat-faced man, the Governor held out Liam's short story.

'First the good news. You've won the writing competition, by a mile if I may say so. There's no doubt you Irish have the gift of the gab. Now the bad news: I am to lose you.'

Liam's heart sank. The thought of leaving the comparative freedom of the open prison was a real blow. To go back into the closed cells – he felt sick, winded.

Seeing his distress, the Governor held out a second sheet of paper. 'Cheer up. You're being released. The Home Office wants to deport the lot of you back to Ireland. All you have to do is sign this agreement never to darken these shores again.'

Liam signed with a trembling hand, hardly bothering to read the terms of the expulsion order the Governor was formally serving on him. It was enough relief to be going home . . .

It seemed strange to be free at last and standing there at the Brighton railway station, clutching a rail warrant that would take him to North Wales and the Irish Sea. He caught the night boat on a cold June night, and watched the grey harbour of Holyhead slip away. It was wonderful, though, to see Dun Laoghaire and the Dublin Hills with dawn breaking over them. He could see the balding slope of Bray Head as the boat manoeuvred its way into the quay.

As he passed through Customs, a grim-faced Special Branch man flicked through his deportation order and looked up from the photograph into Liam's eyes. 'It must be great to be free.'

Liam looked back. 'It must, indeed.' He walked on down the platform to the little train that would take him home to Dublin.

32

Liam should have felt happy, but he did not. Here he was, back in his home town, free from prison yet feeling more closed in than before. For, oddly, the prison walls had provided a safety-barrier against his own self, against his own doubts and torments. Here he was back in the land where the maleness of men must never be seen in doubt. And what about Ria? In truth he hardly knew her, though they had written to each other over the years and she had professed to be missing him. He was dreading his meeting with her now.

Even more, he was dreading meeting the IRA leaders who had sent him over to England. What a whining, snivelling coward they would think him. And if they ever found about himself and Jay Langtry! He could not bear the prospect.

He could feel the familiar atmosphere of the city close in on him as the boarded the bus for Crumlin. At every church on the route - and they must have passed twenty – the bus-driver blessed himself, and so did everyone else on the bus.

The streets of Crumlin looked as grey and mean as ever. He shuddered and thought fondly of the slums around Russell Street, dirty but warm. Great dark hallways where the young would meet to touch and explore each other in pagan love. Here the endless streets of small grey boxes would give no shelter for love. A cold wind swept down from the Dublin Mountains and shrivelled all sensuality.

At the corner of his road he looked up at the immense pile of the new parish church; it stood squat, and enormous, dominating everything and everybody. The pagan anarchy of the slums was here replaced by the cold Catholicism of rent and respectability. The black-frocked

284

priests who scurried by fingering their beads had replaced the old British Imperial power. Strange, he thought, that a people who had fought so hard and so long for freedom should have abandoned it so easily for the religious domination of Rome. Lions would now be led by donkeys. Dublin, once the second city of the Empire, was fast becoming a village dominated by a village mentality. Ireland holy was Ireland unfree, and he resolved that at the earliest opportunity he would shake the clamps off his ankles and leave his home for ever. As he turned up the Sundrive Road he could see a great carthorse laden with turf swaying its way towards Kimmage. What a size the horse was, a full seventeen hands. The carter pulled in beside Flood's public house, and as soon as the cart stopped the great hairy-legged horse spread its legs and sent a flood of yellow urine thundering down on to the concrete.

Piss artists inside and out, Liam thought.

As Liam passed Flood's he almost bumped into his brother Dermot coming out. Dermot's greeting was warm and brotherly, and for Liam very moving. Together they turned and walked towards home.

Liam felt nervous walking round the back of the house – it looked so small. Even as he entered the kitchen he felt the room dwindle around him. He stood there quietly, and watched his mother lovingly. She hadn't noticed him in the shadow and went on muttering: 'Oh, them children have me near murdered. My head is flying round the room.'

Suddenly she turned and saw Liam framed in the door. 'Liam! Oh, you put the heart crossways in a body. And it's fresh and well you're looking. Come in. I'll make a pot of tea.'

Liam smiled. His mother's answer to everything was tea. How he loved her. He sat quietly sipping and relished the familiarity of it all. Home at last!

The first day home passed quickly enough as the other

sons came home and welcomed their brother back. They all seemed pleased to see him and were full of questions about his experiences in England. Liam felt like a hero among them – but his father Frank was much less welcoming. When he came in he barely greeted Liam, but just sat down to wait for his dinner, his shirtsleeves rolled up to his elbows. Then he muttered, 'So *you're* back, are you? Another son to drive us mad and eat us out of house and home.'

By this time Liam had already seen enough. The house seemed so much meaner and poorer than he remembered; the tiny little sink and the ridiculous stove which held only one great cooking-pot. It was nothing as large and commodious as his Grannie's old tenement house with its great hall door, its lovely big fireplaces and endless landings where you could laugh, and play with the other children.

Soon Kathleen and Frank were arguing. She was pressing him to fix a door and he was getting irritable. Finally he flung down his knife and fork and yelled, 'If Christ came down to earth he couldn't satisfy you. If he stayed in this house for any time, he'd go back and nail himself to his cross just to get away from your nagging.'

He glared hard at Liam, who could smell the porter on his breath.

'A right lot of idle jacks you reared, missus!' Then, snatching his jacket, he stood up and left the children and their mother sitting in silence.

'I think I'll go out too, Ma. Lend me some money will you?' Liam asked.

Kathleen sighed and reached for her purse to find some money she could barely afford. Liam walked out into the desolate streets of Crumlin with a heavy heart. Nothing had changed since he had left: the same old arguments and bitterness creeping into the small house, souring the atmosphere and leaving everyone exhausted by the strain of it all.

Back in the city Liam found a lad to carry a message to

Ria Fitzgerald's house, asking her to meet him at the Park gates.

When she arrived she looked as pretty as a picture. His heart rose at the sight and he felt the years drift away. He felt proud to be with her and as they strolled through the darkening evening, he slipped his arm round her waist. They walked slowly up the hill and looked down over the city, its myriad lights burning bright in the night air. Soon they lay down together on the slightly damp grass, and it was then that Liam rediscovered that he could enjoy loving a woman as much as he had loved Jay. It seemed as if all his doubts and fears had gone, like snow melting away before a hot sun. In the distance he could see a train puffing along, its engine throwing up sparks into the cool night air. And then suddenly he was pressing Ria to him and asking her to marry him. She raised her face and kissed him gladly. 'I will, I will.' All she wanted now was a home, a husband and a family, for without them she felt an outcast at life's rich feast.

Ria would never forget the night she told her parents that she was soon to be married to a young man from the Crumlin estate. They were not pleased – not pleased at all. But the bans were called and the wedding was fixed for a month ahead. The reception would be held at their home.

The church service was mercifully short, and as Liam and Ria mumbled their way through the vows, Kathleen gazed at her son so handsome with his auburn hair and slim build – and then at Dermot the best man, so proud-looking. They were like two handsome princes, they were. She held her hanky close to her eyes. Still, Ria was a great girl and she hoped he would find happiness with her.

The Fitzgeralds had not stinted with food and drink. In fact, there was probably too much drink for young men who had little experience with it. Liam drank glass after glass of the porter and whiskey, and as each glass went down he seemed to become noisier, more ready to tell tales that had the stuffy friends and relations of the Fitzgeralds gasping at his irreverence and impertinence. It was obvious now that Liam drunk was a different man to Liam sober, as if two different men lived in the same body – just needing the release of alcohol for one to take over from the other. As his brother grew more raucous, Dermot eyed their mother Kathleen sitting quietly on a chair next to a glassy-eyed Frank, and he felt sorry for his Ma that she should have to watch such a spectacle. His brothers Sean and Patrick and his sister Shelagh were all growing up now into fine young people, and he wondered what they must think of this brother recently back from prison in England. Present too, were Aunt Maggie and Uncle Jim, scarcely able to hide their shame at the sight before them.

Liam was singing now, an uncertain audience listening to his words and he loving every minute, with his arm round the neck of a young male relative of Ria's. The youth's face was flushed with drink and embarrassment, looking for all the world as if he wanted to escape. As Liam finished his song, he turned towards the youth and kissed him full on the mouth to a gasp from the audience.

Dermot could not stay to watch and went into the kitchen. There was Ria, white-faced, her make-up streaked.

She came and stood close to him. 'If I'd known he was going to get like this . . .'

Dermot didn't want to hear her regrets. She was his brother's wife now and he could not turn back time.

'You've made your own bed, Ria. You just get on with lying on it . . .'

Light was just beginning to peep through the curtains when Ria pulled them back and saw an early morning sun rising over the horizon of roof-tops. Tears coursed down her face. Liam had not been a pretty sight when finally he had come to bed in the small hours – with his shirt hanging open, and looking half savage. As Dermot said – she had made her bed . . .

33

Liam had decided that he would be a writer. That was the life. Much better than decorating other people's houses. The search for life was on, and he sought consolation away from the mean little flat he shared with Ria and his three-year-old daughter Susan. He had continued to do a little house-painting to earn a few pennies, but now one or two articles and stories had been published, so he was feeling quite the literary gentleman.

At this time, Dublin was full of all types. Rich young Englishmen, young Americans on grants and all kinds of foreigners mixed and intermingled in the pubs and clubs of a city which seemed to give them a licence to drink all day if they wanted, living cheaply and comfortably amid wide elegant streets and fading grandeur.

Liam played court to them all, singing and dancing the hours away, and telling and retelling stories but they were honed down to the perfect length and impact. For him life was a party, while Ria stayed at home and looked after young Susan.

Mornings in their flat would begin with Liam tapping at his typewriter and muttering to himself. Sheets of paper were torn up, cigarettes smoked, and scribbles made. About eleven o'clock, with the streets well aired, he would set off to McQuaid's for his first drink of the day. It seemed heavenly to lift a glass on a summer morning and watch the crowds go by. Everyone and everything were there for comment or ridicule.

And then there would be jolly jaunts in someone's car out into the Irish countryside, all for the sake of a little after-hours drinking. Or else to the all-night parties held in the basement of some grand Georgian house, where any man could gain entrance if he brought a bottle of liquor.

Liam loved to go out into the city and experience the artist's life among the middle classes who always had money to spend without seeming to strive particularly hard for it. Certainly not as hard as his poor old Da. As he became known for his outrageous behaviour, Liam was soon an essential guest for any host who wanted to give a party to remember. His was the role of social jester, and he lived up to it fully.

He seldom felt much guilt about Ria, who was left to cope on her own most evenings. The nights when Liam roused the rabble were lonely ones for Ria – she had never known such loneliness, even with the child. Her mother and father were no help at all, preferring to ignore their daughter's unhappiness, and Kathleen seemed a great way off in the middle of Crumlin.

Dermot meanwhile carried on with his life, watching as his brother's star rose ever higher in the artistic circles of Dublin. Sometimes he felt wretched with jealousy to see his brother's name all over the newspapers; while at others he dismissed Liam's achievements and antics with a careless shrug. He met him on odd occasions when he drank in McQuaid's, and saw his brother getting fat off his writing – watched as the slim young man who had come out of the English prison turned plump and double-chinned. Yet he dared not say anything for fear of Liam's temper, now well renowned.

34

During the next few years Ria watched as Susan grew up
to be a fine young girl. They moved to a bigger flat which
meant more space for all of them. Liam's fame continued
to grow and he now had a play on the stage at the Abbey
Theatre.

Ria longed for another baby, but somehow it did not
happen. So when Liam received a sizeable advance for
yet another book, she suggested they take a holiday. 'Just
the two of us, Liam. Please. We can leave Susan with my
mother, and it's nearly midsummer . . .'

Finally Liam agreed to rent a house in the west of
Ireland for two whole weeks.

As they lived in the small thatched cottage, the sunny
days passed in perfect splendour. Liam hunched over the
typewriter while Ria went for long walks along the
strand, finding shells and feeling the sun warm on her
body. Then one day Liam decided to accompany her and
they walked all the way round the headland to a small
deserted cove. The rocks around them sheltered little
pools where crabs and seaweed grew undisturbed. Liam
sat down on one as he watched Ria strip off her clothes
and run into the sea. They had been together a long time
now and he was used to seeing his wife's body, yet today
was different somehow what with the sun hot on his
back and the sea surging nearby. She had stood by him,
had Ria, through all his troubles, and he had not been
all that kind to her. His heart went out to her as she
beckoned to him from the gently breaking waves . . . his
Venus summoning him to join her.

Liam took off his clothes and waded out to embrace
her gently. As he did so, he felt desire for her wash over
him, and he carried her back to the warm sand where
they lay together and made love as they had not done

for many a long month. Liam no longer felt himself attracted to his own sex. It was as if he had just taken longer than most to outgrow adolescent fantasies which had been reinforced by the hothouse atmosphere of prison. And now here he was with his own wife, and feeling as if at last he could give himself to a woman. It was like coming home.

His kiss was fierce and hungry, and she matched him with her searching tormenting tongue. He gently undid her bikini top and watched with joy her breasts tumble out firm and delicate in the warm sun. He nibbled her nipples gently, tasting again and again the sweetness of her body. He hauled her closer to him and she wrapped her arms tightly around his waist. Then Ria broke free and, laughing, raced for one of the pools. He dived in after her throwing his powerful naked body about like a seal. Their mouths touched, their lips tingling with the saltiness of the sea. Looking down Ria could see their bodies mirrored in the reflection of the shimmering light. He gathered up palmfuls of water and let the water trickle gently down around her nipples. She closed her eyes in ecstacy.

'Say it, Ria. Say you love Liam and no one else. It's me and you forever.'

She moaned, 'I do, I do,' then dug her nails into his back and cried out 'Liam, Liam, I am yours for ever.' With an exultant yell he moved upon her and her slim strong body drove up against his even after he had spent himself, and went on till she collapsed sobbing with the pure joy of immense relief: it was beautiful, just beautiful.

Afterwards they walked slowly back to the cottage, where a local girl had prepared lunch for them: freshly-caught herrings and oatmeal cakes. They ate and were satisfied.

Suddenly Ria felt like celebrating. 'Come on, Liam. Let's go to the pub. Sure, wouldn't it be grand just the two of us out together for a change?'

He did not feel so sure, glancing nervously at the type-writer and the blank sheet of paper it held. He knew well the curse of the artist: 'the seeking after creativity without toil'. He knew how easy it was *not* to write – to do anything rather than face that empty white sheet staring back at you. Sharpen pencils, go for a walk, do anything so long as you hadn't got to work. The pub was always another temptation, where one could indulge in talking about writing a book rather than actually doing it. How often in McQuaid's had he met people who boasted they had received this or that advance against publication – then watched them as the advance and the book went down the plughole. Writing was hard, serious work. If he did not knock out three thousand words each and every day he felt he had failed. The deadline for this book was fast approaching, so the last thing he should consider was to go to the pub, knowing himself well enough to realise that as soon as they got there the day would be finished.

But Ria persisted, and off they went.

Ria was amazed. 'Look at these men, will you, Liam. Would you ever see the likes of it – men reared just on milk, fish and potatoes and look at the size of them. Never saw red meat, yet none under six feet tall, and some as broad as they are long.'

The locals were busy celebrating a good catch of fish. As they arrived an old man was playing a sweet fiddle, encouraging the younger ones to dance the high cauled cap. Between dances they sang, but none had a sweet voice. They all sounded toneless and harsh, and it was some relief when they asked Liam to sing. At first he modestly refused, but the men challenged him, 'Come on, Dub, let's see what you can do!'

Ria pumped his arm. 'Sing them the croppy boy. You know they'll love that.'

He took a swallow from his full pint and moved out on to the floor beside the fiddler. He listened first to a chord, then threw back his head and poured out the sad lament of the hanging of the croppy boy. As his voice soared to heaven the pub fell silent. Even the men playing cards stopped to look up. It was a most beautiful voice, full of passion, and it held them in its thrall. Ria felt so proud of her man.

As he finished the last verse of the lament, the crowd seemed to breathe again, then broke into wave after wave of thunderous applause, their cries ringing round the smoky pub.

'Good man yourself, Dub. It's yourself that has the magic . . .'

And they begged him for more – then more still – and stacked drinks around him in a great sloppy circle.

Liam sang on and entertained the men for an hour or more. But he was getting drunk, and his eyes took on the bleary look that Ria knew so well. She did not like this anymore, for the drink and the men now stood between her and Liam. He seemed to become a creature of the mob, and they seemed to own him. And she was forgotten in his hunger for their applause. He was like a prisoner of the crowd, who seemed to be able to do what they liked with him. Ria now realised why he went out so much in Dublin. It was like a drug to him: this adulation and praise. He needed it as much as he needed to breathe or eat. She was saddened by it.

She pulled and tugged at his arm. 'Come on now, Liam, let's go home.'

His face was mottled with drink when he turned to her and shouted in her face.

'Eff off now, woman. I have business here, and if you don't like it you can go . . .' He was angry with her now, though they had made love just a few short hours ago.

She went with tears stinging her eyes, and walked back towards the cottage as the sun was sinking towards the sea. She cursed him to hell and out of it, consumed by anger at his contemptuous treatment of her. Oh, wasn't it just like a man – headstrong, untameable, unmanageable, arrogant. If she had had anywhere to go she would have left him years ago – packed her bags and taken Susan with her. But like a fool she had remained. Now as she faced the wind blowing up off the sea, she vowed whatever happened he would never break her; she would survive.

Liam did not return that night, as Ria tossed alone in the bed. When the dawn chorus had barely begun, she set off across the headland for a lonely morning walk.

In her absence an unshaven Liam staggered back through the front door, and looked vainly around for Ria. Then he made some tea and sat at the table, slurping it from a saucer. Where was she? He thought back ruefully to their hour of happiness on the beach. With some relief he heard the latch of the door being lifted — a quick kiss and a hug and it would all be over. He stood up.

To his immense annoyance it was only the postman, holding out an envelope. Liam snatched it off him, barely saying thank-you. It was brief and to the point: Would he consider starring in an interview with John Gooch on the television programme 'Behind the Scenes'. The letter promised him his fare and all reasonable expenses, and ended with the hope that he would see his way clear to fit this commitment in between his many others. Go to London with all expenses paid? Would a duck swim? Probably a couple of hundred quid for a few hours work.

Wouldn't it go down well in McQuaid's? 'I hear that Liam is off to London to be interviewed by Gooch himself.' Oh, how his enemies would squirm as they tried to console each other with the hope that he would make a balls-up of the interview and fall flat on his face.

And what about Ria? He hurriedly packed a bag and left a note: *I'm off to London to make my fortune.*

He reached Dublin by early afternoon. After a quick pint in McQuaid's, just long enough to let the news sink in, he made for his mother's house.

Kathleen was busy sewing when he tore through the door like a town bull.

'Come on, Ma. To hell with poverty, let's kill a chicken.' Kathleen looked at her firstborn son, bearded now – or hadn't bothered to shave more like. God in heaven but he looked a fright. He grabbed her up and started waltzing her round the room.

'Come on, Ma. The taxi's waiting and we're going to do the town. Where's me unnatural brother?'

'Where else but up in his bed.'

Liam bounded up the stairs. 'Come on up now, Dermot, and let's go off and get Ma as drunk as a fiddler's monkey!'

His brother leaned lazily over the rail.

'Oh, for God's sake, can't a man get his rest?'

But Liam was impatient. 'Come on, now. You'll rest long enough in your grave, so you will. Up now and at 'em. I'm on the pig's back. The Brits are flying me over to have an interview with John Gooch.'

So they took the taxi out to the green hills of Tallaght, to a pub called The Embankment and drank and drank.

Finally Dermot pulled Liam towards him. 'You'll have to watch yourself with Gooch.'

'Why so?' asked Liam.

'Why so?' Dermot looked at him. 'Because he makes his money from what he calls in-depth interviews. He'll have you for breakfast if you're not careful.'

Liam's eyes narrowed. 'He will, will he? That's what he thinks. He may have met his match with Liam Kearney just you wait.'

Eventually Dermot and Kathleen deposited a sozzled Liam off at his flat. As Dermot watched his mother embrace Liam with a long hug, he felt a pang of exclusion. No matter what Ma said, she did make a distinction between them. Dermot was convinced she loved Liam more than ever she loved him. Liam, her golden boy. But why? Perhaps it was because of his talent? Wouldn't any woman be proud of him. It just wasn't fair to give so much to one person. The gods had smiled on Liam, and he would always be first among the brothers.

Finally, Dermot escorted a tired, weepy Kathleen home.

*

Liam loved the idea of flying. he marvelled at the throngs of people waiting in the airport lounge for the flight calls. The world and his wife seemed to be on the move. He proudly presented himself to the checking-in desk and smiled in delight when the girl said, 'Of course, Mr Kearney. Your ticket's already here. Would you like a window seat or the aisle?'

'Window seat, if it's all the same to you.'

She smiled and stapled his ticket to the boarding card. It was marked Executive Class, and he felt good. Executive Class – beat that. He was among the top nobs and no mistake. God it was good to be flying like this, and not queueing up for the old cattle steamer!

He smiled to himself as he drank a free brandy, looking down at the Irish Sea beneath him. He thought of himself on the way to talk to millions of Brits. No matter what anyone said about the British, he had grown to find them one of the most tolerant people on the face of the earth. Still, Dermot's warning rang in his ears – watch out for Gooch.

Arriving at Heathrow airport he was met in the reception lounge by a small American girl brandishing his name written in slanted writing on a large piece of card. He let her hire a taxi for them, and lay back in the corner of the cab.

'I'm Janet. I'm the research assistant on the programme. I hope you don't mind, but I need to get some more information from you. Background stuff, you know.'

She had a runny nose and sniffed continuously as she got out her notebook and poised her pen.

Liam was looking forward to this. He loved nothing better than talking about himself. Who could love you more than yourself? Your mother maybe.

She continued scribbling till the taxi reached the centre of London and stopped outside his hotel in Shaftesbury Avenue.

Liam reached the Television Centre the following evening after spending some time in a pub in the afternoon, so he was feeling definitely mellow. There was some whiskey in the hospitality room, so he had a good few glasses of that before entering the studio. He was surprised how dark it was, and Gooch seemed to be sitting in the shadows, his heavy moustache making him look like an old walrus.

He beckoned to Liam. 'Feeling nervous?'

Liam waved cheekily back. 'No, are you?'

Gooch eyed the tousled hair and the open-necked shirt and wondered.

They checked the sound, and the lights, and then the floor manager's fingers counted down. They were on air.

Conscious of the camera staring at him like a great eye, Liam suddenly felt drunk – as if all the afternoon's drinking and the whiskey had caught up with him right at that moment. And here he was in front of millions.

Gooch started quietly enough with routine questions about Liam's upbringing and family. Then he launched in: 'Do you really think, Mr Kearney, that someone like you should make a profit from your criminal background? After all you went to prison for attempting to kill innocent people, and yet here you are selling your books on the back of it . . .'

Liam gripped his chair and forced himself to think clearly, but his anger was aroused. 'And what about you, Mr Gooch? Don't *you* think it's criminal that you're paid to sit on your fat arse and pontificate on subjects you know so little about? And what puzzles me is why so many millions are watching your show. Wouldn't you think, now, that people had something better to do – like walking the dog?'

Liam suddenly felt very tired. Resting his head on his hands, he felt a blackness overwhelm him, and himself falling, falling into a pit.

What the audience saw was a man snoring. He was an overnight sensation. Why, nobody had ever actually fallen asleep on the television!

Gooch was almost beside himself with rage. Far from being the clever tormentor of a foolish victim, he himself looked like he was being baited. Certain that Kearney was only pretending to be asleep, he adjusted his heavy horn-rimmed glasses and looked round for a signal from the producer. It seemed he must persevere and try to rescue things from the mess they were in. He spoke up sharply and loudly, 'Mr Kearney, do you think we might stop playing the fool, and have some consideration for the viewers that are paying your expenses.'

Liam opened one eye to squint at Gooch. Attack, he decided, was the best form of defence. 'Why, aren't you getting ten times as much money as me for this? Haven't you lived off the likes of me and them out there for the last twenty years. What's my poor few bob compared to your thousands?'

By now Gooch was purple with rage. He looked again for a signal from the producer, but found none. This was great television.

Gooch looked stricken, trying to assemble his thoughts. As the startling tirade rolled on and on, mocking, digging, jeering, he felt his blood pressure rising dangerously.

Liam had stood up and now hovered over him, looking down at his victim. 'Can't take it, can we. We can give it out but we just can't take it. Well I'll have you know there's no one yet that has ever got the better of Liam Kearney.'

Gooch simply stared at Liam, his heavy lips quivering, then gave out a strangled cry. 'You bastard, you bloody illiterate Irish bastard.'

35

The morning after, as Liam was walking towards Trafalgar Square, a newspaperman waved to him. 'Eh, Pad, you were good last night. I agreed with every word you said.'

Liam stopped. Fame was nice, he decided. 'And what did you think of Mr Gooch, then?'

The newspaperman cocked his head. 'Mr who?'

So this was what it was like to be famous – people recognising you in the street. And this not just in the streets of your home town but in the capital city of London! Liam glowed with the thought of it. This would give the begrudgers in Dublin something to think about, himself the famous person now!

The next few weeks saw the publicity machine groan into action, and suddenly everyone was running articles on him, wanting to interview him, asking him to come and talk . . .

And the publishers gave him whatever money he asked, so he was never short of cash. He could drink as much as he wanted without worry of the cost. This was it – he was the writer, the talent, the talk of the town.

With the fame came all the invitations to cocktail parties at rich houses. He found it strange that people who once would have thought him below contempt – a jailbird – now welcomed him eagerly into their homes and seemed to lap it up when he poured scorn on their upper-class ways and whiskey on to their furnishings. He slithered on parquet floors, tripped on thick carpet, wrapped himself in floral chintz, and sang while dawns broke. Publicity flowed through his veins like champagne, and through an alcoholic haze he began to believe it all.

Yet he was not writing, and he knew it. It seemed each day began with good intentions which had floated away by noon. And as the months passed he began to develop severe headaches, like monstrous hangovers which could not be dispelled by the noon-tide drink. He told no one about these but just carried on as if he was feeling normal: but the pain would make him bad-tempered, and sometimes when he was drunk he would lose control of himself and the words would come out wrong and his legs lose their strength.

One night he was at a film director's house in Hampstead. Everybody was there, milling around; there were even a few film stars to be seen. The house was big, Edwardian, solid and ornate. Giant fireplaces covered nearly whole walls, and the ceiling cornices were more ornate than he had seen before.

The party was in full swing, with people crushed together talking, talking, and downing glasses of champagne as if it was tap water. Girls were wearing summer dresses with wide skirts and off-the-shoulder tops. As Liam admired them, leaning against the door, he realised he had not bothered to eat that day, so when waiters came round with trays of food he gobbled it all indiscriminately, smoked salmon, chicken or cake – it did not seem to matter.

Then someone suggested that he gave them a song, so he stood and sang 'The Lone Rock'. It was a mother's lament for her drowned loved ones, a song which was one of Kathleen's favourites. When he was as child she had told him of the time so long ago in Galway when she had watched the little coffins being carried to the graveyard, with the women following; and the thought of that poor boy falling off the cliff and drowning had haunted his dreams for many a night.

Young Donal – he was the babe of the three;
Two weeks later he came back to me,
With the wind on the sea and the waves running free,
A pale lifeless corpse he returned to me.

The party-goers listened hushed as he sang. He closed his eyes and could see it all as his mother had described: the blue sky . . . the light reflecting off the water . . . the feeling of fear as he felt himself falling . . . and the blackness waiting for him below in the heaving sea . . .

And then he felt a pain in his head as though it was going to explode.

'For Godsakes, someone do something . . . Fetch a bloody doctor!'

And that was it. A great void opened for Kathleen as she went to the funeral at Glasnevin where the coffin had been brought, and she carried on through the next days, knowing that he had left them. Everyone seemed to agree it was a special grief that a mother should see a son grow up and then have him die before her. The family rallied round and took extra care of her. But they could not do anything about the dark nights when she felt nothing but despair, or the moments in the day when her sorrow would come pouring back and she would weep bitter tears of sadness.

There was one small, bitter consolation she felt. It was a terrible thing but at least he was at peace. Now. Perhaps it was better this way than dragging his life out twisting and turning to avoid the demon drink. It seemed such a little while since he had been a wee lad. How quickly they grew up. One minute at your knee, the next you are looking up at them. Her happiest time had been when they were young. Young women complain now, and cannot wait for their children to grow up. Little do they know they are wishing the best part of their lives away.

How soon life is over. How on earth did she get to be so old so soon? Still, she was content. The rest of the family were well, thank God. She had enjoyed a full life. What had that newspaper man said about her: 'You're a slice of Irish history, Missus.' She supposed she was; she had seen so much, so many great events, so many great men, though no one then ever believed they would be great. It was a pity the Rebellion leaders had never seen the young Republic spring from their efforts. They just thought of themselves as a blood sacrifice, though

302

she remembered how Patrick Pearse, when he hoisted the tricolour flag over the General Post Office had said, 'If our flag flies for one day it will fly forever.' Ah, well, she had been born a republican, had lived as one, and would with the help of God die as one. She regretted nothing. She had never harmed anyone by thought, word or deed. 'If you can't think of something good to say about a person, say nothing' – that had been her motto.

Laugh and the world laughs with you, weep and you weep alone. Her Uncle Ned used to say that. Her people were strong people; they would live on in their descendants. Great red-faced farmers they had been, with hands as big as shovels. Her granny strong as any man standing, her feet ploughing through strong rich earth. Kathleen's roots went deep and she hoped that someday her body in returning to the soil would bear flowers on her grave. She felt united with the universe – a speck, but still part of a great movement that went on and on forever.

She was Dublin and proud of it. They were no petty people. What a great time it had been, struggling, fighting, pushing, but living. And even yet they were turning out energy and talent.

Even though Liam was dead, his progeny would go on. They would become poets, actors, writers. Ria would manage; in the end the women always did. And she had the new baby now, born after Liam's death. A lovely little boy – just like his father had been.

It was a great consolation to Kathleen to see the rest of her family thriving. It was as if she could feel the warmth of a spring sun slowly spread, waking her to a new life. She could see in her mind's eye a sun-filled crossroads with groups of boys and girls dancing to the tune of 'Owen Doyle's Wedding'. The boys in their white pullovers and the girls with red petticoats swirling. She was a young girl again, on holiday on her grandparents' farm. She joined easily in the swirling throng, and felt her body move faster and faster to the fiddler's music.

'I'm sorry, Ma ... I'm sorry we have to go through all

303

this . . .' Dermot looked now at the old woman who was his mother, the tears in her eyes as she looked out of the window remembering the past so clearly. Yet she hadn't been sad for years. She had been his support and had loved all the children and been happy.

'Tell me, Ma,' asked Dermot. 'When I tell this story of yours, what is the most important thing I should write about you?'

Kathleen looked at him, her eyes bright as a young girl's. 'Make sure they know I was a good mother to you all.'

Dermot felt a lump in his throat. 'I'll try, Ma . . . I'll try.'